UNCHOSEN

LISA ANNE NICHOLS

UNCHOSEN

TATE PUBLISHING
AND ENTERPRISES, LLC

Unchosen

This novel is a work of fiction. Names, descriptions, entities, and incidents included in the story are products of the author's imagination. Any resemblance to actual persons, events, and entities is entirely coincidental.

The opinions expressed by the author are not necessarily those of Tate Publishing, LLC.

Published by Tate Publishing & Enterprises, LLC
127 E. Trade Center Terrace | Mustang, Oklahoma 73064 USA
1.888.361.9473 | www.tatepublishing.com

Tate Publishing is committed to excellence in the publishing industry. The company reflects the philosophy established by the founders, based on Psalm 68:11,
"The Lord gave the word and great was the company of those who published it."

Cover design by Joana Quilantang
Interior design by Mary Jean Archival

Published in the United States of America

ISBN: 978-1-68301-606-9
1. Fiction / Action & Adventure
2. Fiction / Fantasy / General
16.03.23

For my twin sister, Erin, my first friend and fan—
thank you for seeing, encouraging, and supporting my gift.

PART ONE

Becoming Unchosen

The Curse

I was not born pretty. Average, perhaps, or plain. But not pretty. And far from beautiful. The day I found out I wasn't beautiful, I cried until my eyes were swollen.

I was seventeen, when a girl becomes a young woman of marriageable age in Zaphon and begins receiving suitors. I had grown up witnessing this phenomenon. When a girl reached her seventeenth year, it was just expected that she would soon secure a beau, and a few years after that, a husband. Most girls already had secret beaus before their seventeenth year; they only had to wait until the proper time to declare themselves chosen.

I was never chosen. The day I turned seventeen, a curse was spoken over me.

The day had begun as it should: I awoke to yellow sunlight slicing through the chinks in the shutters and birdsong being carried on the morning breeze. My family was all smiles and giddiness as they fussed over me that day, surrounding me and pecking at me like hens. I wore the white linen gown with a sky-blue sash that my mother had made for the occasion. My sisters dressed my hair. Ribbons trailed down my back.

The festivities began midday, and nearly the entire village attended. As was customary, games, dances, food, and laughter abounded. At the end of this time, according to tradition, couples recently joined usually gave a toast to prepare for the father's speech and blessing.

The blessing never came.

Before the couples could toast, the wind suddenly changed. It blew heavy and cold, roaring through the trees, and I noticed upon looking up that the sky was thick with black clouds. The change had been sudden and fierce. The merriment died just as suddenly. My guests ceased all action and stared in a long, prolonged silence at the gathering storm. And then I heard whispering—the village people repeating old wives tales, so I thought. Several people had fallen into groups, eyeing me over their shoulders, some with looks of pity or fear on their faces. They spoke quietly with one another about bad omens and curses. Though I don't suppose they intended for me to overhear such words, I did. I was familiar with these superstitions but had never before been the subject of such conversation. And suddenly, I realized that I was in the center of it all; everyone had pulled away from me as though I was leprous.

When the rain came, people began moving indoors or under trees for shelter. I ran to find my papa. Along the way, I passed a group of young people my age whispering together, tossing my name amongst themselves. The wind brought their words to me as I hid nearby around the corner of the house.

"Did you see how no men would dance with her today?" said a girl. "Most girls have many dance partners, especially on this day. I would have been humiliated!"

"She won't be chosen now," another girl chimed in. "My mother says this is the earth's way of declaring her fate. She is to be an unchosen."

A boy next to her laughed. "She wouldn't have been chosen anyway. She's not pretty enough to attract a suitor—certainly not as pretty as you two."

They all laughed together while I escaped as fast as I could.

My heart tightened in my chest at those whispered words, chilling pain that struck my body like a curse and began working its poison inside me. I went home that night, staring in dismay at my image as I peered into our dusty old looking glass. They had said I wasn't pretty enough to attract a suitor. I had never considered myself particularly lovely, but I'd never really noticed that I *wasn't.* I always took for granted that a girl, by design, grew pretty as she became a woman. No, not just pretty—beautiful. And that day, it was my turn.

So I scrutinized myself as their words replayed through my mind. And suddenly, as though my eyes came into focus, I saw what they saw, and I believed those words. I wasn't pretty after all. Somehow I had lived all these years never noticing. Why had my tender mother and doting father never told me? Why had they led me to believe that I was just like every other girl, that I had just as much chance as every other girl for finding love and happiness in this world? My parents' bias had blinded me. Looking into that mirror, it was as though my eyes were opened, and with my new vision, my hope fled.

Although I waited and prayed and tried to hope despite myself, no man ever chose me. My sisters above me in age were chosen, and my sisters below me were chosen, but I was cursed. I became an unchosen.

In the country of Zaphon, from where I come, it's a disgrace for a woman to make her own living. A woman belongs in a family unit, so says the law. She must be in her father's or her husband's household. If her father dies or disowns her before she marries, and no brother or male relative claims her, she becomes one of the unchosen. Whether her father dies or not, and whether she is claimed by a male relative or not, once she reaches her twenty-eighth year and is still unmarried, she becomes an unchosen.

Unchosens are banished from their villages and shunned by mankind. They are a surplus, the law says, unnecessary and useless. As those not belonging to a family unit, and therefore not fulfilling their duty and contribution to society, they are thrown out, like scraps to a dog, to fend for themselves—stigmatized and unwanted.

As I grew in years, I watched the other young women around me become wives, including my four sisters. Some round and plump, others skinny as a stalk, each chestnut-skinned and raven-haired, they were all pretty, and they were all chosen before their twenty-second year. They were married before our father died. I was twenty-three then, and my grief was so deep I had no tears to cry. I mourned my father; I didn't worry about myself.

My father was a believer in the High King, though not all in Zaphon are.

Yet, in a place before time, the High King was.

So says history—or legend, as most have now come to believe. Coralind was first, the seat of the High King and the origin of magic. From there the world spread out concentrically, shaping itself by the High King's power into a sphere until it was complete. All the countries in the Lands of the Seven Kingdoms were once one piece of land and one kingdom under the High King. But misled by a shadow that stalked the earth, men grew selfish and arrogant, and they desired to rule themselves. They banded together and scattered across the face of the earth, and time and war shifted continents and kingdoms of men until there were seven kingdoms. From that time it has been the Lands of the Seven Kingdoms, each ruled by its own master or set of masters. Yet there are some that say the High King still lives and ultimately rules: he wanders like a stranger in his own world as his own people no longer recognize him or believe in him. So he wanders and hides and shows himself only to those who have eyes to see.

My papa was one such person. As a child I was fascinated by his stories of the High King, stories in what he called the history books of the Lands of the Seven Kingdoms, but which few people regard as such anymore. Of course, as a child I didn't know this. I took it for granted that most people knew and believed it all. I learned differently as I grew. I also discovered that though my beautiful mother tolerated my father in his beliefs and allowed him freedom to express his thoughts and opinions about the High King, she took very little stock in the stories herself. But she had been a young mother with a cottage full of little ones all close in age. She had spent a majority of her life pregnant and bearing children. She had lived on the cusp of poverty most of her life and had married my father on a whirlwind, believing it to be her duty and secretly hoping he might bring her into an exciting new life filled with adventure and promise. My mother, with nothing much to root her, went through life jaded and slowly grew more tired and apathetic as it progressed.

My father had many trades, always employing them as the need and opportunity arose, in and out of season, which was fortunate for us because he was never out of work. He worked with his hands and loved to build and create. He could bind books, cobble shoes, mend wheels, and lay bricks. He was also a cooper and a wood worker. His wide range of skills and his sociable personality made him well-liked and an asset to the community. At times he was hired out to muck stalls or plow fields. Nothing was too far above or beneath him. He did it all for his family, uncomplaining and cheerful, to provide for us; and although we did live on the edge of poverty as though tiptoeing along a precipice, we were never in want. For myself and my siblings, I'm sure we didn't know any better until we grew up. I just remember that I was happy.

My father had vowed I would never become an unchosen, no matter my age.

"What about the law, Papa?" I asked him only a few years before his passing. I had been crying, heartbroken, as I picked flowers in the garden, and Papa came and sat next to me on the cottage steps. He tucked my limp, fair hair behind my ears and turned my face to his, which was smiling warmly as though the sun itself reflected off his features.

"Laws can be changed, Bug. Many laws are man's design, and not all are for our good."

"Why then is there still such a law in Zaphon?"

His smile fell and he shook his head, sighing gently. "I don't know. The rulers of this country want all people to be useful citizens and contributors of society, and they feel they know what a man's or a woman's station ought to be in order to make them useful."

"But it's so archaic! All of the surrounding countries have long since abolished that law!"

"Of course they have. And they are right to do so. Unfortunately, we are stubborn in Zaphon, and people cling to the old ways. They raise tradition up on a pedestal and call it ultimate authority." He gave a sly wink then, which caused me to smile despite myself. "However, *we* know that real authority and the true law come from the High King."

I smiled and nodded my head then quickly followed it up with a sigh of frustration. "Why doesn't the High King just show himself and *make* Zaphon change its laws."

"The High King doesn't make anybody do anything. He has given a certain authority to men on this earth, and like it or not, we are to obey them to promote order, develop humility, and become servants of righteousness as we learn to put all our hopes and cares on him."

I sighed again and gently tossed aside the flowers I'd been gathering. "Not everybody believes in the High King, Papa."

"No, unfortunately not. The rulers of Zaphon surely do not. If they did, I cannot believe that they would perpetuate this law and banish women from their homes and families."

I turned my face down, discouragement gnawing at my insides as I thought about my curse. *Will I ever be chosen? Will Papa be able to find a way to keep me after my twenty-eighth year, regardless of the law?*

Papa saw my anxiety and stooped down to gather up the flowers I'd tossed away. He drew them in a bundle, tied his blue linen handkerchief around the stems, and handed them back to me.

"Not to worry, Bug," he assured me. "You are always my chosen. Trust in your old papa. And trust to the High King. If nothing else, there will always be sanctuary with him. Do not forget."

In the next few years, I felt the most security that I had ever known. I stopped waiting for a man to choose me. It was enough to know my Papa would take care of me, that I *was* a part of a family unit and still had plenty of time for marrying. Although I never had suitors, I didn't fear. I only waited.

And then Papa died, so suddenly I had no time for tears. My body just froze up, went into a little cocoon of shock and disbelief. He was gone. No complaints, no prior sickness to offer warning—he just fell asleep one afternoon after working in the yard and never woke up.

As we laid him in the ground, all my sisters watched me from underneath their black veils. I didn't see their eyes on me, but I could feel them. They clung tighter to their husbands' arms. I stood alone next to my father's grave, my gaze fixed on that mound of dirt, and waited. I waited for someone to wake me, to tell me it was all a dream and to take me home. My sisters and mother only touched my arm lightly as they passed me and went home with their new families. My mother would now be a respected widow who, by the law, was promised protection so long as she remained a valuable and useful member of society. She might contribute to charity work or hire herself out to teaching or housekeeping where room and board would be her only wages.

I, however, would not be offered protection unless claimed by a male relative. At that moment I didn't care what happened to me. I just waited, and waited, and waited, hours maybe. I waited until the sun began descending below the horizon and the chill evening wind rustled the edge of the wood nearby. I waited until shadows appeared, stretching across the village graveyard. I stared at that mound. I thought about the curse, the evil words spoken over me that seemed to have sealed my fate. I thought about my papa. I waited for him to come get me, to put his arm around me and take me away from this place—to take me home. But I didn't have a home anymore. The more I thought about those words, the more rooted I became to where I stood. *Soon they will come. Soon they will send me away.*

I finally cried then, warm tears shivering down my cheeks in the icy wind. I barely registered when an arm draped itself across my shoulders and pulled me close into a warm body. I sniffed, wiped my cheeks, and looked to my right, up into a familiar face with eyes half full of pity and half of merriment. For a moment I fancied it was the face of my father, and my heart nearly burst out of my chest with alarm. But as my blurry vision cleared, I saw the face of my elder brother gazing down at me, his fair hair and blue eyes matching mine exactly, unlike the rest of our siblings.

"Well, Bug, what now?" he asked me with the hint of a smile. I nearly winced at his use of Papa's nickname for me.

"Why didn't you come sooner?"

"It took me a long time to get here. One of the carriage wheels broke along the road as I was coming. Besides, I got the news late."

I took a deep breath and let it out slowly. My eyes filled once more. "What's to become of me?"

"You'll come home with me and Emma, of course. You know Father made me promise to take you in if anything ever happened to him."

"Did he?"

"Yes, he did, but you must know it was unnecessary. I would have done it without his asking."

"Would you?"

Brother looked wounded. "Of course. How could you think otherwise?"

"You've been gone a long while. Do you even know how old I am now?"

He gave me a playful shove. "You're not older than I am, and you've still got plenty of time before becoming…well…you know."

He grabbed my arm and gently tugged, prompting me to follow him. The sun had descended completely, and we had to tiptoe our way carefully across the grounds before finding the dirt road leading back into the village.

"Will we live here in Father's house or go to your village?"

"We are going to Father's house just for your things. You will stay with Emma and me in Ghilla."

"How are my nieces and nephews?"

Brother chuckled. "Growing fast."

"Brother," I said, sucking in my breath and hesitating. "In five years, when I turn twenty-eight and am still unmarried, will you cast me out as an unchosen?"

He crinkled his nose at the suggestion, and his shoulders stiffened. "Let's not think too far ahead, Bug. Of course you'll be married within five years."

I grabbed his arm and held him back. "But what if I'm *not*?"

He waited before responding, looking everywhere but at me. He pinched his lips tightly together and shook his head, his hands travelling to his hips. "It's not a matter under my jurisdiction, Alonya," he said, using my given name. "It's a matter of law, and of keeping the law. I would have no choice."

"Do you believe in the High King?" I said suddenly.

"What does the High King have to do with it?" he asked, and my heart thundered to the ground. I knew there'd only be temporary protection within my brother's household. He was merely doing his duty and nothing more.

"Cheer up, Buggy," he said, suddenly affecting cheerfulness, which was lost on me. "Emma and I will help you find a husband. You won't become an unchosen."

I already am, I thought to myself as I followed my brother down the dark road and toward the little cottage that had been my home for my entire life, until now.

2

IN GHILLA

Emmaline didn't like me. Maybe it was because she was beautiful and I was not. Where I was round and shapely, she was narrow and thin; where I was short, she was tall. She had eyes so delicately blue they were like clouds, and long silky russet hair streaked with auburn. Emmaline exuded femininity where I did not. She was a rose; I was a dandelion—or at best, a sunflower.

I'd only met my brother's wife once before: several years ago at their wedding. She had seemed shy and sweet, barely speaking any words but a whisper here and there into her new husband's ear, smiling benignly at the guests and well-wishers, clinging all the while to Benson's arm. The image was that of a devoted, modest, reserved young woman and bride.

When I met her again at my brother's house in the village of Ghilla, she seemed changed. Although a few years older than me, she behaved in a manner more befitting that of a young girl yet unmarried. She was resentful of me and of the intrusion into her home. Her narrowed eyes followed me everywhere when she thought I wasn't looking. When I was looking, she avoided my gaze and turned her back on me as though I was a mere shadow hidden in the corner, barely perceptible. At nights, behind closed doors, I heard Emma and Benson discussing me in hushed, argumentative tones.

"It is *not* our responsibility to find her a husband!"

"Dearest, try to understand. She's my sister and I made a promise to my father. How can you take that so lightly?"

"Your father was fool, spoiling her, feeding her fanciful notions of remaining safe and secure in his house as though the law was nonexistent. Her fate is sealed! Most girls are already married at her age!"

"She still has a few years before the law takes effect against her. There is no reason she shouldn't be given that chance."

"What chance? Even if she had a chance, where are the men? There are very few prospects in this village. Most men her age and older are already married. She would have to marry a younger man, which would be a shame and a disgrace!" Emma stopped then for just a moment. I could imagine her shuddering. "It's already a shame and a disgrace on us to keep her in this house—the poor, unmarried sister. It's a farce, this idea that she has a chance! She's getting too old, and if her age wasn't an issue, her appearance would be."

"What do you mean by that?"

Emma snorted. "Isn't it obvious, Benson? She isn't the prettiest girl in Zaphon. She's not even close."

There it was again—that spoken recognition of my flaw, my plainness, my curse.

"Plainer girls than Alonya are chosen every day," Benson tried to reason.

Emma laughed derisively. "I can't see why. Anyway, the sooner she accepts her fate, the better!"

Countless times I overheard Benson hiss, "Emma, hush!" But Emma never hushed. I was unwanted in her home, which to me was worse than being unchosen.

So as not to prove an imposition, I tried to stay out of the way. Benson made polite conversation over the table at meal times. Whenever I replied, Emma frowned and her jaw tightened. Eventually I kept my head down and ate in silence. At least once a month for the first year of my residence in their home, Benson invited a male friend or acquaintance to supper. Emma presided at these events, ignoring me as usual, but chatty and charming as possible—so much so that she monopolized the conversation and attention of the guest. For my part, I was so discomfited by the obvious attempts at matchmaking that I usually shrank away from the evening as soon as possible. Benson would sigh and splutter as he lectured me later, and eventually he gave up. No new supper guests ever came after that.

I took to wandering the village when I wasn't at my brother's house. I spoke to very few people, but I learned of quiet places to sit and think and oftentimes knit or read. My walks eventually led in a wider arc, to the outskirts of the village at the edge of the wood. I never went in alone, but my curious brain pondered its depths and mysteries as I stared intently into the trees, down the dirt road that threaded its way through the tangle. I longed to have the freedom to walk down that road on my own, to go seek my fortune as it seemed my fortune at present had eluded me.

When I was at the house, I made myself as useful as possible. I rarely watched the children—my nieces and nephews—as Emma seemed to resent my playing with them. I cleaned up after myself, and I did my own cooking and washing. I helped the servants each day so that I eventually became one of them. The old housekeeper was kind to me. Her eyes watched me with pity. The butler was cordial, the cook was comical, and the maids were young and bubbly. They spoke to me as friends and equals. After time I faded into the background; I became the shadow that Emma always treated me as.

One day, without being told, I silently moved my things from my room in the main house into a room in the servants' quarters.

If I could become a meager servant, if I could disappear, if people never knew about Benson's unmarried sister, then perhaps I'd be safe. Perhaps even Benson wouldn't bother with me when my time came.

In time Benson treated me as a servant: he was cold and distant. He never approached me about my voluntary move into the servants' quarters. Perhaps he understood my decision; perhaps he didn't really care. Perhaps he merely hoped to appease his childish and selfish wife.

I found there was satisfaction in usefulness. I kept myself busy from dawn until dusk working with the household servants and taking my solitary trips into the village; and for a short while, in my own little way, I was content with my lot. I kept so busy and distracted with errands and duties that I had no time to concern myself with anything else. I had stopped looking in mirrors long before. There was no need of mirrors. I didn't think about how I looked as a servant. There was a freedom in forgetting about myself, in forgetting my looks, in ceasing to care.

There was a bitterness too, born of the curse and slowly gnawing away at my insides, but I didn't realize it at the time. I didn't realize that I wasn't forgetting myself, I was merely ignoring myself. I often cried myself to sleep at night thinking about Papa and how much I missed him. I wondered what had become of my mother, and why she never wrote to me or visited. It seemed she had already disowned me for the shame of having an unmarried daughter.

There hadn't been an unchosen in that part of Zaphon for several years. When I first moved into my brother's village and ran into town on a jaunt or an errand, I received several sidelong glances and whispered stares in my direction. I never knew for sure, but I had the eerie impression that the villagers put bets out on me as to whether I would become an unchosen or not. As time wore on and the villagers became accustomed to me, they let me alone. The novelty of my situation faded and I was, for the most part, ignored.

Ignored, that is, until the day the peddler came into town.

I was twenty-seven then. I had been four years in Ghilla when the peddler drifted into town atop his rattling cart, pulled by two dusty-brown mares. The dull clang of rusty bells preceded him, alerting the villagers to his presence. Several prospective buyers came out of their houses and cottages and businesses toward his cart. He drove the cart into the village square, stood up as he yanked back the reins, pulling the cart to a sudden halt, and jumped swiftly down from his perch.

"Wares to sell, low prices, high-quality products and trinkets from exotic locations, foreign imports! Come and see! I buy and sell and trade!"

The peddler walked to the back of his cart and pulled aside a large woolen blanket. Dust flew from its folds. Underneath was a mountain of goods and wares. The peddler immediately began pulling things out to display. The crowd inched closer. Fascinated and curious, I watched from a distance across the square, behind a wooden courthouse pillar. This was a new peddler man. I had never seen him before. He was young and seemed energetic and enthusiastic. He spoke easily and freely with the villagers. He made jokes and they laughed. I smiled and laughed in my solitude from my hiding place across the square. And then I heard him say something that grabbed my attention like nothing else had.

"Authentic beauty potions from Coralind. Made with kelp and other rare ingredients found only in the waters of the merrow people. Infused with magical properties."

I skeptically wondered why everything exotic and magical only came from outside of Zaphon, yet I was drawn in by the powerful words, seduced by the promises of beauty. Those words tugged at my heart, urging me forward, but I ignored their pull and stayed glued to my post. I further watched, waited, and listened. The peddler pulled out ribbons, laces, mirrors, fragrances, potions, and other pretty things that I wondered about and longed for. *Oh, to be pretty, to feel worthy to wear such things, to sport beauty, to have the confidence to look into a mirror again!*

I bit my bottom lip and waited. Minutes passed. At least an hour passed, then nearly an hour and a half. The crowed thickened at one point; then finally, slowly, it began dispersing. I seized my chance. When the last customer left and the peddler began packing up, I peered left and right to make sure I was alone then ran across the square toward the cart. I slowed as I approached it, nearly losing my nerve. At the last minute, before the peddler looked up and saw me, I affected a brave front. Squaring my shoulders and lifting my chin, I stepped up right behind him as he was bent over his cart and said, "Excuse me, peddler sir, I am interested in one of your beauty potions."

He turned and gave one quick sweep of my person before saying with a chuckle, "I doubt you could afford such a luxury."

"Oh?" I said, instinctively jingling the coins in my apron pocket. He heard the tinkling and frowned, reviewing and considering me more closely this time. Within such close proximity I was struck anew at his young appearance. Most peddlers were poor, dirty, middle-aged men. This man was by no means well-to-do, but he was clean and spruce in a tunic and jerkin; his dark hair was tame, his face washed, and his beard trimmed. He seemed to have a nice store of merchandise on his cart. The cart likewise looked to have new wooden wheels and was built of a smooth, richly dark wood.

The peddler pulled a couple bottles out of his store and handed them to me. I wasn't sure what to do with them. I turned the bottles over in my hand. I took out the stoppers and smelled the liquid inside. As far as I could tell, there was nothing particularly fascinating about the bottles or what was contained therein.

Uncertain what to do or say at that moment, I handed the bottles back to the peddler. I didn't want to admit that I had no idea what to do with the potions. Did I drink them, smell them, or lather my skin with them? I was too embarrassed to ask. So I merely said, "You've been to Coralind and the surrounding countries?"

"No, but I trade with those who have." He eyed me with curiosity and suspicion, holding up the bottles in one hand. "You don't want these after all then?" Without waiting for a reply, he turned and placed the bottles back in the cart. "They really are made from rare seaweeds."

I nodded but said nothing. I eyed all the products littering that cart, lovely, beautiful, rich things that I had never known and probably never would know. My heart ached for beauty.

The peddler waited for me to say something, to ask to see something else from his store, but all I did was look. I stood mute, transfixed. He continued straightening up his wares, then moved to the front of his cart and began petting and whispering to one of the horses. I watched him. I didn't know why. The longing of my heart held me there.

He saw that my attention had been turned from his merchandise. He leaned against the flanks of the horse and crossed his arms, returning the stare, a smirk pasted to his lips.

"So you feel you need a potion to make yourself beautiful?"

"Of course," I blurted out, as though I had been waiting for him to speak the entire time. "Anyone who looks at me can see that I do."

He took a minute to scrutinize my face. I lowered it from his searching gaze. "I see no such thing," he said.

I kept my face downturned for shame he would see me blush, wondering what kind of a man he was to say such a thing. I pictured him a ruffian fisherman with a large net, tossing it over women like they were goods to be captured and sold. Was he trying to catch me for something? He was a peddler. He dealt in buying and selling. He had probably sold many women compliments to buy their good fortune and their money. I couldn't trust him.

I sucked in my breath. "Yes, well, you know nothing about it." I turned my face up boldly and shot him a fierce glare.

He frowned. "I know nothing about beauty?"

"No—" My lip began quivering with emotion. I quickly bit it and held my chin up higher. "About not being chosen."

The young peddler said nothing, but his eyes softened. That gave me courage to go on.

"In a few months' time, I will be twenty-eight, and then the law will brand me an unchosen. I will be forced to leave my brother's home."

"Your brother's home?"

"Yes. My father is dead, and I have no husband." Heat crept up my face at the confession, yet it seemed to embolden me more to say it aloud, to let it out. A sense of freedom washed over me like a pleasant, fragrant breeze that clears the stale air.

A glint of pain shone in the peddler's eyes—a look I did not expect and could not understand. "Surely your own brother would not cast you out as an unchosen," he said.

"He would have no choice. The law would demand it, and he would become a lawbreaker in trying to keep me."

The peddler's eyes suddenly swept me up and down. "But you are a servant. Does not the law make concessions for the lower classes who already earn their own wages and prove themselves useful by their service? You and your brother may appeal to your employer, who may then appeal to the law."

I had never heard of an appeal process, yet it did not matter. I was no servant. My eyes fell to my feet.

"Who is your employer?" the peddler asked me suddenly.

I shook my head, still looking at my feet. "I am not a servant."

He once again glanced over my appearance—my plain, coarse dress and dirtied apron; my long hair wrapped tightly in a headscarf from my forehead, where tiny wisps peeked out, all the way down to the middle of my back where my split ends were visible; the large wicker basket at my side laden with fruits and vegetables and other shopping items.

"I apologize. I merely assumed because…"

I saw the peddler's confusion and spoke quickly to put him to rights. "My brother is a prominent member of this village, though our father was only of humble origins. My brother has transacted business well and built his own fortune."

He frowned. "And yet he allows you, his own sister, to dress and behave as his household servant instead of sharing his wealth and blessings with you?"

"He owes me nothing. He keeps me in his household out of duty, and I have chosen to make myself useful by becoming like the servants in the hopes that I might…that I might…" My voice faltered, and my cheeks once again began to burn. "That I might become… *insignificant* enough that there would be no need to cast me out."

The peddler watched me intently with such interest and pity that it disarmed me. My bold façade melted, and my eyes began to sting with tears.

"But you said yourself that your brother would have to become a lawbreaker in trying to keep you."

I heard and felt the absurdity of my words before I spoke them. "I'm hoping he will forget me, that he will overlook me when my time comes."

The peddler shook his head, and his eyes flashed fire momentarily. I was perplexed by his passion, his understanding and pity.

"Brother or employer, you may still appeal to him. There is a process by which a woman may appeal to the law and escape banishment."

For a moment my heart fluttered with hope. "Is that so? I have never heard of such a thing."

"Truly there is. You must speak to your brother. It's the only way."

I considered this, but more than that I considered the young man standing before me. He was a man, and he was independent; why should be care so much about an insignificant stranger—a female, no less?

He seemed to sense me pondering his motives. He cleared his throat, wiped his brow, and turned back toward his cart, covering his goods with the large dusty blanket before mounting the wobbly seat at the front. Picking up the reins, he gave me one last pity-filled look.

"Do you still want a beauty potion?"

I had nearly forgotten my original reason for speaking with the peddler. I crinkled my brows and shook my head, stepping back out of the path of the horse and cart. The peddler smiled gently and turned his face from mine. He clicked his tongue and snapped the reins. The horses jumped to attention, and soon the cart rattled out of sight, hidden by a dust cloud left in its wake.

3

Unchosen

Indecision plagued me. Days passed, then weeks. I could not decide whether to appeal to Benson or remain quiet and, hopefully, undisturbed. Benson had ceased acknowledging the day of my birth for the last few years. He hadn't spoken to me in nearly as long. Perhaps he really had forgotten about me. If then I spoke to Benson about the appeal, it would alert him to my presence and remind him that my time was near. I would essentially be sabotaging myself. If, on the other hand, I remained silent and said nothing—if I went about my usual business, quiet and unassuming—perhaps I'd be safe, at least for a while longer. Benson wouldn't really be breaking the law by keeping me, because he wouldn't be mindful of my existence in his house.

I knew it was all too absurd even as I hoped for it. At some point I would be found out, if not by Benson then by Emma for certain. My own brother may have forgotten me, but Emma had not—of that I was convinced.

It seemed my only logical choice was to speak with Benson and appeal to his mercy. I shuddered at the thought of having to remain in the same household with Emma, but if I could go on as a servant, it might be bearable. At least then Emma wouldn't have to acknowledge me as her unmarried, unchosen sister-in-law.

My brother was in the dusty workshop near the house, presiding over a male servant who was sweating over a broken wagon wheel. Benson's shirtsleeves were rolled up and his hairline was rimmed with moisture from the humid air. He pulled out a dirtied handkerchief and wiped his brow as he inspected the servant's progress.

My heart sped up and my breath became labored as I approached my brother. I stopped in my tracks. Everything I'd settled in my mind to say to him suddenly left me. How could I talk to Benson when it had been so long? Looking at him then, I felt I hardly knew him. He was a stranger to me, a brother no longer.

I lost my nerve and turned suddenly, retracing my steps to flee the workshop. My long skirts caught on a fallen board, and I tripped, landing facedown in the dirt and straw. Benson spun around. He watched as I struggled to my feet but did not approach me or offer help. He was about to return his attention to his servant when he finally registered who I was.

"Oh, Alonya, hello," he said as he offered a quick, formal bow.

I smoothed my skirts and ran my hands over my face as though wiping away my fear and humiliation. I did not speak but merely looked at my brother, willing my heart to slow to a regular pace, balling my fists to keep them from shaking so.

"May...May I help you with something?" Benson stammered. Clearly he was as uncomfortable as I was.

I took a deep breath and held it. Benson's eyes looked so sad, so heavy with worry and care. He had changed much in just a few years. My brother was not yet thirty-five, but he appeared much older as I beheld him in that moment. And his body was more wasted, thinner, his back a bit stooped. How I pitied him then. Just as he had forgotten me, I had forgotten him in my own worries and cares.

"Please Alonya, speak if you have something to say. Otherwise leave me to my duties." He turned his back on me, and I stepped forward, kicking the hay and straw with my feet.

"I…I wish to speak to you regarding an important matter."

Benson returned his attention to me and nodded. "You have leave. Speak."

I glanced around the workshop and toward the open door. "May we find a place more remote?"

Benson sighed but honored my request. We left the workshop and entered his private office in the back of the house. Emma's eyes narrowed when she saw us pass by. She tried to follow us into the office, but Benson closed the door in her face before she could get a word in. I nearly smiled but then remembered the heaviness of my brother's behavior and appearance. I knew things were not well at home with his wife, and I knew it was partly my fault. Right then I sensed I couldn't stay. I mustn't stay. I would no longer try to hide. I would ask Benson about the appeal process, but I would not hope for much. It would be better for me to leave.

Benson sat at his desk and folded his hands on the tabletop in front of him, eyeing me expectantly. I remained standing, shuffling my feet before speaking.

"I…it has come to my attention…that is…I have nearly reached my twenty-eighth year. My birthday is next month, to be exact."

Benson nodded but said nothing.

"So…well…you do realize what that means, do you not?"

"I do."

"Did you forget?" I asked suddenly.

Benson's voice filled with regret. "No, I did not forget."

I cleared my throat. "It has come to my attention recently that there exists an appeal process for…women…of my… circumstances."

Benson's eyebrows rose. "It has come to your attention?"

"Yes. I've been speaking with others."

His face registered incredulity for a moment as though he could hardly fathom my speaking to anyone. He unclasped his folded hands and tapped his fingers against the tabletop.

"I see. And you are hoping to enter into this appeal process?"

I shrugged. "Well, I would like to know what my options are. As you can probably very well guess, I would not like to be cast out as an unchosen."

The corners of his lips curled into a smile. "For a woman who has been behaving like a servant for the last many years, you are very well-spoken."

My eyes widened at the statement, partly because it revealed Benson's awareness of my situation despite my hopes otherwise, and partly because of the unexpected compliment embedded therein.

He sat up straighter, and his voice took on a tone of formality and authoritativeness. "As you know, our father is dead, and Emma and I have failed in finding you a husband. In a month it will no longer fall on my hands to keep you. By law I am no longer required to shelter you." He shifted in his seat and once again folded his hands together. "In fact, by law I am *required* to cast you out."

My heart was stung as though with an arrow. I merely nodded. Again, here was Benson performing an office, a duty. He had long ago ceased to think of me as his sister. I ached for him to call me Bug as Papa used to do; that nickname had died on his lips years ago and had failed to be resurrected on Benson's. But Benson had never really tried.

"What do you say to this?" Benson asked.

I wrung my hands then picked up my apron and twisted it for something to occupy me. "Well, I say it is an awfully cruel law that does not allow for differences in gifts and fortunes and circumstances." I cast my eyes sideways before adding, "After all, it is not my fault I am unmarried."

A chortle flew from Benson's lips. "Is that so? I would disagree with you, Alonya."

My eyebrows shot up, and I took a step closer to the desk, challenging him with my eyes to explain.

"Emma and I have tried in our own way to find you a husband, although it was not our responsibility, but you shunned all attempts."

"What attempts?" I nearly forgot myself in my frustration. "You had guests over for supper and nothing more. You never helped me, never coached me, never encouraged me! You never allowed me to feel good about myself, to become confident, to know how to attract suitors!" I was near tears. "You've never believed in me! You and Emma have been resigned to my fate for years. You've merely been biding your time until the day came for me to leave!"

Benson squirmed mildly in his seat before standing to gain ground over me. "We have done what we know to do. It is through no fault of ours that you cannot manage to attract a man."

My response stopped in my throat. Moisture began seeping from my eyes.

"Alonya, try to understand—"

"What about an appeal?" I boldly stated, wiping my eyes.

Benson hesitated a long while before replying, "There will be no appeal."

"Why not? I'm your sister!"

"That has nothing to do with it. I am under the law just as you are."

"And the law makes concessions. Why won't you try?"

Benson let out a breath that was nearly a growl. "Appeals cost money, Alonya. Much money."

"Money? What is that to you? You can afford it."

"I fear it would do no good to appeal. Extra time won't buy you a husband. It's too late."

"I can do other things besides be a wife and mother. Why must it be required for every woman to be married?"

Benson sneered as though he had a bad taste in his mouth. "An unmarried woman is a disgrace. She has no proper place or duty without a husband and children. It is what she was made for."

My fists balled at my sides. "I can't believe that."

"Believe what you will. The law states it."

"Curse the law! Father said men make laws that aren't always for our good."

"Father led you astray with fanciful notions."

"Father would have appealed."

"Father was an old fool, and he never could have afforded it!"

"He would have found a way!"

Benson shook his head in frustration. "Even so, he never would have won. Very few appeals are ever granted, and usually only for laborers and servants."

"I'll be your servant, Benson. Let me stay!"

"No! Emma and I will *not* pay another servant. We have only tolerated you working with our servants because it kept you useful and out of the way. We don't need extra servants."

I moved closer to grab his hands, but he backed away. I fell to my knees. "I'll work for no pay! Please, Benson, don't cast me out! Don't let me be banished! Where will I go? What will I do? I'll die on the streets!"

Benson turned his back on me, but his voice wavered when he spoke. "Don't be so theatrical." He sucked in his breath sharply and spun back around to face me as I knelt on the floor, my cheeks streaked with tears. "This is the way things are. This is the way the world functions here. You must accept your place in it, Alonya."

I remained where I was, my head hung low, the ends of my long hair grazing the floor and hiding my face. Finally I wiped my tears and stood up. I met Benson's eyes bravely.

"You are cruel, brother. Despite what you say and how you attempt to justify yourself, you are wrong. You have not kept Father's promise, and for that you will be judged."

"Unfortunately, Alonya, your many words do not change the law. You have one month in my house, and then you must leave. If you do not go willingly, they will force you out." He lowered his voice to a near whisper. "Please, do not expose yourself to such ridicule and disgrace. Go willingly."

"Is it for me or for yourself that you are truly concerned, Benson?" I said, turning to walk out of the office. Emma jumped back as I opened the door, and I nearly bumped into her in my haste to get out. She turned and quickly sped away, but not before I caught the glint of a smile on her face.

PART TWO

Quest for Beauty

Outcast

That is how my curse came to pass. I became one of the unchosen, the first from my province in many years. Those who knew me—those who remembered me and perhaps cared a little—watched me leave the village with my woolen cloak wrapped about me and a cloth bundle slung over my shoulder, their eyes full of pity and regret. *This is how it will be from now on,* I thought. *Everywhere I go I will be known as an unchosen. I will be watched with pity. Shame and disgrace will follow me. People will never look at me the same. At any given moment, I will be the object of either charity or scorn.*

I went forth branded, stigmatized.

Benson's eyes followed me just out the door before he lowered his pained-filled gaze and turned away. Emma didn't bother to see me out. She scampered outside with her children and ignored me as though it was an ordinary day. For her I suppose it was, but not for me. This was the day I'd inadvertently waited for my whole life. I had known it was coming. I had always feared it, always hoped it wouldn't come to pass, as though with enough wishing I might've deferred or disrupted it from its course. But it came swift as rushing waters downstream and swept me up in its current. I was terrified as I stood at the edge of the village, on the borders of the wood. I had no notion of where to go or what to do. It seemed the end of my life had come. I would now never be chosen. It was too late.

So I stood at the edge of that wood and peered down the ribbon road winding its way deeper in and farther away. Despite my terror, a part of me felt relieved as well. Finally the day was here. I might face it, settle it, and try to move on past it. Certainly nothing good would ever fill my life after this, but I was free. I was branded, plain, unchosen, but I now had the freedom to walk about at will and in a sense govern my own life. It would be a small hollow of a life, but it would be mine. The old chapter of my life was over and closed. I had no idea what awaited me, and my body shivered in fear and excitement.

That day was bright, sunny, and warm. Shafts of glittering sunlight broke through the forest canopy and sprinkled the road. It invited me in despite my trepidation and doubts. I placed myself bravely and resolutely forward and began walking.

I walked blindly for hours. I followed the main road through the forest. Although a long and solitary road, it was dotted with inns every several miles. Once in a while, it pushed out of the wood into open country only to eventually return to the wood as though uncomfortable with the openness of the farms and pastureland by which it passed. I preferred the woods myself. There were fewer people there, fewer farms, fewer crossroads leading to other villages and civilization. I was on my own—yes—and should enjoy company, but I wanted to hide. My braveness in setting out was more of a front, a façade. I had no choice in the matter. Necessity urged my face forward and my feet onward.

I had a small store of coins saved up over the years from gifts and odd jobs. Although Benson hadn't paid me for being a servant in his household, the housekeeper had, after a time, recognized my sacrifice and my service. She had for months past been paying me under the table from her personal savings. She was the only person with whom I'd bid a tearful farewell as I'd left my brother's village. If I was hers, she'd said, she'd find a way to keep me. She'd pay her life savings and live in debt until her dying days to keep me.

I would never see her again.

I thought about her on the road after several aimless hours of walking, keeping my eyes focused forward and my brain numbed to my circumstances. Suddenly, in one fitful moment as the sun was dipping below the horizon, and I looked about me and saw the darkness and felt my solitude like a heavy burden on my back, I fell to my knees in the middle of the dirt road and wept.

Is this what all the unchosen came to? The only tears I'd had before now had been silent, dripping tears as I lay in my bed at night, fearing my future, my curse. Now the tears streamed out, accompanied by a wailing from the deep recesses of my heart that poured out of my throat. I didn't even hear it or understand it at first. It seemed like the howling of some dreadful creature of the wood, low, plaintive, and lonely, carried on the wind toward me. But it was only me. I was the dreadful creature. Truly, in that moment, I was dreadful.

I did not fear robbers or evil men or wild beasts or death in that moment. I wept until my body convulsed and lay nearly lifeless along the side of the road, my face hidden in my scratchy woolen hood. Over and over again I uttered a futile "Why?" into the air, although to whom I was speaking I did not know. I longed to be answered, to be seen, to be recognized and loved and chosen. My cry faded and dispersed on the wind the moment it was uttered, unable to survive for lack of strength and passion.

I was dead.

"Get out of the road, wench!"

A spray of dirt was kicked into my face by the hooves and wheels of a passing horse and cart. I was still lying on the side of the road, having dozed off unexpectedly. As the rattling cart passed by, I shifted a little, my cloak still wrapped about me, and rolled to my other side so that I was facing the wood. Dusk had nearly gone and night was settling in. It was a wonder the traveler had seen me at all; wrapped in my cloak like a large mossy rock, I might easily have been taken for such in the twilight. I had no strength or heart to move. I didn't care if I was trampled.

My stomach lurched and moaned with hunger. I whimpered and pulled my cloak more tightly about me, as though I might fold into myself enough so as to eventually disappear. I didn't disappear. Another traveler came down the road, this time a lone rider on a steed, and he didn't even bother to throw words at me. The thundering hooves came so close to my ears, rattling my entire body that my heart sped up with trepidation. I instinctively drew closer to the wood. My eyes were wide open, level with the grasses poking up out of the dirt. A single blade tickled my nose. It was cool to the touch. The forest floor smelled of fresh upturned earth and dewy grass—sweet and alive. A single tear escaped down my cheek as my stomach lurched again.

It was no use. If I was going to die, it wouldn't be this night. I groaned and heaved myself up into a sitting position. As I did so, two women in plain peasant's clothes walked by with heavy baskets hanging from their backs and bundles wrapped in their arms. The women caught my eyes and suddenly darted to the other side of the road as though I was diseased. I scowled and turned my eyes away, keeping my head down as they walked past, although their mutterings were not hidden to me.

"I heard about her this morning. She's the unchosen one from Ghilla."

"It has been many years since this province has seen an unchosen."

Their tongues clucked—a couple of hens. I imagined their bundles and baskets becoming feathers and those wagging heads growing beaks.

"What a shame," they whispered, none too discreetly. "Such a waste."

I dared a look after the sound of their footsteps had faded. They were still gazing at me with curiosity. I half wanted to jump to my feet, spread out my arms, growl as savagely as I could manage, and chase them down the street. The mere thought of it put a small smile on my face. The women saw my grin and gasped, rightly guessing evil intent behind it. They turned and sped away.

Well, I thought to myself, *I'm no different than I was yesterday, or this morning for that matter, except that the people I love and care about have ceased to protect me under the law. I am healthy but treated as diseased for something I have no control over and had no hand in.*

I mused on this in silence before the grumbling of my stomach became so great it compelled me to my feet despite myself. I hadn't eaten all day besides a few bites of bread and cheese from my bundle. Even now I fished it out and devoured the rest, along with an apple. After the meek repast, my stomach was still unsatisfied, and my legs shook and nearly buckled underneath me with weakness as I stood. I took a step and urged myself forward.

Dusk grew into night as blackness filled the sky, causing the last traces of light to skip away and hide. The air grew chilly. I walked for nearly an hour before the distant cacophony of chatter, music, and laughter met my ears. The woods cleared a bit and a faint light shone through the night. I set my eyes on the clearing and pushed forward. Within fifteen minutes I had arrived at a tavern.

Eerie yellow light glowed from within the small tavern. I hesitated several feet from the door, my heart thudding. I contemplated what would happen when I walked in, whether the people would stare at me, throw insults at me, or kick me out.

Taverns certainly were not where the decent of society gathered, especially not in the dark of night. I had walked most of the day and must have gained at least fifteen to twenty miles from Ghilla. It seemed unlikely I'd meet anyone I knew face-to-face. I comforted myself with the thought that if I did, they'd also have something to feel ashamed of, and I wouldn't be the only one keeping my head down.

Heartened somewhat by that conclusion, I threw up my hood, put my head down, and pushed open the heavy wooden door.

I braved a glance upward once I'd made it inside. My first sight was of a middle-aged woman carrying a tray and running from table to table. The fact that I wouldn't be the only woman in that place further emboldened me. I began walking into the room, casting furtive glances sideways as I did. Dirty, travel-stained men of all ages, some bearded and some too young for beards, followed me with their eyes—curious, but not angry, and not full of pity. I quickened my pace and found a small round table in the farthest corner of the room away from most of the other patrons. I sat without taking off my cloak or lowering my hood. My cheeks were on fire; I sat for a moment, attempting to calm my nerves, which was difficult due to the weight of attention on me. Here was the moment of testing. Would they interrogate me? Would I be taken for a servant or suspected of being an outcast? Would it even matter? In Zaphon there were no laws forbidding an unchosen to move around in public or to use public facilities, or even to attempt finding employment for herself. However, neither did the law protect the unchosen from the prejudiced, cruel public when it chose to exclude or discriminate against them. I was in the hands of the people of this tavern, whether those hands would grab me and throw me out, or offer me a tray of food. I prayed for the latter.

I rubbed my hands together and blew on them for warmth. A fire blazed in the hearth on the opposite side of the room, but I received little of its heat. I was just debating within myself whether I should ask for a tray when a tin mug with steaming liquid was set in front of me. Startled, I looked up quickly. The same woman I'd seen upon first entering the tavern was smiling gently at me.

"Something to warm you up, dear," she said before winking at me and walking away.

I nodded in response. *So kindness still exists for the unchosen.* I longed to do something in return as I watched her walk away to serve the other patrons in the room. Her face was flushed, her forehead soaked with perspiration, and her skin sallow. Her skirts were short and frayed at the hem, and her bodice was tight and stained. I wondered if she had any other clothes. If she could have fit my size I would have handed her my spare clothing from my bundle in that instant. I was disappointed that I could do nothing. A compulsion seized me to remember her face and do something for her, sometime, when I could.

I wrapped my hands around the warm tin mug and held it to my lips. My body relaxed a bit and I slumped in my seat. *What now?*

Noise filled every inch of the tavern. I sat quietly, alone, unmolested. Eventually the curious stares subsided, and I was left just as insignificant and unnoticed as ever. There was a sort of comfort in that. The kind woman came back and brought me food without my having to ask. I could do nothing but smile and thank her with tears in my eyes. Somehow I felt she understood my position and my pain as I saw something of similar circumstances in her eyes and in her manner. At the same time, I questioned whether I would end up like her, and then the tears turned from gratitude into fear.

I lowered my face to hide the shame of my tears, although I was convinced that very few people saw me or cared about me in that moment.

But I was wrong. A man sat opposite me, bold, uninvited; and when I looked up, startled, I saw the familiar, kind eyes of the peddler man.

5

Peddler

He looked tired and shabbier than when I'd seen him last in Ghilla: darkness circling his eyes and his long hair falling clumsily over his forehead. Yet he smiled and his eyes were large with feeling. A mixture of pleasure and embarrassment washed over me at the sight of him. I tilted my head down slightly but turned my eyes upward to peer at him from across the table.

"We've met before, have we not?" he asked.

I nodded.

"Forgive me for being so forward, but I assume your brother did not appeal in your interest?"

I shook my head.

The peddler sighed and tapped his fingers on the tabletop. "I am truly sorry for your misfortune."

Somehow those words did not comfort as I suppose he meant them to. Instead they incited a resentment that spat itself out like venom.

"You? Sorry? How can you have any concern for me? I mean nothing to you. You're a man. Nothing can ever touch you. You have the law on your side." I was shocked at my own boldness.

He sat up and frowned. "Yes, that's true. But I can still sympathize with you in your situation—in your sorrow."

I huffed in derision. "What do you know about being unchosen, about women of my fate?" I looked him directly in the eyes while I upbraided him. "I see that you yourself are unmarried and probably not much older than I. You've probably sent many women to their fates as unchosens." I almost regretted the words as they spilled from my mouth, yet a part of me was unable to stop. "You surely have not redeemed any."

The man's face grew stony. He leaned back in his chair and dropped his hands in his lap. There was a glint of anger in his eyes that softened the more he studied me.

"You do me a great injustice to judge me so without knowing me. I understand your bitterness and realize that you are under the weight of a great sorrow and trouble. But there are many different sorrows in this world. Yours is not the only kind."

I said nothing but merely snorted.

He grew impatient with me and suddenly leaned forward with his forearms stretched out across the table, nearly touching mine. I pulled them back.

"Have you considered the trouble of the man who cannot pay his bills or his taxes? He goes into debt, and consequently his land is taken from him, making him homeless, plunging him into poverty. He loses his rights. His wife and children are then sold into slavery to pay his debts."

I frowned and shook my head. "Such a thing does not happen anymore."

"Such a thing *does* happen, perhaps not where you're from, but in many areas of Zaphon, slavery is still legal. Have you considered the trouble of the children whose parents die or abandon them, leaving them fatherless and living on the streets, eating rubbish and clothed in rags, with no one to tend to their needs or to love them? Have you considered the plight of the man or woman who is wrongfully accused of a crime and sentenced to pay for it in years spent in jail or a rope around their necks?"

His voice rose, passionate. I turned my eyes away. I dared not look at him. I feared that passion, that righteous wrath. But then he took a deep and quavering breath, and when he spoke again, his voice was calmer and more melancholic.

"Have you considered the trouble of the man who is rejected by his sweetheart, the man who gives up everything for her and is repaid in faithlessness? His heart shatters. He loses all hope. He turns to the bottle, or to gambling, or to unchaste women, all in an effort to forget her." He stopped and waited until the silence and the space widened between us, and I squirmed in my seat. Then he went on. "That man considers himself unchosen."

I dared a look at him then. His eyes were cast to the floor, his head lowered. The silence grew between us, thick and heavy. He glanced over at me, and I turned my face away in shame.

"You see, even a man can know what it feels to be unchosen. For all these men and women, the law is useless. It does not protect them—just as in your case."

I'd spouted like a volcano, but instead of feeling relief, I was horrified with shame. I was also too proud and too cowardly to apologize. I let warm, silent tears fall into my lap.

The hum of background conversation, the squeak of chair legs across the wooden floorboards, and the clack of dishware on the tabletops continued steadily and eventually soaked up the tension in the atmosphere between the peddler and me. His voice was soft and kind when he spoke next.

"What can I do for you to help you in your trouble?"

"That's not necessary."

"No, please—I'd like to do something."

I sniffed and wiped my eyes. "Why?"

"Must a man have a reason for being kind?"

"Yes, especially a man. How do I know you aren't offering help as a guise for some darker motive?"

He raised his eyebrows, and one corner of his mouth curved up in a half-smile. "I understand your caution, but I assure you that I can be trusted. Have I not proven that already?"

I cleared my throat and took a half-hearted sip of my cooling drink. "Forgive me, sir, but we've only met twice." I looked him up and down and almost laughed. "And you are a peddler."

"What does my being a peddler have to do with it?"

"Well," I stammered, unsure how to argue my point. Peddlers were businessmen, of course, concerned about gaining as much money as possible, usually by overcharging customers for their wares or embellishing the superiority of their products. I nearly said so then thought better of it and bit my tongue. I looked at the man instead and considered his casual appearance. He looked as if he'd been traveling and working nonstop for days. He was off his guard—off duty—and did seem to be genuine in the words he'd spoken. He *had* been kind to me both times I'd met him. He had sad, honest eyes. I wanted to trust him. I ached for kindness, for a friend.

Yet at the same time, I shrunk away from his openness. He was a man who dealt in buying and selling. He was accustomed to using smooth words to draw people in.

In the end all I said was, "I just don't see how a peddler can be trusted."

Somehow in the silence that followed, I grew cold. The fire was still blazing in the hearth on the other side of the room; the serving woman bent over a large cauldron hanging over it, stirring the warm soup inside, but a shadow seemed to hover in our corner of the room.

"If you must know, I despise what I do," the man replied after a small pause. "I do it only for the sake of necessity—to keep out of poverty," he cleared his throat, "and because it is a quick and easy way to earn money for—"

"An easy way to make money? Just as I thought! Is that all peddlers care about?"

He narrowed his eyes at me. "I warn you, do not be so hasty to judge or condemn me."

I set my hands down forcefully on the tabletop and pushed back my chair to rise. "I've heard enough. Please excuse me. I'll be going now."

He followed me with his eyes. His frustration melted away and was replaced by concern. "Where will you go?"

"What is it to you?" I barked, my voice catching in my throat and tears threatening to squeeze out once again.

"I just want to help."

I ignored him and threaded my way through the tables toward the front entrance. He jumped up and followed behind.

"But you haven't eaten yet!"

I nearly ran as I pushed myself out the door and into the cold, inky night. It had begun to drizzle, and the dirt road was soggy with new-formed mud. I pulled up my hood and hugged my small bundle of possessions to my chest, wondering where I would go for the night. *I should stay at the inn. Why wander out into the woods in the middle of the night?*

I looked about me helplessly and finally stopped only a few feet from the front entrance. The peddler caught up to me.

"Please do not go wandering alone at this time of night. You must stay at the inn."

"What if they won't take me in?"

"They will. As long as you have money they'll let you stay. They've already let you sit and drink, right? So they will let you stay. If not, I will speak for you." He winked at me. "I come here often on my travels."

Everything he did, down to that very wink, heightened my suspicion and sense of caution, yet I allowed him to lead me back into the building. He helped me secure a room and told me I'd see him in the morning.

I, for one, had no intention of seeing him in the morning.

6

Terrington

It was still dark when I left the inn; I stole away quietly in the frosty morning before the sun could stretch out its arms in a yawn and touch the edges of the world with its warmth. My breath froze on the air as I stepped outside. I pulled my cloak tightly about me, lifted my hood, clutched my bundle close to my chest, and set forward resolutely, though once again aimlessly. I had no sense of what direction I traveled—I only knew I was heading farther away from the home and the life I'd known.

In my haste to leave the inn and escape the peddler before he was awake, I had neglected to eat anything for breakfast. After only an hour on the road, my stomach began rebelling. I had but a few crumbs from the previous day left in my bundle. I thought little of it, however. Following the main road would certainly lead me to another inn soon enough.

But the hours elapsed as I walked on, and no inn appeared. The road became narrower, the wood thicker, and passersby scarce. A part of me preferred fewer travelers. I'd already had my share of being stared at. Whenever I did hear the thump of hooves or the rattling of wheels approaching, I quickly dove sideways into the thick of the trees and hid behind a large stump or bush. It was easier to avoid people altogether—no questions, no stares, and no pity that way.

I warmed up as the afternoon progressed, but my feet ached and my stomach twisted more painfully with hunger. My pace along the road slowed and became little more than a drag. Without food I wouldn't make it anywhere. I'd die within a few days. I moved closer to the edge of the wood and peered into it as I walked along, searching for berry bushes or nuts. Yet I was unaccustomed to living and surviving in the wilderness. I hardly knew what to look for.

After the sun had long come up and was cresting the sky, my ears picked up the distant creak and rattle of a cart approaching. I sighed, tossed up my hood, and moved sideways to assume a hiding spot. I squatted down behind a bush, which contained blackberries, and waited for the intruder to pass and leave me in peace. He seemed to slow as he neared, and I slunk down further in my hiding spot, craning my neck to peek through a hole within the bushes and brambles. The driver tugged on his reins, bringing his cart to a crawl. My heart thumped.

Why is the driver slowing down? How can he possibly know someone was in this spot just a minute ago? I then realized that I'd probably been humming absentmindedly as I walked down the road, and my voice must have carried. Even so, I questioned why this driver should be interested in slowing down to seek out a random traveler?

The answer came like lightning even before I recognized his face: it was the peddler. Of course! Nobody else would know or care that I was alone on the road. His cart passed by at a snail's pace while I held my breath and ducked down as low as I could. The leaves rustled and cracked slightly under me.

I was convinced I'd been found out when the cart came to a complete stop. I imagined the peddler's head pivoting from side to side as he gazed intently into the woods. For a moment I considered jumping up and running away deeper into the forest. Before long, however, he snapped his reins lightly to urge his horses forward. I relaxed only when he was around the bend and out of sight, but didn't stir from my spot until later to ensure he was gone. I feasted on blackberries while I waited, though it did little to satiate my hunger. After half an hour had passed and the peddler failed to return in the opposite direction, I finally stepped out of the woods to resume my journey. If he came back, I would surely hear his cart and have time to hide again.

I frowned, wondering why I was so determined to hide from the peddler anyway. I saw myself as I must have looked, sprawled uncomfortably on the ground in the woods behind a blackberry bush, holding my breath, my heart beating fervidly as though my life was in danger. I laughed at the amusing spectacle I would have presented had I been seen. Perhaps I was being silly. *No*, I told myself over and over again, *I'm just being cautious*. Or was I just ashamed, and hiding was the easiest and most natural response?

I didn't see the peddler for the rest of the day. My sense of direction became even more muddled as I arrived at forks and crossroads in the path and turned off the main road, taking unknown ways. The air chilled once again as the sun descended. I had nothing with me but the few extra items of clothing in my bundle and the cloak on my back to keep me warm. I stopped in the middle of the road and took out two spare chemises, pulling them over my head. I put on my spare skirt and stockings and finally wrapped my cloak back around me. The extra layers helped somewhat to shield me from the cold, but they could do nothing for my hunger.

I hadn't the strength to go on once darkness fell around the wood. I stopped and looked about me, whimpering as my hopeless situation crashed fully upon me. There would be no inn this night—no warm drink or food, no roof over my head, no blankets to cover me, and no bed to lie in. Wondering where I was and where all the towns and villages had gone to, I scolded myself for not bringing along a map.

I dropped to my knees and bent over, hunkering down to maintain warmth. At this rate I would freeze before I starved to death. I stayed in that position several minutes, fighting the urge to just lie down again in the middle of the road and await my eventual fate. Somehow I couldn't, though. The servant woman's smile from the inn came to me, and as I remembered her kindness, I knew I couldn't just give up. I had to get up and go on.

Hesitantly and with great effort, I pulled myself back to my feet, hugged my bundle for warmth, and continued on in the dark. At least in walking I had a better chance of staying warm.

I fought the fatigue and hunger as I traveled on. At some point in the night, I made my way out of the woods. The trees thinned and the dark sky opened up before me, displaying the star-speckled heavens. Without aid of the moon to light my way, I discerned the silhouettes of cottages in the distance. Still I came across no inn, just occasional cottages and farmhouses, but I dared not wander to some stranger's door in the middle of the night. I walked on.

I amused myself by watching the stars and guessing the lay of the land. Most certainly I was traveling through pastures and farmland. Clumps of trees and tall bushes could be seen on the horizon as the sky slowly lightened. I barely realized when day finally broke, so weary and fatigued was I, half sleeping as I shuffled along. Once the sun had just risen above the horizon and began sending warm beams to earth, I finally collapsed underneath a grove of trees several feet off the main road. I dropped my bundle, wrapped my cloak about me, and threw myself to the ground. I was asleep instantly.

My sleep was long and deep, like one on her way to death. I dreamed I was on a small island void of tree or bush or animal, surrounded by miles and miles of ocean. It was a small island: twelve steps took me from one side to the other. I was alone, and all I could do was sit and stare out at the waters, waiting for the shimmering horizon to break with the speck of a boat in the distance. But nothing came. I sat and waited and never took my eyes from the horizon. I squinted hard but saw nothing. Tears eventually blurred my vision. Even in my dream I was oppressed by the weight of my hopeless situation.

I awoke crying, my pain not eased by the fact that it was only a dream. *I may as well be on the island*, I thought. *I would be no worse off.*

I curled myself in the shade of the grove and cried for a long time. The boughs above me rustled in the breeze, and birds squawked and chirruped all around. Horse hooves clomped and cart wheels rattled along on the road nearby. In the distance came a clanging of bells. I was near a village.

I sat up reluctantly and heaved a sigh. *How long must I do this—fight to get up and move on when the easiest thing to do would be to lie down and never get up?* I didn't allow myself to indulge that fancy, however. I pushed myself to my feet, ran my fingers through my hair, and wiped my face on my chemise. I grabbed my bundle and slowly found my way back to the road.

The sky was a bright blue and the sun was already in the west when I moved on. My stomach twisted in pain. This was only my third day on the road, and I already felt near starved to death. I didn't know how I would manage. I was all right as long as I could find taverns and inns to feed and house me, but eventually my money would run out. I had no skills for surviving in the wilderness on my own. I couldn't hunt, couldn't trap, couldn't skin, and couldn't build a fire. My only option would be to hire myself out if I could. It seemed unlikely anyone would hire a homeless, unchosen woman as a servant, but there was no other recourse for me except to try. If I had been smart—if I had had any sense of foresight—I wouldn't have hidden in my brother's house until he cast me out. I would have gone in search of work before I'd become unchosen. Of course, it would have been unusual, and people would have regarded me strangely—young women of means didn't just go looking for work on their own—but those looks wouldn't have been half as hurtful and awkward as the looks that would now be awaiting me.

My hands began to shake and my body shivered with fear as I approached the outskirts of the village where a few outlying farms and cottages were basking in the sun, their owners busy in the fields with plow and oxen.

Two children ran in the lane toward me, laughing and chasing each other. They slowed as they passed, and their attention turned from their play to the strange spectacle I provided. Their smiles diminished as they stared at me with wide, curious eyes. I envisioned my dirty, frightful appearance at that moment, and my cheeks burned with humiliation. I turned my gaze from theirs and continued walking, once again wiping my face on my sleeve and smoothing my hair.

I stopped outside the rough-hewn gate of the first cottage. It was like most other simple working-class cottages, constructed of logs and mud with a thatched roof of sticks and straw. More affluent families lived in cottages made with flat planks of wood or even brick! I was less intimidated knowing this was a modest cottage, yet I remained frozen with indecision and fear, having no notion of what to say or what to do. I was as a foreigner in a strange new land. I'd never worked outside my home or earned my own living. In Zaphon it was not encouraged for women to do so unless they were born into the lower classes. Yet even with all the distinction between classes in Zaphon, both a servant girl and a woman of the aristocracy could become unchosen. In that there was no difference. Who I was before didn't matter anymore. I no longer had any protected rights under the law. Once again, I realized that I was at the mercy of society. My fate was in the hands of the people: whether they would accept me or shun me, feed me or neglect me, help me or harm me seemed entirely a matter of chance.

I stared at the simple cottage before me. My heart beat rapidly. I nearly let flow a fresh stream of tears at the idea—the shame—of having to throw myself on the mercy of strangers to beg for work. It seemed unlikely that a family with a modest living would even be able to afford taking on another servant, let alone a nurse or a tutor to the children.

I shifted on my feet, ready to run. Instead, I took a deep breath, swallowed my fear, and pushed open the front gate.

From the corner of my eye, I saw the two children on the road coming closer. Their laughter and talk had quieted to whispers, and their attention was riveted on me. I blinked and focused my attention straight ahead. A curtain at a window fluttered with movement. Before I'd made it to the front porch, the door flew open and a woman appeared, her nostrils flared and her eyes narrowed.

"Get out of here!" she yelled, waving an arm to shoo me away as though I was a fly. "I'll not abide beggars! I've got no food for you."

"Please, ma'am, I'll work for my food." The words came out in a croak.

"No! You don't belong here. Get away from my house! Go find a colony where they'll take you in!"

She continued waving and shooing me away. I turned and hurried off with my head down. As soon as I'd rounded the bend in the road, I hid myself behind a stand of trees and cried afresh, wondering if my store of tears would ever run dry.

I tried appealing at two other cottages that day and was met with the same reception. At a fourth the old woman looked on me with pity as she might look on a stray dog, but her husband bounded out the door at the last minute and ran me off like the others had. The woman caught up to me on the road several minutes later, carrying a small basket, which she handed to me. My throat was so swollen from emotion, I could do nothing but nod as tears flowed down my cheeks. She squeezed my hand and was gone.

The contents of that basket—bread, dried meat, apples, carrots, cucumbers, cheese, and a jar of milk, fed me for that evening and the next day, during which I continued my journey without stopping at any more cottages. Instead I entered the village and managed to procure a sleeping space in the loft of a barn, the proprietor of which was an innkeeper. He refused to rent out a good room to one such as me, but he did allow me to sleep in his barn. I was grateful just to have padding under me and a roof over my head.

I stayed several days at the village, which I came to learn was called Terrington. It was a village I'd heard of but had never been to. I was surprised to have made it that far—I was many more miles from Ghilla than I had originally imagined. It was a comfort to know there was little chance of me coming across recognizable people.

I spent my days as I did in Ghilla, wandering the lanes and outskirts of Terrington and sitting in solitary places, wondering what to do next. My first day there, the innkeeper refused to have a bath drawn up for me in the barn, so I was forced to wander a few miles outside the village in search of a river or a lake in which to bathe. Everything I found was public. The next day, I thought I'd discovered a private corner of a lake and began undressing so as to bathe, but then I heard voices from across the water. I shrank away as a small group of people commenced a picnic on the opposite side of the lake. I moved around a corner to a small bay area where I was out of sight of the party but could still hear them. I merely dipped my head in the water and scrubbed my scalp with some soap I'd obtained from a mercantile. The cool, refreshing water made my scalp tingle. I then sat on the edge of the lake and dipped my legs into the water up to my knees, scrubbing them along with my arms up to my elbows. I dared not get all the way into the water for fear of being discovered. I bathed quickly and was soon off.

Every day I ate a meager breakfast at the inn or some other establishment in town. I then snacked on berries or nuts during the day and bought a paltry dinner of bread and cheese before retiring to bed at night. I returned to the lake whenever I needed a bath. In this way I saved my money and felt satisfied for the time being. I estimated that with such frugal living, my funds would last about a month, during which time I would certainly be able to procure a job somewhere.

As much as I repeatedly urged myself to look for work, I couldn't bring myself to knock on any more doors after my failed experience. So I merely waited, gathering courage and making plans, or perhaps just hoping that some opportunity might present itself.

After two weeks in Terrington, I decided to ask the innkeeper for work. He threw his head back and bellowed with laughter at the request. I began to walk away, but he stopped me.

"Hey, girl—don't leave just yet. I knew you were badly off, but not that bad."

He grabbed my arm lightly and led me to a corner table in the dining area of the inn. Sitting me down, he went back to the bar, filled two tin cups with ale, placed one before me, and gulped the other as he took the seat across the table from me. This was the most attention he'd paid me since I'd been in Terrington.

He eyed me with a smirk of amusement on his face, unhidden by his short red beard and mustache. "I've wondered about you, girl." He leaned in close and lowered his voice. "Do you realize how dangerous it is for a young woman of…of your circumstances to be traveling alone?"

I frowned and tightened my hands around the tin cup, although I had no intention of drinking its contents.

"I would be willing to offer you protection," the innkeeper went on.

My heart lifted and I sat up. "You would? So you'll give me a job?"

"It depends. What can you do?"

"Well, I can cook and clean. I'm very good with numbers. I could manage your books."

He cocked an eyebrow as he took another gulp from his cup. "Is that so? And can you do anything else?"

I bit my lip in realization of my deficiencies. "I'm not certain, sir. I suppose I could teach your young ones, if you had any."

He snorted. "I have no woman or children."

"Oh. Well, unfortunately my skills are mostly untested, but I am a hard worker. I'll do anything. No matter what task you give me, I won't disappoint you."

He hesitated while a slow smile crept across his face. "I'm sure you're right." He emptied his cup and set it down forcefully on the table with a clang. "I'll tell you what. I'm sure I can find something useful for you to do. In the meantime, you may continue sleeping in the loft, and I'll let you know just as soon as I can when I have work for you."

I stood up, my heart lighter than it had been in days. "Thank you, sir. I would be most grateful to you."

"And I you. Run along now."

I was too excited to sleep. I lay awake into the night, wrapped in my cloak on the soft bed of straw and hay, and stared at the sliver of moon in the dark sky through a window high in the barn. Most likely I'd be given menial work to do in the barn or the tavern, which would be less than ideal, but it was a start and would offer me some protection. If the innkeeper was kind enough after I'd worked for him a certain length of time, he might manage to procure me a more desirable situation, perhaps as a servant or a governess in a household.

When I finally drifted into sleep, it was a doze at best, which was instantly interrupted at the sound of a creak from below. Suddenly alert, I listened, my body tense. I heard another creak as of the barn door opening or closing. I sat up and waited, listening. There were steps—slow, quiet, light steps across the floor of the barn.

I reached for a small plank of wood that I kept near my bed every night. The steps stopped momentarily. I held my breath and waited. Endless moments seemed to pass. My heart was loud in my chest. I feared it would burst out and give myself away with its thumping.

Someone was coming up the ladder to the loft!

"Who's there?" I hissed, backing up and raising the plank in readiness.

"It's me," came the voice of the innkeeper.

I lowered the plank and let him continue his rise up the ladder to the loft. I breathed a sigh of relief when his head came into view.

"I thought you might be an intruder."

"Of course not. I keep the barn door locked every night for your safety."

"Do you? I didn't know."

He pulled himself up to the loft and sat down near me. "So I'm the only one who can come in."

I nodded and set the plank down next to me. The innkeeper eyed it quizzically, and in the thin moonlight streaming through the chinks in the barn, I saw him smile.

"I see you're prepared for intruders."

"It's just a precaution."

He inched closer to me and took the plank of wood, turning it over in his hands, weighing it. He then tossed it aside behind him. "It's very good thinking. But like I said, I'm the only one capable of coming into this barn at night, and I'm no intruder."

I frowned suddenly. "Why are you here, sir?"

He waited before answering, his eyes roving, searching me. "Do you not know?"

"No, sir."

He inched closer again, and I moved away instinctively. Only then did it come into my head not to trust the man.

"You told me you wanted work."

"Yes."

"Said you'd do anything."

"Well, yes—I'll cook or clean or keep your books or—" My voice broke.

"I don't need a bookkeeper."

My hopes dissipated as the fear rose in me, choking and paralyzing me. In a quick movement, he forcefully grabbed my arm and squeezed it, moving his body closer to mine.

"You have no one watching out for you or waiting for you to come home, do you? No family, no husband. You are an outcast. So if you'd like to work for me, you'll do exactly as I say. You can't expect anything better."

I gasped, too stunned and frightened to scream. I tried to inch away, but he grabbed both my arms then and pushed me, causing me to fly backwards a couple of feet and land heavily on my back. I kicked my legs wildly. He was not a large man, but he was muscular, and he easily pinned my legs down with his body.

"You've never been with a man before, have you?" he asked, smirking as he held me down by the wrists.

Panic rose in my throat and came out in a squeak, a sob. How could I have been so foolish? An image of Papa flashed in my mind. *Help, Papa!* I entreated, but help did not come.

I mustered all the strength I had and tried forcing myself up, but every time I moved, the man pinned me down again. I twisted my body to throw him off-balance, but he held me down even more firmly. I tried to flail my legs, but his weight was heavy upon me. He seemed to be waiting for my strength to subside. I kept up the struggle for several minutes, and I could tell by his narrowed eyes and frown that he was having a hard time of it and growing frustrated with me. I risked his wrath and continued struggling.

"Keep still, girl!" he yelled at me.

He momentarily let go of one of my wrists and slapped me hard across the face. I took advantage of the moment to grab a fistful of his hair, yanking sideways. He bellowed and lifted himself up slightly to catch his balance. In that moment, I kicked my knee upward into his groin. He toppled sideways, and I crawled backward out of his reach. I quickly grabbed my bundle and dashed past him. He reached out for my skirts and tripped me. As I fell, I spotted the plank of wood he had tossed aside and reached out for it. The innkeeper threw curses at me and began pulling at my skirts, trying to pin me down again. I turned and brought the plank down forcefully upon his skull above his left ear. His eyes registered shock and his hands came up to nurse his head, but no sounds issued from his mouth. I kicked him backward and slid down the ladder as quickly as I could.

The sliver of moon in the black sky seemed to be a wink, as though the heavens were laughing at me as I escaped into the night.

Nona

She found me at dawn. I don't remember falling to the ground in the middle of the night, unconscious with fatigue and cold. But whatever happened, she found me early in the morning when she came out of her cottage and hitched her donkeys to her wagon to drive into town. I was lying facedown on the side of the road a couple miles from her cottage, my arms stuck to my sides as if I'd just collapsed without trying to catch myself.

She told me she thought I was dead. She'd turned me over, and after seeing the faint rise and fall of my chest, she'd determined I was still alive and had hefted me up off the near-frozen ground into the back of her wagon. Delaying her trip to town, she had turned the donkeys back toward home and laid me on her own bed next to the fireplace in the main room. Of course, I didn't know any of this at the time. She told me later—two days later, when I awoke from a restless and fevered sleep.

When I did, I found my cloak and stockings had been peeled off, and I lay covered to my chin in quilts. Disoriented momentarily, I thought I was back in my brother's house in Ghilla, safe and warm in my own bed. Then the woman came into my line of sight holding a bowl of warm broth. She smiled knowingly, and I remembered my escape from Terrington.

"I can see you're in a bit of trouble, girl," she said to me through her thin curl of a smile. It was anything but comforting. I sat up in bed as she handed me the bowl of broth. Wisps of steam snaked upward from the hot liquid inside. I stared and sniffed.

"You've had a moderate fever. That'll help."

I took a sip—it tasted better than it smelled.

"Thank you," I said.

The woman watched me, a disconcerting smirk glued to her face. When I finally got a look at her, I was a bit startled. She couldn't have been more than fifty but was a bear of a woman, wider than she was tall, covered in rolls of flesh. For all that, she was hefty and strong. Next to the fireplace stood a tall pile of firewood that I figured she'd cut and hauled all on her own.

"So I suppose you came from Terrington," she finally said, crossing her arms.

I nodded. "I was there only a couple of weeks. I've been... traveling."

She chuckled—a deep, manly rumble in her throat. "I know what you've been doing, girl. You've been running away. Or, I should say, you've been run out of town. Am I right? You're an unchosen."

I nodded again.

"So what brought you out of Terrington in the middle of the night? Just decided it was time to move on?" Her tone was sarcastic.

I tensed my hands around the warm bowl of broth and remained silent.

"Now, now, don't worry about me. I won't tell anybody. Let me guess: you loitered around town trying to find work, but no one would hire you, so you finally had to sell yourself. You've most likely been used by some man."

"No!" I spat out. "He tried, but I got away."

She chuckled again, shaking her head from side to side, seeming to enjoy my discomfort, getting a laugh out of my expense. Rays of afternoon sunlight slanted through the window and lit her up from behind, producing a glowing halo around her, the effect eerily incongruous to the solid, rude, mocking reality sitting before me.

"Yes, well, I'm surprised you made it two weeks in Terrington without something happening to you. Don't you realize how dangerous it is for an unchosen woman to be traveling alone?"

"So I've been told."

"It's just a matter of time."

"A matter of time until what?"

The bear woman clicked her tongue and raised her eyebrows. "Until she's caught and used by a man."

I was horrified. She saw my look and continued in explanation.

"Girl, an unchosen woman like yourself no longer has any family, nor the law on her side to protect her." She leaned in to emphasize the next words. "You are nothing, you have nobody, and you belong to nobody. A man knows this and will take advantage of it."

My mouth dropped open and my throat grew dry. "What… what happens to the woman then?"

She leaned back and folded her arms across her body casually. "Well, she may become his slave or a concubine of his."

"What?"

"Dearie, many unchosen women become concubines. In fact, it's probably a fortunate thing in one sense to be a man's concubine. At least then you have a roof over your head and food in your mouth." She pointed at me. "Just make sure you find a wealthy man, since poor men can't afford to keep concubines in nice conditions."

My hands shook so badly that I nearly spilled my broth all over the quilts. The woman saw my agitation and took the bowl out of my hands.

"I can see you're upset. What ails you?"

"What ails me? You just suggested that I…I…" I faltered, hardly knowing what I meant to say. "I have no intention of willingly becoming a man's concubine."

"I'm not saying there's any shame in it, especially not for one in your position."

"There *is* shame in it! I have more dignity and self-respect than that!"

The woman nearly rocked out of her chair with laughter. "Dignity? Look at yourself! Dearie, whatever dignity you had is gone. An unchosen woman can't afford to have dignity."

She spit the last word out as if it left a bad taste in her mouth. I shoved the quilts to the side and swung my legs to the floor to leave, but my head swam with dizziness as I stood, and I collapsed back onto the bed.

"Now, don't get so offended, girl. I'm only telling you what's truth. You may be an unchosen, but I guarantee you'll find kindness here if you can put up with me. That's more than the outside world offers you at present."

I sighed and sat back in bed, resolving to give this woman another chance, if only because I didn't appear to have much of a choice in my weak, fevered condition. The woman softened a little as I watched her, and I soon felt more at ease.

"What's your name?" she asked me.

"Alonya."

"Well, Alonya, you can call me Nona. Welcome to my home. Is that better?"

I frowned but nodded.

She gestured to the other parts of the small one-room cottage. "This is my humble home. Out back is a garden where I grow my own herbs and vegetables, and beyond the garden is a shed where I mix and store my potions and powders and other concoctions." She winked.

"Potions?" I snorted. "What are you, a witch or something?"

"Of course I am! That's why I'm so nasty!"

I just stared at her, far from amused.

"A medicine woman, actually, but I've been called a witch. I make and sell natural remedies for common ailments and diseases. My husband, when he was alive, was a physician."

"So you're a widow?"

"Yes, which, as you know, is a notch above yourself. Widows, at least, have some status and a recognizable place in society."

"Do you help many unchosens?" I asked, feeling more at ease.

She hesitated and clicked her tongue. "Well, you're the first one I've seen in a while, dearie."

I shook my head and slid down farther in the bed, wishing I could sink down into nothingness where I wouldn't feel anything anymore.

Nona got up out of her chair—it creaked with a sigh of relief once her huge bulk had left it—and went toward the cabinet near the fireplace. She fiddled with a few things before taking out a long silver spoon, with which she stirred the contents of the cauldron hanging over the fire. She then opened a small, rounded wooden door in the bricks just to the left of the fireplace to reveal a brick oven. From it she pulled out a loaf of steaming bread. The aroma instantly caused my mouth to water and my stomach to twist with hunger. How famished I was from several weeks of barely eating! I hadn't looked at myself in a mirror besides what insufficient reflection I could catch in the river, but I guessed I had wasted away to near bones. My clothing had become slightly large for me in several areas, and even now, underneath the covers, I shivered with cold.

"I suspect you're hungry," Nona said, cutting a large slice of the freshly baked bread and putting it on a wooden plate for me.

"Yes, thank you."

Nona added a lump of cheese to the plate and brought it over to me. I dug into it, but then slowed once I realized Nona had resumed her place in the chair next to the bed and was watching me with that same leer of a smile. She was silent for several minutes, allowing me to eat in peace and quiet.

I finally broke the silence.

"When I was in Terrington, I saw no others like me."

"No other unchosens? Well, that's not surprising."

"No—no other wanderers, no other people without a home. There were servants and workers, but I saw none in poverty—none without a home."

Her grin spread across her wide face. "I suppose they are run out of town, like you."

"But where do they all go? Surely poverty does exist? I remember when I was young seeing men out of work and families with no homes in which to live. They were rare, but I saw them. And the other day, I heard a woman say something about a colony. Are there places where the poor and unchosen and other outcasts go, away from society?"

"My dear, as you well know by now, Zaphon does not very well tolerate those who have no proper position in society. Many of these homeless people are sent to camps."

"Camps?"

"To make them useful."

When I still showed no signs of understanding, the woman threw her head back and belted out a laugh.

"My dear, they are *slavery* camps."

"What?"

"The people are sent into slavery, where they are forced to work—to dig, to build, to do whatever the king asks of them—to make themselves useful members of the state."

"The king? Zaphon's king? You mean, he—"

"Yes, dearie. It is our very own king who sanctions this. I am surprised you know nothing of it." She tilted her head down and narrowed her eyes at me. "For a grown woman of your age, you are quite naïve."

Even then, I recalled the peddler's words to me about a man being sold into slavery to pay his debts.

"They work for nothing?"

"They are not paid, if that is what you mean. Their lives are no longer theirs. They are fed small rations every day, but besides that, they no longer have property nor any rights of their own. They belong to the king—to Zaphon."

"What about their families?"

She looked bored, waving her hand in the air dismissively with her next words. "Their families are usually sold into slavery as well. And most are separated. Many of the women go to work in private homes as servants."

"Servants?"

"That's right, dearie. Many servant women are actually slaves. It works out better economically for the employers because they don't have to pay the slaves." Nona leaned in closer with a wry look on her face before continuing. "Which is why there is no chance of you finding a paid position in a household as a servant, in case you were wondering. Why would somebody hire you to work for them when they can apply to the king for a slave, whom they don't have to pay? And if you wait long enough, you will eventually be picked up and taken as a slave. But that's not the worst that could happen to you, as we've previously discussed."

I swallowed hard. "So most homeless and unchosen women end up as—"

"As slaves and concubines, yes."

I shook my head in disbelief, my eyes fixed on an indeterminate spot somewhere in front of me. "How can that be?"

"It's this world—this unjust, corrupt world in which we live. That's just how it is."

My shoulders slumped, and I pushed my plate out of the way. "What will I do? There has to be another way, another option."

Nona shook her head and clicked her tongue. "For a woman such as yourself, there is no other option."

I began crying again. Nona seemed uncomfortable with my show of emotion and moved silently across the room, leaving me alone. I cried myself to sleep, yet in my mind and my dreams, I was still wandering.

Wandering and alone.

8

MEETING

I stayed with Nona for several more days. At first I remained in bed, no longer because of physical illness but because of heart sickness. I let the darkness creep into my heart, into my thoughts. I saw no light, no hope to lift me from my circumstances. I cried. I longed for death. I defied Nona's every insistence to get out of bed and make myself useful. She told me hard work would give me a will to live. But I didn't want to live if it meant being a slave, as Nona continually assured me it would. What was the point in having a will to live, if that will was just to be taken from me in slavery?

Nona let me indulge in my self-pity for two days before she finally, literally, shook me out of bed. She grabbed a hold of the thick bed covers surrounding me and heaved upward and back, as though shaking out a great tablecloth. I rolled out of bed onto the wooden floorboards, landing on my hands and knees. Nona grunted a laugh and merely told me she wanted her bed back then took the sheets and quilts outside to be beaten and aired.

I stayed on the floor for a long while, fighting the tears. My eyes were sore and puffy from crying. I was tired of crying.

Crying didn't change my situation. I was angry—angry that I had no power to help myself, angry at hateful, evil people who would take advantage of one such as me. As the weight of my hopeless circumstances fell upon me once more, I belted out a scream of frustration and pounded my fists on the floor. I sat back and knocked my head against the wall. That was the moment my heart grew hard. I was fortifying it against hope and faith, although I didn't know it at the time.

Nona heard the commotion and flew into the room. In the only act of tenderness I ever witnessed from her, she gathered me to her cushiony bosom and rocked me back and forth, shushing me with her scratchy whisper. I allowed myself to be comforted. I imagined it was my papa rocking me.

She was careful not to say much to me after that. While I ate breakfast at the table, she heated bucketfuls of water over the fire and then filled a large metal tub with the steaming liquid in order to get me to bathe. It had been days. She told me I'd feel better after a nice warm bath. I didn't argue or resist. I got in the tub, pulled my knees up to my chest, and just sat and stared.

"Scrub yourself, girl," Nona told me.

So I did, slowly. It took much effort. Nona had to help me with my hair, which had twisted and knotted in several places and was congealed with dirt and oil. By the time I'd finished washing, the water had chilled. As I stood shivering by the fire, wrapped in a large sheet, Nona pulled a light pink cotton dress from a chest. It was modest but pretty, trimmed at the neck and elbows and hemmed at the ankles with white lace.

"I made this for you," Nona said without ceremony, holding it out to me. "I also bought you some new underclothes while at market."

So spent with emotion was I that I hadn't any tears left to cry, although I was touched. I nodded my head and took what she offered, going into the bedroom to change. Nona had a large wardrobe sitting in one corner of her room. She came in and opened one of the wardrobe doors to reveal a full-length looking glass on the inside. She ushered me near with a satisfied smile to look at my reflection. I took slow, tentative steps. It was the first time I'd seen my actual reflection in quite a while. I stared wide-eyed at myself, barely recognizing the image in the mirror, uncertain whether it was me or not. But even before I became an unchosen, I rarely looked at my reflection in mirrors.

The face staring back at me was plain as usual, tired-looking, and thin. My cheekbones and the line of my jawbone were more defined, which might have made me look prettier but for the lack of color on my skin—pale and sallow. My hair hung wet and limp around my face, but it was longer, and it still retained its natural highlights. It would still be soft and airy when it dried. That much would be all right. My hair was my only comfort and redemption as I gazed at my unsightly image. The cut and color of the dress was pretty as it attempted to bring out the color in my cheeks, but my frame had lost some of its natural curves and didn't quite fill out the dress in certain parts.

"It's a little big," I commented listlessly.

Nona winked and said, "When you've gained back some weight, the dress will fit better as it should. You'll see."

I sighed heavily, watching myself until I could no longer stand the sight. It seemed as if the longer I stared, the more contorted and ugly my image became.

"We'll do your hair up nicely, and once you get some food in your belly and some color back into your cheeks, you'll be a right pretty thing."

I snorted at that, and a few moments later, the snort grew into a laugh, which then evolved into a cry.

Nona rolled her eyes and stormed out of the room. She couldn't seem to abide strong shows of emotion. Calling out behind her as she left the room, she ordered me to come outside and get some fresh air, being that I was out of bed and all cleaned up. I would earn my bread and my keep, she said.

I obeyed like a robot. I helped her beat the quilts and sheets. Dust flew from them like wisps of smoke. We then moved to tend the garden. After that she took me to her storeroom and showed me how to use a mortar and pestle to crush herbs and plants. She spoke nonstop, giving directions, teaching me the history and methodology behind certain oils and potions.

I lived like that with Nona in her cottage for several days. I helped her cook, clean, wash, and tend the garden. I assisted her with creating her remedies and helping patients who found their way to her cottage. In the beginning, I followed Nona's directions and did her bidding with no heart, as though my soul had been left behind me somewhere along the road, as though prematurely accepting my fate as a servant—a slave. But slowly, as the days passed, I found renewed vigor in keeping busy. Working kept me distracted from my troubles just like it had in the days gone by when I'd been in Ghilla, striving so hard with the servants to keep useful so that my brother might see my value and decide to keep me. Even now I found my heart growing lighter in the strength of renewed hope that perhaps Nona would decide to keep me. Despite her rough personality and oftentimes harsh manner, I thought I'd rather be her helper and companion than someone else's slave—or worse, a concubine.

The first time Nona took me into town with her, my heart thumped wildly against my chest. We would not be going into Terrington, but my experience there had given me a profound distrust of any community of people. I feared I might be recognized as an unchosen in this new town. Would I be taken away and strung up, so to speak? But I was not alone this time. I was with Nona, whom people knew and trusted. Perhaps I'd be regarded as a relative of hers.

Nona sensed my unease as we rattled along in the wagon. She sat in the high driver's seat, cracking her whip at the pair of donkeys leading us. She kept looking over at me with that smirk of a smile she wore so often, as though she knew more than she spoke of, as though dangling secrets over other people's heads. I longed for a comforting word then and inadvertently waited for it from Nona, but it never came. She just kept glancing at me and chuckling. It was maddening. I could never figure out if Nona truly cared for my health and welfare, or if she merely kept me around for her own amusement. I could never come to fully love or hate her.

We went to the town square and set up shop. Nona had done this before, but I'd never gone with her. As it was a market day, several other people were selling various types of food and merchandise as well. Their booths lined both sides of the main road through the village and even snaked along some alleys and side streets.

We stayed all day in the warm, glittering sun. I found myself confident in my new pink dress with matching hair ribbon as I helped Nona fill and sell orders. It was busy, hard work. I couldn't imagine her having to do it on her own. Once again, I found a small measure of satisfaction in usefulness. I felt I had to be worth something to be such a helpmeet. Yet nobody had noticed or cared thus far, not even my own brother. Thus far I'd been nothing but an unsightly nuisance.

I forced myself to abandon such thoughts, as they only brought my heart low to the ground.

After half a day, Nona got an urgent house call from a villager. She grabbed some bottles and threw them into a burlap sack, then charged me to watch the stall for her while she completed her errand. My mouth dropped open in protest, but she was gone before I could utter a word. Fear and timidity overcame me. I shrunk back into the shadows of the stall, hoping to go unnoticed, yet customers still flocked to buy Nona's well-known potions and remedies. They were somewhat startled at first to see me without Nona, but after a few inquiries, they lost interest in me and only wanted to buy what they came for. I began to breathe easily again and forgot my fear as I filled orders and sold

Nona's wares myself. For the most part I kept my head down, but after a while I grew bold and began looking my customers in the eyes as I handed them their purchases. One young man smiled shyly at me and brushed my hand as he took his purchase from me. I was shocked to find that I smiled back instead of putting my head down and retreating.

Soon I began to notice more young men eyeing me and smiling, some customers, some at a distance, leaning against nearby buildings with their arms crossed. My fear returned.

"Where's Nona, and who are you?" a voice suddenly said at my elbow. I turned to see a young man eyeing me curiously with a growing leer on his face.

"I…she's gone on a house call. She'll be back any minute if you need her."

"I wouldn't say I *needed* her. I was just curious who her pretty new helper was."

I blushed despite myself, despite suspicion and a growing fear of this man.

"Oh, um…I'm…I'm just staying with her and helping out for a little while. I'm her niece from Ghilla."

The man's eyebrows rose. "Niece, huh? I didn't think Nona had relatives. None that she speaks of anyway."

"Yes, well, it's true, and here I am. If you'll excuse me, I'm very busy."

I made a show of tinkering with some items, but the man was insistent.

"So, Nona's niece, are you married?"

My heart stopped. I held my breath and then feigned a smile, though my voice quavered when I spoke. "Nope. Plenty of time for that yet."

"Good." The man gestured to a building down the street where some other young men were standing and watching from a distance. "My friends and I would like to invite you out tonight.

On market days they have singing and games and juggling here in the town square. You should join us."

"Oh, no, I don't think so. Nona wouldn't let me go."

He narrowed his eyes. "It seems you're old enough to make your own decisions. What do you say? I could talk to old Nona for you, if you'd like."

I took a deep breath and rebelled against my beating heart. "Oh, well, thanks for the offer, but no. I decline your invitation, though it was nicely thought. Have a good day, sir."

I then turned away to help a woman who had approached the booth. I noticed the man linger for a short while after I had snubbed him. He slowly turned and began walking away, but not before getting a final word in.

"Nona's niece—I'll stop by sometime to see you, now I know where you're staying. Take care!"

My body froze like water icing over in winter. Nona still had not returned from her house call. The sun was beginning to graze the tops of the trees in the outlying wood surrounding the town.

"Hello again."

I looked up and saw the peddler watching me. He approached quickly and eagerly.

"I'm glad to find you well. I wondered where you had gone after you left the inn outside of Ghilla."

I glanced behind the peddler. The previous man had joined his friends, and they were still watching from a distance.

"Have you come to try again where your friends failed?" I inquired harshly.

The peddler's face knotted with confusion. He followed my gaze behind him and saw the men staring. When they were caught with both of us watching them, they turned and left, laughing. The peddler turned back to me, his face sober with a frown of concern.

"I'm not with them. I'm in town for market day, selling my wares. I am a peddler, you know. I go where the customers are."

I nodded and once again assumed distraction in an effort to ignore him. He was not to be easily shrugged off this time.

"Where did you go when you left the tavern?"

"Here, obviously."

When he didn't immediately reply, I looked up at him.

"Are you well?" he asked.

No, I'm not, I thought to myself, but I wasn't about to tell him that. I turned to avoid his gaze before he could see my eyes filling.

"Yes, I'm fine," I finally answered. "I've been on my own these past several weeks. Nona, the medicine woman, has taken me in for now."

"Nona—I've heard of her. Some say she's a witch, you know."

"She's not a witch. She's just a woman."

"I know that. But…is she treating you kindly? Are you her… her…servant or…"

"I'm not her slave, if that's what you're thinking!"

The peddler's eyes grew soft, as they were wont to do whenever he spoke to me. It angered me. What cause had he to care about someone he didn't even know? His interest in me, his apparent pity and concern for me were unfounded and, in my estimation, highly suspicious. I didn't trust him. I couldn't, as much as I longed to. My experience in Terrington had taught me that much.

He sighed. "I didn't mean to upset or offend you. I just…I just want to help you."

"Nona's helping me."

"Yes, but…but where will you go next, if you can't stay with her?"

"Who says I can't stay with Nona?"

"Does she intend to take you in for good?"

"Well, not yet, but she might."

"And if she doesn't?"

I waited and studied him a long while before speaking, growing more suspicious by the minute. "That's not your concern. You think I'm going to tell you, a stranger and a man besides, what my plans are so that you can follow me for who-knows-what purpose?"

"To help you!"

"Go away."

His lips thinned and his nostrils flared. He shook his head and made as though he would storm off, then looked side to side and inched closer. He put his head in and spoke quietly, but sharply.

"Look, there's a place you can go if you need help."

"I'm not going anywhere you tell me to go."

He ignored me. "It's a place where people like you can go for safety and shelter."

"I don't believe you. It's probably some slavery camp."

"It's called the Colony. It's due northwest of here, off the main road, five days' walk."

The Colony. The woman at the cottage in Terrington had spoken of a colony. Could this peddler be telling the truth? I dared not risk it.

Just then, I saw Nona returning. The air had chilled due to the lowering of the sun behind the tree line, and many booths and stalls along the street were beginning to close. I was tired of all the staring, the probing, the questions, and the men. I just wanted to leave. As Nona approached, I grew suddenly nervous at the thought of her catching me speaking with the peddler. I didn't want to confront her mocking humor.

He saw my quick, nervous glance behind him and turned to see what had caught my attention. Nona had stopped to speak with a woman carrying a small child in one arm and a large wicker basket in the other. The peddler turned back to me.

"If you can't stay with the medicine woman then please consider finding your way to the Colony. It's a place you'll find comfort and safety and be amongst other women like yourself. I could help you get there if you need."

"Why are you so insistent?" I snapped. The peddler stopped, pain written in his wide eyes. I lowered my voice to a whisper.

"Just leave, please. Go on your way and live your life, and leave me be."

His countenance fell, and he waited a few seconds before finally conceding to defeat with a nod and walking away.

As we were rolling along back toward Nona's cottage later that evening, she said without looking at me, "I saw you talking to that peddler man just before we closed shop."

"Yes," I replied. I waited for more—for a teasing word, a lecture, or a warning of some kind. I was not disappointed.

"Just keep in mind that slave traders are constantly on the prowl for unchosens, and they travel under many guises, particularly that of peddlers."

Those words haunted and disturbed my thoughts for many days and nights.

9

BEAUTY

I could not decide whether I'd done right in shunning the peddler. I was silent and brooding for many days following my encounter with him due to a sense of confusion and guilt over my treatment of him. I thought of the Colony. More than anything, I longed for it to be a reality. I was drawn to the idea of being with women like me—fellow unchosens with whom I could share my grief and my experiences. I might find friends and a new family amongst them. I was grateful to Nona for her care of me, but her rough personality and her derisive attitude grated on me. Having to abide her presence was like rubbing eggshells up and down my arms. Most of the time I questioned the sincerity in all her words and actions. Despite what I'd said to the peddler and despite my apparent ease with the medicine woman, I lived in a perpetual state of anticipation. I waited for something to happen without really knowing that I was, unconvinced that I could stay forever with Nona, nor certain that I wanted to.

And the peddler—he clung to my mind. He was so unlike the innkeeper at Terrington and that other young man who had questioned me in town. His eyes had shone with sincerity and concern each time I'd met him. I couldn't understand why he should care so much about my fate. I was merely a stranger to him and nothing more. Why should I stick out amongst so many others in need? My nagging suspicion fed and thrived on that thought: he didn't really care about me. He couldn't. It was a ploy, most likely, to lure me and other innocent women into slavery. Based on everything Nona had told me, I could find no other logical explanation.

I had been at least three weeks at Nona's when, once again, my time came to leave. I was stirring the soup in the cauldron over the fire while Nona was sewing in her creaky rocking chair nearby. After I'd hung up the apron on a peg and settled myself on a cushion near the fire, she spoke.

"You do know, girl, that you're not my servant. You're free to go any time. You've been here quite a while, and I'm sure you're more than recovered from your…shall we say, ailment."

She looked at me with narrowed eyes and her familiar pursed-lip smirk.

I cleared my throat and put on a bold front, keeping my eyes on the sewing in my lap. "I'll take that as an invitation to leave." I sucked in a deep breath and let it out in a sigh. "I suppose I have overstayed my welcome."

Nona chuckled. "Welcome, huh? I did what I had to do in bringing you into my home and helping you recover. I am a medicine woman after all. I cannot just ignore a fellow human being in pain and sickness."

Fellow human being. Well, that's something, at least.

Nona went on. "But as you well know by now, I am not naturally given to maternal affection and sensibilities, and despite your helpfulness around my cottage, your stay has been anything but welcome."

My jaw tightened, and I shook my head ever so slightly. *Of course*, I thought. *I might have known this was coming.* It was my fate, after all—my curse—to be cast out of every place I went. It seemed I was not pretty enough, nor helpful enough to be taken in by any decent people, not even Nona. At times I felt as if my curse of plainness and lack of desirability was visible, that it shone on the outside of my skin as dark, pock-marked blotches. It kept people away. Nobody seemed to want me.

I proceeded to get up from my cushion to gather my few belongings and rid Nona of my presence when she stopped me.

"Sit down. I didn't mean for you to take off in the middle of the night. You should know by now not to take what I say so much to heart."

She winked at me, but I was not pacified. I thumped myself back onto the cushion and turned my eyes away from her. I stared into the fire and let my face bask in the glow and warmth of the flames. I closed my eyes as I used to do when outside on a warm, sunny day while turning my face to the sun. I let the warmth caress my skin. It was a kind touch in a world of cruelty and selfishness.

"Nona, why did you tolerate my presence so much if my stay was not welcome?" I said suddenly in an effort to verbalize a building frustration. "Sometimes I can't understand whether your actions are out of kindness or selfishness."

"Oh, a little of both, I'd say. It's true, I don't feel much affection for you, but I do recognize that you're in need, and I suppose whatever kindness is left in me answers to that."

I didn't look at her. I couldn't believe anything she said. She was hard and unkind.

"I know what you're thinking," she went on. "But believe me, I am not so unlike yourself. I may never have been an unchosen, but I know the pain of loneliness and of being branded. People do call me a witch, you know, perhaps not without cause. In the earlier days before my husband passed away, he was given much grief over marrying me. When he returned to the earth, it was rumored for a long while that his witch of a wife had gotten angry with him one night and killed him with her magical powers."

I looked up then, wide-eyed, appalled.

"That rumor never completely dissipated. It just lingered for a time and eventually grew old, fading with age. Yet there are still some who will have nothing to do with me."

I swallowed hard. "Well, I am sorry for your loss and your grief, truly."

"Bear in mind, Alonya, that despite your state and circumstances, you are not alone in knowing sorrow and grief."

The words reverberated in my head, an echo of earlier counsel from the peddler. Suddenly Nona stopped rocking and set her work down firmly in her lap, leaning forward and commanding my attention.

"Girl, what do you think I've been doing all these many days in keeping you? I've been strengthening you, readying you to enter the world again."

"But you said it was dangerous for an unchosen to be out in the world on her own!"

"It is, but it doesn't have to be if you can find the strength to make difficult decisions to advance your own status and cause, and to ensure your welfare."

"What do you mean? What kinds of decisions?"

She leaned back then, rocking absentmindedly, but did not take up her sewing again. She spoke slowly and carefully. "It is not too late for you to seek beauty and find yourself a protector—a man."

I shook my head vigorously from side to side. "No, it *is* too late! No man will marry an unchosen. It never happens! It's unheard of."

"It's not unheard of," Nona said, holding up a hand, "but I am not speaking of marriage—at least, not in the way you think of it." She held my eyes in her knowing gaze, her pupils blazing. I was locked in that gaze for a while as though in a trance or spell before the full weight of her words descended on me.

"No!" I belted out, blinking to escape that gaze and break the spell. "I told you before—I will not willingly degrade myself by becoming some man's *concubine*!"

Nona rolled her eyes. "My dear Alonya, it is not nearly the fate that you imagine. Concubines are treated well by their masters."

"It's just another form of slavery."

"It is scarcely another form of slavery. A slave has no independence, no mind, no will. A slave is forced to work and do the will of her master. A concubine is like a wife—"

"One of many!"

"And as such, she has a small measure of status and say in the household. She has her own rooms, nice furnishings, a fine silk and brocade wardrobe, and rich, luxurious foods to eat. You would be well fed, sheltered, and protected."

"Yes, but despite that, a concubine is still at the mercy of her master, whether he be kind or cruel."

"Dearie, as an unchosen, you will always be at the mercy of another."

That stopped any further argument from me. Nona went on.

"Becoming a man's concubine is one thing, but that is not what I was going to suggest. It's clear to me that your shallow knowledge of the world leaves you with something to be desired, and so I will be plain with you. Instead of waiting for slavers to catch you or some man on the street to ravage you, you may wield the power and choose a benefactor for yourself. That is, you may find a well-to-do single gentleman and offer yourself as his mistress—not one of many, but the only one."

I huffed and rolled my eyes. That proposition was hardly better than the previous one.

"I'm sure you think yourself too far above such things," Nona scolded, "but you have few other options. You have to make the most of your circumstances and work within the confines of whatever power and whatever choice you still have. And since most unchosen women become a man's property anyway, you ought to give yourself the best opportunity by making yourself a desirable commodity."

I watched the floor and breathed in deeply, hearing the logic in her words but also the entrapment. Nona heaved herself up from her chair and kneeled down next to me. She spoke gently but earnestly.

"Alonya, listen to me. I know the world. I've lived and loved and suffered loss for a longer time and perhaps more deeply than you have."

I willed the tears to stay inside. I took a deep breath and steeled myself. My knuckles tightened around the swatch of fabric I'd been sewing.

"You have a difficult decision to make. I am trying to give you helpful advice, but in the end *you* are all you have, and you have to make the decision that will secure your future and bring you refuge, whether it is the future you imagined for yourself or not."

The future I had imagined for myself had vanished long ago. I wrung the fabric in my hands more tightly.

"Alonya, I tell you this for your good. It is not too late to find security and protection with a man."

"I am no beauty. No man has ever wanted me, and no man ever will."

"You may seek beauty for yourself. Beauty will always catch you a man. And the more beautiful you are, even as an unchosen, the less likely you are to be treated badly or taken by the slave traders."

I shook my head, hearing the apparent truth in her words, but unwilling to accept them, because to accept them would mean to enter into a new life wholly foreign from all I'd ever known or been taught by Papa. But Papa was dead. He had failed to protect me, and all he taught seemed to have died with him. Out on my own, I'd seen the world as it truly was: naked, stripped of all my illusions and hopes. It was ugly and harsh and cruel. Kindness seemed a rarity.

"Beauty is power," Nona went on. "Don't wait for men to take you against your will. You can choose to give yourself, to hire yourself out to men who will pay for beauty. *You* can hold the cards. *You* can do the choosing."

I could abide no more words. I stood abruptly and began pacing before the fire. Nona stood up with a grunt and watched the internal battle play out on my face with that familiar leer. She seemed to love conflict, to thrive on it. How could I trust her? Yet how could I not? She was the only person who had shown me any decency despite her harsh ways. Her words were a bitter poison to swallow, yet they made sense; they offered a solution.

I wrung my hands as I paced and forced myself to breathe. In my distress a voice came whispering through. It was the voice of the peddler. He spoke of the Colony.

I stopped suddenly and turned to Nona. Her face flickered in the firelight, a dichotomy of shadow and light dancing, creating grotesque shapes across her features in their battle for supremacy. I wondered if light would win.

"What about the Colony?"

She frowned and shifted so that her face was plunged into shadow. "Who told you about that?"

I hesitated a moment, feeling like a child caught in an act of disobedience. My breathing became labored once more as my nerves tightened. "The peddler," I replied. "He…he told me there's a place for unchosens to live together in comfort and security."

A huge, rumbling laugh belted out of Nona's throat. "Comfort and security! Ha! Those women live in poverty! They have no means of support or income. They rely only on charity to feed and clothe them. And charity these days is hard to come by."

I shook my head and was about to speak once more, but Nona cut me off.

"You can't trust the peddler man! I have already warned you of that. He is most likely a slave trader trying to lure you into a trap."

"But if he's a slave trader and knows about the Colony, wouldn't he have taken all those women as slaves by now? If you're a slave trader and you know about a colony of unchosen women, you wouldn't just let it be."

"That's right. You would lure as many women as possible into this so-called colony and wait until they feel safe and secure, and then take them all as slaves! There have been colonies of unchosens in the past, very quiet, that have been broken up once they were discovered."

I shook my head in protest, but Nona grew even harder.

"Ask yourself, my dear, how this peddler man even knows of a colony. Those that exist are usually discreet. According to the laws of the state, they are legal, but the law does nothing to protect the colonies from slave raids. So even if you did make it to this colony, it would only be a matter of time before you would be taken as a slave!"

I hung my head in my hands. Why did every possible path seem to lead to this eventual fate? Was there no other choice for me?

"Believe it or not, Alonya, you can stop that from happening. You can still earn a small measure of power and independence by heeding my advice."

I finally stopped. I stopped pacing, I stopped fighting, and I stopped ringing my hands. I loosened them and let the fabric fall to the floor, letting go of my last shred of hope and all my dreams in the process.

"What must I do?"

Nona's eyes lit with a fire. She had won.

She took my arms and led me to her wooden rocker, setting me in it. She moved to the opposite side of the room and rummaged in a high cabinet before bringing out a map of Zaphon and unfolding it before me. She set the map on a low table and moved the table closer to where I sat. The table legs squawked as they were dragged across the wooden floorboards.

The map was large and antique, created with beautiful, elaborate drawings and labeled in swirling calligraphy. Pictures of forests and mountains dominated the map, and it was dotted in several places by large inky spots that designated towns and villages. Faint-colored lines showed the boundaries between provinces. I leaned in for a closer look. Nona put a finger somewhere in the middle of the map where we were.

"Coralind is not the only place where magic still exists. Have you heard of the Wild Lands of Zaphon?"

"Yes, on the borders of our country, which is separated on three sides by a vast sea, and on the other by desert." I wanted to show her I was not as ignorant as she supposed.

"Yes. Magic began in Coralind, our most ancient country and the first of the Seven Kingdoms. From there magic spread concentrically to the outlying countries, but over time, with greater industry and civilization magic has lost its potency in many places. It has little part in the lives of many people today, who no longer recognize it or believe in it. This is especially true in Zaphon, since we are the farthest away from Coralind and are the most isolated of the Seven Kingdoms."

I knew little of magic, and even less of Coralind—a faraway country that seemed more legendary to me than anything else. I had never been anywhere outside of my own province before my curse had forced me to wander Zaphon as an unchosen. I had heard stories of places and creatures in Coralind as a child, but that's all they ever remained to me—stories.

"Nona, what exactly is magic?"

"It's power, Alonya. Power in nature."

"Where does it come from?"

"From the earth. The earth itself is infused with power. It is alive."

"Yes, but where did the earth get this power?" I asked, thinking of my papa's teachings. "Didn't it come from the High King in the earlier days of creation?"

Nona's animated face grew stony and her eyes flashed. "There will be no talk of the High King here. They are stories and nothing more! There is no High King. There is only the earth, which has always been here. Magic comes from the earth, not from a mythical High King."

I let the matter drop there, and Nona soon returned to her earlier discourse.

"Since all living creatures come from the earth, we all share a part in its magic, some creatures more than others—like the fairies, for example, or certain animals."

"What has this to do with me and finding beauty?"

"Pockets of magic still exist in certain places. The Wild Lands on the outskirts of Zaphon hold magic still. This magic can give you greater beauty."

"How?"

"Transformation, my dear girl. Your very features would be literally transformed to make you beautiful."

I brought my hand up to my cheek as though Nona's words alone might have done the deed in changing my face. Everything felt the same, however. Both alarmed and fascinated by the suggestion, I dug deeper for more information.

"I know of at least three sources for obtaining beauty," Nona went on. "Zaphon is a big country, and you are sure to find at least one, if not all of these sources if you search in the right places." She rubbed her hands together and took a deep breath. Then, directing my attention back to the map, she pointed to a large wood that ran along the northernmost border of Zaphon. Just beyond the wood lay the sea. "This is Hyacinth Wood, part of the Wild Lands. It is very old and very large. People scarcely travel through it since there are few roads and no village within it. The nearest village is miles away. Here, somewhere in the wood, there are bushes that grow a rare, special fruit. But it is disguised and not easily found. In ancient times this fruit was harvested and used in expensive beauty potions."

I listened, enraptured yet somewhat cynical. I asked how Nona could know of such a thing.

"I am a medicine woman. I have studied the lore and properties of plants and herbs nearly my entire life. The change from the fruit is gradual, and at first temporary. You must eat it over time, and once a certain amount is in your system, the final, permanent change takes place."

"And what if I can't find this fruit, or there's not enough of it for me to eat over time?"

"You may then seek out a mer-pool."

"A mer-pool? You mean the home of the merrow, the water-people?"

"Yes. At one time the merrow lived around here," Nona said, pointing to another spot in Hyacinth Wood. "Merrow love to give gifts. If you chance to meet one and the creature offers you a gift, then ask for a drink from the mer-pool."

"A drink?"

Nona nodded. "The water from a mer-pool has power to bestow beauty when drunk. But it is a gift rarely given, and only then if you can find the pool and meet a merrow."

"Why not just take a drink from the pool without meeting a merrow?" I asked, thinking this was the most logical solution. Nona narrowed her eyes and frowned, but a corner of her mouth still managed to curl up in a sneer.

"Then you'll be drowned for stealing. They'll pull you in before you even get your cupped hands halfway to your mouth. If you want to meet a merrow, that's a good way to accomplish your object."

My skepticism was soon growing into frustration. Each source seemed to have some major obstacle. If I was to take Nona at her word and embark on a quest to seek beauty, I would no doubt have many difficulties to surmount. Most likely the quest would end in futility.

"And the third source?" I inquired with a sigh.

Nona grew quiet and spread both her hands palm down on the picture of Hyacinth Wood so that they covered the entire forest in all its length and vastness. "The last source is the most difficult of all, but the most assured of gaining you beauty." She looked fiercely into my eyes. "The history of magic speaks of enchanted animals with the ability to grant wishes. You must find one of these creatures and ask for beauty. It will be irrevocable beauty, but it will be complete, and you will have gained your object. You will want for nothing, and you will have greater power than you can imagine."

The way she spoke sent an icy sliver of excitement through my nerves. I no longer doubted her words. I wanted what she spoke of—beauty and power. I had no hope of anything else. I needed to secure my place in the cruel world.

And oh, to be beautiful!

THE COLONY

I took a road north out of Nona's wood and through a hilly countryside dotted with groves of leafy trees. It was less a road and more a disused path that wound behind villages instead of going through them. Few travelers traversed the road, and those that did I avoided by throwing up my hood and walking with my gaze fixed on the ground. I was not bothered by anyone, much to my relief.

Nona had equipped me with two changes of clothes besides what I already had on; plenty of bread, cheese, dried meat, and fruit; a skin of water; a rough sketch of the map of Zaphon, which showed my intended course; and—what I hadn't expected—a pocket full of coins. She had surprised me by handing me the small clinking purse, saying it was my earned pay for all my hard work.

"I may be a harsh woman at times, Alonya, but I'm a fair woman," she had said to me. I merely nodded my head as I accepted the gift. If I had distrusted her up until then, I distrusted her no longer. I was grateful to her for all she'd done for me.

I stayed away from the villages and the inns when I could help it, instead keeping to the outer road. After my recuperation at Nona's, I felt much more prepared for being out on the road on my own. I was resolved to my fate and had a vague notion, at least, of where I was going; to that, I had an end in mind. To seek beauty and choose a protector for myself—since none had chosen me—was my course and seemed my only option. It was motivating just to have a goal, though that goal at times turned my stomach sour and made me faint in heart. I tried not to allow my mind to dwell on it but instead focused on the task at hand, one step at a time. I wouldn't cross that other bridge, so to speak, until I arrived at it.

I walked for many days north and westward. Fair weather abounded, which kept me from shivering so much at night while I slept wrapped in my cloak within a stand of trees. I built fires in a way that Nona had shown me. I found small lakes and creeks in which to wash myself. I didn't go hungry. My newfound independence caused my heart to swell with a confidence I'd rarely ever known.

The hilly land eventually shrank into flat, stretching plains, which then evolved into prairieland, high and wild with yellow grasses. Far to the left, hazy in the distance, were the foothills of a soft, low mountain range, rising up from a forest that ran north and south along its base. Through the grasses to my right I could just make out the housetops of a nearby village. I had avoided civilization up to this point. After nearly a week on the road, my food store was growing low. I decided to brave a trip into the village.

It was small and quiet, with only one main road running through the center of town for about half a mile. Farms and cultivated fields fanned out from the center of the village, dotting the landscape with shoddy cottages and outbuildings. It was unmistakably a simple town, not a place of great wealth. That eased my mind as I stepped onto the main road and made my way into the nearest inn.

As it was the middle of the day, the inn was sparsely populated. I took a deep breath and ordered food and drink, put my coins down on the counter, and found a table in the corner of the room in which to hide myself. I ate alone and was left in peace. I wanted to pay for a hot bath but thought better of it, instead gathering my items to leave quickly after about an hour. Outside, the warm sun cast shimmering rays of heat along the dusty road. Few men and women were out, laden with baskets and handling pushcarts. Two women nodded and smiled at me as I passed. Everything was quiet and so nonthreatening I was tempted to push my luck and stay overnight—perhaps a couple of nights. Surely this couldn't be a place where slaves existed. I stood just outside the inn looking up and down the road, frozen with indecision. But then the image of the innkeeper at Terrington flashed into my mind, and with it came pouring Nona's words of caution. I was an outcast. It was better for me to just leave normal people be. I could never expect to assimilate back into ordinary society.

With a heavy heart, I turned westward to follow the road out of town. A rattling cart pulled by two dusty-brown mares came from a side alley, the driver bouncing alone atop the driver's perch, his hands loosely guiding the reins and his tongue making clicking sounds to his animals.

It was the peddler.

I quickly dove sideways behind a building before I could be spotted. The peddler directed his horses down the road and out of town—the very direction I was headed. His usually heavy-laden cart seemed empty. A dirty blanket still covered the back of the cart, yet it was, for the most part, flat and smooth, not bulgy as it should have been if there were myriad items and wares underneath to sell. I wondered what had happened to all his merchandise.

My curiosity overcame my fear. I let a fair distance pass before I moved along on foot, following the cloud of dust kicked up by the cart wheels, which also left shallow ruts in the dirt road. The spectacle of the peddler without wares to peddle only confirmed my suspicion of him. *Surely he hasn't sold everything he owns in this sleepy town, where most are out working their fields and few are actually to be seen on the roads or at the inn. Besides, a peddler goes to the very center of town for business, usually on market days. Today most assuredly was not a market day. What had the peddler been doing down that side alley?*

The cart soon became a speck in the distance then disappeared altogether. At the fork in the road where I'd first spotted the village, the ruts in the dirt showed that the cart had turned left—back the way I'd come. I wavered for a moment before turning left to follow the peddler.

My brisk walk soon turned into a canter then a slow run. The sun began to descend. I strained to see the cart ahead and spied another speck on the horizon. Then the speck was gone again, lost in the tall grasses. At the next fork in the road, I saw that the cart had turned right. I took a brief rest to regain my breath before once again following after the peddler. His pace had slowed, for soon I caught up with him and had to fall behind a bit to keep out of sight. The peddler seemed relaxed and unawares. The tune he whistled drifted on the wind back to where I trailed behind surreptitiously.

The landscape soon changed again as the grassy prairie disappeared and groves of trees rose up, soon thickening into a wood. I had kept my eyes so keenly locked on the peddler for fear of losing him that I hadn't noticed the western mountains looming up above the wood, the sun just beginning to fall behind them, casting lengthening shadows on the road. They grew larger as we approached, then finally disappeared from view when the road ran straight into the forest, like a dark tunnel of trees narrowing the view, blocking out warmth and dimming the light.

When I first entered the forest, I had to stop to let my eyes adjust to the darkness. Behind me, light from the setting sun still clung to the eastern sky, but ahead was shadow, penetrated here and there by chinks of light that managed to squeeze through the thickness of the overgrowth. Below my aching feet was the road—only now it was covered with underbrush. I could see no more tracks. I readjusted my bundle on my back and set forward, again at a quick pace, to catch up with the peddler. As long as the road didn't branch off into other trails, I figured I ought to be able to keep up with him. But if the cart did turn down another path, there would be no way to follow the tracks.

As I walked, my unforgiving thoughts took me over once more. *Surely this is not a well-traversed path. The road is barely more than a trail, thick with fallen logs and twigs! The wood itself sits at the foothills of the mountain. I doubt there's a pass from the looks of things, so surely there can be no village here! Besides, if the peddler wants to get to the other side of the mountains, why not go around them, which would be quicker and easier than going through them? What's out here? His cottage, perhaps? Or a slave trader's hideout? A base of operations?*

Soon I saw the peddler atop his cart ahead of me. Again he had slowed to a crawling pace due to the difficulty of the terrain. I stopped and waited before taking another step. The underbrush crunched beneath my feet, but so also did the cart and horses make noise as they stepped and rolled along. I grew bolder, certain that I wouldn't be heard, and continued to follow behind at a steady pace. My stomach soon grumbled with hunger, but so intent was I on my mission that I ignored it.

A twig cracked as I stepped on it. The cart ahead of me stopped. The peddler began to turn his body to look behind him. I quickly took two leaping strides behind a thick tree and waited, holding my breath. The horses neighed and puffed and stamped the ground impatiently. All else was still.

"Hello?" the peddler called softly.

I wondered if he'd seen me, but he stayed atop his cart. I dared not move. Several minutes passed in silence. My hands gripped the rough bark of the tree I leaned against. I had awkward footing and longed to switch to a more natural and comfortable position.

The cart finally groaned and rattled as it took to the road again. Still I waited for several moments until the sound faded before braving a peek around the tree. Sure enough, the peddler had moved on and was once again out of sight around the bend.

For the remaining distance I followed behind more cautiously. Instead of keeping the cart within my line of sight, I followed its sound around each corner. The sky grew darker and the air chilly. I hoped my pursuit would soon end. I hadn't considered until then that this might only be the beginning of the peddler's journey. *What if he plans on camping overnight in the forest? What will I do then? Sleep somewhere nearby? What if he finds me?* I didn't want to take a chance sleeping nearby a potential slave trader.

I was just about to reconsider and turn back when I heard the cart stop somewhere up ahead and voices speaking quietly to one another. They were female voices. A male voice—that of the peddler—answered them. The women laughed.

Laughter was the last thing I expected to hear.

I crept ahead and peered from behind the shelter of a tree. The peddler's horse and cart stood before the huge mouth of a cave that seemed to retreat deep into the mountain. Barefoot women in tattered skirts and shawls were smiling while they carried baskets and bundles from the peddler's cart into the cave. Standing in front of the horses and petting their muzzles was the peddler, speaking with one of the older-looking women, whose face was glowing with warmth as though the sun shone brightly even in this dark, dank place.

My first fleeting thought was that this was a slave camp and these were slave women, yet that supposition didn't match up with the smiles and laughter I witnessed. As I continued to watch, the truth finally came to me in a sudden flash of understanding.

The Colony. The peddler was bringing these women provisions.

The peddler had told me the Colony was due northwest of where I'd last seen him. I had been traveling mainly north, with a small shift to the west, these last several days. I had unintentionally made my way to the Colony.

But that didn't necessarily mean the peddler could be trusted after all. It seemed possible, based on Nona's words, that he was merely luring women to this place to gain their trust by helping them. He might soon betray them by organizing a slave raid.

Or maybe he was just a kind man like Papa was. I ached for that to be the truth. And as I watched him and the other women for several more minutes, I began trusting him despite my suspicions.

The flock of women finished emptying the cart and disappeared inside the cave, though the older woman stayed behind to speak with the peddler. I could hear them more clearly with the others gone. She invited him inside for supper. He declined with hearty apologies, saying something about having to go south for more supplies, then promised to return within a month's time if he could, depending on how business went. They exchanged a few last words and a hug before the peddler jumped back atop his cart, flicked the reins, and clicked his tongue. The horses turned around to leave the way they'd come. I slunk deeper into my hiding place until the peddler had passed and all was quiet again.

I stepped back out to the road and wondered what to do next. It was far too late to try and make it back to the village for a room at the inn. I could find a soft, comfortable place in the woods to sleep, but it was colder inside the shelter of the forest than it had been out on the open road. And it seemed silly to sleep in the woods alone when there were women like me nearby.

I approached the mouth of the cave and peered inside. Nothing but darkness greeted me. No traces of light appeared. The tunnel seemed endless.

"Hello?" I called. My voice reverberated like a frightened child through the darkness.

I tried again, louder. "Hello? Is this the Colony?"

I considered walking in, but a sudden trepidation seized me. I was rooted to the spot with indecision. This wasn't my mission. I was supposed to be headed north to Hyacinth Wood to seek the sources of beauty in order to offer myself as a wealthy man's mistress.

I shuddered at the idea, although the thought of being beautiful still appealed to me. Perhaps when I was beautiful I might be considered in a better light by all people and really could live on my own in freedom and independence. Perhaps I could still make a decent, honest living without degrading myself. Overall, beauty was preferable.

I wanted to go to Hyacinth Wood to seek out the rare fruit, or the mer-pool. Nona said the women of the Colony lived in privation. I didn't want that life.

But I wanted friends and family. Freedom and beauty couldn't ease my loneliness.

I sighed, still not certain what course to take, when my decision was made for me by a small bobbing light that appeared at the end of the tunnel, growing larger as it approached. Soon the outline of a thin woman holding a lantern materialized out of the darkness.

"Hello. Were you calling in just now?"

"Yes. Is this the Colony?"

A large, kind smile grew on the woman's face. She didn't appear to be much older than I, and she was beautiful!

"I take it you're a fellow unchosen sister," the woman said.

All I heard was "sister," and I knew I was in the right place.

I smiled and nodded. The woman held her hand out to me and I took it.

"Welcome to the Colony. I'm so glad you found us."

She led me in by the hand, and for the first time in a long time, I belonged somewhere.

DANEIN

The woman told me his name was Danein. He came often—at least once every two or three months if he could manage it. He came to help the unchosen women of the Colony.

The cave entrance to the Colony was a tunnel that led through the small mountain to an opening on the other side. It was there, in the forest, sheltered in the shadow of the mountain, that the women made their refuge. They had built huts for themselves made of sticks and mud. Next to each hut was a small fire pit for keeping warm and for cooking. There was a large fire pit in the center of a clearing straddled by a spit fashioned out of thick branches, upon which hung a large iron cauldron used for cooking. A nearby freshwater stream provided water for drinking, washing, and bathing. Several yards away in a grassy clearing was a garden that the women had dug and cultivated, which mainly grew potatoes and herbs. Overall, the Colony was a small camp with no more than thirty women, but it was cozy and provided the most important thing I needed at the time: friendship and family.

I settled in quickly and easily. From those women I learned how to garden, fish, and hunt and how to find the right kind of plants and berries in the wood for food and medicine. I had no notion of how the women originally learned those skills, only supposing desperate times had necessitated it. They had to learn to survive on their own, so they did.

It helped that Danein came to assist the women by bringing them provisions: food, seeds, clothing, blankets, yarn, thread, baskets, tools, and anything else he could procure on his travels.

When Danein came again, I had been at the Colony for five weeks, and autumn was coming on fast and chilly. The days were still warm where the dappled sunlight made it through the canopy and hit the ground in splotches of warmth, but the nights were cold. We were in need of woolen blankets, and Danein was the champion on the white horse, so to speak, who brought them just in time.

It was midday when he came, and instead of just dropping off provisions at the door as he had done before, he came through the cave entrance into the Colony. I saw him from a distance as I kneeled at the stream with the other women washing clothing and dishes. His appearance showed the effect of his life on the road: his clothes were in need of mending and washing, and his hair and beard were growing long. Yet for all that, he was a nice-looking man.

I turned my face away at the thought and began fiercely scrubbing the sheet I held in my hands underneath the surface of the water. Who was I to be thinking such thoughts about a man? I had no right to think any man handsome. It was too late for me.

I turned my thoughts toward my task as I had done many times before and momentarily forgot about Danein. When the washing was done, I loaded the dripping clothing and linens into my wicker basket and began lugging them across the open glade to hang them. Makeshift clotheslines made from rough, scratchy rope pulled tightly and fastened to tree trunks provided the drying area, which was behind a cluster of huts. Danein emerged from one of the huts just as I was walking by, but before he could lock eyes on me, I turned sideways and put my head down so that my hair fell in front of my face.

Hanging the laundry, I wondered at my behavior. I wanted to see Danein to speak with him and to thank him for leading me to this place. I owed him that much. But a part of me was too ashamed at my previous conduct toward him. Another part of me—the part filled with pride—feared that he would gloat at me for having ended up here all along after how I'd doggedly refused to heed his counsel. Yet I couldn't imagine that Danein was the sort of man who would gloat at my defeat.

I watched him secretly from the safety of the trees even as I finished hanging the laundry. The day went on, and I continued to hide, observing him from around trees and huts and sometimes from within the darkness of the cave. He stayed all day. He went hunting in the late afternoon with some of the stronger women to find an evening meal.

I kept hidden within my hut weaving baskets from strips of bark with another woman named Taralyn. She was just a little older than I, and we had become good friends. We shared a hut, and while she sat outside the entrance attempting to soak up the last warm rays of the sun for the day, I stayed safely sheltered just within the opening.

Taralyn was an avid talker, and I loved her stories of her previous life before becoming an unchosen. She had come from a wealthy family and had many suitors in her time, yet felt none of them was right; none truly loved her, so she had rejected them all against the counsel of her family and friends. She said she felt relieved when her time came and she could finally leave her father's household.

"It seemed right," she had said. "I had long wanted to do something important with my life, and it wasn't enough just to be married."

She had traveled for many months using her inheritance, which her father had graciously given her, to help orphans and families in need when she came across them. Eventually she found the Colony and was thrilled at the opportunity to "be a light," as she said, to her fellow unfortunates. Upon meeting Danein, she had given him the rest of her money to be used at his discretion to help fund his business, since part of that business was in helping unchosen women.

Taralyn was known for gathering the women together from time to time for a game, a story, or a song. Nothing excited her more than walks through the forest. She loved dipping her feet in the river and could spend hours watching fish or birds. She saw beauty and wonder in everything around her, despite her circumstances. Somehow she saw the world differently. She believed in the world's magic and from time to time claimed to see the blinking colored lights of forest fairies at night, though Nona had told me the magic in Zaphon was restricted to the Wild Lands in the north. Taralyn occasionally spoke of the High King, and she constantly spoke of being blessed and fortunate. Her words were sweetened with talk of freedom and of life—things that were a distant echo of my past, when I was young and Papa was still alive. I didn't comment much on her words; I merely listened. They brought a smile to my face and a longing to my heart, which were but ripples as on the surface of a pond. I never explored much deeper.

She was a friend, and that was enough.

Danein and the company of women he was with were gone hunting for at least two hours before they returned with a mighty stag. We women didn't usually catch game that large since we rarely had bows. Our meals usually consisted of small rabbits, squirrels, and chipmunks along with the occasional wild turkey. The hunters had circled the stag and closed in on it while Danein drew close enough to hurl a knife into its body.

Taralyn jumped up as they arrived back at the camp with roars of victory, the stag hanging from a wooden pole suspended upside down by its feet. I retreated deeper into the hut and peeked out from the small window opening. Some of the women went straight to work, skinning the animal and preparing it to roast over the fire, while others began chopping potatoes and onions to cook in a stew. I oftentimes helped with the cooking in some way, but that day I stayed aloof from the group.

Danein sat on a log near the fire, carving a stick with his pocket knife and conversing with the women. I just watched him, entranced. He seemed like he belonged in this place—in the wild, among the simplicities of life. Something new began to grow in my heart then: an admiration and respect that I hadn't known for any man except my papa. Watching Danein reminded me of Papa, and that association grew so strong that I had to turn my face away momentarily for the emotion rising within me. When I again glanced out the window, Taralyn was sitting with Danein, and they were sharing a private conversation that I couldn't hear. After several minutes, Taralyn smiled, patted Danein on the back, and returned to our hut.

"How's the cooking coming along?" I asked. Taralyn sat down on the ground next to me and picked up her half-finished basket, rolling it around in her hands.

"It's fine. They've got plenty of help." She took a deep breath and let it out quickly. "I never cared for any of my suitors in my life past, but they were all stuffy, rich, arrogant men. My father never did allow any honest, simple men into my life. If someone like Danein had come along, I would have snatched him up in a second!"

I smiled but hid my face as a twinge of envy sliced through me. I quickly repressed it, confused by it.

"Do you…do you care for him?"

"For Danein? Well, yes, as a brother. I knew his sister when she was here. We were pretty close, she and I."

"He has a sister?"

"He *had* a sister. She died a while ago."

All of a sudden, I understood him.

"I've been cruel to him," I abruptly admitted. Taralyn's face flashed confusion, and I went on in explanation. "I've known him for months now. I kept meeting him on the road here, and he continually tried to help me, but I didn't trust him. I was rude, and even now, I can't bring myself to face him."

Taralyn's eyes widened with amusement, and she leaned in conspiratorially. "You mean to say you've known him all the time he's been here today and you never said anything?"

I shook my head. "I followed him here. That's how I found the Colony in the first place."

Taralyn's mouth dropped open. She abandoned her basket and pulled on my arms with both her hands. "Go talk to him, Alonya. Now! He'll forgive you. He'll be so happy to see you."

"How do you know?"

"Because he was just speaking to me of a girl that he met weeks ago whom he hasn't been able to find, though he's been looking all over for her! He's talking about you, I know it! It would ease his mind to know you're here, safe and sound!"

"He said that?"

"Yes, now go!"

Taralyn pulled me to my feet and shoved me out the door. I hesitated, mere feet away from where Danein sat, and stared at his back. He threw his head up in a laugh at something one of the women said, stick and knife still in hand. I approached him tentatively.

"Go on," Taralyn whispered from the hut.

I waved my hand to shush her and quickened my pace, then stopped when I was a mere five steps from Danein. I stood, waiting, watching his back. He seemed to sense my presence because he stopped what he was doing and suddenly stiffened, then slowly turned around. I lost my courage and dashed sideways as if on an errand so that he would only catch the form of my retreating backside. I bent over quickly to grab a large basket of dried laundry and began walking away, hoping he wouldn't recognize me after all.

"Hello."

I stopped in my tracks.

"Always running away, aren't you?"

I turned slowly, timidly. He was on his feet and had followed me a few steps, but a smile showed underneath his beard.

"I'm sorry, I just…I…well…I feel bad about…"

"It's all right," he said, and his eyes shone with a kindness that made me want to cry in relief.

"I'm glad you came," he went on. "I've been looking for you, you know."

"I know. Taralyn told me you'd been asking after me." I let myself smile. "I followed you here."

His eyebrows flew up. "Did you?"

"Yes, for nearly half a day."

His eyes grew wider, and it took all my strength not to laugh, though I dearly wanted to.

"I am truly impressed," he said. Then, seeing the heavy bundle I carried, he took it from me and led me to a place where we could sit away from the center fire pit.

"I never learned your name," he said.

"Alonya."

"I'm Danein, and I hope you're not afraid of me anymore."

I shook my head, feeling the heat creeping up into my cheeks.

"I'd like to be your friend, Alonya."

"Are you friends with all these women?"

"Well, no, but I do know most of them pretty well."

My eyes narrowed suspiciously. Danein chuckled.

"Because of my sister," he explained. "She lived here once."

"That's what Taralyn said."

He nodded then leaned forward with his elbows on his knees and turned his attention toward the group of women busy at work. As he watched them, his stoical countenance slowly softened, as though melted by the memories of his sister, as though he could see her even now among the throng of familiar women. I kept my eyes on his face, fascinated by the flickering emotion I saw there—his dark eyes deep in thought and the line of his jaw tightening, then slackening.

I don't know what possessed me to ask it, but I did: "What happened to her?"

His eyes clouded over. "She died here, a few years ago."

"What was she like?"

He sat up and rubbed the tops of his legs distractedly. "She was just like you, just like these women. She was so good, so smart. She always took care of me when we were growing up. When our mother died, she became a surrogate mother to me." He shook his head, reliving his past, somewhere I could not see and could not touch. "She worked so hard to be mother and caretaker, even to our father. He became distant and cold, and then when she was still too young to become an unchosen, he died.

"I was nineteen then, and I barely had an occupation—I was still apprenticed and lived in the home of my master—but I did what I could to support both of us so that she could stay with me, under my protection as her brother. My master understood our predicament, and he prematurely employed me as a journeyman under him. I began making a modest wage and moved back into my father's house with my sister. She tried to get some employment as a household servant, but none would hire her, and we had a difficult time financially." He stopped as his voice caught in his throat and a tear escaped. He wiped it away quickly. "You see, although I had claimed her after our father's death and she wasn't therefore lawfully considered an unchosen, the town still looked upon her as one and treated her as such, partly because I could not support her as I ought to have done."

"What happened?"

"I failed." He took in a deep breath and exhaled slowly. "I came home one day to find her gone. As I found out later, a stranger had come and taken her while I was away."

"A slave trader?"

He nodded. "He was a stranger to our village. He couldn't have known she was an unchosen unless someone had told him."

I gasped. "You were betrayed?"

"Yes. I never found out who betrayed us, but I had my suspicions, especially as a certain person in town suddenly had a significantly larger purse than his income allowed. But I never had any proof, and so I finally left the village of my birth and went in search of my sister. I traveled to the royal city but could not get an audience with the king. I took to slinking around the palace, waiting for hours for his carriage or a hunting party to come forth so that I could get close enough to speak with him, or at least with one of his advisors, which was equally difficult. I was eventually caught and arrested and spent several months in jail. I tried taking my appeal to the guards, but they did nothing but taunt me. Nobody would pass my message along."

I listened, horrified yet enraptured by his story, scrutinizing every furrow of his brow, following every lick of his lips, and tracing every flicker of firelight on his face with my eyes.

"Somehow through palace gossip, I suppose, it came to be known that I was jailed for trying to get an audience with the king to find my missing sister, so the king's daughter came to see me one evening in the cell. She had pity on me and released me in her father's name, then through some means of which I know not, set up an inquisition to look into the matter. But she told me right away that since my sister was an unchosen, and therefore no longer under the protection of the law, there was very little she could do." He paused and wiped a hand across his face, his body slumped by this time. He let out a sigh. "I do believe she tried, but in the end, it was fruitless. I was angry at myself for wasting so much time—time that I could have been out there searching for her myself. So I took to the road and somehow fell into peddling because it was a way of making a living that also allowed me to travel the whole countryside. Everywhere I went I looked for my sister and asked around for her. Months went by. I never stopped searching. I earned more and more money so that when the time came I could buy her back from whatever slavers had her. I found slaving camps, but she was never among the people there.

"And then I heard, very surreptitiously, about this place—the Colony. I didn't think she'd be here, but I came to look anyway." He chuckled slightly. "Believe me, it was very hard finding this place and then trying to earn trust enough to be allowed in. The first time I came, the women fairly fought me off, thinking me a slaver. I was even injured. I told them I was looking for my sister, gave them her name, and produced an old sketch drawing of her. Sure enough, they knew her. She was here. I'd found her.

"She told me she'd endured several months of"—his voice faltered—"of *abuse* at the hands of her master and had finally escaped. She'd found her own way to the Colony. I told her I wanted her to come with me so that we could start a new life somewhere, but she wouldn't come. She felt safe here, and she wouldn't leave no matter how I implored her. I finally relented and accepted her choice to stay, yet I knew I couldn't just go back home. I couldn't return to the life I'd lived before. It came to me so clearly then—like a light shining down from the heavens, as though the High King himself was speaking to my heart—a new purpose, a new mission."

"Helping the women?"

"Yes. I wasn't able to protect my sister, but I would still try to take care of her and the women with her. So I used the money I had saved up for her to buy provisions, and I've been doing that ever since."

"And may I ask how your sister died?"

He shrugged. "Grief, I suppose. Grief from being an unchosen before her time, grief from being kidnapped and abused, grief from being forced to live in poverty as an outcast in hiding. She grew sick and weak here and stopped eating, and eventually, her body wasted away. There was nothing I, nor any of the women, could do to give her back her will to live. She'd lost it long before."

He leaned forward and put his head in his hands; tears were dripping down his face. I sat quietly at his side, uncertain what to do or say, my heart breaking in a way I didn't know it could. Finally, hesitantly, I put my hand on his back and held it there. Once upon a time, this would have been considered improper, but I was an unchosen, so the rules of propriety didn't apply to me anymore.

"I'm sorry I doubted you before," I said, finally understanding his eagerness to seek me out and help me. It seemed ridiculous now—my suspicion of him.

"I failed my sister. I couldn't protect her. I'm haunted with that every day of my life." He inhaled deeply and wiped his eyes, sitting up straight. "So now you understand my grief and pain—the grief and pain a man can feel, even though he is a man."

"I'm truly sorry for what I said before—"

He held up a hand. "It's in the past. You're forgiven."

He held my eyes for a long time, his suddenly shining with a new light. I fancied a sense of relief and peace behind those eyes, which was just what I felt at that moment. I was glad to have helped him merely by listening, and I wondered whether he'd ever shared his story with anyone else before. I smiled at him, and he smiled back, and our smiles turned into chuckles. We understood each other.

And it was good to have a friend.

12
CHANGES

I had been at the Colony for nearly ten months when a woman named Shessa went out for a walk one morning and never returned. The night elapsed, then another day, and still she didn't return.

"She must've wandered too far and gotten herself lost," Taralyn suggested in the secrecy of our hut.

"How could she have been so foolish as to go walking by herself?"

"One gets too comfortable after living here in peace for a length of time," Taralyn said. "We start to feel safe and forget what's out there."

I still couldn't quite fathom the danger that existed out in the world for unchosens, though I had experienced a little of it myself.

Taralyn went on. "She probably ended up on a main road and stopped someplace to ask where she was and get directions back." She gasped and her hand flew to her mouth. We held each other's gazes a long moment before Taralyn spoke her concern. "She could inadvertently lead them here by her questions."

"Lead who?"

"Slavers."

A few of the younger women suggested forming a search party and venturing out to look for Shessa, but the older women adamantly forbade them to leave, lest they go missing themselves. Against the elder women's advice, they spent a day searching the outskirts of the camp. They all returned safely but had found no traces of the missing girl, not even a corpse.

The days went on in silent work, a fever of anticipation and fear hovering in the air amongst the women. They either spoke in hushed whispers about the missing girl, or they didn't speak at all. Nobody seemed to want to voice—and thus bring to life—what her likely fate was: she had been taken by slave traders. It was as if everybody was waiting for something to happen, for someone to come. But nobody came. And after a week, Shessa was still absent.

Then Danein returned. His visits had become more frequent since I'd moved to the Colony, and he stayed longer each time he came, sometimes for several days on end. He hunted with us, prepared food with us, cooked with us, and ate with us. He helped us through the winter by bringing extra blankets, food, and boots where he could afford it. He helped us build and repair our huts. When two women died from illness—compounded by lack of nourishment and warmth—Danein helped us bury them.

Instead of bringing only provisions, he began bringing gifts, pretty but impractical things for the women—small decorative trinkets, woven tapestries to hang across the walls of our huts, necklaces, bracelets, ribbons, sashes, rich and brightly colored fabric for making clothes, and flowers. He would saunter around camp, giving a tulip or a daffodil to each woman; the younger women blushed and giggled while the older women joked with him, beaming maternal affection. He always gave me my gift last, lingering as he did so—not just a tulip or a daffodil, but a rose. Sometimes it was white, sometimes yellow or pink, but it was always a rose.

I looked forward to his visits, not just for the gifts and provisions he brought with him, but for his company—for his friendship. Despite the gifts and the roses, I never imagined my relationship with Danein to be more than that. I never allowed my imagination to dwell on what might be or let my heart fly away with fanciful notions of love and romance. I had given up those dreams long ago. But—I told myself at the time—if I couldn't have a husband, at least I might have a friend in a man. My mutinous heart rebelled at times against this and would often swell at the sight of Danein or even just the mention of his name. I quickly squelched it. I hadn't been created to receive the love of a man. I knew that much.

When Danein came again, he hadn't time to pass around his customary gifts before word of the missing girl reached his ears. He spent the majority of that day in private conversation with some of the elder women, sober-faced with his arms crossed rigidly in front of him. The rest of us hung back and maintained our daily work, but I continually stole glances at him, curious as to what thoughts roamed his mind.

At the evening meal, he sat on the ground near the center fire, barely eating his stew. He set his bowl down and began absentmindedly prodding the fire with a stick. His eyes glazed over from staring into the flames. He appeared to want to be alone, but as I walked by to refill a bowl of stew for one of the women, the spell over him seemed to break and he glanced up at me.

"Hello, Alonya."

"Hello."

"How have you been doing since I last saw you?"

I handed the bowl off and stuck my hands in my apron pocket, my shoulders coming to my ears in a shrug. "About the same as always. Things don't change much here."

He nodded and shifted his position on the ground. "Come sit by me."

I took a seat next to him, wrapping my arms around my knees and staring into the fire, too aware of Danein's physical presence near me and the weight of his eyes on me to be completely at ease.

"Are you happy here, Alonya?"

I nodded. "I'm satisfied enough for the present."

"And what about in a year, or two years, or five? What then?"

"I don't know. I can't think that far ahead or I…I…"

"You what?"

I shook my head and swallowed hard. "I get sad sometimes. I know I should be happy and thankful for what I have here, but I oftentimes wish my life had turned out differently." I gave him an awkward half-smile. "I know it's futile to wish such a thing."

He sighed. "Sadness is a very potent, slow-working poison. I wish I could do more for you here."

"You already do so much."

"Even so, this isn't the kind of life for a woman—for any person—to be hiding in the woods, living in harsh conditions, barely surviving, constantly in fear of intruders."

"Do you think Shessa was taken by slavers?"

Danein didn't even blink. "Yes."

The way he said it—so confident, so convinced—sent a ripple of alarm through me.

"I've met many people on my travels throughout Zaphon and have learned to identify the slave traders. There have been quite a few about lately." He met my gaze with those familiar concern-filled eyes. "I'm not sure it's going to be safe for you women here anymore."

"But where will we go?"

"I don't know yet. But I'll figure it out."

My alarm grew into frustration. "The world should not be so."

"No, it shouldn't, but it is."

"How is it that I grew up with this injustice happening under my very nose, and yet knew nothing about it?"

Danein smiled, but there was sadness in it. "You had a good father who protected you and shielded you from the ugliness."

"But I've lived my life in ignorance and naivety!"

"Innocence," Danein said suddenly. "You've lived in innocence, and that is a great and rare treasure."

"Perhaps," I conceded, "but I'm beginning to think my brother was right."

"About what?"

"That my father filled my head with fanciful notions about the world and its goodness and the High King."

Danein sat up straighter, alert. "But your father was right about that."

My eyes filled with tears. "But how could he have been in a world where people are mistreated so, in a kingdom where there are unchosen women who aren't protected or cherished or loved?"

"It *is* unjust, Alonya, but it is men creating the injustice, not the High King."

"Why doesn't the High King abolish the unjust laws, then?"

"It is not for him to make or abolish everyday laws." Danein leaned in, and his face was suddenly alive with a passion I hadn't seen before. It disarmed me, but I, nonetheless, was held in the words he spun over me. "The High King gave the Great Laws long ago, and he has given authority to the lesser kings to govern by these laws. But many men no longer believe the High King or govern by the Great Laws. They pay them no heed. They know that all mankind are under the Great Laws, but they do not acknowledge it. They do not want to admit that ultimately their own dominion and power will cease. It was never theirs to begin with. It was given them by the High King long ago. They simply ignore this fact, and place all their faith and trust in kings and men—in their own power."

His words stirred a longing in my heart. I let out my breath, unaware that I had been holding it. "Do you really believe that?" I asked.

"Yes. There will come a day when the High King will reveal himself in power, and all authority and dominion will be his alone, and every knee will bow to him. The way it is now is not the way it will always be. It is only a temporary trouble. We must hold tight, Alonya. We must keep true to the High King and his ways."

I wished then I could have his confidence and his assurance. I wanted to tell him so, but my heart was so tight with longing and emotion that I felt any attempt at words would burst it to pieces and send me into a fit of crying. I did not want to expose myself so openly to Danein, so I kept my heart to myself.

He watched me intently for a long time, his eyes searching me for any words of response. I smiled, but it quivered on my lips and ultimately failed. I turned my face back to the fire. The camp had emptied during our conversation—the women had finished their suppers and retired to their huts for the night. It was strange to me how, even when surrounded by other people, I always felt we were alone when I was with Danein. I never saw anybody else but him.

"Have you ever seen the High King?" I asked, breaking the silence.

Danein shook his head. "Not in person, no."

"Then how can you know so much?"

He smiled—nearly laughed, so I thought. "There is much in this world that we don't see, most of which is hidden and only revealed to those who have eyes to see."

"And how does one obtain these 'eyes to see'?"

Danein inhaled a long, slow breath and let it out. "By choosing to believe, even when one does not see with one's eyes. There are other senses, you know, besides that of physical sight, which reveal truth."

I waited a long moment, unresponsive, until Danein suddenly stood and motioned me to follow him. "It's a warm night. Shall we go on a walk?"

I stood up, and to my surprise, he took my hand—took it as if it was the most natural thing in the world, as if we frequently walked side-by-side with hands clasped. He led me away from camp and into the thickness of the trees, shushing me when I asked him where we were going. After five minutes of walking, he stopped and dropped my hand.

I could barely see his face in the failing light, and it grew darker as we waited. I kept trying to speak, but each time I did, Danein just held up a hand to silence me with a grin of amusement on his face. He looked around in all directions while we stood there. Clearly he was waiting for something to happen.

Soon, all I could see of Danein was an outline. His dark form blended in with the thick wood around him, but as it did, small dots of light began to appear. They were yellow flashes of light, flickering on and off, only a few at first. Then more appeared, like stars waking in the night, surrounding us—fireflies. Soon these blinking lights were followed by quick streaks and flashes of color darting in and out from behind trees. I gasped when I first saw it and thought my eyes were playing tricks on me. Yet unmistakably, there they were—greens and blues and reds and oranges, like fiery color flying all around us. I watched it all, unblinking, caught in a moment of sheer delight and magic. And then a memory, buried deep in my heart, thrust itself to the forefront of my mind's eye. I had seen this before, once long ago when I was very young and had wandered out late one night, chasing fireflies and crickets to the edge of a wood. From the interior of the forest had come strange-colored lights, and I had puzzled over them until my papa found me and carried me home with a sharp rebuke for wandering so far.

It was then that Danein spoke.

"The forest fairies create their own light, similar to that of fireflies. They're nocturnal creatures, so they do most of their work at night, which is why they are rarely seen; but as you can see, they are alive and real."

I couldn't speak for emotion, so I merely nodded my head, though I knew Danein could barely see me. In the dark, he somehow found my hand again and took it, this time more tenderly.

"It's like that with the High King, Alonya. People don't always see him, but he's present, and he's still at work. As High King of the Lands of the Seven Kingdoms, he *does* know what's happening in Zaphon, even if it doesn't seem that way. And he *will* always show himself to those who have eyes to see, to those whose hearts seek him wholeheartedly, the way your heart seeks beauty and magic. You see, the forest fairies knew. They showed themselves to you, because you *do* believe."

"Truly?"

"Yes."

"I saw them when I was a little girl. I knew I had, but I'd forgotten."

"I just wanted you to see that there is more to our world besides pain and loneliness and injustice."

We stayed a little longer and returned to camp when it grew too cold to be out in the night. All was quiet at camp; no whispers or murmurs even came from within the interior of the huts where the women dwelt. The supper things had been cleared away, and the fire had diminished to embers that barely pierced the darkness with their faint glow. Danein walked me to the entrance of my hut where he lingered, squeezing my hand and searching my face before letting me go. He turned and walked across the clearing to a small tent he had set up on the outskirts of camp. He went inside without looking back.

I lifted the hide across the entrance to my hut and stepped quietly inside, hoping not to disturb Taralyn. She, however, was wide awake, sitting next to the flickering glow of a candle. She looked up at me with a smirk when I came in, and without fully knowing why, my face suddenly flared with heat. She didn't say anything but just watched me as I undressed and lay down on my pallet bed, burying myself with my quilts. I closed my eyes, trying to ignore her smug countenance, but even after several moments, I was uncomfortably aware that she was still eyeing me.

"Will you please turn out that light, Taralyn?"

"When will you admit to yourself that Danein cares about you?"

"We just went on a walk."

I could see her roll her eyes without even looking at her.

"You know better than that, Alonya. Everybody else can see it. You're trying not to."

"I'm an unchosen, Taralyn. I don't have the luxury of thinking well of myself in regards to men. Who am I that any man should love me?"

She clicked her tongue and lay down. From the muffled sound of her voice, I could tell that her back was to me. "We're all unchosens, Alonya, but that doesn't mean we're unworthy of love. You know, your self-loathing can be quite infuriating at times."

I was stunned to silence. Taralyn blew out the candle, and the hut was plunged into darkness. My heart was suddenly heavy again.

Danein left the next morning with a resolve to look into Shessa's disappearance. He promised to return as soon as he could. He advised us, in the meantime, to ready ourselves for sudden flight in case our camp was discovered and we had to leave in a hurry. This alarmed many of the women, but we immediately set to work, packing bags and bundles of food and clothing, and determining escape routes. Days passed, and we all waited in suspense and anticipation, but nothing happened. No one came. A week elapsed, then two, and still we were safe. So we grew comfortable again. We maintained our normal mode of living. We began venturing out again for hunts and food gathering.

It was in that moment, when our guard was down, that they finally came for us.

We were caught defenseless.

Still Danein had not returned.

13

PRISONERS

I smelled the smoky aroma of the morning fire from within my hut before the muffled screams reached my ears. They intermingled with the noise from my dream. Once I finally realized what was happening, I opened my eyes and shot upright to find Taralyn watching me with wide eyes. She put a finger to her mouth and shook her head. We scooted deeper into the recesses of our hut and covered ourselves in quilts and blankets, hoping to go unnoticed.

They came suddenly, like a swarm of locusts, from the trees and hills surrounding our camp, destroying everything in their wake. They smashed our huts, stole our goods, and captured us. The women who fought, screamed, and resisted were beaten into submission, some left unconscious. Taralyn and I didn't even try to run when our hut was torn down around us and we were pulled from the wreckage.

Crying and wailing drowned all other sounds as we were bound hand and foot, gagged, and tossed into the back of covered wagons with iron bars over the windows as though we were animals in a cage. I'm sure in that moment our assailants considered us little more than animals to be hunted.

Soon we were rattling along the road through the wood. There was one prison wagon for the thirty women and another open wagon for the goods and provisions stolen from us. The men who captured us—at least twenty-five of them—walked along beside the wagons or traveled on horseback.

Inside our prison, the other women whimpered, tears streaming down their dirty cheeks. Some closed their eyes. Others rocked back and forth. Still more stared blankly, wide-eyed in shock. The air in that jail was charged with a panicked anticipation of what evil fate awaited us. I knew the answer only too well from Nona's descriptions. This was it. A part of me had been waiting for it, like I'd waited to become an unchosen, so that part of me also felt a sense of relief that it had finally happened. It was too much to hope for and expect that we all could have lived happily ever after in the wood, free and unmolested. So I didn't cry. I let my mind empty into a state of resignation.

Taralyn, however, was sitting up, alert, shifting her body and looking around with wrinkled brows.

"What are you doing?" I asked her below the din of crying women.

"I'm planning a means of escape."

I shook my head. "There's no way to escape."

She didn't even look at me. "Alonya, you give up far too easily. There is always a way."

Her words stung me, just as they had when she had called me out on my self-loathing.

"We have *right* and *good* on our side, which is more than I can say for those louts out there."

I didn't reply; I merely contemplated her words. Taralyn had such strength of spirit and such a positive outlook on life, even when circumstances weren't in her favor. I wondered where it came from but knew the answer even as I asked the question of myself.

The wagon continued to bounce along. Thin slants of sunlight came peeping through the barred windows as the party exited the thick wood and approached more open road. The other women had calmed a bit, and many were whispering amongst themselves or leaning their heads on one another's shoulders, their eyes closed. I couldn't tell whether they slept or prayed.

"You're right," I finally whispered to Taralyn. "I always seem to be waiting for bad things to happen to me. I never expect any better."

Taralyn turned her eyes to me then. They were filled with compassion, not irritation, as I had supposed. "You must remember that the whole world doesn't hold by the laws of Zaphon. Just because Zaphon has deemed you an unchosen doesn't mean that you *are* unchosen. I have chosen you as a friend, and so has Danein."

My mind turned to Danein. I wondered what he would do when he returned to find us all gone. He might hold himself responsible, as he did with his sister. His heart would be broken, and at that thought, *my* heart broke. It put a little life back inside me, though.

"So what's your plan?"

In the shuffle and confusion of being discovered and kidnapped, Taralyn had managed to slip a small dagger underneath the waist of her skirt. She was planning on using it to free the women when the party stopped for the night.

"If they let us out of here for the night, we may have a chance to run away. If they keep us locked in this wagon, it will do no good to cut our bonds."

We spent the remainder of that day contemplating all possibilities as the wagon bounced along, shifting us uncomfortably to and fro. We were squeezed so tightly in the back of that vehicle that despite the cool spring day, there was little breeze sifting through the barred windows, and we seemed to stew in our own perspiration. We saw little of our captors except what glances we could catch through the narrow slits between the bars. A few were large men, but most were of average height and build. They all wore similar plain black tunics and breeches that were dirty, worn, and ripped in several places. Some wore sandals or boots; others were barefoot. They were, on the whole, a dirty, ragged bunch who clearly lived in the wild and rarely joined the ranks of civilization. They were most likely uneducated ruffians and criminals who had found a meager living hiring themselves out as slavers. Taralyn considered this to be in our favor. I thought that even if we could outwit them, they had the advantage of speed and muscle over us.

We were fed nothing all day, and we didn't stop until hours later, after the sun had descended. Chains clinked and rattled as the door to the back of the wagon was unlocked. It opened, letting in a cool, fresh breeze. The women all sat up and seemed to cower as one body toward the back of the wagon. Two men jumped in and began hauling them roughly outside. A few women tried to run once their feet hit the ground, but they were quickly overtaken. I watched in horror as one of the younger, more defiant women was slapped mercilessly by one of the men and dragged off into the darkness of the wood beyond.

"This'll teach you to defy me!" the man bellowed at her as they disappeared.

I was careful to make myself as small and unnoticed as possible.

Miles from the main road, in the midst of a large glade, a small camp had been set up. Tents surrounded a glowing orange fire in the center. We were all herded to a clump of trees and told to sit. I continually glanced at Taralyn, who was right next to me. She only smiled serenely at me, or gave me a wink of reassurance. I dared not speak, but I was certain then that we were both of the same mind. We hadn't told any of the other women about the hidden knife, but most likely some had overheard our conversation in the wagon and were merely waiting.

Our captors proceeded to cook a large skinned deer over the fire, laughing and exchanging crude language, all the while stealing glances at us women cowering nearby. They sneered and occasionally lowered their voices while watching us, as though planning unspeakable evils.

One of the men who had stayed aloof from the others and was more nicely dressed than them—albeit still in black—approached us with several skins of water. He was little and thin but seemed to command authority. He called over another larger man and ordered him to help us drink. We tipped our heads back while they poured some cool water from the skins into our mouths. It seemed these men were intelligent enough to realize that if they completely starved and thirsted us, we would be useless to them once we arrived at the slave camp.

An older woman—one of the matrons of the Colony named Jillian—was stubborn and refused the drink. The nicely-dressed man knelt down until he was eye level with her.

"I implore you, madam, to drink lest you lose your strength. You will need it for the journey tomorrow. We've a long way yet to go."

Jillian's lip quivered as she gazed steadily at the man. She then turned her gaze away, lifted her chin slightly, and replied, "I would rather die than be used by you men for whatever foul purposes you have in mind!"

The larger man stepped before his comrade and slapped Jillian hard across the face, eliciting a cry of surprise from several women.

"Let me teach her a lesson, sir!"

The leading man stood, stared at him with a stony expression, and then glanced at Jillian, who was white-faced, her eyes popping with fear.

"She says she would rather die than do our bidding," he said coolly. He turned to the large man. "Give her what she wants."

Jillian shook her head fiercely and began screaming as the larger man pulled her from the group and dragged her away into the wood, a large hunting knife brandished in one hand. She disappeared, just as the other woman had.

I was too terrified and stunned to speak or cry.

The small man finished giving us water and walked away, saying, "You'll get food tomorrow."

The night deepened, and we stayed still, quiet, and alert as the group of men slowly retired to their tents. We knew they wouldn't all go to bed. Sure enough, as the rowdiness tapered down and the camp grew quiet, three men were left to guard the group of women. They sat near the fire—at least fifteen feet away—with their backs to us, occasionally glancing backward to check on us. Any time one of us tried to speak or began whispering amongst ourselves, we were quickly shushed. From time to time, one of the guards would approach us with vile gestures and threats, but they never touched us.

The wood came alive with the clicking and buzzing of insects and the rustling of small, hidden ground animals. These were sounds I was accustomed to by then. I shivered with cold despite being crowded next to the other women, several of whom had fallen asleep with their heads on their chests or on another's shoulder. Taralyn was still wide awake, as was I. Her strength and resolve infused me with energy. I knew she was just waiting for the right moment, though she, like myself, was uncertain when that was.

Several hours later, during the deepest part of night, that chance came.

The guards had rotated shifts. A new set sat around the fire, but since most of the women had fallen asleep—and those of us who hadn't had nodded our heads to feign sleep—this second shift of guards was less attentive than the first had been. The fire had died down significantly, casting us in shadow. The guards played quietly at a game that involved sticks and stones on the ground next to the fire. So occupied were they on their game that they seemed to forget us, their charges, indefinitely. Taralyn had only to nudge me, and I shifted my body slightly to reach with my hands—which were bound in front of my body—into the back of Taralyn's skirt. I felt at the waist and found the hidden knife, keeping my eyes ever on the guards. They didn't even glance in our direction. I pulled out the knife and brought it forward. Clutching it tightly between my fingers, I began sawing at Taralyn's bonds.

One of the guards yawned and flung his arms out wide in a stretch. As he did so, he turned his body to check on us. We quickly put our heads down and closed our eyes. There was no noise but the whispering amongst the guards. I waited several minutes before risking a peek. The guards were back to their game. Taralyn nudged me again and I continued sawing. A few of the other women were roused by this time and watched silently, holding their breaths.

Once Taralyn's hands were free, she took the knife from me and began cutting the rope at her feet then worked to free me from my bonds. A woman named Eloise, close to our age, sitting behind us, saw what we were doing and whispered that she had also smuggled a knife into the front pockets of her apron. Taralyn turned slightly and began sawing at her bonds. Between the two knives, which we passed around quietly from woman to woman, we managed to free nearly everybody. We were continually on the alert, but as more women woke up, shifting and whispering restlessly, it was difficult to continue feigning sleep. We were soon found out.

The guards turned and noticed something amiss. The moment they stood to approach us, several of the freed women suddenly fled in panic. They took off in all directions. My initial impulse was to up and run as well, but Taralyn held me down. The guards' attentions were fixed on the fleeing women. They shouted an alarm and began pursuing the escapees.

"Now!" Taralyn called.

We stood up along with Eloise, who had wisely stayed put with us until then, and ran along the outer edge of the camp in the opposite direction the rest of the women had fled. Men began pouring out of their tents, half-clad, looking sleepy and confused. They quickly assessed the situation, however, and came to attention. Most of them went off in the direction of the clamor while the three of us snuck away quickly and quietly toward the road, back the way we'd come.

Unfortunately, the tree cover was thin, and we soon came out of the glade into open land, broken only by large hummocks and rock formations. Stars and a near-full moon threw down light at us. We ran hard, not looking back. My chest ached and my legs grew weary, but still we ran on.

After what seemed ages and miles of running, Eloise suggested we slow down for a rest. We had just thrown ourselves against a large boulder when the unmistakable sound of hoof beats rang out from the darkness behind us.

"Go!" I shouted.

We kept on at full speed. My lungs burned and felt near to bursting, but I ran on. The hoof beats grew louder, and men's voices carried on the air with them.

We entered a shallow, rocky valley between two large hills. My body sliced the cool air before me as I flew through the night, overtaking Taralyn and Eloise. We raced as fast as we could, but still our pursuers closed in, nipping at our heels. Soon they were right on top of us. I stole a sideways glance to see Eloise struck to the ground. Still I kept on.

Taralyn and I swerved to the left just as the dark outline of a horse and rider appeared on our right side. The road became narrower as the hills on either side grew steeper, and soon we were dodging larger rocks and boulders that were strewn along the ravine floor. We could barely see by the faint light of the moon, but we managed to elude the rider by climbing atop boulders and swerving left and right of them. He, on the other hand, had a more difficult time of the terrain and fell slightly behind the farther we ran on.

He was soon joined by another horse and rider, which surprised us by swooping down from the steep incline at our left. He herded us out to the middle of the road. The riders were merely feet behind us. My heart nearly burst from my chest and my feet were wet with blood, but I continued on. The thumping of my heart in my ears was doubled by the heavy panting of the horses directly behind us. And then something happened.

One of the horses stumbled, throwing its rider into a boulder with a sharp crack. We ran on without looking back, now pursued by only one horse and rider. This one gained on us.

"He'll take us both down!" Taralyn shouted at my side. "You have to keep going! I'll stall him."

Then she slowed down.

"Taralyn!"

"Keep going! I'll be right behind you!"

I did as I was told and shot forward. I heard a scuffle, a snort of nostrils, and a loud thump. Thinking Taralyn had been knocked down, I stopped suddenly and whirled around. Taralyn stood next to the fallen rider with a large rock in her hand. She pelted him with it before throwing another, all the while backing up as though readying to flee again. The rider struggled to rise; he had apparently hurt himself during his fall. Taralyn pelted him again. He cursed at her as the rock bounced off his arm. She turned and saw me watching.

"Go!" she screamed, waving her arm at me.

She then pulled out the knife with which she had cut our bonds. The silver moonlight reflected off the sharp blade as she ran to the animal and plunged the knife into its side. It cried in pain and backed away, kicking and flailing; its legs buckled under it, and it fell to the ground.

The rider was on his feet again. He cursed and shot straight at Taralyn. She turned and ran on toward me.

"Go!" she screamed.

I started to run again then stopped and turned, hoping to help Taralyn. We were, after all, two-to-one now. But the man was big and strong despite his injuries. I hesitated on my feet, trapped with indecision. I had just made up my mind to stand my ground when the man's big arms, open wide like wings on either side of Taralyn's smaller body, came crashing down on her, encircling her like a rope. They both tumbled to the ground. Taralyn struggled to break free, but the man soon had her pinned down.

Her eyes met mine, not full of fear but of courage and resolve.

"Go now!" she screamed with all her strength. "Seek sanctuary with the High King!"

The man yelled at her and brought a hand down forcefully across her cheek. She was stunned to silence, but still she watched me while her hands were tied up. She nodded and winked at me, and only then did I turn and flee back into the night. A cloud flew past the moon, and I was plunged into darkness, tears streaming down my face.

14

ESCAPE

I was alone again.

I had run blindly into the night after Taralyn was captured, fearing that the rider would come after me next. I had no sense of time. I merely followed the path along the ravine as it grew steeper, climbing the mountains until it entered a wood. The glow of the moon was my guide when it shone freely in the sky, unobstructed by cloud cover. At times the light dimmed when overtaken by the clouds chasing it, and I would freeze on the spot, peering around me, trying to penetrate the shadows and inky silhouettes on all sides. The night was full of noises I'd never known so intimately before: scratches and rustlings and cackles and howls. I wasn't sure what I feared the most: my human pursuers (if indeed they were still pursuing me), or some unnamed, unseen creature of my imagination, waiting for me somewhere in the darkness.

Then the clouds would move past the moon, and my eyes would focus on the old, knotty tree stump that had seemed like a crouching beast ready to pounce, or on the tall, spindly tree that resembled a monster with arms outstretched. I ran on. I ran until my head hurt and my legs seemed to liquefy beneath me. Every time I considered stopping to rest, a squawk or rustling noise from somewhere above or behind me would propel me forward.

So I traveled the remainder of the night that way. It seemed hours until the stars disappeared and the sky finally lightened. Only then did I slow down. The night noises dissolved into harmless, familiar forest noises—among them the gentle sound of water on rock. I followed it until I came to a narrow and shallow stream, overhung by a canopy of drooping branches and leaves, very hidden and quiet. I bathed my face and drank my fill of water before sitting back on a boulder to rest. It was then that I considered my situation. I had been in this position before—wandering, lost, and alone—and thus could approach it in a more composed frame of mind. I had also lived in the forest for many months as part of the Colony and knew how to subsist in the wild—where to find food and water at the very least.

I inhaled deeply, ready to do whatever was necessary to survive.

My thoughts flew to Taralyn and the other women. *What would happen to them?* I asked myself. *Would they be punished for attempting escape? Had any actually escaped? Where was this slave camp to which they were being taken?* I guessed we had been traveling in a northerly direction the previous day. *The slave camp must be somewhere to the north, perhaps a ride of a day or two.*

I looked around at my tranquil little haven, realizing I was lost. I had no idea what direction I had run last night. The path I'd taken hadn't been straight or clear-cut by any means. I knew I was in a wood in the mountains somewhere in the north; that much was obvious. *If only I had a map!*

A small strip of sandy shoreline ran parallel with the stream. I suddenly jumped from my perch on the boulder, pulled out a stick from the nearby brush, and ran to the shore. I picked out a few broken twigs and dried leaves from the sand before smoothing it over with my hands. I stared at the blank sand, picturing in my mind the map of Zaphon that Nona had given me. Slowly, meticulously, I began drawing in the sand with the stick, recreating the map as well as I could remember. I'd looked at it very little in the previous ten months while at the Colony.

As soon as I'd finished a rough outline of the country, I filled it in with the basic physical features—lakes and rivers and mountains—that I had learned as a child during geography lessons. I then indicated some of the major towns and villages by writing the first letter of its name, and finally put an X in the general location of the Colony, somewhere in the upper middle of the map.

I sat back to inspect my work. It was, of course, not accurate to scale, but that was no matter. I took the stick and, beginning at the X, drew a squiggly line in the direction I'd guessed we had travelled the previous day while bound by the slavers. Twice I smoothed over my line to fix it. I closed my eyes. I tried to feel the swaying movement of the wagon again, to picture my few glances out of the barred windows and recall the direction of the sun as it descended. We had certainly traveled east. The camp where they held us had been in an open area somewhere near these mountains, perhaps on a mountain plain. The Colony was in a forested nook in the foothills of a mountain range.

I glanced at the sand map, and after a few mental calculations as to time and distance, I made a rough estimate of where the camp must have been, marking it with a stone, and guessed that my current location was somewhere on the same mountain range as the Colony, but farther north and east.

Reason suddenly came crowding into my thoughts. *What now? I've guessed the direction the slavers are heading, but that won't necessarily help me find their base of operations. They might turn at any moment. They might have days farther to ride. And even if I do find it, what am I to do then, a defenseless woman on my own? I'll most likely fall into a trap and get myself back into the mess I've just escaped. And Taralyn…*

Taralyn. I stopped reflecting and took a moment to grieve for my friend, for my loss. Taralyn had sacrificed so much to help me escape. She had given up her life, essentially, for mine. And what was my life? Nothing.

She had told me to seek out the High King. I had more notion as to how to find the slaver's camp than the High King. He was said to dwell in Coralind—the sacred country—but others said he had no permanent dwelling place, that he went about from country to country, living in them all at once. Yet these were just ideas, just tradition or legend, kept alive by those who still believed—people like Taralyn and Danein.

I wondered if I would ever see Danein again.

It struck me that I ought to make my way back to the Colony to be found by Danein when he returned. I glanced back at the sand map. I figured I could probably make it in a two-day walk. Most likely nobody would be there, but—

But what if slavers returned to loot and to pick the place clean like meat off a bone, to ensure they'd captured all the women, or to hide in waiting for any escapees who might ramble back to the only place they could think to go?

No, my gut told me I couldn't go back to the Colony. Yet my heart ached for a familiar face, for company, for my friend, for Danein. I needed help—the other women needed help—and he was the only one I could trust to help.

The sun was nearly topping the trees and came through cracks in the forest canopy. It fell on my back and warmed me. I sat a long while, unmoving, my eyes fixed absentmindedly to the sand map. They roved over it while my mind wandered to faraway places—the people I'd known, the places I'd been, the circumstances I'd found myself in. I had never anticipated any of it when I was young. How had my life turned out so oddly? How had I ended up so alone and disappointed? Disjointed thoughts roamed in my brain. And somewhere in the mess I tried to bring myself out of my abstract reverie and get back to the situation at hand. I lingered a bit too long, perhaps—a method to ignore all my trouble—but then from the muddle of faces and voices in my mind, I heard Taralyn telling me that I give up far too easily. So I snapped back into alertness.

When I did, I found I was still looking at the sand map. My eyes refocused to the top part where I'd drawn symbols identifying a huge expanse of forestland in northern Zaphon—the Wild Lands. Then I saw the small indentation in the sand that designated my current location.

I was on the outskirts of the Wild Lands of Zaphon. I had unintentionally trekked back into my original quest.

Everything Nona had taught me came swooping back into my consciousness. Aside from Danein turning out to be trustworthy after all, she had been right about everything. Even in an obscure forest colony of unchosen women, there was still no refuge. The camp had been raided and all of us had been taken. Some had already died; some would still die while others would become slaves. It seemed no matter where I went or what I did, this fate stalked me as though I were its prey. There was nowhere safe I could go to live a normal life.

I decided then I would rather choose my fate than have it catch me in its clutches, unaware. Nona had advised me to trust in magic, to go to the Wild Lands and seek the sources of beauty. I had been bent on that purpose up to the second I had accidentally found my way to the Colony, which had sidetracked me for months. I was now free to renew my original quest.

The sun was clear above and shone down great puddles of light through the boughs. I had been sitting for quite a long time in one spot, and thirst suddenly overtook me. My limbs ached when I moved. I groaned in pain as I made my way slowly back to the water's edge. As I dipped my cupped hands into the cool, clear mountain water, I thought of Nona's words about the merrow pool. She had said that to take water without asking was treacherous. I glanced up and down the stream. Clearly this was no merrow pool, and I had already drunk once. But could it be true? I had seen the forest fairies myself. Surely merrow were still in the world as well.

My life had been sheltered growing up. I'd never seen anything or gone anywhere except in stories. Papa had often spoken of magic and of the High King, and I'd always just taken it for granted that those things were true until he was gone. I had never worked out for myself what I truly believed.

I wanted to believe. I wanted it all to be true. I wanted to see it with my own eyes and to touch it with my own hands. If there was a High King, then perhaps the best way to find him would be to start with magic. Although Nona didn't seem to agree, in my mind the two were inextricably linked, as they had been in Papa's mind. I told myself that perhaps one might lead to the other—that perhaps seeking the magical sources of beauty might help me find the High King as well, since I was uncertain where he was to be found.

Bent over the clear water, I caught my reflection—the first time I'd seen it in months. There had been a few small mirrors at the Colony, but I'd never looked into them. Nor did I try to catch a glimpse of myself in the stream when we would bathe, wash, or collect water. So I finally stopped and looked. It was difficult to see the image clearly with the ripples along the surface of the water as it moved. I crawled onto a large boulder that jutted farther out into the stream where it was deeper, once again bending over the side to look.

My hair was much longer than I'd remembered, and it was a mess, dirty and knotted. Dark circles rimmed my puffy eyes, given to me from a mixture of crying and exhaustion. I continued to stare, searching for some redeeming quality in the face I saw looking back at me. I saw nothing of consequence, nothing to stand out; and the longer I looked, the worse my reflection became.

I pulled away from the image in the water and sat down heavily upon the boulder. I still was not pretty. It was my curse.

It had been spoken over me on my seventeenth birthday by my schoolmates and had run its course, ruining my life.

But that was years ago and long past. I had to make plans to move forward. I still ached for beauty. If I had been beautiful to begin with, my life would have taken a different course. Perhaps by following Nona's advice, I could still remedy some of the damage that had been done. I might still turn the course of my fate by going to the Wild Lands and seeking the sources of beauty. If, in my quest, I came upon answers regarding the High King's whereabouts, so much the better. But it was beauty I was after—a sense of self-presence and confidence with which to govern myself and others—and nothing else, so I thought. The High King—wherever he was—couldn't help me.

After refreshing myself by the stream and collecting some berries and edible roots, I once more checked the map. It had been slightly altered by insect tracks in the sand but was still legible to read. I glanced up at the sky to check the direction of the sun, determined a route, and walked blindly into the forest away from the stream, once more determined upon my course, ignoring the nagging pull in my heart and mind that sounded a lot like Taralyn.

The Fruit

I didn't know what I was looking for. A fruit, Nona had said. A fruit that was disguised and not easily found.

I stopped midstep and shook my head. *How am I to do this?*

Hyacinth Wood. This should be Hyacinth Wood, I told myself as I gazed at my surroundings. Hyacinth Wood was part of the Wild Lands where the fruit could be found.

I had walked all afternoon, my mind occupied with the direction of my quest. Undoubtedly, I was in the mountains and had not come upon any other people or villages. That fortified the certainty in my mind that I had, indeed, stumbled upon the Wild Lands. It was only then that I began considering the logistics of my mission.

How was I to find a disguised fruit? I had no notion of what to look for besides a very brief description from Nona that was all but faded from my mind. I took a moment to reach back into my memory, to the day I had left Nona. She had instructed me on how to go about my journey and reminded me of what to look for. The fruit grew on very short plants that were often hidden beneath or entwined by other bushes. The fruit was sometimes the color of earth, sometimes the color of berries, and sometimes the color of foliage, for it constantly changed colors just before being picked off the vine. To ensure positive results in the way of beauty, the fruit had to be picked at the precise moment it was transitioning from one particular hue to the next. But I could not remember which ones. If I found the fruit, I would just have to try all possibilities.

I spent the remainder of that day with my face downward, searching the area at my feet as I walked. I saw nothing resembling what I was looking for—and yet all the time, despite my hazy recollection of Nona's description of the plant, I wasn't even completely certain what that was.

It soon grew cold as the sun set and shadows populated the wood. I quickly gathered sticks and brush before the sky faded completely to black and built a fire easily on my own. My stomach grumbled as I lay down next to the fire, yet I was too weary to attempt hunting. I hadn't seen much game besides a few small squirrels and birds, and even then I had no knife with me with which to kill and skin an animal. I would have to try to survive off of berries, nuts, and plants while I could, until I found what I was looking for.

Until I found beauty.

Somehow, I thought that once I found beauty, everything else would be well. That was my only aim then, my final object.

I quickly drifted into sleep.

The sudden crack of a twig breaking underfoot startled me from sleep. My eyes popped open and I listened in rapt attention, lifting my head slightly off the ground, peering into the night.

The fire had died down to faint red embers, but all else was black. In the tense stillness, the ceaseless chirping of cicadas was magnified in my ears. I waited, listening for several moments until my neck grew sore from holding my head up.

I heard no other sounds. With relief I let my head fall back to the ground and closed my heavy eyelids to resume sleep. The cicadas' song soon lulled me into a doze. My body felt heavy, listless. I had the sensation of falling, as though I was sinking through the ground into a cavity beneath the earth. I drifted slowly, floating. Then I stopped.

In my dream I stood in a vast grassy meadow. I began searching for something. I knelt and examined blades of grass and flower petals; not finding what I was looking for, I moved on to another spot in the meadow. The meadow seamlessly evolved into forest, and still I continued to search.

Then there were hands in front of me: strong, beautiful, masculine hands. They took my arms and turned me from my search. I watched the hands as they gripped me gently, and a sense of relief and peace coursed through me. Yet my heart beat rapidly, nervous and scared and exhilarated. I followed the length of the arms up from the hands—muscular, firm arms—and my eyes continued moving up to the shoulders, the neck, and finally the face.

Danein's dark eyes stared back at me, bright with mirth. He looked different from when I'd last seen him, but it was him. Different, yet the same. A stranger, yet familiar. He held my hands and just watched me, smiling. I knew he cared about me. It was him. He loved me, and I loved him. We were together as it should be. I wasn't alone. I wasn't unchosen or unloved. And somehow it seemed it had always been this way.

Quiet footfalls intruded upon my dream. The sound of scuffling and crunched leaves underfoot awakened me with a start. The embers were gray. I was shivering and gasped at the sudden onslaught of cold and dark as I sat up straight, rubbing my hands up and down my arms. My heart pounded in my chest, as though something inside me was trapped and fighting to get out.

It had only been a dream. Danein wasn't there, and I was alone. I sighed heavily and forced myself to hold back tears from the weight of disappointment pressing down on me.

The dream fragmented and disintegrated as quickly as it had come while I stoked the dead embers with a stick to try and revive the fire. Through cracks in the forest canopy above, the sky was beginning to lighten. Just as I was about to plop myself back down to the ground, I heard whispering.

I fell instantly to my stomach to keep myself out of sight and once again lay stiff and silent, listening. Men's voices, muffled and low, came from somewhere through the thicket of trees at my right. They stepped lightly through the underbrush, but the sounds grew louder as they approached. Through a chink in the foliage, I saw—several feet away but unmistakable—the black hide boots of the slave-traders that had raided the Colony.

Pressed as low to the ground as I could manage, I scurried around the fire and into the dense woods opposite the men's voices. Clearing my campsite, I stood and ran, weaving back and forth through the maze of tree trunks. Before long, I stopped and leaned against the rough, shaggy bark of a hickory to catch my breath. A small fox darted out in front of me in its chase of a rabbit, startling me. I chuckled in relief, but my heart barely had time to settle from its panic before I heard the men's voices again.

"This way. She's here!"

I bolted without looking to see how many of them pursued me. Like a deer in flight from her hunters I fled, bounding this way and that, plunging straight into thickets and plowing through thick overgrowth. The sounds of pursuit behind me were close, but I doubted I could be seen in the dense forest. They were following my sounds of flight. I needed a place to stop and hide.

After I'd put a little more distance between me and my hunters, I suddenly ducked sideways behind a small stand of shrubs and changed direction. I ran several more yards before coming to an area of the wood where the trees were blacker, thicker, and more formidable in appearance. The branches were low-lying and gnarled. I stopped momentarily just to ensure I was out of sight from my pursuers before leaping up into an ancient cedar with more speed and agility than I knew I possessed. I climbed as high and deep as I could, hiding myself within the thick tangle of needle-bearing branches.

I waited. My chest heaved as I gulped the air, struggling to regain my breath. I flicked a red ant from my leg and noticed that the skin beneath my dirty, ragged skirt was scraped and bleeding. My arms too were streaked with blood and suddenly throbbed with pain. I bit back tears and stared downward. From my position high in the tree, I could see little of the ground.

My breathing soon became less laborious, but I was unable to relax completely, rigid with apprehension as I was. Before long, I once again heard the voices of my pursuers, though I couldn't see them. They were close and had obviously slowed to a stalking pace. In the stillness of the moment, frigid with fear, I managed to strain my ears to hear every word.

"She's gone."

"No, she wasn't that far ahead of us. She must be hiding."

They searched the area around the tree, yet never once looked up. I waited with my breath held, leaning as far back into the tree as I could, as though I might melt into it. Minutes passed, long interminable minutes, during which they wandered out of sight and sound in their effort to discover my hiding place. Soon they returned, and although they weren't directly beneath my tree, they were close enough for me to hear.

"Perhaps she scrambled up a tree."

"Would she have had time for that?"

There was silence as they considered this possibility. My heart raced, and I tried to dig myself deeper within the boughs of the large, gnarled cedar. Although I dared not peek downward, I imagined the hunters peering up into the boughs, possibly seeking out the trees with low-lying branches, testing out their durability.

"She could be in any of these trees. We can't possibly search them all."

"We can, and we will."

My heart nearly stopped.

"But what if she didn't scramble up a tree? She might have gotten away on foot in any direction."

"I think not. There are no traces that she fled in any direction but up."

I was done for. This would be it. My only option would be to try and run again. I considered sneaking down quietly and making my escape as soon as the men's backs were turned. They would hear me, if not see me, but perhaps I might still outrun them.

Before I could act on my plan, a rustling directly underneath indicated that one of the men had begun climbing upward.

I had nowhere to go. I was trapped!

I flung myself back against the trunk, willing myself to shrink, to disappear. Without knowing why, I closed my eyes, turned my face skyward, and whispered to the High King. "Help me! Help me!"

Just then, a stampede of hoofbeats rang throughout the woods, and the ground trembled, shaking the tree with the vibrations.

"Get out of there!" the man on the ground shouted.

I leaned forward to peek downward; the man who had been climbing my tree jumped down and dashed away. The rumbling grew louder, and I held onto the tree as the shaking became more thunderous. Streaks of white bodies and feathery manes flew past underneath me. Wild horses.

The stampede didn't last more than a minute. The wood was silent once it had passed. I held my place for several moments until a neighing and stamping drove me out in curiosity. I climbed down for a better view. I saw no sign of my pursuers anywhere. A single white mare stepped directly underneath the tree, looking up at me as though waiting for me to descend. The herd had passed, but she seemed to linger behind intentionally. After further observance that she and I were the only two bodies in the area, I climbed all the way down and jumped to the ground with a soft crackle of underbrush beneath my feet.

The mare stood tall and majestic before me. It was only then that I saw she had a single horn of ivory, smooth and glistening, protruding from her forehead. My breath caught in my throat. Just to be certain of what creature was before me, I glanced at her feet: cloven hooves, unnatural for horses but typical of unicorns. Her tail flicked on the other side of her body, and another quick glance revealed a long, slender appendage with a tuft of hair at the end, like that of a lion's tail.

Even as I stood she seemed to approach me. My heart thumped wildly, yet at the same time I felt calmed, as though the creature knew me, as though she had known all along that I was in that tree, and she had chased the men away. As I'd heard, unicorns were very discerning of evil. Anything or anyone with evil intent could never stand in the presence of a unicorn for long—the creature would impale it with its horn.

We stared at each other for a long time. The wood around us seemed to disappear. I heard nothing but the heavy breath bursting out of the unicorn's nostrils. As she watched me with her dark eyes, I felt judged. Suddenly sheepish under her gaze, I wanted to lower my head in shame. I began to tremble, and tears flooded my eyes.

My papa had told me once that unicorns, the purest and most innocent creatures on the earth, had the power to judge—to peel back the flesh and see the soul, to discern motives and read the heart. It was rare to see a unicorn, and when one did, it was for a specific purpose. The unicorn had chosen to reveal itself to that person. That person was chosen.

The unicorn approached until she was mere inches from me, then slowly lowered her head so that her horn was level with my body. I feared for a moment that she might run me through, but her head continued to lower until her horn touched the dirt, as though bowing. When she raised her head, she neighed happily and rubbed her face against mine. I instinctively wrapped my arms around her neck, burying my head in her soft, silky mane. My tears flowed freely, though for what reason I cried I knew not.

"Thank you," I whispered over and over again.

She seemed to let me cry as though comforting me. Finally, she began backing away.

"Did the High King send you?" I asked her.

She did not respond.

"What do I do now?"

I got no answer but a stare.

"I don't want to be alone. Will you go with me?"

She snorted, tossed her head, and turned to leave.

"Wait!" I called, never once thinking it absurd that I was speaking to an animal. Somehow I knew she understood me, even if she couldn't answer me.

The unicorn fled into the woods and was gone.

I spent the rest of that day walking on in a daze, comforted by the unicorn's appearance, yet disturbed by emotions that were in conflict within me. I thought continually of Danein and then cursed myself for doing so. I saw Taralyn's face in my mind, so calm and resolved when she'd been captured, tranquil and strong like the unicorn. She and the unicorn were the same, part of the same magic and faith that pointed to the High King, and I longed to be a part of it, but I didn't know how. I didn't know how to find the High King. I knew then with certainty that he was alive and present in the world. Perhaps I had always known it. I'd just forgotten. I'd ignored it.

"Where are you?" I whispered.

I continued to wander. The farther I walked, the deeper I went into Hyacinth Wood and the Wild Lands. I had long ago ceased to walk along a path. The land was hilly, the wood populated by dips and valleys. The broadleaf beeches, oaks, and hickories gave way to a forest dominated by cedar and pine, which continued to grow thicker and more ancient in appearance, the trunks tall and erect, towers stretching up to touch the sky. I didn't stop, nor did I eat all day. My arms and legs were covered in streaks of dried blood, yet I had not come across a river or pond. It wasn't until dusk that I realized I was weary, thirsty, and hungry. I finally stopped to make camp. I built a fire and went in search of something to eat.

In the failing light, it was difficult to make out more than shapes and silhouettes. I fumbled along for quite a while, circling my camp various times, but could find very little besides a few nuts and some edible plants. I sighed heavily and was just resigning myself to another night on an empty stomach when, from across the orange flickering of the fire, I saw a faint green glow near the ground. My first thought was that it must be a fairy, so I stood still and continued to watch, waiting for more colors to appear. None did, and the green glow never left its place near the ground.

I stepped around the fire to get a closer look. As I did, the glow changed from green into a ruddy red, bright like berries. I nearly dove for it when I realized it must be the fruit Nona had told me about. I knelt down and inspected it with my hands. It was oblong in shape, like a leaf, and just barely thicker than a leaf. It had spines and veins running through it as well. Aside from the color, it looked like an ordinary leafy plant, not like a fruit at all. So this is what Nona had meant when she said it was disguised. I had only seen it because the color glowed in the darkness, giving it away. In the daylight I might have missed it completely!

I pulled at the fruit on its vine, revealing more glowing colors behind it, hidden within the bramble. I pulled and dug until I had uncovered more of the fruit. I knew there was even more to be found, but I was too famished to continue searching. Knowing the fruit had the property of giving beauty, I hesitated before picking any, curious and uncertain. My stomach growled, pawing at my insides. I idly questioned whether the fruit was safe for eating. Would it even satiate hunger, or was it only good for magical purposes like bestowing beauty?

When a piece of the fruit suddenly began fading from crimson and shifting to a dusty orange, I impulsively plucked it from the vine and bit into it. It was sweet and soothing like milk and seemed to melt on my tongue. I was instantly awash in warmth and a sense of comfort. Even as I finished the last bite, my body seemed to ache for more. My hunger was not appeased. I waited until another piece of fruit began transitioning between colors before plucking it, and then another; I ate these with as much relish as the first. How long I sat there in the dark with the fire to my back, eating the nameless fruit, I know not. But each new piece, even as it satisfied me, only seemed to leave me wanting more—filled, yet empty.

It was pure exhaustion that finally drew me away from the bush and back to the fire. I crawled on my hands and knees, suddenly overwhelmed with fatigue, as though oppressed by a weighty object. When I finally reached the fire, I dropped down to the ground next to it and was instantly asleep.

The Merrow Pool

I awoke on my belly with my face in the dirt, in the exact same position in which I had fallen asleep. My mouth was dry and my throat parched despite my little banquet of the previous night.

I needed to find water. I hadn't drunk in nearly two days.

I got up, unsteady at first, beset with dizziness. My stomach lurched. I dropped back down to my knees and vomited.

Clutching my stomach, I stood again and wobbled along, listening for water. I ambled for several minutes, paying little heed to my direction, desperate for a drink. The ache in my stomach deepened into a painful cramp. The pain throbbed on and off, and at times was so severe that I doubled over and had to wait for it to pass before I could stand and walk again.

Nona hadn't told me that eating the fruit would cause such an adverse reaction. She said people used to cultivate the fruit for use in potions and such. Perhaps it wasn't meant to be eaten in its pure, most potent form. In any case, I wished I hadn't devoured so much. It had done nothing but make me sick.

Perhaps it had done some good, though. I wouldn't know until I could find water and look at my reflection. I might be changed—I might be prettier! I ran my hands over my face but could not determine any noticeable differences.

The woods in the morning were quiet and tranquil: a light breeze sifted through the boughs high above, and birds sang their morning songs as the soft sunlight dappled the ground; yet pain and chaos reigned inside me. I vomited several more times along the way toward water. It seemed my body was rejecting the magic of the fruit.

Finally, after what seemed an hour or more of wandering, the faint trickle of water met my ears. I ran toward the sound. It led me to a small freshwater stream overshadowed by tall, thick willows and oaks and strewn with large, mossy boulders. I fairly dove in and stuck my head underneath the cool liquid to get a drink. I sat in the water, which rose to my waist, splashing my face and wetting my hair. My stomach soon settled down, but I stayed where I was, letting the water flow past me, over my legs and through my toes. My skirt rippled in the flow, and I scrubbed my arms and legs until all traces of dirt and blood were gone.

As the sun rose, the early morning shadows fled from the water and it became clearer. I caught my reflection in the stream and nearly jumped out of my skin when I saw an unfamiliar face staring back at me.

I swung around at the waist to see who was standing behind me, but there was no one. I looked in the water again. As I bent my head down for a closer look, the reflection staring back at me seemed to move her head closer toward the surface of the water. It was me. And I was different, but only slightly: enough to make a difference, but not enough to lose sight of my familiar self. The eyes were the same, though perhaps a little larger. Or maybe the rest of my face had shrunk. My nose was mildly different—slightly upturned—and my lips were fuller. Or were they? Hadn't my lips always looked like that? Even as I stared at the reflection, it seemed to waver as the features continued to change. One second my eyes looked as they always had, and the next I couldn't recognize them. One moment my chin seemed round, and in the next blink of my eyes, it was narrower.

I watched, mesmerized, confused, until finally my old familiar self was staring back at me. Several moments passed until I realized that the changing of my features had ceased, and that indeed, there was no permanent change. It was to be expected; Nona had said the fruit's effects were temporary, and I had expelled most of what I'd eaten that morning.

I sat back and sighed. A chill crept up my body and goose bumps popped out on my arms. I stood and moved to the shore to dry myself. I sat on the dry ground in an open patch of sunlight, feeling hungrier than ever. My disappointment over the failed magic of the fruit did not strike me as heavily as I expected. In fact, I was surprised to find myself relieved. That first glimpse of my unfamiliar self in the water had been startling enough to make my heart nearly jump from my chest. It was as though I had disappeared and someone new had taken over my body, like a parasite latching onto a host. Perhaps the magic was a parasite.

I was lost.

I spent the remainder of that day foraging for berries, nuts, and roots with lackluster effort. I came across more of the magic fruit and heartily avoided it. Along with the fruit I saw an odd assortment of berries and fruit trees, yet knew none of them, and I dared not take a risk in eating anything unfamiliar. Yet I was wandering ever deeper into the Wild Lands, where little to nothing was recognizable. Truly, if ever this forest was traversed, it no longer was. Traces of old roads and paths were wildly overgrown, and twisted branches and vines hung down messily from the canopy. Very little sunlight broke through.

Why had Nona sent me here, alone and defenseless? It was a forest wasteland. If magic existed in this place, it was long forgotten. Surely stories had developed about this deep, dark wood to keep out intruders. Only a mad person would venture in! And who knew what kind of creatures lived within its depths.

My recurring thought all throughout that day was that I had to get out, or I would die alone in the Wild Lands.

I attempted to follow the line of the sun as it descended, but it was difficult to calculate. I turned in many directions and tried several paths, most of which were unnavigable. At the end of that day, I was no nearer to escaping. The forest had shown no signs of thinning out.

I had traded one prison for another.

Toward dusk, howling in the distance caused me to speed up my pace, although I had little notion of where I was going. Ahead was a small glade with a patch of sky showing through. I raced toward it and came to a circular pond, a spring near the base of a colossal oak, its waters clear and pure and glistening in the evening sunlight. I stepped toward the water, and without thinking, I knelt down and dipped one hand in, bringing it up to my mouth to drink. Before my lips touched the water, though, I caught a rustle of movement to my left and shifted my gaze.

There was the unicorn, standing just at the edge of the clearing.

I suddenly remembered what Nona had said about the merrow pools. I let the water slip through my fingers and backed up with alarm. I had nearly drunk from a mer-pool without permission!

Just as the realization came upon me, there was a movement in the water—a single ripple that traveled from one end of the pool to the other—coming straight for me. I backed up rapidly and stood, moving toward the unicorn. I watched the movement in the water with terror, yet the unicorn's presence calmed me. Somehow I knew she was there again to help and protect me.

The movement in the water came to the pool's edge where I had just been, and a head slowly emerged, the long hair sleek and dripping, plastered to the fair, pale skin of the merrow. She raised herself until her bare shoulders were exposed, then lifted up her arms and crossed them, leaning on the bank of the pond. I was momentarily distracted by her hands, which were webbed between the fingers. I moved my gaze from her hands to her face to find that she was smiling, the large black pupils in her silvery gray eyes gazing intently at me.

"Hello, human."

Her voice was like music, with an airy, tinkling quality. I could not tell if she was speaking or singing to me.

"I have seen little of your kind in many years."

"I have seen none of your kind ever," I replied.

"Well, come closer then and get a better look," she proposed.

"Where did you come from?" I asked, noting that the circular pond was relatively small, certainly not as large as a lake, and couldn't possibly be that deep. As far as I could tell, it wasn't connected to any waterways.

The water-girl turned her body halfway and pointed to the massive oak on the opposite side of the pond. Its tentacle-like roots jutted out the side of the bank and dove into the water.

"There is a cavern underneath the water below that tree. It goes back very far underground and joins other ponds and lakes." She turned and gestured for me to come closer.

I stared at her for a long while without moving. Her gaze became more devilish under my curious stare, as though she enjoyed being looked at. She swayed from side to side, and as she did, something shimmered in her dark hair. On the crown of her head and coming down over her forehead was a woven cap. It was silvery-white, matching the creature's eyes, and thin and delicate like a spider's web.

The girl laughed and splashed water at me. "Come closer. I have nobody to play with!"

"Don't you have others like you down there?"

Her lips pursed into a pout. "We merrow are very lonely creatures, especially here in the Wild Lands. We get so very few visitors."

I tried to recall what Nona had told me about merrow. They loved to give gifts, she had said, and they'll drown anyone who tried to drink from their pools without permission. I dug inside my memory for more information but found very little. Merrow were playful and tricky. Although some could be trusted, as with every race on earth, there were some that couldn't.

Can this water-girl be trusted? I asked myself while watching her. *Will she give me a drink from the pool? First she has to offer me a gift, and I'm to ask for a drink. But will it truly transform me? And what if she doesn't offer a gift? Am I to just ask for it?*

As I considered these things, I found that my curiosity grew. I was parched for water, but there was another, stronger tug at my heart—the one that promised something I had long yearned for. The merrow girl was wispy and graceful and beautiful. In watching her, I wanted to become her. The water from the merrow pond would both satiate my thirst and give me beauty, and in being so close to the object of my desire, I forgot my sense of alarm from that morning when I hadn't recognized my own reflection, and the relief I'd known when I had changed back to my own identifiable features.

Whether of my own volition or because of an unseen power the merrow might have had over me, I took a step forward.

"Yes, please come," the girl sang. "We'll be friends."

The unicorn stamped a hoof heavily on the ground. I turned my head at the sound, distracted from my course. I had nearly forgotten about the magnificent beast standing beside me. She, too, was beautiful and graceful, yet in a different way—in a regal and ancient way, the embodiment of love and wisdom. I took a step back.

"I'll stay where I am, thank you," I told the water-girl.

"But you must be thirsty. Come, take a drink from my pool."

I stayed where I was. The girl watched me, her gaze boring into me as though she could yet convince me with an unnamed power. As I waited, her smile once again turned into a pout.

"I see you do not trust me," she said, casting her eyes downward.

"Your artifice doesn't fool me," I said, becoming bolder, knowing that aside from her powers of persuasion, she had no means to harm me.

She immediately brightened up again. She pushed herself off from the bank and began swimming backward, keeping her head above water to talk with me still.

"Come, I will not hurt you. Do you not want a drink? Do you not know that a drink from the mer-pool will give you beauty?"

"So I've heard, but I thought that I was supposed to ask you for a drink once you offered a gift."

The merrow's eyes narrowed suddenly, and all mirth was gone. "So you are. That's usually the way of it. You know more than you should, human. You almost took a drink from my pool without permission. Since you are so well-informed, do you know what your penalty for that would have been?"

"I do, and I apologize. I forgot myself for a moment. I admit, I was thirsty."

The merrow came forward again. "By all means, if you're thirsty, do drink. I give you permission now."

I hesitated and put my hand on the unicorn's mane, feeling greater protection the nearer I was to the creature. It stepped forward and I walked with it, toward the pond. The merrow's eyes widened and the pupils seemed to shrink until her eyes looked entirely white. She backed away in the water as the unicorn approached. They locked gazes for a long while as though in silent combat until the merrow finally relented. From the opposite side of the pond, she gave me a nod, and I bent down to the water, thinking entirely of my thirst.

I cupped my hands and drank from the pond. My thirst was immediately satiated—and my hunger as well!

"It won't give you beauty," the merrow suddenly said from across the pond. "We only give beauty in exchange for something else. It's a very pricey gift and not freely given."

Once again, a small measure of disappointment cut through me, but not enough to cause true regret. Somehow, knowing the unicorn accepted me was enough—for now.

"I should've known," I said, sitting up but staying at the edge of the pond. "I'm guessing it's pricey enough to demand one's very life."

She giggled. "Not always. Usually you pay service to the merrow, or have the years of your life shortened. Are you willing to pay?"

I stood and moved away, disgusted. "Thanks for the drink."

I followed the unicorn out of the clearing and back into the forest.

We walked along, my hand on her mane, for a long time, even after darkness enveloped the forest. The merrow water had given me renewed energy and alertness. At some point in the night, I looked up and was able to see the bright arc of the moon. My heart leaped at the realization that the forest was thinning out and that the unicorn was leading me out of the Wild Lands.

It wasn't until the sky glowed a pale orange that I was finally overcome with exhaustion. I lay down in a patch of wild, overgrown grass and was almost instantly asleep. The last thing I remember was feeling the warm body of the unicorn as she lay down beside me with a soft neigh and a shake of her mane.

When I awoke, the unicorn was gone. Shivering in the late-morning chill, I felt her absence before I saw she wasn't there. The air, cool and damp, pricked at my skin. Sensing it was going to be a gray day, I opened my eyes to look and saw a man sitting on a rock in a relaxed manner, watching me from a few feet away. I shot up, startled, before I realized it was Danein. Relief washed over me, yet I said nothing as I continued to stare at him in surprise. I had dreamt this once before. I dared not breathe lest I awake and find him gone.

Danein's smile grew as we watched each other.

"I expected some words at the least—perhaps even a hand shake or an embrace," Danein chuckled.

"So you *are* really here?"

"Yes, I'm here. It took everything in me not to wake you the moment I found you sleeping here."

"When did you find me?"

"Only just over an hour ago." He shook his head as though in disbelief. "Thank the High King you're safe."

I shifted onto my knees suddenly and leaned forward. "I asked the High King to help me the day before yesterday, and he sent me a unicorn. Did you see it?"

Danein frowned. "A unicorn? Truly? I never saw it."

"It lay down beside me to sleep this morning. It must have left before you came."

As I spoke, I searched the ground for signs of the unicorn's recent presence. The grass in the spot next to where I'd been lying was upright and fresh-looking. There were no tracks heading away back into the woods either.

My face fell. "I...I don't understand. She was here." I implored Danein with my eyes. "I mean it. She was here. You must believe me."

"I do, I believe you." Danein came to where I was still sitting on the ground and helped me up. "Ancient creatures of magic rarely leave traces. Why do you think they're so hard to find and to see? Why do you think people have forgotten about them and stopped believing?"

"I wish you could have seen her, Danein. She was beautiful. And she knew me! It was as if she'd known me my entire life. She helped me—" I started to mention the mer-pool but stopped myself.

"She helped you what?"

"Well, I was being followed...by the slavers who captured us from the Colony."

I informed Danein of all that had passed since I'd last seen him: how the women were captured, how we traveled the entire day in the back of the barred wagon until we stopped to make camp, how we waited hours to free ourselves with the knife

Taralyn had smuggled, how we managed to escape and nearly get free until being followed, and how Taralyn had sacrificed herself and been captured again so that I could go free.

"And you've been wandering, lost, ever since? Did you try to find your way back to the Colony?"

I hesitated a moment before replying, wondering how much I ought to divulge to Danein, knowing that I hadn't, in fact, tried very hard to find my way back, but instead had spent the last two days in a fruitless quest for beauty. I nearly blushed for the shame I felt.

"No…" I began. What could I say that wouldn't be a lie? "I didn't go back to the Colony. I went north and got lost."

"North?" Danein's face registered confusion before quickly brightening into a mirthful smirk. "And that's how you ended up in the Wild Lands! Not the safest place to be!"

Before I could reply, several drops of rain plopped down onto our heads from the gray sky. Danein took my hand and led me back into the woods a little deeper under the shelter of the trees.

"I was horrified when I arrived at the Colony to find you all gone! I learned that men were coming, so I made haste to get there in order to warn you and help evacuate the camp. When I saw I was too late and that you were all gone, I…" Danein put his head down, caught in a moment of unmasked emotion. "I nearly despaired. I followed your tracks as well as I could, but a rain had washed away most of the traces. I went back to the Colony to see if I might find any clue as to your whereabouts, or in case any survivors straggled back."

"Did any?"

Danein shook his head. "No, none came back, but I did find some tracks and clues suggesting that a few of the women—maybe two or three—had escaped during the raid in another direction besides that which your captors had taken. I followed them and eventually ended up here." He stopped and glanced up at the sky, heavy with rain clouds. "It's so strange: at some point

I just found myself wandering, having lost all traces of who I was following, and yet I made it here. In our wandering, without even trying, we found each other."

I smiled at the sentiment, but knew my own story hadn't been as simple or innocent as that.

The rain came down hard, and we ended up retreating farther into the woods. We kept on the outskirts of the Wild Lands as much as we could manage. Yet it wouldn't have made a difference to me how far we traversed into those woods; I was with Danein, and I knew my unicorn was out there somewhere watching me.

The clouds were above us, but I was floating on one.

A Toad

We walked that entire morning and into the afternoon with not so much as a rest. I did not tire once. My stomach did not demand food, nor was my throat parched for water. It was as if the benefits of drinking the merrow water still lingered. Perhaps that was the true magic of the water: not in its power to bestow beauty, but in its power to satisfy hunger and thirst and to restore energy. As the day progressed, the clouds drifted away, the rain stopped, and a pristine blue sky showed underneath. In that moment, the weather seemed a beacon of hope and good tidings to come.

I let Danein do most of the speaking. He had much to share, yet not about any of the goings-on in the outside world. He spoke mainly of himself, his family, and his history. Some I had heard before, but some was new. I let him speak. Despite myself, my heart overflowed just to be near him. In the joy of our reunion, I believe we both momentarily forgot the plight of the outside world: the injustices of the law in Zaphon, and the kidnap of Taralyn and our other friends, the unchosen women.

When pressed, I hesitantly spoke of myself. I told Danein I had grown up the middle child of four sisters and one brother. I had had a carefree and happy childhood. My parents had been loving and had never lost nor forgotten me in the muddle of so many children. I admitted I had been a favorite of my papa's—probably for being the only daughter with light skin and fair hair.

"And did you see your siblings much after they were married?"

"I saw my sisters and their husbands quite a bit as they lived nearby. I never saw my brother and his wife until my papa died and he took me in. After that, I never saw my sisters."

"And your mother?"

I took a deep breath. "I did not see my mother after that either. She bore the shame of having an unchosen daughter, and I can't blame her for that. It is the way of things in Zaphon."

"True, but you weren't unchosen then. You were still years away from your twenty-eighth year, and your brother claimed you."

"Yes, I was twenty-three then, but despite that, I believe my entire family considered me unchosen. For most women, twenty-three is already quite late. I don't believe any of them truly had any hope for me—none but my papa, that is. My only ally died when he did."

Danein was quiet for a long moment after that. I was grateful for the lapse in conversation and hoped the attention would soon be turned from me. The more we talked of my past, the heavier my heart became. I didn't see what good could come of resurrecting memories of things that had already happened and couldn't be changed. I was just about to broach a new subject when Danein went on.

"Why is it, Alonya, that you believe you are unchosen?"

I stiffened as we continued our walk through the wood. "Well, I am unchosen because no man has chosen to marry me."

"Yes, but *why* do you believe no man has chosen you?"

Although it was midday with the sun warming our heads, the air around me seemed to grow chill all of a sudden. I shook my head, at a loss as to what I could possibly say without revealing the deepest part of my heart to Danein. A piece of me wished to speak, to let him see my heart in all its weakness and vulnerability, but I felt he would despise me if he knew.

I stammered out a few unintelligible words; Danein laughed gently.

"Alonya, I don't wish to upset you. I want you to know that you can be honest with me and speak the truth."

"You won't like the truth."

"Perhaps not, but what you consider the truth might not really be the truth, but only your perception of it. But if it's too difficult for you, I won't press you any further."

"I'm sure you have your own ideas about it," I finally said.

"I do, but I'd rather hear it from you."

I sighed, defeated. "I'm unchosen because I'm not beautiful." There…I'd said it. But I wasn't prepared for the hand of emotion that seized me. I furiously held back the tears that surfaced.

Danein nodded. "It's as I supposed. Do you remember how we first met?"

I thought for a moment. "You came into Ghilla with your cart and your wares."

"And you came over inquiring about a beauty potion."

I could feel my face begin to burn. "You must have thought me silly."

"No," Danein said soberly. "You reminded me of my sister even then. Like you, she struggled with the question of beauty. Most of the women of the Colony did as well. I have come to learn a lot about women, as you can imagine, and I see the role that beauty—or the lack of it—plays in their lives."

"And what do you think of it?"

Danein's brows came together in thought. "At times I think I understand, and at other times I grow confused and frustrated. Why do women seem to think that beauty is an objective thing, that it has rules and definitions and boundaries into which only a few fit? Don't you see that beauty is wide and unlimited, that it changes from eye to eye? What one person sees as ugly, another may see as beautiful."

Danein skipped ahead of me a pace, suddenly animated, and turned to me while still walking. "Alonya, is a snake beautiful?"

"What?"

"Do you think a snake is beautiful?"

"Well, no, not particularly."

"I do! The various colors and patterns of the skin, the design and function of the body—it's fascinating and beautiful."

I crinkled my nose but could not help smiling.

"Is this forest beautiful?" Danein said.

"Yes."

"Why?"

"Well… it's bright with color and life."

"And what of a desert?"

I nearly laughed. "What of a desert?"

"Is a desert beautiful?"

I hesitated. "I suppose…"

"A desert is not so bright with color and life, but does that make it any less beautiful to some eyes?"

"No."

"Exactly!"

I rolled my eyes good-naturedly. "I know all of this…I do. It's only—"

Danein stopped suddenly. "Do you think me handsome?"

I came up short, nearly bumping into him. "What?"

"It's a simple question: do you think me handsome?"

Once again, I fumbled for words.

"Come now, be honest. Tell me what *you* think. You won't upset me. I've made up my mind how I feel about myself, and nothing you can say will change that."

Knowing he was half in jest loosened my tongue. "Well…yes, I…I think you're handsome."

"You do?" He frowned. "Not many women have."

"Why do you say that?"

"Like you, Alonya, I am unmarried and have had little fortune in love. I do believe I have hinted at a previous situation with a woman I once courted?"

"I believe so. What happened?"

Danein's face grew sober once again. "She chose another because I would not forget my sister, and I would not stop helping other unchosens. I have lived a very lonely life since then, albeit one of my choosing, and I would not trade it."

"Would you like to be married one day?"

He held my gaze. "I would, but it seems unlikely I could find a wife who would join me in my venture and not be jealous of my dealings with unchosen women."

"I can see how that would be frustrating," I admitted.

"So, as you can see, women have shown me very little interest or care. Should I then assume it is because I'm unhandsome?"

"Well, of course not."

"Then why do you assume that of yourself?"

"I…" My eyes fell to the ground. "I never had a suitor. Not one."

"Did you never have young men in your growing up years that showed you any attention?"

"Well, yes, I suppose I did. They were friends or acquaintances, but never anything more."

"And you think it's because they found you unattractive?"

I was growing frustrated. "Well, what else could it have been?"

"Many things. Having no suitors is not a measurement of your physical beauty."

"I don't know how else to interpret it."

"No, most women don't, and that's where the pity lies."

We continued on in silence. The sunny, carefree mood of earlier was gone. I was brought back to myself and my recent errand before Danein came along. He had spoken of beauty as being subjective to the beholder, but he had never said he thought

I was beautiful. To me that seemed to disqualify all his earlier words. And suddenly, instead of being comfortable and confident in Danein's presence, I grew more ill at ease.

Danein seemed to sense my change of mood. He tried to revert to earlier conversation, but I answered half-heartedly in monosyllables, and soon we both grew taciturn, lost in our own thoughts. The day waned into night, and we made camp. Danein built a fire while I searched out some food. As we sat around the fire sharing our meager repast, Danein looked at me with an apologetic glint in his eyes.

"I'm very sorry for upsetting you earlier."

I shook my head. "You were right about everything you said. I wish I could truly allow myself to believe it and find comfort in it."

"I wish you—and many of the other women from the Colony—could see yourselves through another's eyes. Maybe then you'd be more forgiving. You might see something there you've never seen before."

"I'm sorry, but can we not speak of this any longer?" I asked. Danein seemed hurt by my abruptness, but nodded nonetheless.

"Of course."

"I'm going to bed. I'm tired."

"Well, have a nice sleep. I'll see you in the morning."

I held back tears as I lay near the fire with my back to Danein. I lay awake a long time, trying to fall asleep yet unable to for the rush of thoughts and emotions coursing through me. I listened to the creaking of the boughs above and the clicks and chirpings of insects nearby. I heard the steady, even rhythm of Danein's breathing. It was a long time before he finally lay down to sleep. Like me, he seemed restless and deep in thought, though for what reason I couldn't imagine at the time.

I awoke the next morning to the smoky fragrance of roasted meat. Danein was sitting on a rock nearby, bent forward, his elbows resting on his knees. His eyes and forehead were knit into a look of concentration. He didn't notice me until I sat up, and the movement distracted him from whatever serious thoughts pervaded his mind. He sat up straight and his features softened instantly.

"Good morning." He sighed heavily. "Did you sleep well?"

"Not really," I admitted. "I had strange dreams."

"Yes, you were tossing and turning a lot last night."

"And you? How did you sleep?"

"Like you, not well. Many restless thoughts kept me awake most of the night."

I nodded but didn't respond. I was curious to ask Danein about his restless thoughts, but fearful that they might regard me and possibly be unpleasant, I refrained from asking him.

A small skinned rabbit was hanging over the fire on a makeshift spit. I stood, stretched, and inched closer to the fire to gain some warmth from the early morning chill.

"I took the liberty of catching us our breakfast this morning," Danein said, standing to inspect the cooking meat.

"It will be nice to have meat again," I confessed with a little chuckle. "I have been living off of berries and roots and nuts and other things I can't quite identify."

"I am amazed at you, Alonya, having been out here in the Wild Lands all alone."

"Yes, well, I've been out on the road alone before."

"I know," said Danein. "It's a very dangerous place to be."

"So you keep telling me. I haven't had much of a choice, though." Even as I said it, I knew it wasn't true. I had had a choice. I had chosen to pass through the Wild Lands. It seemed unlikely I could tell Danein that.

He took the rabbit from the spit and set it on a large rock, cutting it apart with his knife. Along with the rabbit, he had also found some berries. He handed me some food, and we ate our breakfast in silence while the sunlight slowly filtered into the wood.

We were on our way again before long. We spoke little, mainly just observations about our surroundings. I knew Danein was lost in his own thoughts, as I was in mine. We hadn't spoken of where we were going, but we were walking east, back in the general direction I'd come, opposite the Colony. I wondered if Danein hoped to look for the other women. Perhaps he thought that had been my aim all along as well. And suddenly I felt like a fraud. Danein didn't really know me, and if he did, he wouldn't like me.

My thoughts disturbed me most of that morning as we walked back through the wood. I struggled within myself as to what course to take next. Once again, I'd been thwarted on my quest. I didn't want to leave Danein, nor have him leave me, but somehow I felt I was deceiving him just by being with him. There was also the matter of my security. I was still a homeless, unchosen woman with no rights and no protection from the law. I had to figure out what to do.

"Alonya," Danein said, breaking a long silence heavy with tension. "Are you angry with me?"

"No, of course not."

"You have been so quiet and thoughtful since last night, and I'm sure I upset you with my questions yesterday, although that was not my intention at all."

"I know. I can be sensitive about my past. I apologize."

"There's no need to apologize. It's only—I feel there are things you wish to share, yet you still seem distrustful of me, though it's now been nearly a year since we first met."

"I trust you, Danein."

He reached out and lightly grabbed my arm, pulling me to a stop. "Then please talk to me. What is it that ails you? There has been a shadow hanging over you since yesterday evening."

I wanted to tell him—I longed to tell him everything. But even as I tried to get the words out, I swallowed them back.

"I…I just don't know what to do or where to go from here," I said, which was partly the truth. "There is no more Colony, and

I have no family that will claim me. Taralyn told me to seek the High King, but I don't know where he's to be found, or *if* he can even be found. I feel very confused and alone."

Danein's face lit with relief as if that was a problem easily solved. "But you're with me! You're not alone. And we'll find the other women and help them. We'll find a new place for you women to live."

"You said so yourself," I suddenly spat out. "Living in the woods in harsh conditions is no place for women! How long can we keep that up before more slavers appear? It's not a life, Danein. It's survival. I don't want to just survive! I want to live!"

"Then we will find a way to appeal to the king of Zaphon and have the law changed."

I shook my head and turned away to continue walking. "You tried that yourself once. It didn't work."

"That was a long while ago. Things may have changed."

"Danein, please," I implored. "Can we refrain from this conversation?"

"We can, but then nothing will ever be solved. You can't continue to just hold everything inside and ignore it. Your passivity will accomplish nothing!"

I spun on him. "Passivity? If I was operating on passivity, I would have given up long ago! I would have let the slavers take me and do with me whatever evil purposes they had in mind! I wouldn't care about my life or preserving it!"

Danein was taken aback by my abruptness. "I'm sorry. You're right. I was…I was thinking of my sister. She gave up, you know."

"Yes, I know, and I'm sorry."

Danein heaved a great sigh. "Why don't we take a break? This looks like a nice place to build a fire and have our midday meal." He whipped out a knife from the pack across his shoulders. "I'll go look for something and be back." He disappeared into the woods, and I was left alone.

I was frustrated with myself. Danein had gotten a glimpse of my fiery side. Already I feared I'd started to push him away. *Well,* I told myself, *maybe it's for the best. I can't stay with him forever. Eventually we'll have to go our separate ways.*

I walked lazily around the wood, collecting stray twigs and fallen branches, gathering them into a pile for firewood. My heart was not in the task, however. I dropped the bundle in my arms and plopped myself down onto a fallen tree trunk nearby.

The wood was quiet and tranquil, like a place out of time. Although being part of the Colony was not an ideal way of life, I had enjoyed living in the woods. I considered staying with Danein if he would still have me, if he could tolerate me after my childish outburst.

A movement to my immediate left distracted me, and I turned my head to see a large brown toad sitting on the log next to me. I jumped up in alarm and moved away from the log, turning to stare at the creature. The thought of its slimy, lumpy skin touching me made my body shiver. It hopped along the fallen trunk until it was sitting in the place where I'd just been. I waved my arms at it to shoo it away.

"Oh, you are an ugly thing," I whispered. As suddenly as I said it, a stab of guilt hit me. Who was I to call a fellow creature ugly or treat it as unwanted? I was just like that toad. It may be unsightly, but it was a creature of the Wild Lands just as the unicorn and the merrow were. It couldn't help how it looked.

I gingerly stepped toward the toad to get a closer look. Certainly it appeared harmless. The longer I gazed at it, the more pity I felt. I absently wondered what it would feel like to touch a toad, whether the skin was slimy, rough, or smooth. I found courage enough to reach out and stroke a finger across the toad's back. It seemed to stiffen at first, but soon relaxed and let me touch it. Its skin was surprisingly soft and not wet as I had supposed.

"You're not so bad after all," I said. I then took both my hands and scooped the toad up into my outturned palms. "You just need a friend."

I continued to stroke its back with my finger. As I did, a sense of calm and peace overtook me. I found comfort in the little creature as I imagined it found comfort in me. I was seized with a sudden impulse to kiss the toad without knowing fully why. I bent my head down and lightly kissed the creature on its back.

"There now," I soothed, "you're not alone."

"I'm afraid, Miss Alonya, that kissing the frog won't turn it into a prince."

I turned at the voice. Danein was smirking, standing near the small pile of brush I had collected for the fire. He had a dead fox in his hand and dropped it near the sticks.

I set the toad down. "I was merely trying to treat it as I'd like to be treated. I found a kindred spirit in it."

"How do you mean?"

"Well, just look at it. It's ugly, lonely, and rejected."

"Alonya, please, there is no need to speak of yourself so."

Before I could respond, the toad croaked loudly. I turned to it. It seemed somehow changed. It continued croaking in a peculiar assortment of sounds. I glanced at Danein, who had stepped closer, a mystified expression on his face.

"That seems an odd sound for a toad."

The strange discordant croaking continued, eventually smoothing out until it resembled an ordinary human voice.

"Because you have shown me kindness," the toad said, "I will grant you one wish only. Choose well."

I swiveled around toward Danein. His eyes were wide with disbelief. "It's an enchanted animal!" I cried.

"So it seems."

"I found one—or it found me!"

"You found one? Were you looking?"

"Well, no," I stammered. "That is, Nona had told me they could be found in the Wild Lands, but I didn't imagine I'd actually encounter one!"

Danein grabbed my arm and squeezed it lightly. The toad had reverted to its usual discordant croaking. "Wait—so you *did* come to the Wild Lands intentionally? You didn't just wander in by accident?"

I turned my eyes down. "Well...yes, I knew where I was going. Nona sent me here."

"Nona? That medicine woman you stayed with outside of Terrington? Why would she send you here?"

I knew I had given away too much already. I couldn't retreat now. "You must know that she helped me—she saved me. She took me in and looked after me and got me back on my feet." I took a deep breath. "She told me my only chance of a true life, as an unchosen, was to become beautiful. Only then would I have any kind of power against men, and I might manage to find a decent situation for myself."

Danein's eyes narrowed. "What do you mean by a 'decent situation'?"

I looked him in the eye and spoke slowly to still my wavering voice. "She said I might still procure for myself a wealthy man to look after me in comfort and ease."

Danein's jaw was clenched, his face livid. "You were going to become a man's mistress?"

"It's better than being taken and forced into such slavery!"

"It's just the same, Alonya! Do you really think that's going to make you happy?"

"I don't have the luxury of choosing happiness! I'm an unchosen. The entire world is against me!"

Danein's eyes softened a little, but his jaw was still clenched and his nostrils flared. I made one last attempt at explanation in hopes he might come to understand my place.

"Nona was kind to me. She was the only person I could trust. She encouraged me to come up here into the Wild Lands and seek three different sources of beauty. I didn't know what else to do."

Danein moved away from me suddenly and began pacing, his head shaking in disbelief. "You were in the Wild Lands seeking magical sources of beauty? That's why you traveled north when you escaped the slavers instead of coming back to the Colony?" He stopped pacing and looked at me, his eyes fierce.

"Don't judge me so!" I said, covering my face in my hands. "You know nothing of it!"

"Why didn't you come back to the Colony? Didn't you trust me? Didn't you know I would have been looking for you? I would have taken care of you."

"Stop!" I cried, shaking my head furiously back and forth. I took my hands from my face and glared at Danein. "You are not my husband, and you are not my brother! Why should I expect you to take care of me indefinitely—or any of the other women for that matter?" I took a deep breath and tried to calm my shaky nerves. "I was trying to make my own way with the few options available to me as an unchosen woman. And I was on my quest before I even found the Colony. If you must know, that was by accident. I followed you because I suspected you, because Nona told me I couldn't trust any men. I didn't even intend to go to the Colony. I wanted to find out what you really were."

Danein was still for a moment, pain in his eyes.

As if taking advantage of the silent moment, the toad, momentarily forgotten, burst out in another series of loud, cackling croaks, then suddenly choked out, "I will grant you one wish. Make your decision now."

Danein and I glanced at each other. He held my gaze long, his eyes beseeching. He shook his head slightly and took a step toward me. I sighed in defeat and turned back toward the toad.

"I wish for beau—"

"No!" Danein called, lunging forward. He grabbed me forcefully and turned me toward him. "Do not wish for beauty. It is a treacherous gift. There is always a price to pay."

"But it's a free wish."

"No, wishes are never free. They come with a sacrifice. There is always something to give, something that's taken away. You won't be yourself anymore if you wish for beauty."

I frowned at him. In my mind, he was saying that only plainness befitted me.

He seemed to know my thoughts because he suddenly winced in embarrassment, let me go, and held his hands out. "No, that's not what I meant. What I meant was, you don't need it. It may completely change your appearance. You won't be like yourself anymore. Part of who you are is in your appearance, whether plain or not. But you're not plain, Alonya. At least…that is…you may be plain to some people, but not to… not to…"

I held my breath, waiting for I knew not what.

The toad croaked loudly again and repeated its offer. I glanced back to it, the desire to accept growing stronger in me every moment, despite the sacrifice or the compromise involved.

"Besides, who knows what this toad's idea of beauty is!" Danein went on.

"Not to whom?" I asked with tears in my eyes. "You never finished what you were trying to say. I may be plain to some, but not to…?"

He stood there, eyes wide, face reddening. A heavy sigh escaped him, and he finally spoke. "You're not plain to me, Alonya. Not in any way."

I smiled bitterly and shook my head. "I want to believe you, but I wonder if you're just saying that to keep me from making the wish, not because you really believe it." I turned back to the toad.

"But I do believe it!" He came forward again and held my arm. He looked wounded. "Alonya, why would I lie to you? Have I ever lied? Have I ever been anything but truthful and kind to you?"

I wrenched my arm away, tears streaming down my face. "I don't want your pity! Leave me be! You only feel sorry for me! You only want to help me because you're trying to redeem yourself after failing your sister!"

His mouth dropped open. "How could you think…that's partly true, but it's not…it's not why I—"

"It's not your fault that she died, Danein. It's just something that happened. At least you tried to keep her at the beginning. My brother didn't even try to keep me or help me or look for me. He did nothing. He never fought for me. Nobody has ever fought for me."

"I'm fighting for you now, Alonya. Can't you see that?"

"Out of pity! I don't want your pity."

He stood up straight, suddenly full of resolve. "Not out of pity—out of love."

He did something then that I hadn't expected, nor ever could have expected, and still can hardly believe. He took my head in both his hands, looked directly into my eyes, and said, "I don't pity you, Alonya—I love you."

And then he kissed me.

That convinced me, if nothing else had.

PART THREE

A New Course

The Great Sea

Knowing Danein loved me made all the difference. It buoyed me. I was stronger because of his love. His faith gave me confidence. And suddenly I had new vision; knowing Danein believed in me helped me to see myself in a more forgiving light. If a man could still love one such as me, surely I wasn't beyond redemption or hope. Perhaps life still held good things for me.

No longer alone and helpless, I felt I could do anything: jump off a bluff and soar over the ocean to find the High King if need be. He was our only hope now as Danein and I faced an immense task: finding our friends and rescuing them, as well as all the women throughout Zaphon who were being mistreated at the hands of the law. In the meantime, I was still in danger. Only until we could find the High King and seek sanctuary with him would I, or any other unchosens, be safe. Knowing of no other place to look besides the first and most ancient of all the Lands of the Seven Kingdoms, we decided to travel to Coralind. We felt that would be our best course to find him since from times of old he was said to dwell there, though nobody knew for certain where he could be found either inside or outside of Coralind.

So we traveled north, around the eastern border of the Wild Lands and toward the coast. A few villages and lone farms dotted the countryside, and we were able to stop each night at inns to sleep in warm beds and fill our bellies with warm food. Danein kept a close eye on me any time we were around people, insisting that we pose as brother and sister and always rent adjoining rooms to avoid suspicion. I reveled in his watchfulness over me. After being on my own and trying to take care of myself for so long, it was refreshing to have someone like Danein care for me. I could have burst with joy. At times when we were sitting together at a table at the inn, or taking a stroll down a village road, I could do nothing but smile. Danein spoke, and I just smiled. Sometimes I didn't hear what he said; I only noted his presence beside me and would think of his hands on my arms or his lips brushing mine, and I would smile. Then Danein would stare at me quizzically, let out a little laugh, and say, "If you don't stop smiling so much, people will certainly guess that you're not my sister."

That would cause me to laugh and smile even more.

Then his eyes would sparkle with mirth, and he would lean in closer to me and say, "I hardly know you, Alonya. I've never seen you smile so, but it's beautiful. You're beautiful."

I would blush and be even more lost for words.

"I mean it, you know. And I'm sorry it took me so long to tell you. I was trying to work out the proper moment to do so, and… well…I was afraid."

"You, afraid?"

He chuckled. "It's true! I, too, wondered if I had only misread your attentions all that time. I also wanted to secure your trust in me as a friend before making such declarations. At least, that's what I told myself, but it was mainly my own fear and insecurity that held me back. I hope you will forgive me."

"As you told me once, it's all in the past, and you're forgiven," I said.

Danein hadn't kissed me since that first time. I knew it was because we were out of the Wild Lands and back into civilized country. Although we often held hands as we walked along the country roads, once we entered a village, Danein was careful to behave as nothing more than a brother to me. For my part, it was enough to know he loved me.

Our trip was just short of a week. We made it to the port town of Fynn Harbor on the northern border of Zaphon where the land met the Great Sea. We were to take a boat across the channel toward the country of Kerith. From there Coralind was far to the west. It would be a long and arduous journey, and Danein would certainly run out of money before we made it even halfway. I addressed this concern to him the afternoon we arrived in Fynn Harbor as we scouted the wharf for a vessel to take us across the channel.

"Let me worry about that," Danein assured me. "I have many more skills besides peddling, which is a very valuable skill in and of itself. But I *did* work as a clerk before taking to peddling."

"Yes, but…how will that help us on the road?"

Danein's eyebrows rose as he thought about this. "Well, I'm not so sure, unless someone needs help in their counting house." He laughed. "I suppose it is a very impractical trade for a traveler. Well, harvest time is coming on, and I can always hire myself out as a laborer in the fields." He winked at me. "But don't underestimate the import of someone who can read, write, and count. Those skills are always in demand."

It was difficult to find inexpensive passage. Most of the vessels were small and nondescript—fishing boats that didn't travel far. The merchant vessels didn't ordinarily take passengers unless they could pay extremely high fees. It was a long while before we could secure one, and even then, Danein had to find temporary work to pay the passage for both of us. He did some hauling and loading of goods for about a week, and then, sure enough, his skills as a clerk came into good use. He was hired to help keep records for a warehouse of goods belonging to a wealthy merchant and trader.

In the meantime, we took up residence at the Restful Sea Inn, a clean, modest establishment near the docks. From my room on the top floor, I could see the boats anchored to the piers, watch the men march to and fro busily, and view the water reaching out toward the horizon smooth and flat, broken only by the occasional ship coming or going. Far to the left of the docking area was a pillar of rock, atop which sat a huge torch that when lighted provided a beacon at night for the seafarers.

We were both restless to leave, but Danein more so than me. While he was away at work each day, I was forbidden to leave the inn. Only when Danein returned would he allow me to step outside for a walk or a short trip into the main district, accompanied by him. Each day he returned from work fatigued and disheveled, yet managed to rouse up the extra energy to escort me around town. I was grateful to him for his sacrifice, but it caused me guilt. Danein shushed me anytime I tried to apologize.

"Can I not find work, too, and help contribute to our passage?"

"Absolutely not. I'm not taking any chances that you might be discovered."

His devotion brought me to tears many times. During the first two days we were in Fynn Harbor, I walked around the inn, up and down the stairs, listless and bored. After I explained to Danein that I needed something to do to pass the day, he procured me a sewing kit, some fabric, and two books. During the following days, I spent long afternoons sitting near the hearth in the main parlor of the inn mending our clothes and traveling cloaks. Yet neither of us had much, and sewing was a quick job for me. I finished the two books quickly as well. I wished for more employment to keep me occupied—some gardening to do, or cleaning. Danein suggested that I make us some new garments and offered to buy more fabric as well as more books for me to read. I shook my head. Spending his earned money on more fabric and books would only lengthen our time in Fynn Harbor and delay our passage.

The inn was managed by a skinny, middle-aged man with thinning hair and a matronly woman whom I later came to realize was his mother. Despite the hard, weathered lines on his face, the innkeeper was quiet and seemed kind. I never spoke to him, though. I'd seen Danein making small talk with him but nothing more. He was frequently absent, hiding out in the back rooms of the inn or running errands. The matron, on the other hand, was a large, bustling woman who had more direct charge of the guests and the servants. I often noticed her eyeing me curiously, but she would say nothing, always too busy with other tasks. I had often considered approaching her to offer my services, but then I would remember what had happened at Terrington with the innkeeper, and I kept my thoughts to myself.

One cloudy afternoon as I stood downstairs near the hearth watching out a window, the matron approached me.

"Miss, you appear out of sorts today. Indeed, forgive me for saying so, but you often seem sad and lonely during the afternoons."

I was slightly shocked at her directness but was nonetheless grateful for the kindness in her voice. "I have very little to do while my brother is away," I said.

"Why don't you take a walk and get some fresh air before it rains?"

I smiled but shook my head. "I can't. My brother is very protective of me and doesn't like me to go out unescorted."

She nodded in understanding. "I suppose that is wise, as it seems you are strangers in this town."

"Yes, we are waiting to book passage to Kerith."

The woman seemed to note my reticence and didn't press any further. She put her hands in her apron pockets, looked around the room, and said, "Well, it's an empty house today, and the servants have everything all under way. Why don't you and I take a little walk outside? I can be your companion while your brother is away."

I hesitated, though I was drawn to accept the offer. The woman's eyes looked kind and eager. Yet besides Danein, I knew

I could trust no one, and I didn't like to think he might be upset with me.

"I'd like to, but I'd better not."

"We can make a meal to take to your brother while he's at work. Would that be all right?"

She was gentle, so unlike Nona, and so eager to help me, that I couldn't say no after that. She ran to the kitchen and put together a picnic of bread, boiled eggs, cheese, and fruit, tossed it all into a basket, and fetched her cloak. She seemed excited, and I was pleased to have a new friend. The wharf was a short walk, and we were there within minutes. The woman spoke nonstop the entire time, expounding on the inn business and talking about her son, the innkeeper. She asked me nothing about myself, and I was glad of that.

We only had to walk up and down along the quayside a few times before we found Danein. He carried a barrel over his shoulder and was calling out orders to other men marching like ants back and forth along the docks. Seagulls circled and squawked above in the graying sky, and mist hung above the water

Danein's brows knit into a concerned frown when he first saw me, but then he noticed the woman beside me, and his face registered surprise.

"What are you doing here?" he asked, setting down his barrel and approaching us.

"Please don't be angry with your sister," the woman said. "It was my idea to bring you a meal. The poor thing looked like she needed some fresh air."

Danein nodded as he wiped his hands on his trousers and looked back and forth at us. "Well, I thank you for accompanying her," he replied. "As she's probably explained to you, I have asked her not to go out during the day without me."

"She did, and I understand. Yet if you don't mind, I would like to employ her at the inn."

I turned to her in surprise. She continued on without noting my expression.

"The most she would have to do is walk a block or two for shopping and errands. But I would keep her mostly indoors."

Danein watched the woman steadily. "And what would you have her do?"

"I can see from the past few days that your sister has some skills in mending and sewing. I advertise that as a service to my guests, but my hired help works poorly with the needle. I would like your sister to be a seamstress and laundress." She turned and looked at me then. "It is very difficult work and would keep you busy most of the day. Really, you probably wouldn't get out much at all. So if that's something you might like to try, I could pay you room and board." She nodded at Danein. "For both you and your brother."

I glanced at Danein, and we shared a long, quiet stare, me nearly dancing on my tiptoes as he considered the offer. We would be able to save money more quickly with our room and board taken care of. And I would have employment during the day to occupy me and help contribute to earning our passage.

Danein could see the plea in my eyes, and he finally relented, nodding his head in answer. I flung my arms around his neck without thinking then quickly drew back, turning my face to the ground lest the woman catch on to our secret. She was oblivious, however. I assumed it was because sisters embraced their brothers all the time, although I couldn't be certain. I had never been close to my own brother.

The woman took Danein's hand tenderly. "Thank you, sir. Your sister will be a great help to me, and I'd like to be of help to you as well."

"Well, we both appreciate it. I *am* sorry Alonya has had to sit alone these past several days. I'm glad to know she has company now."

The woman turned to me. "So that's your name—Alonya. Such a pretty name for such a pretty young woman."

I smiled and blushed, still unaccustomed to such compliments.

She then turned back to Danein. "And who might you be?"

"I'm Danein."

"It's nice to officially meet you both. My name is Janna, and I think it's about time we found a spot to share this meal before it rains."

With Danein's promotion at the wharf and my earning us room and board, we were able to save money quickly. Within a month we had more than enough for our passage. Danein suggested we stay in Fynn Harbor for another month to double our earnings. That way, once we made it to Kerith, we wouldn't have to worry about money for some time. I enjoyed working at the inn with Janna and agreed to the plan. Although it was an unconventional situation—living and working at an inn and being cared for by a man not my husband, but my friend—it was the first time in a long while that I felt safe and at home.

In my preoccupation at work, and in my happiness at being near Danein, I forgot the outside world at times. My heart often told me we should stay in Fynn Harbor and make our lives and our home there. I forgot I was an unchosen by law. I forgot that Danein was not legally bound to me and could not offer me true or lasting protection. Those truths were my ties to reality and to the pressing matter of our kidnapped friends. Despite my heart often urging me away from the facts, a stronger tug began to emerge beside it—a tug that kept me fixed on our mission and drew me onward with it. It was so urgent at times, and the temptation to abandon it so strong, that it was I who finally suggested to Danein that we be on our way soon. He was reluctant at first, and I could tell he wanted to stay a while longer. I thought I had been the only one, but perhaps we both had gotten too comfortable in our stay. Our vision had become too narrow to see anything beyond our current circumstances.

EMMALINE

Fynn Harbor was pleasant in the autumn. Cool breezes wafted inland from the sea, blowing their fresh breath across the town. A light woven or knitted shawl was enough to keep me cozy on our shopping jaunts. The air always smelled like salt and fish, and I enjoyed the clacking of our shoes on the cobblestone streets.

Laden with baskets one afternoon, Janna and I left the Restful Sea Inn and weaved our way through the familiar streets and alleys toward the market district. Janna always kept a close eye on me. As was our agreement, I was not to leave her side. This day we were in a hurry, with fewer than two hours to run our errands. Janna quickly busied herself at a fruit and vegetable stall while I stood nearby, absentmindedly gazing down the street.

"Alonya, dear, hold out the basket, please."

I apologized and came forward so that she could drop some onions and peppers into the basket. I continued to watch the street. It was a wide thoroughfare lined with shops and portable booths, busy with a mass of shoppers. Horses clip-clopped up and down the street, trailing carts and wagons behind them.

I often took to watching people, curious about their lives and stories, wondering if there were any like me out there. If there were, how would one really know? Several women shopped alone. They could be servants—or wives or daughters sent on errands.

The sun was bright in the sky. I put my hand up to shield my eyes and that's when I saw her: a slight woman with long dark hair swept back into a thick plait. Even with her wide straw bonnet atop her head, I could see that it was Emmaline, my brother's wife. She was several feet away on the opposite side of the street, browsing the booths. I took a few steps sideways to get a better look. A cloud moved in front of the sun, muting its brightness, and I was better able to see. There was no sign of Benson anywhere.

For reasons I knew not, I was suddenly alight with curiosity and eager to speak with my sister-in-law. I glanced at Janna, who was still focused intently on her produce.

"Janna, I think I ought to run down to the baker's to speed up our errand."

"Hmm?" She looked up, studied me, then turned to glance down the street at the baker's shop on the corner.

"You know Danein would not be pleased if I let you wander down the street alone."

I heaved a frustrated sigh. "I feel so like a child! I am approaching my thirtieth year! Please, Janna, let me go. It's just down the street."

She narrowed her eyes at me, but her lips were smiling.

"Do *you* fear for me," I asked, "or are you merely following Danein's orders?"

"All right, go on," she said, waving her hand at me. "There are enough people in the market that I doubt you will be taken from under my nose. Be quick, though!"

She had barely spoken the words when I was off, hurrying down the street, searching for Emmaline with my eyes.

"Get five loaves and one large sack of flour!" Janna called after me.

I dodged shoppers, horses, and wooden carts. Emmaline came in and out of view. She had turned and was walking away in the opposite direction. At one point she stopped and looked over her shoulder directly at me. I waved and called out to her, but she turned and fled down the street to the baker's shop and around the corner.

I followed her. At the corner I stopped and peered along the side street down which she'd disappeared. I saw no trace of her.

"Emmaline!" I called. There was no answer.

I glanced back to where Janna was. She had moved on from the produce stall but hadn't noticed me. I started to follow Emmaline but hadn't taken five steps when I stopped just as suddenly. It was a narrow street, more like an alley, paved only with dirt, and nearly abandoned. I bit my lip. My conscience tugged me back. I had already deceived Janna and defied Danein by coming this far unescorted. I couldn't go any farther. As much as I longed to discover why Emmaline was in town and why she'd run from me, I knew I had come to a wall in the maze and was forced to turn around.

I made my way into the baker's shop, basket dangling from my arm, and searched for a large burlap sack of flour.

I told Danein about Emmaline that evening as we sat alone in the parlor next to the blazing fire in the hearth.

"I wonder what she's doing in town. I suppose she's with Benson. He could very well be here for business. They did travel often when I lived with them."

"I wish you would be more careful, Alonya. Did you consider that perhaps she was purposely leading you away from the market to get you to a place where you'd be alone and defenseless?"

"Why would she do that?"

"Well, why would she run then? It's more likely that you should run from her." Danein's eyes widened and he grew suddenly restless. "You said Emmaline always had ill feelings toward you. Now that she knows you're here, what if she gives you up as an unchosen?"

I considered the possibility, but it seemed far-fetched. I shook my head. "She may have never liked me, but she's still family. She's married to my brother. I can't imagine that she'd betray family."

Danein's brows rose. "Alonya, you know an unchosen woman is considered to have no family. I doubt Emmaline has any sisterly affection for you."

I shrugged, unsure what to make of it, yet not inclined to think ill of Emmaline.

"You say your brother wasn't with her?"

"Right. She was alone."

"Did she have a basket?"

I frowned. "No, she just seemed to be looking."

"She may have been looking for you, waiting for you to spot her. If she didn't have a basket then she wasn't shopping."

I smiled and leaned back in my seat—a high-backed wooden chair furnished with knitted cushions. I took one of the cushions and rolled it around my hands. "No, it can't be."

"Why not? We've been here nearly two months. This may be one of the major port towns in Zaphon, but it's not *that* large. There are more visitors here than locals. Emmaline could have easily spotted us somewhere in the past few weeks."

"If Emmaline had wanted to turn me in then she would have done it by now."

"Either way, we have a problem on our hands." Danein leaned in and lowered his voice. "We know for certain she's seen you. If Emmaline comes knocking on the door of the inn with the authorities, we have no papers to give them to prove that you're legally bound to me, that you're not an unchosen. Ordinary people may take us at our word, but the authorities won't. Many of them are corrupt and work in conjunction with the slave traders. At any hint or suggestion of an unchosen woman in their midst, they will be like dogs to the bone."

A new fear rose in me. Whatever Emmaline's purpose or intentions were, it seemed I was not destined to find out. We would have to leave Fynn Harbor as soon as possible.

"Tomorrow I'll begin making arrangements for our passage out of here," Danein went on, his voice low like the soft flicker of the candle on the table next to us. "It may take a few days, perhaps a week, until we can set sail, so I want you to stay inside until then, understand? No more market visits, not even with Janna."

Three days passed uneventfully. It was given to me to tell Janna that our time had come to leave. She was disappointed but understood. I made every excuse possible for not going out with her, and she didn't seem to suspect anything. It was easy to keep myself busy and useful around the inn, but every so often, as was my custom, I would sit quietly in the parlor or take a rest in my room and look out the window. I always tried to find Danein in the crowd of men scurrying to and fro along the waterfront, but I never could.

The fourth day arrived. We were set to leave Fynn Harbor at dusk the following day. Our few belongings were already packed. Though I understood the necessity of leaving, a part of my heart had found a home in Fynn Harbor, and I regretted having to leave so soon, so suddenly, especially when the danger was still so uncertain and undefined.

As I watched out the window that morning, I saw a hooded figure standing near the inn on the opposite side of the street. From the size of the figure and the dark brown curls protruding from the hood, I knew it was Emmaline. She *had* known where I lived and hadn't come knocking with the authorities after all. Perhaps she too desired to speak with me and only wished to be cautious.

My curiosity overcame my judgment, and I grabbed my cloak from the peg on the wall and dashed down the stairs. At the bottom, I stopped and glanced around to make certain Janna wasn't in the entrance hall. I then made my way lightly to the door and opened it quickly, slipping quietly outside and shutting the door behind me. The cobblestones were wet from an early morning drizzle, but the sky was clearing up, its clouds moving fast as though being shooed away by the sun.

I looked across the street to where the figure was. Emmaline stood there, watching me. She slowly let down her hood so that I could better see her. I opened my mouth to speak and took a step forward; in that instant Emmaline turned and fled down the street, her footfalls kicking up water behind her.

"Wait!" I yelled, running after her.

I fastened my eyes on the edge of her bright cloak trailing behind her. She ran left and right, down one street and up another, going at a constant sprint. I had her just in sight, though she kept at least one block ahead of me.

"Emmaline! I wish to speak with you! Stop!"

She made another turn down a street I recognized. Being familiar with the area and guessing her exit point, I took a separate way to meet her head-on. I slowed as I came upon the meeting point so as to catch her unawares. As I expected, she came out upon the same street I occupied, just a short distance ahead of me. I quickly ducked sideways behind a lumber wagon. She turned to find I was no longer pursuing her from behind and stopped, glancing around the intersection. Confusion was written on her face; she lingered and continued to scan the area as though looking for me. I was only mildly struck by the paradox that she would be looking for me after having successfully lost me. Isn't that what she had wanted—to lose me?

I slipped up next to her as she was looking in the opposite direction and grabbed her arm. She turned to me, startled, instinctively pulling away. I held her firmly.

"What are you doing, Emma? Why are you running from me?"

For an answer, she only glanced left and right in a nervous gesture. A few people walked up and down the street, going in and out of shops and other buildings. We hadn't seemed to have drawn much attention.

I went on when Emma remained speechless. "You were waiting outside the inn. Did you want to speak with me? Is Benson all right? The children?"

When Emma still didn't reply, I gripped her arm even more firmly, resisting the urge to shake her. "Speak to me!"

Her look suddenly changed from apprehension to disgust. It so confused and frightened me that I released her arm and took a small step backward to gain some distance from her.

"I've been watching you," she finally said. "I saw you days ago one evening walking with that man of yours, so I followed you. I've been following you for a while. And here you are, living a free life on your own. I wonder if Danein knows you're an unchosen."

My brows contracted in bewilderment. I was especially surprised that she knew Danein's name. "He does. He's known from the beginning. And it hasn't been an easy road."

"And the innkeeper woman? What did you tell her? Does she know she has an unchosen woman living freely under her roof?"

It was my turn to grow concerned about drawing attention. I hastily glanced to the side and tilted my head downward, leaning in toward Emma. "Please lower your voice. Why are you here?"

"Your brother has never let you go. In all this time you've been gone, he hasn't forgotten you. Why can't he just forget you?"

I said nothing.

"He is haunted with guilt because of you." She scowled as though she had a bad taste in her mouth. "He feels he failed your father for not fulfilling his charge completely. He won't listen to me. He has shut me out." Her hate-filled eyes leveled on me, blue as ice. "I have been supplanted in my own home by an absent sister…by the ghost of an absent, unchosen, disgraced sister."

I had no words to reply. Although I knew I'd done nothing wrong, her words stabbed me with pain and guilt. I had been angry at my brother for not taking care of me, for casting me away. Yet the last thing I wanted was for him to suffer guilt in my absence, to jeopardize the well-being of his family because of me. It seemed I had caused trouble without intending to, without even being present.

"I…I'm sorry," I said, wishing to appease my sister-in-law, whom I had never truly cared for but now found myself sympathizing with. "I believe Benson's heart is pure. He does not mean to shut you out—"

"What do you know of it?" she spat.

We stood nearly in the middle of two intersecting roads. Several men on horseback rode by, and we stepped back to keep out of their way. People were still busied about their usual tasks; I let my stiffened shoulders relax a bit in the knowledge that nobody seemed concerned about the spectacle of two women arguing in the middle of the street.

I was just about to speak again when Emma went on. "The irony of it all is that I am a chosen woman. I have a husband, a home, and children. That's what all women in Zaphon long for to be happy and secure. But I'm not. I'm not happy. But you are."

"Emma, I don't understand what you're getting at."

"Why should you be happy with a man who loves you when I am not? Why should an unchosen have the privileges of ordinary people?"

"I don't have the privileges of ordinary people. I have to live my life in hiding. I'm not free to roam or be my own. I live a lie. That's not privilege."

"And yet here you are, living an ordinary existence alongside a man who loves you. You work, you earn your bread, and he takes care of you as a husband would. That seems a privilege. But tell me this, Alonya. Why is it he has not yet married you?"

I turned my face from hers and looked at my hands. "He will. The time isn't right for that."

"Perhaps he knows he doesn't need to marry you to have you."

"It's not like that," I shot out, meeting her penetrating stare. "We are on a quest to find the High King, to get the unjust laws in Zaphon abolished. There's more that binds us together than what you think."

"I'm sure you're right. Silly and idealistic, but right. You and he are united in heart. Benson and I have never been. No..." She lowered her head and bit her lip, becoming momentarily unguarded. "I have never truly loved Benson. I've never known what it is to be so closely knit to someone."

She studied her hands closely as though looking for something, as though recalling a time long past, written in the lines of her skin. "I never truly loved Benson," she repeated. "My mother died when I was young, and as I grew older, my father pushed me to marry as soon as I could. He was harsh and greedy and wanted to remarry. He didn't fancy having an unwed, unchosen daughter strapped to him. For as long as I can remember, he was after me to marry. I, like you, never had any serious suitors until Benson came along. He was the first one to really care about me. So though I personally didn't think much of him, I snatched him up, partly to escape the fate of an unchosen, but mostly to escape the intolerable conditions of my father's household."

Emma looked so pitiful sharing her sorrows that my heart nearly broke for her. Despite her hatred toward me, I related with her fear when young and understood her actions. I even sympathized with her current plight. I'd never earnestly considered that a chosen woman could still be unhappy, could still feel unchosen. I'd never realized how the unchosen law could drive a woman to marry prematurely due to fear of its ramifications. Which was the lesser evil, I wondered: not marrying and becoming an outcast according to the law, or marrying prematurely for fear of the law? Truly, the world was a backward place.

Emma hastily wiped a stray tear that had escaped down her cheek and looked away from me. Once more she glanced around, and her face registered a sense of alarm as though suddenly remembering something. Without a word, she turned and fled once more down the street.

Assuming she was mortified by her emotional outburst, I followed her in order to finish our conversation, to discover what her true purpose was in seeking me out. Surely she hadn't meant merely to insult me.

"Emma!" I called after her once more. "Please stop!"

A supernatural speed seemed to urge her onward. I kept her as much within my sights as possible, hoping that if I could not stop her, at least I might discover where she was staying. If Benson was there, I could speak with him to make sure everything was all right.

Emma threaded her way up and down shorter, curvier streets, disappearing around a corner just as I was rounding the previous one. So intent was I on my pursuit that I didn't notice when the streets narrowed and emptied. The buildings, mostly crumbling and abandoned, began to thin out. A sudden panic filled me; I slowed, realizing I was in an unfamiliar area. I stopped and looked around me. It seemed to be an old shipping and trading district on the edge of town, but I couldn't be sure. I could hear seagulls and the sound of water far to my left, which told me I was on the eastern edge of Fynn Harbor. That knowledge didn't give me much of a bearing, however. I was certain only that there were no other people around.

"Emmaline!" I called. I heard a scuffle of feet on ground, then silence. The thump of my heart beat heavily in my ears. "Emmaline," I said once more, quietly.

I had lost her, and I was alone in an abandoned part of town, far from the inn.

I turned to leave the way I had come, and suddenly there were pounding steps behind me. Without looking, I knew it wasn't

Emma. I flew forward to escape, but from around the corner ahead of me appeared a tall, muscular man with unruly beard and dirty clothing. He came at me, and I stopped short. Someone grabbed me from behind, wrapping his arms around me and lifting me off my feet. My arms were pinned to my sides. I screamed and kicked and struggled. Laughter from my assailant drowned out my screams, his breath putrid and hot on my neck as he carried me back around the corner where I'd last seen Emma.

A prison wagon hitched to a team of horses waited there. There were narrow barred windows near the top of the cab—just like the slavers' wagons into which we'd been tossed after the raid on the Colony. Although I didn't recognize these men as the same captors from then, I knew they must belong to the same group of slave traders.

The man carrying me set me to my feet. I let my legs go slack and slipped to the ground, nearly out of his grasp. He was quickly on top of me, pinning me down, while the other man used a rope to tie my hands in front of my body. I was then picked up and tossed brusquely into the back of the wagon. The door slammed shut behind me.

At first I was too stunned to cry out for help. What had happened to Emma? Where was she? I stood on my toes to reach the barred windows and peek outside. Emma was there, standing mere feet from the wagon.

"Emma!" I called through the bars, my heart lifting for a brief moment. "Help me!"

She continued to walk slowly and steadily toward the wagon, her eyes narrowed and her mouth pursed tightly, seemingly unconcerned with my plight. One of my captors came into view behind her, his arms crossed, watching the scene before him. Confusion rattled my brain, and my heart sank. I then realized that she had done this to me. She had led me into a trap.

Before I could say anything, the door to the back of the wagon opened. I turned at the sound and retreated further inside. Emma appeared at the doorway, but she did not come in. We stared at each other for several long moments. She seemed to be appraising me. I wondered why she didn't speak.

"Why are you doing this?" I said, my voice trembling.

"Because you're an unchosen, and this is the fate you deserve."

I shook my head. "You can't really believe that. I've done nothing to you to earn this injustice, to cause you to hate me so much."

Her eyes flicked away from mine and her face softened, but only momentarily. Quickly the anger flared up again. "You should have ended up in the slaving camps long ago. I am merely ensuring that you be put in your proper place."

"You treat me like a criminal when I've done nothing. Don't you see that?" When she didn't answer me, I sighed and dropped my shoulders. "Why do you hate me so much?"

Her words from earlier flashed through my mind in an instant, giving me my answer. *Your brother has never let you go. He is haunted with guilt because of you. I have been supplanted in my own home by the ghost of an absent, unchosen, disgraced sister. Why should you be happy with a man who loves you when I am not? Why should an unchosen have the privileges of ordinary people?*

I grasped for words to say to comfort Emmaline, but none came. Yet I needed her to continue to confide in me, to trust me. Perhaps then she'd come to her right mind and release me from this prison.

"Emma," I finally said, my heart knocking frantically in my chest, "I know my brother does care for you, despite your feelings for him. And you and I—we *are* family. I'd like to be family to you. I can see that we have both been outcast and abandoned in different ways. We ought to help each other."

Whatever Emma may have wanted to hear, that was not it. She moved closer to the wagon, and without getting inside, she leaned in so as to better gain privacy from the men outside. Her voice was firm and cold.

"If once Benson loved me, he no longer does. He despises me now."

"Then why do this? Why make him despise you more?"

"I'm doing this to punish him, and to put you in your place."

She turned away and nodded to the men, waving her arm dismissively in my direction. I ran to the door of the wagon, but it was shut in my face with a click of the lock. Once again, I stood on my toes and reached up to see through the barred window at the top of the wagon.

"Emma, please!" I called out to her retreating form. "Don't do this! You're wrong about me, and about Benson. Please reconsider. Emma! Don't go! Don't leave me!"

My shouts became more frantic and my voice hoarse, but Emma was soon gone. There was a whistle and a snap of the reins before the wagon began rattling down the road. I threw myself against the walls of my prison, causing it to rock side to side, screaming for help all the while.

"You be quiet in there!" my captors warned me. I ignored them and continued kicking and screaming. Soon the wagon stopped abruptly, and I heard crunching gravel as one of the drivers jumped from his perch and came around to the back. I stopped and watched as the door was swung open and one of the men leaned in, pointing a menacing finger at me.

"You'd best stop that noise now, missy, or I'll give you something to scream about. Don't think I won't!"

I feigned meekness and lowered my head. As soon as the man turned away to close the door, I ran with all my strength and threw myself at it. The door slammed hard against the man, and he stumbled backward. I flew out, crashing to the ground. Momentarily dizzied, I fumbled on the gravel road, attempting to stand, which was difficult with my hands tied in front of me. Before I could take two crawling steps, I was grabbed from behind and heaved to my feet. I began to cry out, but the man slapped me hard across the face, the force of it knocking me to the ground once again. I was stunned silent as hot tears ran down my cheeks. A drop of blood splashed on the ground below me, and I touched my mouth with a shaky hand. My lip was cut.

Again, I was heaved up from behind and dragged back to the wagon. The man threw me inside, cursing at me all the while.

"What'd I tell you, missy? I mean what I say, and there'll be worse coming next if you don't mind me properly! I can do much worse. Take that as a promise and a warning."

The door slammed closed once again. I was too weak and shaky to do anything but hold my stinging cheek and pray for help.

20

Captured

For a short while I could still hear the sea to the distant north, its soothing rhythm a lullaby that lulled me to sleep amidst my living nightmare. I don't know when exactly sleep claimed me, but when I awoke, the friendly voice of the sea was gone, replaced by the crunching of wheels on gravel and sand, and the occasional lonely cry of a wolf. My body on the floor of the wagon rocked gently back and forth. Looking up, I saw the bright night sky through the bars, broken frequently by the top of a pine or a fir tree. It was evening, and we were passing through an open wood. Cool night air streamed in from the windows. I shifted my position, and the white-gray moon came into view, nearly full, beaming down on the earth. I stared at it for a long time. It was like a friend, the way the sea had been. I clung to it as something beautiful and familiar.

Danein would know by now that I was missing. He would have known hours ago. Janna had probably discovered it soon after my flight from the inn and had gone to the wharf to find Danein. They had most likely scoured town looking for me. But they wouldn't find me there. They wouldn't know where to look. This time I was gone for good.

Self-loathing and self-condemnation began circling like vultures, closing in. *How insufferable I must be to Danein,* I thought, *always getting myself into trouble, not heeding advice or warning.* He had already gone to the ends of the earth to find me after the first time I'd been captured. How could I expect him to do more, to come after me again?

He loves you, a voice seemed to whisper to my heart. *He would die for you. You are a precious jewel to him, of greater worth than you think.*

I knew I didn't deserve that kind of love, but tears of gratitude for the reality of it flowed down my cheeks, and those truths began to chase the vultures away.

A man called out "Whoa!" and the wagon came to a halt. I sat up abruptly. I heard the voices of my captors, low and indistinct, yet nobody came to claim me. My stomach twisted in hunger. I hadn't eaten anything all day, nor had I once been out of my rolling prison since we'd set off. There were sounds of footsteps shuffling to and fro, twigs breaking, horses snorting and neighing, and finally a fire crackling. We had stopped for the night, and still I was neglected. I waited and listened. The men were talking low, but one would bellow out a laugh from time to time. Soon the aroma of roasted meat occupied the little space of my prison and tightened my stomach even more. A passing wave of dizziness hit me as I stood, but I managed to walk timidly to the door and push on it. It didn't budge.

"Hello?" I said weakly. The men continued to laugh and converse. I cleared my throat and took a deep breath. "Hello!" I said more loudly. "I'm hungry. I've been in this wagon all day, and I'm faint with hunger."

"Quiet, you!" bellowed one of the men. "You're not going anywhere, you fiery wench! I don't trust you."

"Please, just a little water and bread would suffice."

I received no immediate response, but within a few moments the sound of heavy steps came toward me, and there was a sudden pounding on the side of the wagon. I jumped in fright.

"I said shut your mouth!" the man warned.

I waited a moment, gathering my thoughts and my strength before speaking. "So be it! But once we arrive at your slaving headquarters, a weak, sick, near-dead girl isn't going to be a great deal of use to you. You won't get much for me. What a wasted trip it will have been!"

There was silence then. I heard one of the men cursing under his breath before there came a scuffling of feet and the click of a key in the padlock. The door was opened. I recognized the man who had slapped me earlier when I'd knocked him to the ground. He threw in a leg of roasted meat along with a stale piece of bread. Just on the inside of the door, he placed a tin mug of water.

"Anything else, Princess?"

"Yes," I said coolly. "I need to relieve myself."

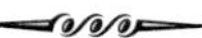

I slept inside the wagon that night, but I'd managed to negotiate a rag of a blanket before they locked me in. I lay awake a long time, uncomfortable and frightened despite my bold front earlier. My thoughts took me back to the women of the Colony, especially Taralyn. I had some comfort in the idea that I might possibly be seeing some of my old friends soon, if indeed I was being taken to the same place as they were. I would enjoy seeing Taralyn again. I wondered how she fared. She had always been so strong, so full of hope and faith. Had the slaving camp broken her? Had she been sold? Did her master treat her kindly or cruelly? These questions gnawed at me. It was partly my fault she had found that fate. Now that I was on my way to the same fate, her sacrifice had been in vain. I had been so close to freedom but had lost it. Danein and I had nearly been out of the country, but then I had been foolish and followed a whim, and now that freedom was gone.

Yet I was not willing to accept that fate. Something new arose in me then—not a resignation, but a will to fight. And with it came an image of the unicorn from the Wild Lands that had appeared after I'd called out for help from the High King, hardly knowing what I was doing. And so, instead of giving up, I took a deep, shaky breath, and with my eyes on the silver moon like a tiny discus in the sky, I said again what I'd said before: help me. I didn't know what would come of it, if anything, but a peace settled over me, a sense of hope in the seemingly hopeless circumstances in which I found myself. And in the warmth and comfort of that peace, I was able to finally sleep, though my bed was hard and my cell cold.

The rocking movement of the wagon roused me. I sat up, my body full of aches. The scratchy rope around my wrist had loosened a little but not enough for me to slip my hands free of the knot. I put my back against the side of the wagon and tried to ready myself for the remainder of the trip. I wondered if we would arrive at the slavers' headquarters that evening. The thought made me nervous and fearful, yet at the same time I was eager to get out of the back of the wagon. I hoped I might really see Taralyn or some of the other women. That thought was the only kind of comfort I had; that and the continued presence of the unicorn in my mind. I fancied it might even then know where I was. Maybe it was following me. Perhaps it had followed me along my entire journey. Although I hadn't managed to find the High King, somehow I felt like he and the unicorn were united, as if he'd sent the unicorn. And if he'd sent the unicorn, then somehow he knew about me. He knew where I was. Even then I was sure he could see me, and that was enough—knowing he saw me.

It was early morning. Birdsong flew to me on the wind through the bars of my prison. The air was chill. I had been offered no breakfast, though I smelled the smoky remains of a fire. I had little energy to do anything but sit and think and pray. Not long into the journey my head dropped to my chest as I dozed in and out of sleep; confused and disoriented images swirled in my brain.

Then the back of my head hit the wall behind me as the wagon came to a sudden halt. I was jolted awake. My captors called out in distress and yelled at each other, their words mixed with other sounds. From somewhere in the distance came the hiss of an arrow splitting the air, and then moments later, a heavy thud. I heard the grinding of feet on gravel. The horses whinnied and pawed the ground restlessly, moving forward slightly, then backing up, as though unsure what was happening or what to do. There were a few more shouts, then another hiss. A man cried out in pain and fell to the ground. We were being attacked!

I stood and looked through the barred windows but saw nothing except the forested hillside. From the front of the wagon came a sudden scuffle accompanied by cursing and cries of pain. Then there was silence. My eyes roved back and forth as far as they could reach, expecting to see a gang of men come into view, yet I saw nobody. Then somebody was right outside the door of the wagon, handling the lock, attempting to get in. In the next instant the door flew open, and Danein stood there, looking worried and ragged. I hadn't known who to expect, but it certainly wasn't him. I flew forward into his arms. He caught me and set me down to the ground. Tears flowed uncontrollably.

"Danein! How did you…"

"There were only two of them," he said, winded, breaking the embrace and cutting my bonds with a knife. Harsh red marks circled my wrists. He took a moment to rub them tenderly then took my hand and led me away from the wagon.

Across his shoulder was slung a bow and a quiver of arrows. As we fled from the scene, I looked back to see the two large men who had been my kidnappers lying motionless on the ground in front of the horses.

"Did you kill them?" I asked, horrified at the thought.

"No, I only wounded them, and then was forced to knock them unconscious to get the key."

"Did you come alone?"

He tugged at my hand, dragging me along quickly up the hill. For my part, I was too weary to run. "Yes. I rode all night when I heard. Benson told me what had happened, how you'd been taken."

"Benson?" I said, out of breath.

"I'll tell you later!"

We crested the hill and ran several more yards down the other side. Though I doubted the men would wake anytime soon, we ran as though wolves were nipping at our heels. Two horses were tied to a tree at the bottom of the hill. Danein helped me up on one and leaped onto the other, and away we flew, back toward Fynn Harbor. I followed Danein as we took a path that wound through the woodland before stretching far into open countryside, north of the main road. We ran hard then slowed after a couple of hours to rest the horses. At midday we came into a small village and stopped for a quick respite.

"This village is off the main road, so we should be safe for a little while," Danein said, tying the horses' reins to a post outside a common stable.

"I don't think those men came by way of the main road," I said.

"No, they came by this road, but they'll not care to be inconspicuous if they choose to follow us. They will go the quickest route to get back to Fynn Harbor, which is by the main road."

Danein dropped two coins into the groomer's hand at the stable for care of the horses, and we proceeded to spy out an inn where we could eat a midday meal.

Danein was mostly quiet, his mouth set firmly in his face so that it was almost a frown. We chose a table in the corner of the dining room of the inn and ordered a simple meal of bread, cheese, apples, and water. As we waited for the food to arrive, Danein put his elbows on the table and buried his face in his hands, weary and fatigued. I watched him as he remained in that position for a long time. Finally he sat upright and heaved an enormous sigh. His eyes were rimmed with red.

"Are you angry with me?" I asked timidly.

Danein didn't answer right away, but when he did, I knew he was sincere. "No. I'm angry with myself."

I frowned. "Why? I'm the one who didn't listen to you. You were right about Emmaline all along. I should have heeded your warning."

"Perhaps, but I might have done the same thing if I was you. No—I'm angry with myself for not heeding *you* several weeks ago when you suggested that we think about leaving soon. I agreed with you then, but I made no move toward leaving. I neglected to make arrangements for our departure, thinking it harmless if we stayed. I just…" he faltered. "I was happy with the way things were. I didn't consider us to be in any hurry."

"Nor I," I admitted. "That's where the danger lay."

"So you see, I'm also to blame."

I took his hand from across the table. "Thank you for coming for me."

"I'm so sorry this happened to you. I forget sometimes the true danger out there for you. I'm sorry that it took almost losing you again to be reminded of it."

The food came then and we ate in silence, occasionally sharing glances and smiles.

The horses were swift after the half-hour rest. We rode hard all afternoon until the sun was directly ahead of us on its descent. There had been no sign of pursuers all day, although, if Danein was correct in his assumption, they could have taken the main road back. The possibility that we might yet have to deal with them loomed over me like a black cloud. I tried not to think about it as we slowed the horses to a trot to give them another rest. I looked over at Danein. His body slumped and his head drooped slightly in fatigue. The poor man hadn't slept for hours.

He had ridden all night on his own to find me. I knew the slower pace was as much for him as for the horses.

"How much longer until we arrive back in Fynn Harbor?" I asked.

"It should be within the next hour or two. We have only about that much sunlight left. Our ship is due to leave this evening just after sundown. We should make it."

I nodded. "Danein, you said earlier that Benson told you what had happened to me. How did he know? He wasn't a part of it, was he?"

"No, he knew nothing about it until Emmaline came home yesterday afternoon. Janna and I had looked for you all around town, and in the evening when we arrived back at the inn, Benson was waiting there. He asked for me, and we went into the parlor to sit down. He told me that Emmaline, in a sort of smug rage, had confessed what she'd done. He had been so alarmed and shocked that he sought me out, not knowing what else to do."

"I am grateful for my brother's help, but I wish he had come himself so that I could've seen him before we sail."

Danein looked at me, his eyes tender. "He wanted to come, I believe, but he seemed ashamed. He said he hoped that by coming to me and informing me of the situation, he might have paid even a little of the debt he owes to you and your father."

"I am sorry for him. It seems his own life hasn't been so easy."

"Nobody's life is easy, Alonya. Everybody has troubles of their own kind, whether unchosen or not."

The ambush came as we entered the outskirts of Fynn Harbor. My two assailants, plus three other men, jumped out in front of us and blocked the road. They brandished clubs and knives. We stopped our horses and looked on. My heart hammered in my chest. From the wharf close by came the shrill blast of a whistle—some vessels were making ready to set sail, and one of them was most likely ours.

"All we want is the girl," growled one man. "Give her up and you can go freely on your way."

"No!" snarled another who was limping on one leg. Dried blood covered his trousers where he'd been pierced by Danein's arrow. "He's the one that shot me and knocked me out. I want vengeance!"

They walked toward us, and we backed up our horses. Danein whipped out his bow and strung it with an arrow. He pointed it directly at the man who'd last spoken.

"I aimed to wound before. This time I aim to kill. I promise you—if you do not back down, I will shoot you."

My horse shuffled nervously, blowing steam out of its nostrils.

"You can't shoot us all at the same time," another man answered, stepping forward slowly.

"Would you like to place a wager on that?" Danein challenged.

For a moment the men stood still, looking back and forth at one another. Danein kept his bow fixed straight ahead. Then, without warning, one of the men flung his knife at Danein. It flew too far to the left and missed, but the motion had momentarily distracted him. At the same moment, the others had run forward, brandishing their weapons and rallying a cry for vengeance. I backed my horse up and turned to fly in the opposite direction, but in the confusion of the noise and movement, it was too baffled to heed my pull on the reins and ended up circling several times, rearing up, and nearly tossing me to the ground. I managed to still the animal just in time to see Danein, recovered, fell two men with his arrows. Another came toward me, and the other two—the ones who had been earlier wounded by Danein—backed off, not swift enough to capture me nor foolish enough to risk being shot again.

Danein turned his bow toward the man approaching me and commanded him to stop. He ignored the warning and drew closer. I held out my leg, ready to heave a blow with my foot when, with a flash and a swish, an arrow penetrated the man's chest.

He stopped in his tracks, glanced down at the blood soaking his tunic, and collapsed backward.

Danein then trained his arrow on the two quickly retreating.

"Stop!" he commanded.

The men held up their hands in surrender, waiting.

"Go, Alonya," Danein told me firmly, not taking his eyes off the men. "Head toward the wharf. I'll be right behind you."

I kicked the flanks of my horse and it flew to action. The men followed me with their eyes as I escaped them a second time. I flew through the village streets and alleys where men with large torches were lighting the lanterns along Fynn Harbor's thoroughfares. Before long, I heard a second set of hooves clacking on the cobblestones and glanced behind me to see Danein close at hand. Together we reached the wharf just as our vessel was blowing its last whistle, signaling departure.

I was surprised to see Janna awaiting us.

"Quick, you two! I've already had your belongings transferred to the ship, and I spoke with the captain earlier to convince them to wait, but they won't wait any longer!"

I embraced Janna quickly. Danein shook her hand, and together we rushed down the dock, my heart nearly bursting from exertion and breaking from once again having to leave a place that had been home, even if only for a little while.

So before our second month in Fynn Harbor was up, we were aboard a midsized merchant vessel, its white sails flapping in the wind, bound northwest across the Great Sea for Kerith.

Wanderers

The winds that carried us along were fair and peaceful, tinged with the fresh, salty fragrance of the sea. Above us the sky spread out in all directions, clear and soft. I stood against the railing on the upper deck of the bow of the ship for several hours a day, leaning into the wind as we sailed along. Sometimes I watched the endless sea stretch out before us; other times I attempted to discern shapes in the clouds. I scanned for land across the horizon, but I mostly closed my eyes to feel the sun kissing my cheeks and the wind whip softly across my forehead, playing with my hair. Inside, my heart exulted in the adventure—in the sense of peace and freedom that being on the sea afforded me. Always, though, the reality of my circumstances would cast a shadow over these reflective moments, turning me melancholy. I knew Danein and I were on the right path, doing what must be done, but a part of me wished that our course wasn't so necessary.

Danein often joined me on the deck, but being more garrulous than I—even more so than I realized—he spent a lot of time walking about and speaking with the sailors or the captain or the cook. I had little to do with these conversations, and the men never approached me of their own volition. I preferred it that way, and I believe Danein did too, although he was easier about me wandering the ship alone than he'd been about me wandering Fynn Harbor.

The first time we were asked to dine with the captain in his quarters below deck, I was glad for the occasion. I wore my best dress of the few I carried with me and smoothed my flyaway hair. The sun and wind had put some color into my cheeks, and both Danein and the captain complimented me.

The captain was a jovial man, tall and bulky, wind-beaten and sea-weathered, but his dark skin and the creases in his face told a story of a fascinating life of travel and adventure. He was full to the brim of energy and mirth, and he spilled it out heavily on Danein and me while we enjoyed roast lamb, vegetables, and soup—a more extravagant meal than I would have expected on a ship. The captain was a wealthy man, we came to learn, having been employed most of his life by merchants. He told of his exploits around the eastern world, how he'd never lost a ship nor any merchandise. This gave him an unparalleled reputation among the merchants of Zaphon and elsewhere.

"Have you ever sailed to Coralind?" Danein asked as we sat at the dining table in the captain's modest quarters. He sat at the captain's right hand, while I was on his left across from Danein. A single servant dressed in livery stood like a statue behind the captain, awaiting orders. Next to him on a short table was a tray laden with wine, extra glasses, and utensils.

The captain swallowed a large piece of lamb and cleared his throat before speaking. "Ah, Coralind! Now there's a place to which I have always wished to sail. The finest of silks and fabrics, the sweetest of fruits, the rarest of beauty potions, the riches of wines, the most potent of medicines—all come from Coralind. An exotic place indeed—but alas, no, I have never myself captained a ship that traded with Coralind."

"How then does Zaphon come by products from Coralind?" I asked.

"My ships trade with ships that trade with Coralind. We make many stops and do considerable business with merchant ships from the eastern and the western world."

"It's a very lucrative business," Danein interjected, looking at me. "When I was still young and apprenticed, I considered gaining employment on a merchant vessel to travel and see the world while making my fortune."

My smile widened to learn this new information about Danein. "Truly?"

"Yes. I have always had an interest in travel. And I have always wanted to go to Coralind."

"Then why didn't you, son?" the captain asked.

Danein appeared mildly uncomfortable before answering. He exchanged a quick glance with me. "Oh, life circumstances prevented it any sooner than now. I have traveled around Zaphon as a peddler and made a good living by it, but I never had the opportunity to travel overseas."

"Until now!" the captain beamed, lifting his glass to toast Danein. "To new adventures and opportunities!"

Danein and I laughed and lifted our glasses.

"To Coralind," Danein added. He looked at me.

"To the sea," I said.

The captain took a long, heavy draught of the wine and clunked his glass down on the table. "So your final destination is Coralind?"

"Yes. My sister and I are looking to visit an old friend there." Danein had a way of answering questions without disclosing too much information.

"Well then, I wish I could take you farther than Kerith. Unfortunately, this is a routine trip for us, and not a long one. But I could give you some contacts of people I know along the way who might be able to offer assistance."

"Thank you kindly, sir. I would be glad of it."

"Truth be told, I wish I could go with you myself," the captain continued. He rested his hands on the tabletop but still held the utensils in them. His eyes had a faraway, wistful look. "I have always wished to see Coralind—the Holy Land, you know."

My eyes met Danein's in surprise. The captain went on, gesturing with his hands as he spoke, his fork and knife waving in the air with the motions.

"I have always been a wanderer, seeker, and adventurer in body and in spirit. I have never seen the High King in person, mind you, but I have always wished to. Coralind is the best place, I would imagine, for coming into contact with him."

The smile slowly grew on Danein's face. "So we've heard."

"You believe in the High King?" I asked, still staring at Danein, noting his reactions.

"Well, call me a fool, but I do, I do. I was brought up to it, and I suppose it's always been a part of me. It seems a beautiful thing to believe in. Somehow it makes the world less nonsensical to think that there is a true king over all the other kingdoms of this world who knows all and is in control of all and will eventually make all the wrongs right."

Danein nodded. "Indeed."

The captain suddenly waved his hand as if to dismiss his words. "Well now, I suppose I'm an old sentimental fool, but that's that. I'm sure you two would rather talk of other things."

Danein set his arms upon the table and leaned forward. "Actually, sir, I must tell you that my sister and I are hoping to meet with the High King in Coralind."

The captain's hand stopped midway from his plate to his mouth. His eyes searched us back and forth. For a few moments we were silent, rocking to the movement of the waves beneath us.

"So that is your errand to the Holy Land? To seek the High King?"

We both nodded. The captain dropped his hand and shook his head in disbelief, but his eyes were gleaming and his cheeks flushed, either with wine or excitement or both. I wasn't sure.

"You two are brave, faithful souls. May I ask the nature of this audience with the High King?"

"It concerns injustices in Zaphon that need to be addressed."

"There are many of those, indeed," the captain said. "Now I truly wish I could help you more along your way." He stopped and seemed to consider for a moment. During the short lapse in conversation, the servant ambled over with a large tray held in one hand to clear our plates from the table. The captain waited until he was back at his post before addressing us.

"I'll tell you what: duty keeps me tied down for the present. But I do believe you will meet the High King and find what you're looking for. If ever in the future you need a friend and ally, I'm your man."

Danein nearly jumped from his seat to shake hands with the captain. "Thank you, sir! I will certainly take you up on that offer!"

After experiencing Janna's kindness, and with the captain on our side, our mission suddenly seemed less formidable. If there were people like Janna and the captain out in the world who fought injustices every day with kindness and friendship, certainly there were more, and Danein and I were not alone. After that day, though I was still prone to bouts of melancholy, I felt more equal to the task at hand. I stopped thinking of the High King in terms of *if* and began thinking of him in terms of *when*.

We sailed for four days before coming to land, but were only halfway across the sea to Kerith. A small island between Zaphon and Kerith aptly named Haven was one of the stops for merchant ships traveling our route. A small harbor and port village offered a supply and trading post. We dropped anchor there so that the ship could restock provisions and the sailors could have a rest.

We took a rowboat into town from the anchored ship. It was a small village without a name, merely called Haven after the name of the island. We rowed ashore with the captain himself and four other sailors who took charge of the large oars. The waves rocked us gently back and forth as we approached the village.

"I have business to transact here, which will take up the majority of today and tomorrow morning," the captain explained. "You are welcome to stay overnight on the ship or find lodging in the village. Many of the sailors like to stay ashore to feel the solid ground beneath their feet as long as possible."

"That is understandable," Danein replied, squinting in the bright sunlight. "I believe Alonya and I would enjoy losing our sea legs for a day. What do you think?"

I nodded my assent, and we were soon at the wharf, stepping up onto the docks. Behind us were several more boats from the ship loaded with crates and barrels and rowed by sailors bringing goods to shore for trading.

We followed the captain up and along the dockside. He stopped several times to speak with clerks and sailors, then finally addressed us outside a small wooden structure that served as an office.

"This is my stop and where I leave you two." He pointed to the right where a wide dirt road—the main thoroughfare—led into the rest of the village. "That's where you're wanting to go. You should find all you need for a comfortable stay. If you need any help, don't hesitate to come down here and ask for Captain Lynch."

He informed us of the ship's departure time for the following afternoon. Danein beamed and shook his hand, and after saying good-byes, we turned and walked into Haven Village. It was a small place, surprisingly busy, with the main street extending no more than a half mile from the shore and several smaller roads leading into the surrounding country. Vendors and merchants stood on either side of the street inside booths or underneath awnings. The air was full of the chatter of people milling about.

It wasn't long before we found a tavern in which to eat. There was an inn attached to the tavern, but it was a busy, dirty place and seemed nearly full. After our noon meal we wandered about town, looking for lodgings. The inns were few, and they were mostly full. The innkeepers charged high fees to fill their last rooms, knowing that overnight accommodation was scarce. Danein tried negotiating with the last innkeeper we met, but he was stubborn and ended up turning us away. I could tell Danein was frustrated as we stepped down into the dust of the road.

"We should just stay on the ship tonight," I suggested. "That way we'll save our money."

"Yes, but I had wished to give you a holiday from the sea for at least one night."

I took his hand between both of mine, uncaring whether we were seen or not. "You've already done so much for me. I really don't mind going back to the ship."

His face softened and he smiled. "Well, let's take a walk and explore this island. If we still can't find any lodging by tonight, we'll go back to the ship."

I thought he would let my hand go, but he didn't. We followed a dirt road out of the village, one that looked old and disused, down which were no people. It stretched for a couple miles through overgrown fields of grass. Far to the left, we could see the water and hear the waves crashing against land. Soon the road took a sharp turn to the right and began to twist more inland, eventually going straight into a wood.

"There doesn't seem to be much on this island, does there?" I remarked.

"Just the village, and maybe a few outlying cottages."

"No farms?"

Danein shook his head. "This is a trading harbor. Everything on this island comes from outside. Most people come here for business, and those that do live here permanently make their living from that business."

We had wandered into the wood and continued down the road, which seemed to grow narrower until it was nothing more than a footpath. An old, overturned wagon was lying in the thick of the brush off the side of the path. Creeper vines and bushes had grown around it, almost completely veiling it from plain sight.

"Well, it seems to have been awhile since anybody has been this way," Danein said.

It was a peaceful wood, thick with quiet that muffled the sound of the sea and eventually drowned it out altogether. Sunlight filtered through the canopy, beams that sliced across the shadow to reach the forest floor, painting the wood a dusky sepia. We continued walking on, mostly in silence, enjoying the moment and enjoying each other's company. Every so often one of us would make an observation and comment on the surroundings, but we were mostly quiet as we walked on. In my heart, during that moment, I was content. Yet, as often happened when I imagined the moment ending—when I foresaw us eventually walking out of the wood and rejoining the world in the noisy village—I grew melancholy. I longed to be with Danein—to *belong* to him. I didn't want to be an unchosen any longer. I often wondered why Danein didn't ask me to marry him, but deep in my heart I knew the answer, so I never asked him. I knew certain things needed to be made right and to be put into place before Danein and I could be together for good. Our time together then was like a whisper, a promise, of what was to come. But it couldn't yet be fully mine. And even then, as we walked through the wood, I had a strong sense that our present time together was coming to a close. I didn't want it to, nor did I understand it, but I felt it. The farther we walked, the deeper this presentiment grew.

Eventually Danein noted my uneasiness and stopped, turning to me.

"What's wrong?"

I shook my head, uncertain how to explain. Danein put his hands on either side of my face and drew me to him. He kissed me like he had that first time.

"Don't be sad," he said.

"I…I feel as though something is going to change soon."

"Many changes are happening all around us," Danein said. "Change is necessary. It's what helps us grow."

"I know. It's just…there is still so much I long for. I feel as though everything we're waiting for and working toward is going to take much longer, and be much more difficult, than we anticipated. I don't always feel up to the task."

"Nor I. But we must stay strong and keep on course." He held me to him in a close embrace, and I let the tears flow.

"You do know that I love you, do you not?" he said, his voice muffled in my hair.

I nodded, unable to speak.

"Then, no matter what happens, take comfort in that and in the promise of 'one day.'"

I moved away and looked up at Danein, confused. "One day?"

"One day, Alonya," he said quietly. "One day things will be right and we can be together."

I put my head against his chest again and closed my eyes tightly. "Why not now?" I asked, knowing the question was futile. "I've waited so long already."

"We both have," Danein said, stroking my hair.

I don't know how long we stayed there, but the wood darkened around us as evening descended. Night sounds surrounded us, amplified in the stillness.

"Come, we must go," Danein whispered. He pulled away from me and took my hand as we turned to leave. Although we had followed a footpath on our way in, and it had made no more than soft curves through the wood, in the deepening dusk it was difficult to discern the way back. Other paths seemed to spring out of nowhere, and we could not recall which way we'd come.

"It seems we've gotten ourselves lost," Danein said coolly. His nonchalance steeled me, but having spent several nights in the woods on my own, I wasn't worried. We would be able to survive one night in the wood on our own. Besides, it wasn't yet too late to try and make our way out. We could wander all night if we had to.

I laughed softly. "I guess we weren't as heedful as we ought to have been."

Danein looked at me tenderly. "You distracted me with your presence so that I had no notion we had wandered so far."

I only smiled. At that moment we both saw it: a distant light far to our left, somewhere in the thick of the woods off the path. We both stared for a while before speaking.

"It can't be a firefly or fairy," Danein said. "It's unmoving and looks larger. And it's too high to be a fire."

"A candle in a window, perhaps?"

"My thoughts exactly. It seems there are people living here." He tugged at my hand. "Come. Let's investigate."

The source of the light ended up being closer than it seemed; although, having to find our way in the dark, we were long in getting there. We kept our eyes fixed to the glow. Every now and again it seemed to go out but was only temporarily hidden behind the foliage. My eyes grew sore from staring so intently at it in the darkness, but I held fast to Danein's hand while he led. The air around us grew cold, but sweat edged my brow from the exertion of the walk.

A dark crumbling hut nestled between two large trees and hidden behind hanging vines awaited us. As we suspected, a single candle was lit in the window. It faintly illuminated the front of the hut, revealing a lopsided wooden door.

A curtain hung in the window behind the candle, blocking our view into the building. I sidled close to Danein. We looked around but saw no one, nor did we hear anything, not even from within the hut.

"It seems abandoned," I said.

"Yet someone must have lit that candle."

"Who do you suppose it was?"

"Maybe a fellow traveler, someone who got lost in the woods just as we have."

"But why put the candle outside the curtain?"

"Perhaps it's a signal of some sort."

We were still a long time, attempting to discern sounds from inside the hut, whether voices or footfalls—anything to suggest the hut was occupied.

"I don't think anyone's in there," I finally said. "Maybe whoever lit the candle took off to do some hunting."

"Unlikely. It's difficult to hunt after dark."

"Then perhaps someone's hurt in there."

Danein was silent for a long moment as he considered the possibility.

"Well, I suppose since we're here we ought to investigate. I would hate to think we'd missed an opportunity to help someone."

After one more cursory glance at our black surroundings, we walked toward the front door together, hand in hand. Danein reached out his free hand to the knob on the wooden door. He gave it a slight budge, pushing and then pulling on it. It was stuck tight. He let go of my hand and used both hands, pushing his weight against the door. It jiggled and loosened and finally fell inward. Danein nearly stumbled inside.

As soon as the door was open, light came spilling out of the doorway. I stepped inside with Danein, and we both squinted against the brightness shining into our faces.

"Hello?" Danein called. "Is anyone here?"

"We're sorry to intrude. We were wandering in the woods lost and saw the light in the window."

Slowly the light began to fade and objects came into view. The room seemed larger on the inside than it had appeared from the outside.

"Wanderers?" a voice suddenly called from directly ahead. I felt Danein's body tense next to me, and I reached out to grab his arm. A man's form began to appear in front of us as the light dimmed and our eyes adjusted. "Wanderers are always seeking something. Whatever you are seeking, your search is over. You have found it. Or, I should say, you have found *him.*"

Finally we were able to see the man clearly. And without having seen him before, looking into the unfamiliar face suddenly familiar, I knew that he was the High King.

PART FOUR

IN THE PALACE OF THE HIGH KING

THE HIGH KING

He was dressed in plain brocade with embroidered cuffs. Tall and straight in stature, the High King was nearly half a head taller than Danein. He had a short, dark beard, and a circlet of gold, shaped in the form of a vine, lay on his head. It had golden leaves and pointy protrusions, like thorns, hanging from it.

"Welcome, Alonya. Welcome, Danein: children of Zaphon."

A sense of elation washed over me, and I felt weightless as though my troubles were over for a time. My heart beat heavily in my chest, yet I could not tell whether it was due to fear or excitement. I just knew that something was happening. Something had changed, and there was no going back. This was no ordinary person before us.

I clutched Danein's hand as we stood mute. The man before us smiled gently, looking back and forth between us. Although the light had dimmed and was no longer blinding us, we yet basked in a glow that seemed to radiate from within the High King. But the longer I watched him, the more he became like an ordinary man. Or perhaps Danein and I had been so enveloped by the radiance that it no longer seemed extraordinary after a while.

Finally the High King nodded at us, said "Follow me," and turned. Danein instinctively moved forward and took me with him. I kept my eyes on the High King and therefore saw little of our surroundings. I faintly registered that we were walking through a maze of stone corridors. The passageway down which we traversed finally opened up into a large hall of gleaming marble hung with portraits and elaborate tapestries. Although it had been nighttime outside just minutes ago, light poured in from high vertical windows along one wall, revealing bouquets of flowers in large glass vases that sat on tables beneath the windows. At one end of the hall were wide steps that led to a dais, upon which sat a throne upholstered with red velvet cushions. Two sets of polished carven pillars ran the length of the hall, one set on either side, going from the throne to a double archway covered with a curtain that led out of the room.

The High King swept his hand out as we passed through, only allowing the briefest stop to gaze at the room before moving on again. "This is the throne room—a place for general meeting and council."

As we followed the High King through the immense room, I caught sight of the massive woven tapestries covering two adjacent walls. There were four of them, each depicting a different living being beautiful in form, gentle of countenance, and regal in bearing. One showed a man as though sitting for a portrait, another a lion as though stalking prey, a third an ox pulling a plow and threshing grain underfoot, and the last an eagle in flight.

My eyes lingered on these tapestries until we were through the archway and down another corridor toward another room. This one was smaller but had the same tall ceiling painted with murals of various designs and colors. Many other archways opened up from the room, leading to more corridors and chambers. Each door was tall and ornately carved with depictions of gardens or fairies or other magical creatures. The tiled floor was covered with a large woven, patterned rug. Tables standing on elaborately carved legs and inlaid with gold sat along the walls and in the corners with vases of flowers or other ornaments on them. One larger table sat in the middle of the room, directly in front of a massive grand staircase.

"This is the entrance hall," the High King said. "The center of the palace. Every chamber in the palace can be accessed from here."

I was nearly speechless with the opulence of it all. What had happened to the dark wooden hut we had entered just minutes ago? I was dizzy with bewilderment in the strange dream, for it did seem like a dream; the only real, solid thing I knew was the warm press of Danein's hand in mine.

The High King motioned with his hand as he continued to walk before us. "Come this way." We followed obediently up the grand staircase, down several more corridors carpeted with rugs and lined with tapestries, and finally stopped outside two large wooden double doors. The High King turned to look at us, and with a very pleased smile, he pushed on one of the wooden doors. It opened into an expansive library with polished floors and gilded walls. The ceiling rose several feet in the air, and shelves like mountains of books reached up just as high. Tables, chairs, benches, and other furniture were spread out in several places throughout the room. The High King led us to a corner with two upholstered reclining sofas and motioned us to sit. Danein and I sat together on one while the High King sat adjacent to us on the other.

"I imagine you are filled with questions," he said after a brief pause to let us gain our bearings.

I nodded while Danein replied, "What we've seen here is a great mystery. My mind is still grappling with it."

The man before us chuckled. His smile was beautiful and radiant. It seemed to me he was full of age and wisdom, yet his skin appeared smooth beneath his beard, untouched by age. His eyes were a rich brown speckled with bits of blue and green and purple and other colors, so that they were one and many colors at the same time.

"Sir," I finally piped up, "if you don't mind me asking, where are we?"

"You are in my palace: the palace of the High King."

"Yes, but…we entered through the door of a little woodland cabin. Did it disappear? Did we get transported to some other place?"

"The cabin did not disappear. It is still there, though you are not."

Danein and I exchanged glances. When our faces still registered confusion, the king elaborated. "Think of the cabin as a doorway. It led you here, to my palace, which is not located in any particular place or time. It is everywhere. There are doorways all throughout the Lands of the Seven Kingdoms. The doorways can only be seen and found by those who are seeking, by those who know how to look."

"Was it magic then?"

"Everything wondrous to behold that stirs the heart is magic, Alonya. The melody of a song, the beauty of a flower, or the intricacies of a spider's web—all these can be magical."

Now that I sat in the presence of the High King, a compulsion urged me to speak. I recalled my conversation with Nona about magic. She had dismissed my notion that magic had originated with the High King, saying it came only from the earth. I hadn't known until then how bothered I'd been by the idea—how, despite the opposition I'd faced, I had longed to see evidence of the High King in my life and in the world around me. Perhaps that's what my journey had been about all along. And here it had led me.

"Sir, what exactly is magic? We see so little of it in Zaphon."

"It is a resource given to the earth and its creatures. And, like most resources, it gets exploited. Magic can be used for good or ill, and there are those who would manipulate it and use magic for their own evil, selfish purposes."

"Because it is so powerful?"

"Yes, and it is a great temptation for men and beasts alike to hold power over their fellow creation. They use the power that's been given them to usurp my authority and set themselves up as kings and gods to be revered."

I thought of the fruit and the merrow pool in the Wild Lands. I would have used the magic of the earth for my own selfish purposes. It all seemed so silly and trivial at that moment. I should have known better. I did know better, but I had ignored the warning tug in my heart and moved along despite it. As though a beam of light was falling on me and exposing my failures, I felt suddenly sheepish in the presence of the High King.

The High King went on, eyeing me closely. "And then there are those who don't desire what I've given them. They do not acknowledge me, and so they are blind to the magic all around them."

Yes, I thought. *I was one such person. Danein and Taralyn helped me to see.*

"Only those with eyes to see can see the magic," he continued.

It was an echo of what Danein had shown me that night in the wood before the Colony had been raided. I nodded, tempests of emotions battling within me. The king watched me as though waiting for me to speak, but I merely turned my face away. He frowned.

"What troubles you, Alonya?"

I shook my head, longing to speak but unable to. How could I bear my soul to this man, blackened as it was?

Silence permeated the air around us, though the passing moments seemed to tick loudly in my ears. The king was being patient, waiting for me to speak, yet I couldn't. I braved a look at him. There he sat, watching me with his soft, fathomless eyes.

"Alonya, you will soon learn that there is nothing you can hide from me. Your soul is not blackened as you think, nor is your heart evil. I have washed you clean. I am in the business of making all things new. Do you believe this?"

Knowing he saw me as I was, and yet did not condemn me, freed me to speak. "I want to believe it, sir."

His face broke into a smile. "Well then, that is why you are here. That is why you have sought me from the beginning and why your search has finally led you here, through the doorway, to my palace."

I nodded, though I was still mystified by it all. "So we are no longer on Haven Island?"

"In here you are not. When Danein goes out through the doorway in which you came, he will once again be on Haven Island."

"When Danein goes?" I said, glancing between Danein and the High King. Danein stared fixedly at the placid face of the king but said nothing. "Do you mean to say that…that…"

"You know what it is you have to do, my daughter. Danein knows too. He knows that for a time you are meant to stay here to be in my presence and learn my ways."

I moved forward to the edge of the sofa. "But…why must Danein go? Can't he do those things too?"

Danein remained speechless. His gaze had fallen to his lap, yet his eyes were serious, his countenance resolute. The High King smiled and shook his head.

"Danein already knows me. He has brought you to me, which was part of his task. Now his task is finished, and there is no need for him to stay."

I turned toward Danein beside me. Tears pooled in my eyes. "I don't want you to leave me."

Danein sighed and put his hands on mine. The High King stood to leave. "I will give you some time to share good-byes."

He swept past us, across the large library and out the double doors. They closed behind him with a thud. For several moments, neither Danein nor I spoke. My throat was tight with emotion, and the silence between us hung thick like the damask curtains lining the windows. For my part, I was hesitant to begin speaking, as though I might delay the inevitable by keeping silent.

Finally, Danein spoke first. "I knew that if we found the High King, I would have to leave you with him."

I nodded. "I believe in my heart, I knew it too."

"I am at peace leaving you to the keeping of the High King. My aim has been to protect you, and there is no safer place to be than here."

"For how long?" I asked, knowing it was a fruitless question.

"I don't know. For as long as the High King wills."

"When will I see you again?"

Danein seemed to break with those words. I watched his face tremble as he tried to withhold the tide of emotion that surged forth. He lifted a hand to my head and gently stroked my hair. "I don't know when we will see each other again, but I know for a certainty that we will."

I couldn't help myself; I let a tear slip, and then another. "It seems a cruel fate to have to be parted from you after waiting so long to find you." My voice broke and I fell into Danein's arms, sobbing.

"Alonya," he whispered. "Be comforted knowing that wherever I am, and however long we are parted, I love you, and that will not change."

"How can you be sure?"

He continued to hold me, and I could feel the beat of his heart against my cheek. "Because I've chosen you. There will be no other for me as long as I live, Alonya."

I watched Danein leave out the door by which we'd come. The wood was aglow with the fresh, promising light of early morning—a new day. Danein hadn't embraced me or kissed me or said any other parting words. He had merely looked at me, smiled, and then turned to walk away. My heart cried out within me. I longed to run after him. I scuffled forward a bit but held tightly onto the wooden frames of the doorway. Until that moment, I thought I'd experienced the most difficult trials that life offered. Watching Danein leave me was the biggest blow I'd yet encountered. Despite what he'd told me in the library, a venomous fear rose up inside and began to spread throughout my heart, whispering to me that I'd never see or hold Danein again.

"I will not tell you what is to come, child," said a voice behind me. I wiped my tears and turned to see the High King. "I can only tell you to hope and to trust. It will not let you down. *I* will not let you down. Nor will Danein."

I turned back to the woodland view before me. Danein had disappeared. "Anything could happen," I said with a sigh. "Where will he go? What will he do?"

"He will go on doing what he was doing before."

Then a bitter thought struck me. Until the raiders had come to the Colony to kidnap the women, Danein had been working steadily on his mission to help unchosens for years. Then I had come along and had essentially pulled him away from that. As I was one of his charges, he had felt responsible for me after I'd gone missing and was compelled to find me. Despite his personal feelings, he had been merely doing his duty by me in helping bring me to safety. Now that I was here, he was free to continue the life he'd had before I came along.

With that thought my heart seemed to squeeze within me, suffocating my life, and I slid to the floor, weeping. After several moments, I felt a body next to mine and a hand on my shoulder.

"Alonya, it wasn't despite his feelings that he helped you, but because of them. Do not give any room for wayward thoughts to slither into your heart. They will only poison you and blind you to the truth."

I met his gaze with my red-rimmed eyes. "How do you know my thoughts?"

"A true king knows his subjects, inside and out. Everything is mine, and there is nothing that can be hidden from me."

And then, in the presence of that great man, shame replaced the fear. My thoughts and beliefs about the High King had wavered so in all my years of life, and yet he had always been there, knowing me and watching me. A sudden conviction crashed and swept over me, and I lowered my head. "I'm sorry," I said, unsure what else to say, yet feeling it was enough. "I'm sorry."

"And that, my child, is where it begins." He raised me to my feet, took my hand, and led me back inside to the palace.

DOORWAYS

I was brought to my bedchamber—a luxurious, majestic apartment with several separate rooms and a small library—and tended to before being left to sleep. The room was suffused in gentle candlelight. Thick, dark curtains covered the immense windows along the far wall. I pulled one aside and peeked out to see bright light shining down on a large garden dominated by lawns, flower beds, and groves. The garden was enclosed on all sides by other walls and wings of the palace, though it was so large it was difficult for me to see far across to the opposite side. Above was a clear blue sky. Yet I'd just come from an area where night had fallen; my body was still weary and my feet sore from walking most of the afternoon. I let the curtains drop, extinguishing the shaft of light beaming into the room, and made my way to the four-poster bed. I didn't bother to change out of my traveling dress as I pulled back the gauzy muslin drapes and crawled into the thick downy covers. I was almost instantly asleep.

I had no sense of time when I awoke, nor during the following weeks as I went throughout my days. The light from outside the window was ever present as though it was never nighttime. Yet the palace ran on a strict schedule of meals, lessons, free time, and rest; and so the days passed.

Attendants helped me with my wardrobe every morning, dressing me as royalty in richer clothing than I had ever worn—soft cotton chemises and finely embroidered gowns of velvet, silk brocade, and cotton. I joined the other guests in the palace for a meal before moving on to a group lecture or lesson with either the High King himself presiding or one of his representatives—usually an advanced student who had been at the palace a long while under his tutelage. After the midday meal was a time of private study and rest followed by supper and evening festivities, during which the palace guests would participate in readings, recitations, games, and musical or dramatic performances.

I spent at least half an hour every other day in the presence of the High King, just the two of us. Sometimes we would converse as we walked along the palace corridors or in the garden. At other times we spoke little or not at all, instead sharing companionship through quiet reading in the library or fruit picking in the garden orchards. Often the king would do the speaking and I would listen as he related old tales of the history of mankind in the Lands of the Seven Kingdoms.

The palace was expansive; the greatest portion of my days was dedicated to wandering, exploring, and speaking with others that I met. Every day I saw new faces and met new people, and just when I thought I had traversed the entire palace, I would discover a new, unknown wing or chamber. The sprawling garden situated in the center seemed to be the only outdoor region. The doorways to the outside world were along the outer perimeters of the palace, and from time to time, a new person would arrive or leave. But no one who was a guest at the palace would come and go frequently. No one, that is, except Marcus Du'Karafin.

My stay had lasted several weeks at that point; it would have been difficult not to notice the tall man with hair and trimmed beard the color of soft sunset and eyes gray as granite. I'd not spoken to him, but I had often crossed paths with him. He was one of the main speakers during our lessons, so I knew he had been with the High King a while. I would often find him sitting alone in some corner of the library or garden, or see him walking along, hands clasped to his mouth as in deep thought or prayer. While many of the palace guests congregated in group socials or games during free times, Marcus remained aloof. He spoke little during meals. And despite everyone at the palace being dressed finely, Marcus stood out from them. He wore his clothing with dignity and ease, as though he was used to wearing such fine things. His mannerisms were of high breeding and training. Something inexplicably drew me to him, and I longed to speak with him.

In hopes of gaining an audience with him one evening after supper, I followed him down several corridors leading away from the entrance hall. I knew he was heading toward the "outside" doors. He didn't slow or stop or look around. He walked straight on at a steady, determined pace. I kept my distance and finally stopped where two corridors intersected. I watched from around the corner as Marcus moved straight toward a door, pushed it open, and walked out, closing the door behind him. I stared at it for a long moment until curiosity propelled me down the passageway toward the door. I pushed on it, but it didn't budge. I looked for a handle to pull it open, but there was none. I put my ear to the door and listened, but only silence and the cold press of the wood on my skin answered.

"You cannot go through that door, Alonya."

I jumped at the High King's voice behind me and spun around, clutching my chest. "You have a way of sneaking up on a person," I said.

"I tend to know what goes on all over the palace," he explained with a smile, approaching me. "Don't think of it so much as me sneaking up on you, as me just always being present."

I motioned toward the door. "Why can't I go through?"

"It's not the door by which you came. You cannot go except by that door, nor can anybody else come and go except by the door in which they came the first time."

I nodded in understanding. "Was it all right for him to leave like that?"

"Of course. No one is a prisoner here."

"Will he be back?"

"Yes."

"So I can leave if I want to—by my door, the door on Haven Island?"

The king lowered his head and narrowed his eyes jovially. "Do you want to?"

I almost laughed. "No, not exactly."

He offered his arm, and I took it as he turned and led me back to the interior of the palace. "Everything you need is here. There will come a day when you will go just for a visit back to the world, and then you will return. You will come and go as you please. Then one day you will go, and when you try to return, you will not find the palace again."

"What?" I gave a small tug on his arm. He continued to walk but looked down at me tenderly with his clear, speckled eyes.

"You will not need to return. Your time with me will be over, and though you will not see me, it doesn't mean you won't be in my presence."

I shook my head, filled with a sudden melancholy. "I don't understand."

"You will," he said, squeezing my hand. "In time you will understand."

We made it back to the entrance hall. The High King let go of my arm, bowed, then turned to leave.

"Who is he?" I asked, still thinking of Marcus.

There was a glint in the king's eyes. "Why don't you ask him the next time you see him?"

"Well, he's somebody important, that's for certain."

"Alonya, everybody here is important."

When next I saw Marcus, it had been nearly a week. He was in his usual nook in the library, sitting in the alcove of a tall bay window that overlooked the gardens down below. He was reading, his knees drawn up with a book resting on them.

"Hello," I said tentatively as I approached. He looked up, blinked several times, and smiled.

"Hello there."

"I'm sorry to disturb you."

"Not at all. I'm always eager to meet a fellow guest here at the palace."

I nearly snorted. He wrinkled his brows.

"Did I say something funny?"

"I'm sorry. It's just—you keep to yourself a lot. I wouldn't imagine that you cared to meet many people or keep much company."

His eyes widened at that; he took a deep breath and let it out in a prolonged sigh. "Yes, I suppose you're right. You've learned my secret." He smiled and gestured for me to join him in the window seat. He swung his legs down to make room. "I must admit, I seek solace because, where I'm from, I'm constantly surrounded by people. It is not from a desire to dissociate myself from common people that I keep aloof."

"Common people?" I asked. "As opposed to uncommon people?"

He laughed at himself. "I apologize. As you can see, I still have a lot to learn, which is why I'm here. I'm trying to rid myself of all vestiges of conceit."

"And why, in your former life, were you taken to such conceit?"

He hesitated for a long moment, seemingly unwilling to divulge too much information. "Unfortunate personality trait," he said finally, "given to nobles and royals."

My heart leaped inside me. My suspicion had been confirmed. "So you're a noble?" I asked.

His smile widened as he stared at me. "Here I'm not."

I grinned, but it seemed clear he was not going to elaborate. "So how long have you been a guest in the High King's palace?"

He frowned. "I can't rightly recall. It's been so long."

"And what keeps you away for days on end?"

He gave me another grin. "Oh, business at home. Things I need to tend to."

"I apologize," I said, stepping down from the window seat. "I'm prying."

"You don't have to go. It *is* nice to speak with someone for a change."

"I can understand wanting to hide who you are," I said. "I've done it most of my life."

He looked at me a long while, his countenance thoughtful. "I'm Marcus," he finally said.

"Alonya."

"Where do you come from, Alonya?"

I again sat next to him. "Zaphon. And you?"

"Coralind."

I straightened up and turned toward him. "Coralind? Truly?"

He chuckled, noting my enthusiasm. "Yes. What is so fascinating about that?"

"It's Coralind! The center of the world. The seat of magic and of the High King."

"Yes, well, as you can see, we're both at the High King's palace now, and it's not in Coralind."

"Yes, but Coralind! I have always longed to see it. My friend, Danein, and I were on our way to Coralind to seek out the High King before we found the hut on Haven Island with the door leading here."

"Is your friend here now?"

I looked at my hands. "No, he couldn't stay. He only meant to bring me here. Now he's gone."

Marcus's eyes were soft and understanding. "He did a good thing."

"Tell me, Marcus—is there an unchosen law in Coralind?"

His brow wrinkled. "An unchosen law?"

"Yes—a law that brands a woman unchosen if she is unmarried and unclaimed by male relatives?"

"No, we don't have such a law, although I have heard of it. It's barbaric, if you ask me."

"I am an unchosen," I admitted.

"No, you're not. Not here, anyway. Here the outside laws don't apply, only the laws of the High King."

"Danein and I are hoping to eventually appeal to the king of Zaphon to get the law abolished."

Marcus seemed to consider for a moment. "Well, perhaps I can help you with that."

"You? How can you help?"

"I've got some standing of influence in Coralind," he said with a glint in his eye and a furtive smile. "I've dealt in international trade and politics. I have connections in many places around the world. I'm sure I could think of something to help you and your friend on your mission."

I eyed him quizzically. "Even as a noble, what kind of man has enough influence to affect foreign policy from across the world?"

He winked at me. "A prince."

I lost my voice momentarily. "You…you're a prince?"

"Here I'm not, but out there I am."

"You're the prince of Coralind?"

He laughed. "Yes. Now you can understand what keeps me away for days on end. I have national affairs to tend to. There are, in fact, three kings in Coralind, each ruling a separate territory, and my father is only one of them, but one king just died childless and the other has only an infant daughter, so right now, I am the heir of all of Coralind until the girl grows up and marries."

I stared at him incredulously. Here I was, sitting and speaking with a noble—a prince! And in the house of the High King, we were equals. I felt neither the jitter of nerves nor any feelings of inferiority as I had on the outside.

When I didn't speak, Marcus went on. "So between my learning here at the palace and national affairs at home, I have been busy." He sighed, and his eyes moved away from me and fixed on some faraway spot. "I can sense my time here coming to a close. I will miss it, but I feel better equipped now to lead and rule my people. I was never strong like that before."

"What were you like before?"

"Oh, I was silly and vain and selfish." He chuckled suddenly, as though at himself. "I tried to force a woman to marry me once. I thought she would say yes of her own accord, but when it was clear she wouldn't, I locked her up and threatened her."

"You didn't!"

"I did!"

"But why?"

He shrugged. "I thought I loved her. I was momentarily infatuated. However, there was a curse on me that could only be broken by love, and so I tried to orchestrate the breaking of my curse by trapping the woman. It didn't work."

"What happened to her?"

Splinters of sunlight shone through the window, and Marcus held up his hand to one, watching the light play on his fingertips. "She loved another, and she escaped with his help. They were on their own mission, you see, and I had the privilege of joining up with them to aid them later in their quest. Then she went back to her own land, and I never saw her again. It was shortly after that that I sought the High King for myself."

I took a moment to absorb all his words. "That's a great story, Marcus."

He looked at me, doubtful. "Is it? I always feel rather sheepish to think I was such a man."

"I think you must've cared for her a little to help her in the end. And you let her go, which was right. Ultimately it led you to the High King. So you see, there was purpose in everything."

"I know I am not that man anymore, and I am grateful for it." Marcus then fixed his attention fully on me. "And what about you, Alonya? You call yourself an unchosen. Yet you have a friend called Danein whom you have been traveling with, and whom I am sure isn't only a *friend*."

I squirmed under his gaze, never intending the conversation to fall on me. "Well, Danein has confessed that he cares for me, but now that I'm here and don't know how long I'll be here, I wonder if Danein will still love me when I see him again. He says he will, but it's difficult for me at times to trust a man's word. People are weak and inconsistent. Their minds change easily."

Marcus nodded in understanding but said nothing.

"And anyway, as long as a woman is a certain age and unmarried in Zaphon—which I am—she *is* an unchosen by law. So I still feel like an unchosen, though in my heart I know I'm not and that the law is wrong."

Marcus leaned in close and lowered his voice to near a whisper. "Well, let me tell you this, Alonya. None of that matters here. Believing yourself an unchosen is only going to weaken you, and I sense that there's going to be a time when you'll have to stand against that. Whether Danein loves you or not is irrelevant because it's the High King who will show you who you really are, and that's what you must believe."

I nodded, knowing he was right, knowing that was why I was there, knowing I might never see Danein again—might never have him hold me or hear him tell me he loves me—but realizing that was also part of the journey—giving him up for something greater, some bigger purpose that I didn't know at the time and couldn't see then but had to trust was there. There would be a time for Danein's love, but it wasn't then. That was the hardest thing to accept.

It was difficult at the beginning to let him go. I spent many nights crying into my pillows for loneliness, for the ache of desiring my own earthly love, for the pain of having something so close to me torn away. No matter how I missed him or ached for him, he wasn't there with me, and he wasn't coming. I had to learn how to live without him, how to live in the waiting and in the meantime.

The days passed into weeks; the cycles of the moon came and went. I soon advanced in my studies and came into the service of the High King as a lady-in-waiting. My lessons became less frequent. I tended to other new guests in the palace as I had been tended to and still was. Once again, I found a simple satisfaction in being useful and in serving, yet I was no longer working merely for myself, trying to hide behind my usefulness or trying to find safety and security in it, and that made the difference. There was purpose in knowing that I was working for the High King, that he saw everything I did, that he knew my work and praised me for it.

And so the time passed, and so I lived in the palace. Winter arrived in the outside world, soon followed by summer, and then another winter; and though I did eventually learn to stop thinking so much of Danein and to stop inadvertently waiting for him, I never truly forgot him.

BEAUTIFUL

Time was a vague, insubstantial thing in the realm of the High King, like a mist that slips through your fingers and dissipates when you try to grab it. I lost track of time in the palace, and it was often difficult for me to remember that the outside world existed at all. Even when I was given leave to visit Haven Island, I never did. I never forgot what the king had told me: how one day while in the outside world, when I tried to return to the palace, I would not find it. In my heart I wanted to stay always. I was safe there, and comfortable, and at home. I knew the outside world couldn't offer me that. Even the idea of one day meeting Danein again wasn't a strong-enough temptation for me to go through the door. Though I often thought of him and wished him well, a part of me believed I would never see him again, and I reconciled myself to that.

Yet I knew, like Marcus, that one day I *would* have to leave the palace, and so I tried to relish every day as though it might be the last.

I was sitting on an upholstered stool near my bed one morning as a chambermaid dressed my hair when there came a soft knock at the door. The maid moved across the room to answer it while I inspected the stitching on my gown to pass the time.

"May I come in?"

I turned at the High King's voice to see the chambermaid kneeling with bowed head as the king strode into the room. I stood in his presence and bowed my head likewise.

"Good morning, Your Majesty," I said, surprised at such an early visit.

"How are you this morning, Alonya?"

"Very well, sir. Thank you."

The chambermaid crossed the room quickly to open the curtains further and straighten the covers on the bed. While she bustled along in the background, the High King bid me sit and pulled up a chair for himself next to my stool. He settled himself comfortably and watched me for several moments before speaking, as was his custom.

"Alonya, have you been happy here in my palace?"

"Yes, sir," I replied with a frown, confused at the question.

He nodded, a satisfied smile gracing his lips. "Yes, you have learned much and grown much while here. Yet I sense a lingering doubt and melancholy in your heart."

"Doubt, sir?" I shook my head furiously. "No, no, I do not doubt you—"

He held up a hand. "That is not what I mean, Alonya. I know you do not doubt *me*. I am referring to you. You still doubt yourself in many ways, and though you say you enjoy living at the palace, I know much of that is fueled by fear."

"How do you mean, sir?"

He threw a question back at me in answer. "Why is it you never go through the doorway to Haven Island? Why do you never visit the outside world?"

I put my head down and stared at my hands in my lap. "Sir, you know why."

"I would like to hear it from you."

"I…I don't know. I suppose I'm afraid of being left on my own again, of being abandoned. I am afraid if I leave, I won't be able to find you again."

"You have to understand, Alonya, that whenever you leave my palace, I will go with you. My love and my wisdom will guide you, and you will always be able to find me if you seek me with all your heart. I don't only reside in this palace, you know."

"I don't understand, sir."

"You will. For now, let me assure you that the day you leave is not today. It is yet a short while off and…"—he paused until I looked up at him—"none of your concern. You will miss what you are to do here and now if you continually run ahead to see around the bend at every turn of what will be."

"Yes, sir."

There was another long pause before the king spoke again. "I know you fear what the outside world holds for you, but my palace cannot merely be a hiding place for you, Alonya."

"Oh, sir, it's not."

"I hope not. There is still much in you that is unsettled, despite your time here." He sighed and sat up, hands resting on his knees. He took a moment to let his eyes sweep the room before they rested on me once more. The chambermaid had ceased her frenetic movements and was now standing silently by the door, attending us.

"So, Alonya," the High King began again, "we have never spoken of that thing very close to your heart, and it is now time."

"What thing?"

"Come now, Alonya. You know of what I speak."

Once again, I lowered my eyes like a child being chastised. "How I've always wished to be beautiful?"

The king nodded. I shrunk under his gaze, but he laughed at me.

"You are not the only woman who desires such a thing. All women long to be beautiful. It is part of how they are made."

I said nothing, waiting for him to continue.

"What is beauty, Alonya? Is it merely being pleasing to the eye?"

"No, sir," I said, though I knew I had always treated beauty as such.

"Worthwhile beauty goes much deeper than being pleasing to the eye and involves a pleasant and contented heart, one that delights in the truth. To love another selflessly, and to know you are loved selflessly by another, helps develop this beauty." The High King cocked his head toward me with a grin. "I know of at least one person—though truly there are more—who loves you selflessly, and his love has already begun its work in you."

My face warmed at the obvious allusion to Danein. "But he's been gone so long."

"He is mine—as you are—and he'll return."

The king stood and made his way to the corner of the room where a full-length looking glass sat neglected in the corner of the room, a white sheet draped clumsily across it. The king grasped a corner of the sheet and pulled it off with a flourish, letting loose a cloud of dust that floated slowly down to the floor as it settled.

The king motioned to the mirror. "In the meantime, please take a look in the glass."

"Sir?"

"Do as I say, Alonya."

I rose from my seat slowly and took tentative steps toward the corner. Though I admit I had thought little of beauty while at the palace due to preoccupation with my many studies and duties, the habit of avoiding mirrors was still ingrained in me. I inhaled deeply and swallowed a lump in my throat before stepping in front of the looking glass.

I looked at the glass itself first. It was large and oval-shaped, framed in polished, carven wood and set upon a stand. I then looked at my image in the glass, starting at my feet, letting my eyes slowly drift upward to the hem and bodice of my gown. Yes, my clothes were nice, I knew that much. My figure didn't look entirely unbecoming in the cut and style of the gown.

"Look at your face, Alonya."

I turned to him in appeal, but he gave me a firm look, so I returned to the mirror. I bit back tears and my heart hammered in my chest as I forced my eyes to travel up the reflection of my neck, then above my chin to my nose and finally my eyes.

My eyes. They seemed different.

I let my eyes roam the rest of my face, wondering who was staring back at me. Was it truly me? I took a step forward and reached out as though to catch the imposter, but the reflection moved just as I did, reaching a hand back toward me. I stopped. The image in the mirror stopped. I frowned. So did she.

She was pretty. The hair was the same as mine. The body shape was the same. The face was even the same, yet somehow different—more elegant, graceful, and lovely.

"Is that me?" I finally asked.

"It is you, Alonya."

"What did you do, sir?" After all my futile attempts to make myself beautiful through magic, had the High King done it himself?

"Me?" He laughed—a sweet, warm-hearted laugh that seemed to reverberate from the high-arched ceiling. I relaxed immediately. He went on. "I did nothing. You've always looked that way. But do not forget that beauty is more than what is pleasing to the eye. You have sought truth and trusted in me, and now your eyes are opened to see not only what is pleasing to the eye, but what is pleasing to the heart." He stood behind me as I continued to gape at myself, and he lowered his voice to a gentle whisper. "Alonya, the king is enthralled by your beauty."

I smiled and wiped a tear from my cheek.

He made to leave but turned around at the door to address me once more. "Now tell me: why are you here, Alonya?"

It was the first time he asked me that, and I thought the answer was obvious, especially considering how long I'd been there. "Well, I am here to find sanctuary from the unchosen laws in Zaphon."

"Yes, but what else?"

I looked again at my reflection in the mirror. "To see myself as you do."

He nodded. "And?"

I inhaled deeply and shook my head. "I'm not sure I know."

"To learn what it means to live—to go forth and do my work in the world. You are meant to be my hands and feet to the people, to be the reflection of my glory; only then will you find the greatest reward."

The beginnings of a fire stirred in me at those words, a hope for what I might do to help other women like me. "What is your work for me, sir? I will gladly do it."

"I think you know, Alonya, for it is already in your heart."

I thought of his words when he said his love and wisdom would guide me when I left the palace. "And you'll be there too, sir?"

"I will. I've already gone before you. It's why everything has happened the way it has."

After that, I visited with the High King for lessons less frequently. I knew that my stay at the palace was coming to an end. I don't know how I knew; I suppose I sensed it the way Marcus had.

I did learn to venture out to Haven Island. I needed to, to fortify my trust in the High King. I went for walks in the woods and sometimes visited the village and watched the ships dancing on the waves in the harbor. Often I would bring myself a picnic meal from the palace stores and find an outcropping of rock near the harbor on which to sit and enjoy my repast alone. When I was back in the outside world, my thoughts strayed more towards Danein. I wondered how much time had passed since I'd last seen him. I wasn't rightly sure. From the looks of things on Haven

Island—the movement of sailors along the docks and shoppers along the dirt roads through town, the calls and whistles from the ships in harbor, the cries of gulls circling above, and the flight of wispy clouds across the sky—it could have been only yesterday that I was with Danein when we had gone wandering off to find the small cabin in the woods.

I often sighed at the remembrance of him, though in my heart I was fulfilled in knowing he had loved me. In my mind, my future with Danein remained uncertain. I knew I had to make choices for my life apart from him, so I had been considering what I ought to do. I knew that somehow, someway, I would fight for the rights of unchosens in Zaphon. I would return to my country and spend the rest of my life if need be working toward justice in Zaphon.

At times I grew so fervent in this new passion of mine that impatience plagued me. Though I once feared being unable to return to the palace after an outing, I began to endure a small stab of disappointment every time the small woodland cabin came into view through the brambles off the main path. I would smile and laugh at myself while the High King's voice in my head reminded me that all things happened at their proper time. As soon as I returned after one particular outing, he was waiting just inside the door with a jovial gleam in his eye, arms crossed, to greet me with, "In due time, Alonya. In due time."

"I know," I answered. "I feel more ready than ever to rejoin the world and take my proper place in it."

"You are ready, Alonya," the High King told me to my surprise and delight. "You lack only one thing."

I frowned. "What's that?"

He put his hands behind his back, gestured with a flick of his head for me to follow him, and turned to walk down the corridor back into the palace proper. I sidled up alongside him. "You seem to think you're meant to walk your path in the world alone, Alonya."

"No, sir. I know you'll be with me as you are everywhere at all times."

"That is true, though that is not to what I refer."

"Then what, sir?"

He smiled and swept ahead of me quickly. "You'll see," he said, soon disappearing around the corner and out of sight.

I saw it in a dream that night. Danein was in the throne room before the king of Zaphon. I watched as though a spectator, hiding discreetly behind a pillar in the back of the room. The conversation was indistinguishable at first but soon became clearer. I found that I, too, had somehow come nearer, so that I was standing just behind Danein, facing the king of Zaphon.

Though I had never seen the man, I knew who he was. He was little and fat, commanding an attitude and claiming a power that was far bigger than him. In his hand was a large, glowing scepter made of the power and authority that didn't rightly belong to him. It brought pain to his hand and weighed him down so that he eventually set it across the lap of his throne, though his white fist still grasped the thing tightly.

I whispered Danein's name, but he went on speaking to the ruler of Zaphon, heedless of my presence behind him. And though I looked into the eyes of the king on the throne, he didn't see me.

Then I finally heard Danein speak, and what he said nearly stopped my heart, though it was but a dream.

"And what if a man wishes to marry an unchosen woman?"

The king leered and chuckled. "A man needn't marry an unchosen woman in order to take her."

"You misunderstand me, sir. What if a man desires to marry an unchosen woman, out of love?"

The king stroked his round cheek in thought, peering carefully at Danein. "Well, I suppose there is no law against it, although it is rather rare as I understand. Men who marry unchosen women rarely do for love. Many are widowers who are in need of a woman to run the household, to raise the children. I would call those women lucky. That's the best an unchosen woman can hope for."

Danein shook his head. "You're wrong, sir."

The king leaned forward on his throne, his scepter suddenly brightening as the room seemed to grow darker. Shadows cast on the king's face gave him a devilish look. "You dare to contradict me, man?"

Danein went on, undaunted. "I love such a woman and desire to marry her. It is not of her making that no man chose her before I did. It was not a curse, as she supposes. It was a matter of course and timing. She didn't come into my life until she was meant to, and that just happened to be when she became an unchosen according to law. But in my heart she was never unchosen." Danein's motions became more demonstrative as he spoke his passion. "Sir, how can you say, based on arbitrary conditions out of one's control such as a woman's age, that a person's life is not valuable? Why should a woman be any less desirable or worthy at thirty years than at twenty? When you place such conditions on a woman's life, you condemn her prematurely, before she's been given a proper chance. For such people, you stunt the growth of their lives. We need to help the people who need help, not use them and exploit them!"

"How dare you question my authority and my governance!" the king shouted.

"You have only as much authority as the High King allows, and he can take that away in an instant!"

With that, the light in the king's scepter went out suddenly, and my vision disappeared. I woke up with a start and sat up in bed. Perspiration had dampened my forehead. I flung my covers off and stood, my mind whirling with the vision I'd seen. I went to the basin on the table near my bed and drew some water. I drank half of it and used the rest to soak a cloth and wipe my brow. I paced the room, trying to make sense of what I'd seen. Why had the High King given me the vision? I thought of his words to me earlier that day, about thinking I was meant to walk my path in life alone. In my dream Danein had been before the king of Zaphon, appealing to him, as I knew he'd done in the past. Danein had fought for the rights of unchosens, just as I hoped to do once I left the palace. In the dream, he was also asking permission to marry one. Is that what all this had been about—all my time and training at the High King's palace—about joining Danein in his work?

It seemed too much to hope for, and despite myself my heart seemed to inflate as hope rose in my breast. In all the time I'd been away from Danein, I had learned and resolved to live without him, but it seemed he had not resolved to live without me.

I was glad of it.

PART FIVE

A New Quest

REUNION

I stood at the familiar spot as I had many times before while the red-orange forest canopy swayed above me, moving with the motion of the sea breeze off the coast. It was quiet that mid-autumn day but for the rustling of the trees. Scurrying squirrels were busy at work gathering and storing for the oncoming winter. I stepped lightly across the ground, which was thickly carpeted with fallen leaves that crunched underfoot. Though I knew the place, it had changed. I had changed.

When I was certain of my location, I dropped my sack, in which were the remains of my midday meal, and sat down atop a short stump. I stared at the spot where the cabin had been; it was no longer there. My doorway had finally closed. I would not return to the palace.

My sense of adventure and expectation for this moment had fled from me. Instead, a weight of sorrow descended upon me. I hadn't thought it would be so difficult, that I would grieve. Although I knew I was going forward into new adventures and that I wouldn't be alone, I was again facing the loss of a life I'd known for so long, a good life I was sorry to see pass, though I knew in my heart that its loss was the seed from which another good season in my life would grow.

And so I let myself grieve without shame. At first tears came, warm and silent, flowing down my cheeks and falling onto my hands in my lap. Once the tears were spent, I merely sat where I was and thought. I stayed in the wood all afternoon and into the early evening, recalling the time I'd spent at the High King's palace, as immeasurable as that time was, and trying to fix my mind on all I'd learned. I knew I would need it for the coming days. The High King had promised I wouldn't be alone, but he hadn't promised that my road would be easy or that I would not have difficulties or experience sorrow from time to time.

Hours went by, and the air chilled quickly as the sun lowered in the sky. Soft beams of light still penetrated the wood and dappled the ground in many places, glistening in the drops left from a morning rain like the light of fireflies or fairies. That is what the High King would call beauty and magic, and I was there amongst it, as part of it, enjoying it as a gift given specifically for me. I heaved a great sigh. I knew it was time for me to rejoin the outside world, to enter into that purpose for which I had been made. I would have to begin by making my way into the village on Haven Island. From there, I didn't know immediately where I would go or what I would do, how I would earn my bread and lodging, but I trusted the High King would guide me by some means.

Just as I stood to go, there came a movement and a sound of rustling to my far left; I swung around to see a large white, horned beast emerge—my unicorn.

I nearly cried again at the sight. I walked forward to her while she received me with what I interpreted to be enthusiasm, snorting loudly and tossing her head as she trotted toward me, quickly closing the space between us. I buried my face in her mane and was comforted by her warm body and soft, silky hair.

"I am so glad to see you," I whispered. "I don't know how you got from the mainland to Haven Island, but I am glad, nevertheless."

Once again, the High King was showing me—reminding me—that I was no unchosen after all.

"I feel you need a name," I said to her. "What shall I call you, hm? Liora, how about that? For you have been a light in the darkness for me."

The unicorn neighed and tossed her head in response, and I took that to be an approval of my suggestion.

Then I heard a voice that made me start, but also made my heart quicken with gladness.

"Did you know that unicorns rarely show themselves to humans, and even then, only to the purest in heart?"

I lifted my head and turned to see Danein leaning against a tree, arms crossed, watching me, as though it was only yesterday that he and I had come to this place together in search of the High King. Indeed, he looked little changed, except that his hair and beard were shorter and he was better groomed than when I'd last seen him. I smiled.

We watched each other for some moments before he moved from his position and approached me slowly. "In fact, unicorns have a great sense of discernment. They have the power to sense evil and righteousness." He nodded toward the magnificent white beast next to me. "You have been given a great gift in her."

"I know."

Danein closed the distance between us and stopped when he was only an arm's length from me. "Hello, Alonya."

"Hello, Danein."

"It has been awhile, has it not?"

"At least two years, I think."

"You look much changed."

I laughed, ready to cry with joy. "You are not! Here we meet again in the place where we parted, and it's as if no time has passed at all."

"I might believe the same, except that you look so well."

I cocked my head as my hands absentmindedly stroked Liora's mane. "Did I not look well before?"

"I only mean, you were always sad before—even when you were happy, you were sad."

"I'm sad today."

"But it's not the same kind of sadness. You are sad today, but well." He frowned, as if he didn't understand his own words. "Does that make sense?"

"It makes perfect sense." I sighed, betraying my confidence with a quiver in my breath as I exhaled. "I'm sad today because I cannot go back to the palace of the High King. The doorway has been closed to me."

"Why?"

"Because my time has come to leave and rejoin the outside world, so here I am." I then noted Danein's presence anew, as if for the first time. "But how did you come to be here? How did you know I'd be here?"

He chuckled as a hand went up to touch the strong, broad back of the unicorn. "I didn't know. I only hoped." He turned his face down then, suddenly timid. "I've been to Haven Island at least three times since our parting, and I always came here just to see…just to see if I might find you, to see you again and speak with you. But I could never find the cabin. I realized I wasn't meant to, and yet I continued coming." He rubbed the back of his neck and his face reddened slightly, but I didn't laugh. I only smiled a little. "This last time was different. It was as if the High King himself spoke to me. I had a great sense of compulsion telling me I had to return to this place. So I came. I docked this afternoon and ran through the village and through the countryside and didn't stop. I came straightaway to find you, hardly breathing, hardly daring to hope that I might see you again." His eyes locked on mine and his hand dropped from Liora. "There were times during these last two years I feared—" His voice broke, and my eyes clouded with tears at the sight of him so disarmed. "I feared I might not see you again. I feared that in giving you up to the High King, I had given you up for good. I know things are different now, and you have changed much and learned much under the tutelage of the High King, but still I feared the possibility of you being out in the world alone. I didn't want that to happen. At times I felt I had abandoned you—"

"You didn't abandon me," I interjected. "You led me to where I was meant to go."

Despite my words, Danein's features grew more cloudy and troubled. "Though I knew it was the High King's will that you should stay with him, I only remembered how distraught you were the day we parted, and I always felt responsible. You must know how sorry I am to have left you, Alonya, and that I always intended to come back for you."

I nodded my head but said nothing, the emotion quickly rising in me at Danein's agitated state. "I was restless so often," he continued. "I feared you might forget my words or forget me, and I…well, I suppose that's partly why I came so often to Haven Island when I could manage it." He took a deep breath, waited a moment, and smiled feebly. "I must confess, Alonya, I feared you might learn to live without me, and I, well…I hoped that by trying to find you I might prevent it. I was impulsive and selfish, and I know that's why I was never able to discover the doorway on my own. Can you forgive me?"

I realized my heart was thundering in my chest and my hands shook. I grasped them tightly together. I tried to speak but no sound came. Tears were my only reply.

Danein grew more in earnest than ever. "Alonya, why do you cry?"

"There is nothing to forgive," I said, my words coming out in little more than a squeak. "I am surprised—you feared I might learn to live without you. Well, I feared you would learn to live without me. I thought, despite your love, that our lives had been sundered from each other. I couldn't live with the pain of such a loss, and so I *did* try to forget you. I tried to move on, and for a while I thought I had, but it was all because of fear." I met his eyes, unblinking, steady and resolved. "And then I saw you. I saw you in the throne room of the king of Zaphon, appealing for the rights of unchosens…appealing for the right to marry one."

I watched Danein closely as he processed my words until realization brightened his countenance. He jumped forward and suddenly took my hands in his. His eyes were wild with delight and confusion. "You saw me there? But how did you know? Were you there?"

I shook my head. "No, I wasn't there. The High King gave me a dream. It was weeks ago. I think he meant to reassure me of your constancy, to relieve my fears."

Danein's mirth dissipated momentarily. "Did you doubt me, Alonya?"

My eyes nearly overflowed, and the next words came out in a sob. "If I did, then I do no longer. Forgive me."

He wrapped his arms around me and held me long. I had forgotten the feel of being in his arms, the sense of security and love and peace it afforded. It had been a ghost of a memory, one I never believed I would have experienced again. I nestled in his embrace as his arms continued to wrap more tightly, but gently, around me. My tears dampened the front of his tunic. I thought he might never let me go this time, and for my part I felt I could stay there with him forever.

"I do want to marry you, Alonya," he finally whispered into my hair, "and I will, but not now. The time is not right yet."

"I know. I trust you. I will wait. You are here now and I am happy."

"Yes, I am here, and I won't leave you again, ever." He pulled me away somewhat reluctantly and held me at arm's length. "You must know there is still danger out there for you. I have been several times to see the king of Zaphon these last two years. Do you remember the tale I told you once, of when I first lost my sister to kidnappers and tried to gain an audience with the king?"

I nodded.

"Do you remember what happened then?"

"Yes. You were denied an audience and then imprisoned when you tried to waylay the king outside the palace."

"Yes, and the king's daughter eventually heard of my plight, released me from prison, and tried to help me."

"I remember," I said, glancing about the wood. The sun had set and we were quickly enclosed by the gathering darkness. "Perhaps we ought to get out of this wood first and find shelter in the village before you finish your story."

Danein nodded his agreement and took my hand. He began to pull me along in one direction, but Liora, who had been momentarily forgotten, snorted and stamped a hoof impatiently. We turned to see her shaking her mane and backing up as though she wanted us to follow.

"I suppose she knows a shortcut," Danein said.

"Well, let's follow her then. I would trust her with my life."

Liora cut a path through the wood, weaving in and out and around thick trunks and staying clear of thorn bushes and brambles, her lion-like tail whipping out and swinging behind her as if to clear the trail for us as we followed. The canopy above thinned out, and soon full moonlight was streaming down on us. Liora's body shimmered like water in the soft glow of the moon's light, providing a beacon for us to follow in the dusky wood. At first, Danein attempted to continue his narrative as we walked along, but it was too difficult for him to concentrate on that in addition to navigating the path, so for the most part we both remained silent, content in each other's company.

In less than an hour, we came out of the wood somewhere on the outskirts of the village. There were few houses and cottages dotted about the open land. We found a road—nothing more than shallow wagon ruts carved into the dirt—and began following it into town, still hand in hand. Stars shone bright and clear overhead alongside the moon, and it was much easier to see our way in the open country. Liora fell behind, but I continued to listen for her stamping hooves as we walked along in the cool air. I wondered how long she would choose to walk with us. She had a way of appearing at precisely the right moment and disappearing when I least expected it.

Soon, small dots of light appeared in the darkness ahead and grew as we approached—the firelight through windows and from street torches. A sound of water lapping shore became more pronounced, and we knew we had reached the village. When we were yet a quarter of a mile off, I turned around, expecting to find Liora gone, but there she was! But she had changed. Still of the same height and breadth, her slender lion's tail had transformed into an ordinary tail of hair. Her hooves were no longer cloven; she had the smooth, round hooves of ordinary horses. Most noticeable of all was that her horn of ivory had disappeared!

My mouth gaped open when I saw her. She tossed her head, neighed, and came forward to nuzzle my face as though reassuring me it was her.

"What happened to you, Liora? You look like a common mare."

"A beautiful common mare," Danein added. "I think she means to follow us into the village. She can't show herself to just anybody after all."

"How strange, but I'm very happy she has decided to join us."

I patted Liora's back, and Danein and I continued making our way into the village. When we had obtained lodgings and stabled Liora, albeit somewhat hesitantly on her part, we took a walk through the village, hand in hand, while Danein finished his story.

"After we parted, I began searching out any remaining colonies of unchosens," Danein explained, "but all the ones I'd had contact with had been raided, the camps left deserted and overturned, just as yours had."

"Wait—you had helped other women besides us?"

Danein nodded.

"Why did you never tell us? Perhaps we could have helped."

"Unchosen colonies are best kept small and secret. Even amongst fellow unchosens, there can still be betrayal." I frowned at Danein, uncomprehending, so he elaborated. "People in desperate circumstances will do desperate things to pull themselves up and out of the mire. Do you remember that girl from your colony that went missing?"

My eyes widened with understanding. "Yes, but wasn't she taken by slave traders?"

Danein shrugged. "We can't know for sure. She may have been, but…" He turned a determined glance my way and lowered his voice. "I suspect she may have gone to meet them intentionally."

"But how—"

"There was no evidence found to suggest she just got lost and was taken by force."

"But some of the women had done a search."

"They were looking specifically for evidence that she may have been hurt, so they didn't find anything. I did a little searching of my own in a wider radius. Her movements, as far as I could tell, were very purposeful and methodical, not random and sporadic as would have been the case had she been lost. I found the remains of a fire where she may have camped overnight. She managed to keep at a consistent bearing for at least a day and a half and then came out at a clearing not far from a road. I found wagon ruts in the dirt far off the side of the road, and no sign of a struggle."

"She had predetermined to meet them?"

"Yes, that's my guess. She must have had contacts and been working with someone else, but whatever the case, I believe she betrayed you women, and most likely she sold out the other unchosen colonies as well. I spoke to some contacts of mine to discover any information regarding the other raided colonies, but could determine very little, so the only other option was to go once more to the king of Zaphon."

"And that's when I saw you in my dream?"

"No, that was much later. I've had several audiences with the king thanks to the princess. I sought an audience with her first. She remembered me from my first failed mission to find my sister, but she was, and is, sympathetic to the cause of unchosens, so she agreed to help."

Horns blew and whistles clanged from the harbor. Danein and I changed direction to walk along the edge of the sea while the moon shone full in the clear sky, shedding its light on the dark waters—a lamp in the Great Sea.

"You found an ally in the princess," I marveled. "That's amazing, because I also met one from the royal house sympathetic to our cause."

Danein's eyes lit up with curiosity. "The royal house of Zaphon?"

"No, of Coralind. I met the prince of Coralind at the High King's palace. He was a guest there for a while, like me."

"You befriended the prince of Coralind?"

"Yes, and he agreed to help us if ever we needed it."

Danein shook his head, disbelieving. "It seems the High King has shown us his favor by sending us such powerful allies."

"Please continue with your story," I implored. "What did the princess of Zaphon do then?"

"She gained me several audiences with her father, and in the meantime employed her own spies to discover any information she could about the whereabouts of the missing women. It seems that most of the kidnapping is connected to the same group of slavers; that is, they're not all random incidents. Something of this caliber usually isn't. It's highly organized and strategic. They probably have a large base of operations where they sell the women as slaves to be used as…well, in whatever manner their masters wish."

I was speechless for a moment. "How can that be?"

"There's no law against it. A lot of nobles and wealthy citizens are involved in the buying and selling so that the upper class of society profits."

"But how can anyone treat people so?"

"In Zaphon, the outcasts are considered of no value to normal-functioning society. Turning them into slaves makes them somewhat useful, and it's a convenient way to deal with the...well, with the problem."

"With what problem?"

Danein squirmed under the question. "The poverty problem. The unchosen problem. Any problem where a human being loses his or her place in the community."

"But it is oftentimes the law that causes a person to lose his or her place to begin with! And then the law determines that the solution is to hand these people over to slavery?"

"I know it makes very little sense."

"It makes no sense!" My blood rose, heating my face despite the cool night air washing across my skin. "It sickens my heart, and it makes me feel ashamed to—" My voice caught in my throat, and I stopped to swallow down tears. Danein put his arms around me and pulled me in protectively. "I am ashamed to be called a Zaphonian. How is it that I am part of a country that throws people away? They just...throw people away..." I began sobbing then, partly for myself, but mostly for all the others in Zaphon who were suffering at the hands of the law.

"Yes, they throw people away," Danein said, "but we will help bring them back. I don't know how, but we will."

"If being with the High King taught me anything, it was that all people are equal in his eyes, and they all have value and a purpose of his determining. He cares for them all, and if the Lord of all the Lands of the Seven Kingdoms cares for every person, then we ought to as well."

The wind grew fierce, and the ships moored far out in the harbor groaned and creaked, swaying atop the waves. A gull cried out somewhere in the distance, piercing and lonely, and then the wind stilled and all was silent once more.

"Once upon a time, I had no place," I said into the night, still nestled into Danein's embrace. "I lost my family one by one. They abandoned me, and without them I didn't truly know who I was or where I belonged. Zaphon tells me I have no place in society, no real value as a human being in this kingdom, but right now I know my place and my purpose more than I ever have before. I was meant to become an unchosen to have my eyes opened, to find the High King, to discover things and purposes greater than myself, and to help other people like me find who they truly are."

"And to become mine, of course," Danein added with a chuckle. "If you hadn't been unchosen, I would never have met you."

"Yes," I said, pulling away and looking up into his face, "it was always meant to be you."

PRINCESS

The Great Sea and Haven Island were long behind us as Danein and I clattered down a narrow dirt road, the wheels of the cart kicking up dust behind us. The high grass in the wild meadows on either side was dry and bent over, broken and withered in the heat like a farmer too long in the field, crooked and parched of water. Yellow hills rose up before us, huge treeless mounds that broke the horizon and would eventually level out into the arid wasteland of eastern Zaphon: the Outlands.

We rode along quietly into those hills atop the seat of Danein's peddler cart. Months had elapsed since our reunion on Haven Island, months in which preparations had been made for the next step in our plan to recover Taralyn and other unchosen women from the slavers. We had spent the majority of the winter back in Fynn Harbor with Janna at the Restful Sea Inn, having taken her into our confidence and employed her assistance. When once the snows subsided and buds began appearing on the stark limbs of the trees, Danein had taken to the road again to gather information and supplies, leaving me in Janna's care until a more definite plan could be reached. At first, Danein did not want to involve me at all, but I had insisted; and once it was determined that we would need all the bodily help we could procure, he had conceded and let me come along.

He had kept in touch with the princess of Zaphon during that time and made a few visits to the royal city. She and Danein both had been unable to get her father to move regarding any of the unchosen laws. He seemed to tolerate Danein's visits because of his daughter's connection to and fondness for the peddler. The king had himself become fond of Danein to such a degree that he often engaged in business with him to Danein's profit, but whether he did it from a sense of amusement or duty to pacify his own conscience, Danein was never certain. Perhaps the king was hoping to deter him, to buy his loyalty. Either way, Danein remained steady on his course. The time was close at hand.

So it was that on that hot summer day we found ourselves winding through a narrow valley, enclosed on all sides by the bare yellow hills, their slopes broken here and there by a single shrub or a huge boulder. I had just wiped my forehead with a handkerchief and opened the water skin to take a drink when we turned a corner to find a small train of men on horseback in the road before us. In the midst of the train stood a nondescript boxed coach with a single door and two curtained windows, one on either side of the vehicle.

We approached slowly, and as we did, the curtain to the coach window was drawn aside, and a woman's face peeked out. She gave a slight smile when she saw us, then let the curtain fall back over her face. The door was opened by one of her men a moment later, and the princess of Zaphon stepped out, helped down by the same man.

I had never before seen her, and I suddenly grew excited. She stood, awaiting our approach; she was as tall as many of her men. Thick, creamy brown locks fell in waves behind her shoulders, brought together in the middle of her back by a single loose plait. Even attired as a peasant in a plain woolen skirt, linen chemise, and bodice, her entire bearing and posture spoke of confidence, intelligence, and regality. Though I'd heard reports from Danein of her gentleness and kindness, I suddenly felt shy and self-conscious in front of her.

Danein clucked his tongue and pulled back on the reins. The cart stopped. Danein jumped down and came around to the other side to help me down. We both approached the princess in the warmth and stillness of the moment. Not even the wind stirred. We stopped just in front of her, Danein bowing his head and me offering a small curtsey.

"Princess, may I present to you Alonya, my betrothed."

It was the first time I'd heard him say it that way, and I beamed despite my rapidly beating heart and dampening brow. I gave another curtsey, and the princess came forward with her arms outstretched to me.

"There is no need of all that formality," she said, embracing me. "We are equals, friends, and sisters. After all, look at me!" She held me at arm's length so I might study her attire. "Do I not look like one of you?"

I laughed. "Yes, but even as a peasant you still look tenfold more stunning than I ever could!"

"Oh, nonsense," she said, dismissing my compliment with a wave of her hand. "You are just as stunning as I am!" She winked at Danein, and I swung my gaze around to see him nodding, on the edge of laughing. The princess took my hands.

"Please, call me Zhara—not Princess, not Your Royal Highness, not My Lady, but simply Zhara. Though I am a princess by earthly right, we are all brothers and sisters in the eyes of the High King."

Her words brought me back to the palace, to my conversation with Marcus, the prince of Coralind.

"Come, we have much to discuss," she went on, turning and gesturing for us to follow. She led us around the next bend in the road and up a small trail to a flat, shady area between two hills. A small stand of dry-looking trees sprouted in the shade, and as we sat on the blanket that had been laid out for us beneath the trees, two blackbirds in the boughs cackled and fluttered away at our intrusion. Here in the higher land we caught a cool breeze that danced over the surface of the hills and refreshed us from our travels.

Half of Zhara's men stayed behind with the vehicle and horses while the other half stood guard at the foot of the hill, close enough to keep watch from a distance, but far enough away to give us privacy.

The princess's dark eyes glittered with anticipation. "I have been eager to share with you what my spies have discovered. It has been a long and arduous task, and especially difficult keeping it a secret from my father. He is not, as you already know, Danein, sympathetic to our cause."

She shifted position on the blanket, glanced left and right to make sure we were completely alone, and went on. "We have confirmed that this operation is taking place in the Outlands, far east of here. There are a number of large, highly organized slaving camps there, in the uninhabited land beyond the Great Desert."

"Beyond the Great Desert?" Danein asked with a frown. "It's a rocky, dry wasteland. Nobody goes out there!"

"Which makes it perfect for an operation of this sort," the princess said. "It keeps it invisible to the public."

"How can they survive out there?" I asked.

"They have discovered underground water sources, so there are several wells in the area. They also have food, water, and other goods shipped by way of sea. From the place of harbor, it is another two days' travel to the camps. Even now there are laborers digging a huge canal from the Great Sea to the camps in order to easier secure goods for survival. It seems this business has been in operation for several years."

"Who are these laborers you mention? Are they paid workers?"

Zhara shook her head. "They are slaves, mostly men, some women and children."

"So they're not just camps for unchosen women," I noted.

"No. They have the poor, homeless, orphaned, disabled, and injured as well as unchosen women—anybody unable to help themselves, essentially. The laws of Zaphon justify this type of slavery by saying that these people are being given occupation, but most of it is debilitating or degrading—selling women into prostitution, working the children and the disabled for hours on end in menial tasks, assigning hard labor to everyone else, and the sword for anyone who does not comply." She stopped for a moment, her eyes glazing over as she pondered her own words. "I have not seen the camps myself. This is merely what has been reported to me by trusted spies of mine. Of course these people are kept like animals in improper living conditions. People die every day, but they just round up more and more to replace them, as if people are that expendable."

I was horrified. Danein's face was rigid, his mouth tight, his head shaking back and forth. "Are the families kept together or separated?" he asked.

"I believe most of the families are kept together while on base. Most of the people except the unchosens remain on base to work the camps. But the unchosen women are kept separate from the others, sold into prostitution or to wealthy men who take them to their own homes as personal slaves. Many of them do not end up staying on the base for long, unless they remain unsold, or unless they are strong enough for physical labor. Some are kept on base for the"—Zhara's face reddened—"for the use of the guards and soldiers."

I wiped away tears as they ran down my cheeks. My thoughts strayed to Taralyn. She could be anywhere. Danein patted my arm, and I quickly wiped the tears away and sat up straighter to compose myself. A fly buzzed around my head and I swatted at it angrily.

"Those that remain on base," Danein said, "those that work the camps, as you say, in menial tasks and physical labor—what is it for? Why aren't all the slaves sold to buyers?"

"I believe there are a few buyers who want other slaves besides women, but most of them remain at the camps to help make the Outlands habitable. They're digging canals, hauling rocks and water, making bricks, building structures, things of that sort."

"Zaphon wants to make the Outlands habitable. Why?"

Zhara shook her head. "I am not sure. As you can guess, I haven't spoken to my father about any of this, but I do not doubt that he knows of it and even has a hand in it. Although he has never mentioned the slaving camps to me, I have been in company when he has spoken to advisors of his plans to expand this country, to grow it and fortify it to have greater influence, greater reign, and greater control over our neighbors. The Outlands constitute a huge portion of this country, nearly half, but throughout our history that land has been unused, wasted, just sitting there for any rival country to come and claim. I suppose, in a way, he sees the potential in the land."

"But he's using slaves against their will to work that land," Danein pointed out. "Exploiting the helpless. That's not right!"

"No, it's not," Zhara agreed, "and I am full of shame for it. I want with all my heart to believe my father ignorant of the evils going on under his very nose, but I know he's not." Her body seemed to slump under the weight of her grief. "I have seen too much and heard too much in my years to believe him innocent. Even my mother, the king's very own wife, even she—" Zhara's voice caught in her throat and she covered her mouth with her hand momentarily.

I reached forward and took her free hand in mine. She sniffed, gathered herself together, and spoke. "When I was a girl, my mother displeased my father—I was never completely sure why—and so he sent her away. He said she had done something bad and had to go away, and I was never to ask of her, so I never did. But my nurse would hint at things which led me to believe she was sold into slavery because she was unable to give him a son after my birth. My birth was hard, you see, and it damaged her. She could not conceive after that. Well, these are things my nurse mentioned when we were alone. She was furious about my mother being sent away. Soon after my mother disappeared, my nurse was gone as well, and a new nurse was hired to look after me. I haven't truly trusted my father since then. Oh, he loves me—he adores me. Though I am by the laws of Zaphon considered an unchosen myself, my father, of course, says I am exempt, that the common laws don't apply to the royal house, and that he would rather see me unmarried than married to the wrong man."

She gave a wry smile and shook her head. "But I have other ideas as to why he would not like to see me married besides fatherly affection for his only child."

A basket of food and a pitcher of water sat nearby; from these the princess took a plain ceramic cup and poured water into it. She offered the cup to Danein and me, but we shook our heads. I patted the water skin tied to a belt around my waist, and Zhara nodded before taking a long draught from her cup. She pulled a handkerchief from a pocket of her skirt and dabbed at her forehead.

"Shall we find a shadier spot?" Danein suggested.

"No—it's not just the heat," Zhara said. "I am much more apprehensive and agitated about this ordeal than I thought. It is good to have friends whom I can trust and speak candidly with about these issues, but it is difficult feeling as though I am working behind my father's back, betraying him, in a sense."

Danein and I nodded but kept silent, waiting for the princess to go on in her own time.

"I'm sorry, what was I saying before?"

"Why your father doesn't want to see you married."

"Oh yes. I am unmarried partly by choice: my suitors have never truly inspired respect or admiration from me. They have, for the most part, been vain and haughty and selfishly ambitious. Many noblemen are, you know, because of their privileged station. Those that weren't so haughty were typically dull, without much life or spirit. I have never been caught by any of them. My father has also never truly pushed me to marry."

She pulled the basket of food closer and rustled inside, pulling out a lumpy, folded cloth. She unfolded it to reveal bright red cherries cut in half and pitted. She offered some to us before popping one into her mouth.

"There was a man once that I did come to care about. He was a duke from Kerith. I met him during a visit when he served as ambassador in some trade dealings between Kerith and Zaphon. I had been with my waiting women out in the palace gardens, painting, and he on a tour of the grounds with a manservant. I was introduced, as was the custom, and although I was usually irritated by such obvious matchmaking techniques, I was intrigued by this man. I waited for the usual flattery, the obsequious manner, but there was none. There was nothing of affectation in him. He offered his arm and I took it, telling my ladies and the manservant that I would guide the remainder of his tour.

"I liked him right away. He seemed genuinely interested in knowing me, not just for my position but for my person. We spent a great deal of time together. In private—when we could manage it—we spoke of marriage, of being together."

Zhara's eyes had been lit with a small smile during this speech, but her countenance suddenly fell.

"There came a short stretch of days where I didn't see the duke, but I didn't think anything ill of it. There had often elapsed a day or two at a time where I wouldn't see him due to his travels and business. I decided to speak to my father about him one evening, about how I liked him, how I would accept him were he to offer his hand. I thought his courting me was partly the reason the duke had been invited to the palace to begin with. After all, my father had seen what had been developing between us for many weeks.

"But the king merely gave me one of his patronizing smiles, covered my hand in his, and told me that the duke had returned to his home in the north of Kerith. He had spoken nothing of marriage to me, my father said. He had not been courting me, but merely entertaining the king's daughter.

"I was devastated at first—heartbroken for the first time. I kept to my rooms and cried day and night. I wrote letters to the duke and received nothing back. I was also restless, confused. Despite everything, I couldn't truly believe that the duke had not cared for me. Something must have happened. My father must have sent the duke away just as he'd sent away my mother and my nurse all those years ago.

"So I wrote another letter and sent it privately by way of a trusted waiting woman of mine and two men from the village. I didn't trust the guards not to be in my father's power. After nearly three months, my woman came back with a message from the duke. He had indeed asked for my hand, but had been told by my father—a devious lie—that I was betrothed to another, that I had known this and was only clinging to the duke as a way out of my betrothal. I think other falsehoods were told as well, but that was the main thrust in the duke's heart. He had left quickly, without word to me, without giving me a chance to clear myself. In the months that followed, he had traveled to other parts of the world and met another woman whom he was promised to marry at the time. He had never received my earlier letters, and he did not want to break his current betrothal."

She stopped, her head down, her finger tracing the stitching on the rough woolen blanket beneath us.

"He said he was sorry, but that too much time had passed, and too many things had changed for him to go back. He wished me well, and that was all."

Zhara's voice had broken at the end, though she held back the tears. She merely brought her handkerchief up to her eyes and nose to dab away the moisture. After several moments she squared her shoulders and straightened up.

"Princess, allow me leave to say that he was partly at fault for never fighting for you," Danein suggested softly.

"I know," Zhara replied. "It took me a long while to come to that realization, but I know that he's gone, and he wasn't the one for me. There will be another. But it was after that—after I had recovered—that my distrust of my father grew, and I began to see ulterior motives in everything he did, every decision he made."

"And you believe your father doesn't want you to marry at all?"

"I have begun to suspect that, yes, especially after the duke. He was perhaps one of the most eligible of all my suitors, and an alliance between the royal houses of Zaphon and Kerith would have been advantageous to us."

"What motive do you think your father has, then, to keep you from marrying?" Danein asked.

The princess had resumed eating the cherries, though it seemed mostly out of a nervous, absentminded habit rather than hunger. I believe we were all too ill at ease then to eat.

"I don't know whether you understand how succession works in Zaphon, but a daughter doesn't inherit the throne unless she is married, and that to a nobleman. When she does marry, her husband succeeds the king after his death."

I didn't quite understand yet, and Danein looked confused. "So you essentially have no rights to rule at all then?"

She sighed. "That's right. My purpose is to provide the next king by marriage and to bear sons to the throne, although many kings do allow their queens to rule alongside them. My father wasn't one of them."

"But if you don't marry at all," I said, "then there's no heir to the throne. You father will die eventually, and there will be no king."

"Well, my father has the right to name a new successor before he dies, as long as I remain unmarried. I believe he is keeping me from marriage at this time because he knows I will gain power by it. He sees that I am bright and intelligent and already have much influence in many matters just as princess. I have been schooled well in foreign policy and warfare and will be a great commodity to the future king. My father knows and sees all this, and I believe it is a threat to him. So my father keeps me as his pet. Where all other unchosens in Zaphon are driven from their homes into self-sufficiency, I must remain at home to lose mine."

"So your father is waiting for a successor that will be sympathetic to him, but not pose a threat?"

Zhara nodded. "It seems that way."

"What about elopement?" I asked. "Can you marry without your father's consent?"

"No, I cannot without forfeiting the throne. You see my options and my choices are limited. But now"—she looked both of us squarely in the eyes—"you can understand why I am so sympathetic to your plight, and to the plight of the unchosens in Zaphon. I will do whatever is in my power to help you and to change the terrible state of things in this country."

The long, dry grass blowing in the wind tickled my legs as the sun slowly descended into the west. We spent the afternoon gaining more information about the camps and sharing maps, plans, and strategies for our mission, heedless of the passing time. It was only when one of the guards from below gave a little whistle to signal that it was time for the princess to leave did we stand up, our legs aching from sitting so long, and take the trail back down to the road. We said our good-byes to Zhara as she embraced us both briefly. As her coach pulled away, she drew aside the curtain to one of her windows and watched us until her train disappeared out of sight, hidden in the failing light of dusk.

I sighed and rubbed my arms together. It had grown suddenly cold with the sun low in the sky behind the hills, plunging us into shadow.

"Well, where do we go from here?" I said.

"We return to Fynn Harbor," Danein replied, as sure of himself as he'd ever been. "We gather some supplies and reinforcements there and then travel east."

My body shivered with both cold and the anticipation of the venture. "A rescue mission."

"Yes, and it will be dangerous." Danein put his hand on the small of my back to guide me back to the peddler cart. "When did Marcus say he could meet us?" he asked.

"The middle of next month," I replied. "That's only two weeks away."

"Perfect."

Everything seemed to be falling into place. Danein helped me into the cart and jumped up behind me. He clicked his tongue and snapped the reins, and we were off, rattling down the road by which we'd come. As night descended, the air grew noisy with the song of crickets and cicadas and other insects hiding in the tall grass around us. Danein hummed a soft tune next to me. I smiled at him and let my own imagination wander. Everything was in place, yet my heart grieved for Zhara. I had seen that her broken heart over a lost love hadn't been as fully healed as she'd led us to believe.

Then I thought of Marcus, and it all made sense.

A smile grew on my lips, but I kept my thoughts to myself.

27

PRINCE

Prince Marcus Du'Karafin of Coralind stepped off the ship full of marked confidence and resolution. It showed in his stern-with-a-hint-of-a-smile countenance; his steady and straight step down the docks spoke of it. He spotted me when he was halfway down the dock, his eyes and his smile growing large. He unfastened his traveling cloak and hung it casually over one arm, then bounced the rest of the way down the dock, breaking into a trot once he reached land. He moved toward me like he might scoop me up into an embrace, but upon approach seemed to recall propriety, so he slowed, finally stopping directly in front of me. Danein stood by my side. Marcus bowed, and Danein followed suit while I offered a curtsey.

"Dear Alonya, it is good to see you again after so much time."

"And you, Your Highness."

"Please, call me Marcus." He turned slightly and nodded toward Danein. "And who, might I ask, is your distinguished gentleman?"

"Marcus, this is Danein," I said, glancing sideways at him, "my betrothed."

"Yes, of course. Alonya has spoken of you."

"Have you?" Danein asked me.

"Of course!"

Marcus cleared his throat. "If I may, sir, Alonya spoke of you often during our stay together at the High King's palace. She also mentioned you in her letters to me. Allow me to say how grateful I am to have been enlisted in such a noble mission."

"Truly, Marcus, when you offered to help back at the palace, and when I wrote to you for help, I only expected you to write a few letters to the king of Zaphon, or to send an ambassador from Coralind. I never expected you to come in person yourself!"

Marcus let out a good-natured laugh as we all turned to walk down the wharf toward Janna's inn. "Well, I am always up for an adventure, and this escapade of yours sounds like it may well evolve into one." He turned toward me as we walked along, and his expression suddenly grew serious, like the clouds covering the sun. "You may still keep my presence here a secret. As you can see, I have come in more common clothing. I intend to go all the way with you in this mission, beyond just a visit to the king of Zaphon. That means secrecy is of the utmost priority."

I glanced at his clothing—polished leather boots, finely-stitched breeches, and a sleeveless embroidered doublet over a freshly cleaned tunic. I giggled and exchanged glances with Danein, who brought a fist up to his mouth and cleared his throat. Marcus gave us a questioning look.

"What is it? Do you not believe I am in earnest about giving you my aid?"

"It's not that," I assured him, stifling another giggle. "It's just—" I patted him on the front of his doublet, which felt soft enough to be silk. "If this is what you mean by common clothing, then even the peasantry in Coralind must have finer tastes than we do in Zaphon and be better off financially."

Marcus stopped and gave himself a looking-over. Then he studied Danein's plain belted tunic with loose-fitting breeches and laughed. "But these are my plainest clothes. Look—no bright colors or patterns."

I shrugged my shoulders. "Common people don't wear silk, unless they can afford it, and then only for great occasions."

"This isn't silk—it's fine cotton."

I started laughing, and Danein shook his head at me, averting his eyes to his feet. Marcus glanced back and forth between us; his face suddenly lit up with a smile. He rubbed the back of his neck. "It seems I do stand out a bit. But have you no doublet, sir?" he asked Danein.

"I have an old coat with patches on the elbows, if that's what you mean by a doublet."

"Well, Danein, you will have to give me some lessons then." He then met my eyes with a somber, earnest look. "I do wish to make a difference in Zaphon. And with whatever earthly power, authority, and influence I have, I will do it."

The cry of gulls circling the harbor faded as we drew farther from the wharf. It was a busy day in Fynn Harbor, and the cobblestone streets were swarming with horses, ponies, and goats pulling carts that clacked and rattled behind them. It wasn't long before we made it to the inn and stole inside, taking refuge from the noise and bustle outside. Janna expected us back with the prince and, though it was midday, had prepared a small fire in one of the private parlors off the main dining room. A feast had been laid out on the sideboard near one wall. The room had been tidied and decorated: carefully stitched and embroidered pillows graced each seat and couch, clean new linens were spread across each tabletop, unused candles sat in each candlestick, and freshly-picked flowers from Janna's small garden out back filled vases on each table, washing the room in a soft, pleasant fragrance. I was surprised to see the wooden floorboards underneath our seating area covered in a beautiful, brightly woven, though slightly threadbare rug. The inn had never had so much as a foot mat in any of the rooms. Marcus was astonished at the simple grandeur such a rude, modest room could showcase. He highly praised the inn, turning Janna's face red with his compliments. After she had seen to his comforts and refilled the kettle over the fireplace with fresh water, she hesitantly left the three of us to meet and talk in private.

The plain curtains over the windows had been drawn for privacy, shutting out the small bit of daylight from outside. The room was dimly illuminated by the dancing, yellow-orange flames of the fire, which chased the shadows into the far corners. Marcus settled himself in one of the cushioned chairs opposite the fireplace, letting the light play directly on his features. I took a plate and loaded it with meat, vegetables, and bread, and handed it to Marcus while Danein helped himself and sat down.

"Thank you, Alonya," Marcus said.

"You ought to try Janna's woodberry juice," I said as I poured Marcus a cup. Glass goblets had replaced the usual tin, wooden, and clay cups. For an instant I worried at the cost to Janna. "It's better than any I've tasted in Zaphon."

Danein nodded. "She's right. You don't want to miss out."

"Well, you've piqued my interest. I've tasted many a cook's woodberry juice. It's a difficult recipe to get right."

I handed him the glass, and he brought it to his nose for a sniff.

"Janna uses a few different ingredients of her own," I bragged with a smile of anticipation.

Marcus matched my smile as he held the cup to his lips, hesitating.

"Oh, come now! Stop teasing. Drink it!"

Marcus cocked his eyebrows and finally took a long draught of the dark liquid. He hadn't even time for reflection before his eyes went wide and he uttered a surprised, "Wow."

"Good, right?"

"It's delicious—very sharp and tangy—by far the best woodberry juice I've tasted. I'll have to give my compliments to the chef."

I sat down next to Danein. "She'll color all the way to her feet. Janna's very excited to have you here."

"She seems a kind, trustworthy woman." Marcus suddenly cleared his throat. "Are we certain she can be trusted?"

"Oh yes. She has been like family to us. She knows all about my situation and our plan. We've nothing to fear from her."

Marcus emptied the glass in another long draught and set it down. "Good. I'm satisfied hearing it from you. What about these other friends of yours? Will you tell me more about them, and what parts they are to play in this mission?"

"Certainly," Danein said, sitting up on the edge of his seat. "Captain Lynch runs a merchant ship. He has agreed to ferry us east along the coast under the guise of traders and merchants. The slave camps regularly receive provisions, so it should be easy to go in undetected."

"Yes, but don't the traders who go in have papers?" Marcus interrupted. "Inventories and records of the sales? Not just any merchant can walk in. It's meant to be a highly secretive base of operations, am I right?"

"Yes, you're right. They also have special papers from the king allowing their entrance into the camps. That's where Zhara comes in."

"Zhara?"

"The princess," I jumped in, unable to hide my smile. "She's been helping us."

It took a moment for Marcus to process the information. His face had frozen in an expression of thoughtful curiosity. "The king's own daughter is working against him?"

"I wouldn't say that. She and her father do not have similar agendas. She's doing what she believes is right, just as we are."

Marcus remained silent, staring into the fire. Danein and I exchanged glances.

"She's an unchosen, also," I added.

"Is she?"

"By the king's own doing."

Marcus came to attention suddenly. "That's very curious, indeed."

"Well, as you know, royals aren't subject to the same laws as the common people. He hasn't yet wanted her to marry, for reasons about which I'm sure you'll find out soon enough. Zhara sympathizes with the cause of the unchosens and the outcasts, as you do. In fact, I think you'll find that you two share a lot of common interests."

Danein turned to me and raised his eyebrows in question. I answered him with a smile, and I believe he understood my mind at that moment. He gave me a reproachful look, though it was belied by his growing smile.

"Zhara has told her father that she has discovered the camps and would like to visit them to bring goods and provisions to the outcasts there. The king has consented, thinking it merely a charity mission. She has named Captain Lynch and procured the necessary papers for him, so we're covered there."

"I see you've considered every angle," Marcus said, seemingly impressed.

"That's the easy part," Danein said. "What comes after will be much more difficult and unpredictable. We're not certain how close we can get to the actual slave houses once we're in."

"Well, there's desert all around, so I can't imagine the place is heavily patrolled or guarded."

"No, I don't believe it is," Danein agreed. "Not according to our sources. Very few people attempt escape. Those that do are usually caught quickly or perish in the desert. That's one of the reasons for the camp's location."

"What exactly will we be attempting once inside?"

Danein looked at me, but I was quiet in thought, staring at the uneaten food on the serving table. I let a moment pass before responding.

"We need to find Taralyn, and any of the others from the Colony, and get them out."

"Princess Zhara also wants to see the state of things at the camp for herself. She'll be making a kind of diplomatic visit, which will be the basis for us to get in, find the women, and get back out."

Marcus thought on this for a moment. "How far a journey is it from the sea to the camps?"

"About two days on foot according to Zhara's sources."

"If we do manage to get out undetected, we'll have several weak, malnourished women with us who will most likely not survive such a journey in the Outlands."

"While we're returning from the camps, Captain Lynch will bring horses, supplies, and reinforcements to meet us. He has trustworthy men of his own."

"We will most likely be discovered and pursued," Marcus pointed out. "Even with these supplies and reinforcements, who's to say we'll escape?"

Danein and I were silent. Marcus understood our silence and nodded. He poured himself another glass of woodberry juice and leaned back in his chair. "All noble endeavors come with some measure of risk."

"Perhaps it won't be discovered until too late that the women are missing," I suggested.

"Let's pray they don't keep close watch on their slaves. Even so, it's a risk worth taking."

"Thank you," I said. "Your help will be invaluable to us."

"I am yours to command," Marcus said, raising his glass as if to toast.

I retired early that evening after Danein and I had taken Marcus on a small jaunt through the village and along the harbor. We arrived back at the inn just as the sun was bleeding orange into the horizon of the sea. The fires in our upstairs rooms had been lit; serving trays laden with bread, fruit, and drink had been set out; and our beds had all been turned down. Janna had been attentive to the smallest detail, serving even Danein and me as though we were prominent guests. She refused to hear of me helping her, as was my usual custom. I drew the curtains over the windows, which swathed the room in the dusky light of the fire, and then dressed into my nightgown. Janna came in to check on me.

"Is the prince satisfied with his accommodations?" she asked with a small tremor of worry in her voice. "I fear even my largest room is not quite up to the standards of royalty."

I went to her and put my hand on her arm reassuringly. Though she was my elder by several years, she seemed a child under my gaze, her face lined with anxiety in its innocence and eagerness to please. "Janna, you should have heard him earlier as we were in the parlor. He is much impressed with your inn." I turned to gather some of the garments draped across my bed. "And besides, he is not so stuffy and princely as you might imagine. You may call him Marcus if you please."

"Oh no, I dare not!"

I picked up a woven basket from the floor and tossed the garments into it before turning back toward Janna. "Truly, there's no need for all the ceremony and formality. I wish you would let me attend to my daily duties at the inn. The laundry is piling up, as is the mending and the sewing." Janna moved to take the basket from me, but I held onto it tightly, pulling away from her with a smile.

"Alonya, you and Danein are on the cusp of your great mission. That is where your duty lies now, not here at the Restful Sea Inn, washing, mending, and sewing!" She gave a little chuckle and pulled the basket forcefully from my hands.

I smiled then turned away quickly before she could see the tears pool in my eyes. "You have been more than good to us, Janna, even when we were keeping secrets from you."

"I understand everything you've done and why you've done it. Yours has not been an easy road."

I fussed with the covers of my bed, then moved to the small table with the washbasin and began rearranging and straightening items in distraction. I sighed. "A part of me wishes that there was nothing else except the Restful Sea Inn, Danein, and you. What else do I really need?" A small hand towel had fallen on the floor; I picked it up.

"I will always be here for you, Alonya, as will this inn. I won't be going anywhere for the rest of my life, I'm sure." She moved across the room and took a seat on a small wooden chair near my bed. It creaked slightly under her weight. "This inn is my life. Oh, I doubt my son will carry on this business for much longer, though we've had the inn his entire life. It will fall to me. My husband and I started it, you know, years ago. But it's already been five years since the sea took him, and poor Havley continued running this place out of a sense of obligation to his father, I think. He isn't happy. That's why he's so often absent. I think he would like to travel some, and see the world, and find himself a wife."

"Well, maybe whenever Marcus goes back to Coralind, he can take Havley with him," I suggested, holding a thin white candle into the fire to light the wick. "I'm sure he can find some employment for him."

"Do you really think he would?"

"Oh yes. Marcus has a great heart. I'm certain I can get Danein to suggest it to him."

Janna's face instantly lit up, and her eyes reddened with emotion. "I would never have believed in all my life that I would host a prince under my very roof! And to think you and Danein have won the favor of the prince of Coralind!"

"And the princess of Zaphon!"

"Praise be the High King!" Janna exclaimed. "How he watches over us and orchestrates events to bring everything and everyone exactly where they're meant to be is a wondrous thing, too marvelous to fathom!" She stood and came to me, looking into my eyes for a moment before embracing me. "You and Danein would do me a great service to suggest employment for Havley with the prince of Coralind."

I returned the embrace. "Of course, Janna. It's the least we can do in return for all you've done for us."

She smiled, wiped her eyes, and hastily retreated without another word, closing the door softly behind her. I sighed, contemplating her words and all that was before me—the path I had taken and the path I was still to take. She was right: that path was leading me away from the Restful Sea Inn, away from the sheltered, inconspicuous, and obscure life I'd once led and hoped to always lead, a path with comfort and safety, void of troubles or worries or risk.

I snorted at the thought. What kind of a life would that have been? I discovered then, though not for the first time, how everything I'd experienced—all the difficulty and sorrow and suffering—had been a part of my path all along. Those things brought me to where I was at that moment and helped me become all I was meant to be, like a dying plant that withers in the desert for a time until the rains come, causing it to grow and strengthen and bloom and become more beautiful than it ever could have imagined.

I sat on the edge of my bed and let the tears come and drip into my lap, tears of release and freedom that shed the last vestiges of hurt and pain from my past. The sting of my life was gone in that moment. I accepted where I'd come from and even embraced it.

When a soft knock came at my bedroom door several moments later, I hastily wiped my face clean and smoothed back my hair.

"It's Danein," came the warm, familiar voice from the other side of the door.

"I'm coming."

I stood and looked about for something with which to cover myself since I was not properly dressed to receive male visitors. I finally pulled the top blanket off my bed and wrapped myself in its folds. I opened the door to admit Danein. He was slightly taken aback to see me wrapped in a blanket, but I merely shrugged and told him I was getting ready for bed.

"It's still an early night. Are you feeling unwell? You look as if you've been crying."

"I have, but not because of any complaint or illness. I was thinking about how grateful I am for my life, and for you and Janna, and I was emotional. That's all."

Danein stepped into the room but kept the door opened behind him for propriety's sake. He took my elbow and guided me to the far window opposite the door, lowering his voice.

"I have something for you," he said, taking out a small envelope from his trouser pocket. "As you know, our courtship has been a little unconventional. You never received any token of my promise, though that is the custom."

My heart began beating rapidly in nervous anticipation as though Danein and I had only just met and were only newly betrothed. I took my eyes from the envelope and watched his face.

"Well, an unchosen woman becoming promised to someone is far from the norm," I said with a smile in my voice. "I don't suppose there are any accepted societal mores for such a thing."

"Yes, but if I had given you something at the beginning, I might have been able to better protect you. My only excuse is that I felt I had nothing worthy to offer."

"A woman who belongs to nobody is always a target, no matter whether she has a token of promise or not. I wish you wouldn't blame yourself."

"Even so, I don't want you going any longer without the assurance of my promise and my affection." He inhaled a shaky breath. "We are about to embark on a dangerous mission. I know ultimately the High King guides and protects us, but I hope this will give you comfort and a sense of safety in the midst of the battle, so to speak." Danein emptied the contents of the envelope into his outstretched palm, then lifted up a tiny, delicate silver chain on which was hung a shiny silver ring. I gasped when I saw it, for though I knew it wasn't overly expensive by any means, I also knew that Danein had saved up to buy it. Danein held up the chain while I fingered the ring, scrutinizing it. It was plain but for a simple floral pattern etched along one side all the way around. On the inside was engraved a message: My chosen and beloved, you have captured me.

I stifled a sob as Danein unclasped the chain to put it around my neck. "When we are married, you shall wear the ring on your finger."

"It's more beautiful than anything I could have asked for or imagined." If necessity and propriety hadn't dictated that I hug the blanket around me, I would have embraced Danein at that moment. Even so, I fell into his arms as he wrapped them around me.

Kissing my hair, he whispered, "You are more than I could have asked for or imagined, Alonya."

DEPARTING

It was a warm, breezy day when we prepared to leave Fynn Harbor for the second time. I prayed it wouldn't be the last. Though our plan seemed flawless, especially with the security of Princess Zhara's authority behind us, there was no telling what unforeseen circumstances might arise to hinder us. I just kept thinking of Taralyn. No matter what, I prayed we would find her. In my heart, she was the main reason for formulating the plan, embarking on the journey, and taking the risk. Of course I would be happy to find any of the other women from the Colony, but Taralyn was my dear friend, and I owed a debt to her—the debt of my life.

We met that day at Captain Lynch's ship, which bobbed on the surface of the water at the end of a wooden pier. I waited with Janna at the edge of the wharf as Danein and Marcus, tunic sleeves rolled up to their elbows, helped Lynch's men load our belongings and the provisions into the vessel. The wind stirred up the water wildly; waves crashed against the wood and stone, spitting and spraying water like a hissing cat. I backed away to avoid the spray and saw Zhara arrive in the same plain, boxy coach she had used to meet us before. I knew she was trying to avoid notice from the townspeople, though I doubted many in Fynn Harbor had ever actually seen their princess as the royal city was leagues from the small village.

Zhara's men handed her down and gathered her luggage. I sent Janna back to the inn to fetch Liora and then skipped forward to meet Zhara. Again, she looked ravishing to my eyes despite her plain woolen kirtle, which was cinched around her waist with an equally plain belt. Her hair was plaited down her back and wrapped in a long head shroud. The only color that stood out was a light blue woolen shawl draped around her shoulders to fend off the sea chill.

Before I met her, I looked back anxiously at the ship. Danein and Marcus were unaware of Zhara's arrival, still busily loading crates and barrels onto the ship. I bit my bottom lip and smiled, holding my hands out to Zhara. She took them and greeted me warmly.

"Oh, my sister. I am so glad to see you again."

"How was your trip to Fynn Harbor?" I asked.

"A bit tedious. We were delayed along the way by some rain and mud, but nothing serious. We only arrived in Fynn Harbor just this morning, though I'd hoped we would have arrived an entire day in advance. That was the reason for my message late last night."

"Yes, we received it and were sorry to have missed you, but glad you arrived safely." I looked back again to discover that Danein had stopped his work and was motioning to Marcus to come down off the ship. He had seen us. I turned back to Zhara. "I am eager for you to meet someone." I took her hand, pulling her along the wharf toward the pier.

"Would this be the prince about whom you wrote me?"

"Yes, and he is eager to meet you as well. You were a secret to him until just a few days ago."

Zhara gave a good-natured laugh but tugged on my hand to slow our progress. "Alonya, should I consider this a matchmaking endeavor?"

I stopped and turned to her. Her skeptical eyes and waning smile said that she was less than enthusiastic about meeting yet another seemingly hopeless prospect, and I understood why. She was worried that Marcus would turn out to be just another disappointment. I sobered my expression but squeezed her hand.

"No, it doesn't have to be. Only if you so desire."

She sighed, but her eyes traveled above and beyond me to catch a glimpse of the stranger. "Is he even looking for a wife, Alonya?"

"I don't know, but he doesn't have one yet, so that's hopeful!"

Zhara chuckled. "Well, I suppose it speaks well of him that he's joined us on this mission all the way from Coralind."

Zhara straightened her shoulders then and nodded to me, and I continued leading the way. Just ahead, Marcus descended the platform from the ship to the pier, joining Danein as he stood awaiting our arrival. The prince bowed deeply before either Danein or I could say a word of introduction. When he stood, his earnest gray eyes locked firmly on Zhara's. Neither spoke for a moment; the prince and princess merely stared at each other, Zhara with tentative curiosity, Marcus with solemn fervor. Finally Zhara offered her hand. Marcus took it and kissed it according to custom.

"Lady, I am beyond honored to be in the presence of the king's daughter."

"Do you know my father then?"

"Indeed, no, I have met him but once and it was years ago when your father made a diplomatic visit to Coralind. I don't believe I had the pleasure of meeting you then, but I must say I am glad of it."

Zhara's brows rose in surprise. "Glad of it? Why so?"

Marcus released her hand and retreated two steps, casting his gaze down to his feet. He cleared his throat. "Well, to speak frankly, Your Highness, I was a bit of a presumptuous, arrogant toad in my younger days. I would not have been worthy of you, and I don't think you would have liked me."

Zhara seemed pleasantly surprised by the confession and put a hand to her mouth to cover her smile.

"Oh, it's true, I assure you. I'm not just saying that for the sake of making conversation and being charming."

Danein stared incredulously at Marcus and slid closer to him to knock him in the side with his elbow. I laughed, which freed Zhara to laugh aloud as well.

"Do you normally consider yourself charming then?"

Marcus smiled, but his cheeks reddened to near the shade of his hair. "At one time I suppose I did, but I've learned my lesson."

Zhara looked from me to Danein, then back to Marcus. She had grown comfortable in his presence, realizing she had the upper hand. "Well, sir, there's no 'Your Highness' with me. You may call me Zhara, and I am pleased to have made your acquaintance."

Marcus bowed again respectfully. "And I, yours. Call me Marcus, if you please. What I've seen of your country is lovely, thus far as I can tell." He kept his eyes on Zhara as he spoke. She seemed momentarily disarmed, but quickly regained her standing.

"Yes, Zaphon is a beautiful kingdom, albeit small and obscure compared with the other kingdoms of the world. Geographically we are the farthest from Coralind, are we not?"

"It's true, which is why I've never had the good fortune of visiting myself."

"Zaphon has great strengths, but unfortunately, we are also prideful and stubborn. Some traditions we have abandoned easily, like our belief in the High King. But then to some traditions we cling: for centuries my father has walked in the policies and dictates of the kings before him, upholding laws which are unjust. You see, Zaphon's pride is in these traditions and laws—

traditions and laws that give our country the lowest percentage of poverty and crime in any of the kingdoms of the world, yet in so doing promote slavery. Those that fall in the margins of society are banished and driven from their homes, eventually ending up in slaving camps." Zhara put her head down, which until then had been raised high. She inhaled a shaky breath, and when she again raised her eyes to the prince, they were rimmed with red. "We exploit our people, Marcus. We exploit the needy instead of helping them. We conveniently get rid of our poor and sick and unchosen, and by this we boast that Zaphon has the lowest rate of poverty and crime." She shook her head. "The crime may not be exposed to the populace, but it's there. It's quiet, hidden within the legislative system of Zaphon."

I reached over and gently took Zhara's hand in mine. That silent act let loose the emotional flood in the princess, and despite herself tears ran down her cheeks. She took a handkerchief from a pocket of her garment and hastily wiped the tears away. The world seemed to quiet and slow around us. Gulls cried above; the waves slapped the piers, and men's voices sounded from the ship, calling out orders to each other. And I held Zhara's hand and let her cry. Marcus dropped his gaze to his feet once more, his brow rippled in thought and concern. Danein watched me with a small, compassionate smile.

"I'm so sorry," Zhara said, sniffing, wiping away the last traces of tears on her cheeks and depositing the handkerchief once more into her pocket. She squeezed my hand and let go. "I may be immune to the common laws of Zaphon, but this is my country and my people, and I feel for them—with them. My father has not chosen the path of righteousness and justice, and that brings me deep despair and shame. I long to make a difference, but I feel so limited and useless, what with being a woman and an unchosen myself."

"And have you so little power and influence, then, as the daughter of the king?" Marcus asked.

"Yes, it means almost nothing to be the daughter of a king here in Zaphon, at least in national affairs and policy. But"—she took a deep breath and squared her shoulders, again locking eyes with Marcus—"what little influence I have, I will use to the best of my ability to help these that have been forced against their will into slavery. And I'll keep praying and hoping that one day there will be change."

Marcus nodded, his face lit with compassion, and sadness swimming in his eyes. "Allow me, Princess Zhara, to be your champion in this cause. My heart is stirred with the plight of Zaphon's unfortunates. I offer you my services insofar as they may be useful to you. I join my influence and power with yours, and together, with the aid of the High King, I do sincerely believe that Zaphon will see change coming swiftly as on wings of an eagle."

"Thank you, sir. You have no idea what that means to me."

Just then, Janna came down the pier loosely clutching leather reins, Liora clopping along behind her. The unicorn had remained all these many months disguised as an ordinary mare, and I frequently forgot that she was more than she appeared. I had now grown so accustomed to seeing her as a mare that I often wondered whether the unicorn was nothing more than a mere illusion, something I had somehow conjured from my imagination. I often longed to see her again as a unicorn—to relive those moments of magic and wonderment. The unicorn had appeared as a guide and guardian in my most desperate times of need. Although I realized I was beyond that need, I still longed for the experience of magic as a kind of reminder that we weren't alone in our quest. I craved assurance that everything that had happened before—meeting Liora and the High King and staying at his palace—hadn't been merely a fancy of my mind. Already it seemed like a faraway dream, the recollection of which lessens and fades as time elapses until it's gone, forgotten except as a faint, shapeless impression on the heart.

All eyes fixed on Liora, creamy white but for small flecks of dirt and mud on her legs near her hooves. She moved ahead of Janna and approached me, thrusting her head forward near mine. I laughed and held her head in my hands, stroking her face. The others stroked her mane as they stood by.

"Hello, beautiful Liora," Marcus greeted. He had met her during his stay at the inn.

Zhara's eyes were wide with delight and surprise. "What a magnificent horse!" Her hand strayed from Liora's mane and roamed her flanks and her legs before moving up to her face. "Wherever did you get her? Even some of my father's horses aren't this well-bred."

"The High King gave her to me," I said, smiling broadly at Danein. He shook his head and lowered his face to hide a smile. He and I alone shared the secret that Liora was a unicorn.

"Then she must be very special indeed," Zhara said.

"Oh yes, she's much more than she appears to be," Danein added. He gave her a hearty pat and took the reins from Janna, who had drawn near. "I believe we are just about ready to embark." He turned to signal to a man on the ship and received an affirmative signal. "Yes, Captain Lynch says we're ready. I'll take Liora up and let you say your good-byes, Alonya." He kissed Janna on the cheek then turned away with Liora to ascend the platform to the ship's deck.

"We will follow," Marcus said, rolling his sleeves down over his muscular forearms and offering an arm to Zhara. "Shall we, m'lady?"

Zhara took his arm and allowed herself to be led by Marcus. As they walked away, they seemed to easily reengage in conversation. The waves and gulls soon drowned out their voices, and I was left with Janna on the pier.

"I am glad this time there is no need for such a hasty departure," Janna said with a weak chuckle. "The last time you left it was over two years until I saw you again."

I nodded as tears filled my eyes. "I know. I wish I could say when we might see each other again…*if* we will…"

"Of course we will!"

"Yes, of course, you're right. I should speak with more hope and expectancy." I inhaled a deep draught of the sea air and let it out quickly, willing myself not to cry. "*When* we return, you can be certain that Havley will have a place with Marcus in his employment."

"Oh, my dear, I know that. That's not what's foremost on my mind right now." She took my face between her hands. "Don't you worry about me or Havley. You are on a righteous mission, and may the High King bless your journey, guide your steps, and grant you success, and I will trust Him for your safety. I *know* we will see each other again."

I nodded, my throat tight. Janna went on.

"Your life has only just begun—you have this adventure and many more before you, my dear Alonya. You have family and friends and love. You have the favor and strength and blessing of the High King. Don't ever lose that or forget. Never forget."

"I won't."

Janna brought my head down and kissed me on the forehead, then let go of my face to wrap me in an embrace. I returned the hug, too emotional to offer any words. The lump grew tighter in my throat. Janna stepped back, surveyed me with a smile, and then turned to make her way back up the pier. She offered a wave to those already on the ship as she walked along the wharf toward the inn. I watched her all the way, but she never looked back.

THE OUTLANDS

The ensuing weeks saw Marcus, Danein, Zhara, and I eastward across the Great Sea, roughly following the shoreline of Zaphon. For the first two days, the wind favored us, filling out the sails of Captain Lynch's ship, and we bounded along as though sprinting atop the water. After that our journey became more laborious as the winds changed, and the captain had to order his men to the oars in the ship's hold. We trudged along in this manner for another four days, so that in just short of a week we had made it to our place of berth on the northernmost borders of the Outlands of Zaphon.

The landscape that spread out before us was dismal. To the west rose up dunes of sand; a bare, rocky wasteland stretched south and eastward, dotted with small hills and buttes. Far on the distant horizon in that direction, mountainous terrain rose up. Our intended destination lay somewhere beyond that.

Sand and dust swirled on the wind as we disembarked on the shore. Next to the small, crude wharf, at the base of a high sandstone butte, was a camp. At least fifty small canvas tents and several fire pits surrounded a stone well in the center—the living quarters for the slaves and laborers working there. There also stood nearby a large, weather-beaten barn in which to stable the working animals.

We left the ship and drew near the camp. As Zhara's "lady-in-waiting," I walked beside her and pulled Liora along loosely by her reins. I knew it would be assumed that Liora was the princess's horse. She had been restless from the sea voyage and now tossed her head and whinnied with excitement to have freedom of movement. I whispered to her softly and stroked her mane as we strode through the camp. The air reverberated with the sharp clang of metal on rock. Hundreds of men—and even some women—were at work digging along a wide canal with pickaxes and shovels. The canal began at the water's edge and stretched southward toward the mountains. My eyes fixed with fascination on the workers as we walked past them; many stopped to survey us as well. I was surprised to find that most of them, even the women, appeared very strong and sturdy. I wondered which were the paid workers and which the slaves. There were a small number of taskmasters standing watch over the workers, but none with whips or angry voices.

Princess Zhara and Captain Lynch strolled ahead of the rest of us to seek out the foreman of the digging operation to show him our papers and thus secure our passage through the area. A short, stocky-looking fellow with little hair and a greasy head, the foreman was expecting us and bowed deeply to the princess, immediately ushering us to a specially prepared place just south of the workers' camp—within sight, but far enough away to allow for a greater sense of privacy. A high wedge tent had been erected for the princess, with openings on either side, and a cot and small table on the inside. The rest of us, as the princess's "staff," were meant to fend for ourselves. Captain Lynch and his men would stay the next several nights on the ship. I would stay with Zhara in the tent. Danein and Marcus planned to construct a small tent from our stores and supplies, just big enough for two men to sleep in.

As the four of us unpacked and settled into our sleeping quarters for the evening, I couldn't help but chuckle at the disproportionate accommodations between Zhara and Marcus—both royalty, yet unequal in their sleeping arrangements. I mentioned my observation to Marcus, and he merely shrugged his shoulders.

"Zhara has come as herself—the princess of Zaphon—whereas I have not. I am here for her, for you two. Even if I had made myself known and been given a furnished tent, I would still have offered it to you, Alonya, for you are a lady, and I"—he bowed, smiling broadly—"merely your humble servant."

"You're a silly goose, is what you are!"

"What was it he called himself at the wharf in Fynn Harbor?" Zhara said, her arms laden with blankets. "A presumptuous, arrogant toad?"

Marcus affected a look of insult. "Now, now, that was *before*, in my old life."

Zhara laughed and continued on into her tent.

"I am no longer like that," Marcus called after her. "Truly—I am a reformed man!" When he didn't receive an answer from the tent, he shot a glance of helplessness at me and shrugged his shoulders.

"She likes you," I assured him, beaming. That elicited a smile from him, and he continued on with the construction of his modest tent.

That night, after the sun had touched the tops of the sand dunes, glazing them with a glossy golden hue on its descent downward, and the sky had darkened and lit up with stars, we built a fire near our small camp, attempting to stave off the desert chill. Liora stood by freely, untied to the post that had been set into the ground earlier just for her. I knew that if she was to wander away at any time during the night, she would be back the next morning. The clamor from the digging crew had lessened, though not stopped. Captain Lynch and his crewmen had helped us cook and then joined us for a meal, after which they quitted us to mingle and carouse with the canal crew before eventually making their way back to the ship. Early the following day, we would strike out south- and eastward toward the craggy mountains to seek out the slaving camps. My heart beat rapidly within me at the thought of seeing Taralyn again after more than two years. I hoped and prayed that we would find her well—that we would find her at all.

The fire warmed us, and as we sat around it, looking deeply into the dancing flames, I was reminded of the Colony. How long ago that life seemed and how completely foreign to who I was now. I thought of all the evenings, just like this one, I had sat next to Danein and spoken with him, how I had come to look forward to his visits, how my heart would light up and come alive whenever he was near. There had also been sorrow in that happiness because I had doubted myself so, and I had doubted Danein's intentions. Oh, how I had longed for his affection, yet didn't dare hope or believe it could ever be mine.

That night, with Danein beside me, as he had been for many days and nights since the Colony, I was astonished anew at what favor the High King had shown me, at what hope he had given me. Danein must have been thinking along similar lines because he quite unexpectedly took my hand in his and kissed it. My face warmed, and I blushed at the evident, outward sign of affection in front of our friends; but Zhara and Marcus were deep in conversation on the other side of the fire, as were Captain Lynch and the foreman, who had come over to check on the princess's accommodations.

"Do you have your ring?" Danein asked me quietly.

I nodded and pulled the chain out from the neck of my garment to expose the ring dangling on the end of it. "I never take it off," I told him.

He nodded and stroked my fingers. "I promise that you shall wear it soon."

"I'm not worried," I assured him.

Again he brought my hand up to his lips and kissed it, never taking his eyes from mine.

"I bid you good night, young people," came the captain's hearty voice. He stood and was followed by the foreman.

"I ought to be saying g'night as well. Must check on my crew. Some o' them can get a bit wild durin' this time o' night." He smiled sheepishly at the princess. "Don't want none o' them disturbin' your Highness."

"You have been more than accommodating, sir, and I thank you."

"Well then, g'night, ladies and gentlemen." The foreman nodded to us and was gone. The captain watched him go, waiting until he was out of earshot before turning once again toward us and leaning in close.

"I made arrangements with the foreman as planned. He's going to lend you horses and mules for your journey tomorrow to help pull the wagons."

"Nice work, Lynch," Marcus said.

"I'll make sure my men are up early to have everything prepared for your departure. We'll follow you after two days and meet you at the halfway point on your return trip. I'll try to convince the foreman to lend me extra horses—I'm not yet sure how, but I'll think of something."

"Tell him you must meet us with extra supplies," Zhara said. "That will be true enough. Of course, they'll be for the women we bring back, but the foreman doesn't need to know that."

"Yes, I might just say that. Good night then. See you in the morning." The captain took his leave.

Marcus chuckled suddenly. "'They will be for the women we bring back,'" he said, repeating Zhara's words, "'but the foreman doesn't need to know that.' Truly, Princess, you never cease to amuse and surprise me."

She laughed. "It's true, all the same. I wouldn't want the poor captain telling an outright lie, but neither can we expose our plans. Everything we've done and said so far is the truth: we *are* on a charity mission to bring provisions to the slaves at the camps, and also so that I can determine the state and condition of things there. You are all on this mission with me as my trusted servants and advisors. That's what these people understand our visit to mean, and that's the truth. There's no need to mention anything beyond that."

"No need to mention what? That we're really here to steal back the women that were kidnapped from Zaphon?" Marcus said with laughter in his voice. Zhara shushed him and glanced around at the darkness beyond our circle of firelight.

"Do not fear, Princess. There is nobody here but us."

"You, sir, are too free with that loose tongue of yours!" she scolded, but there was no mistaking the smile on her lips.

"Even if we are found out and caught, there is nothing legally that can be done to us," Marcus went on.

"How do you mean?" I asked.

"Correct me if I'm wrong, Zhara, but this entire slaving operation is neither legal nor illegal. It is merely *permitted*. The king knows of it and sanctions it, but there are no rules or laws by which it is governed. This base is given free rein to operate independently of the laws and statues of Zaphon. If it weren't so, it would be more public, and the king would have to acknowledge it publicly."

"That's true," Zhara added. "There is nothing in Zaphon's law regarding slavery. Indentured servitude, yes, but not slavery, especially not of this sort. Our law is yet so incomplete, and much is left to the discretion of my father. Where there are gaps and holes in the law, unjust things are allowed or tolerated or ignored, and those responsible go unpunished."

"Therefore, there is no danger for us from the law," Marcus went on. "The danger, if any, will come from the men in charge of this slaving operation, because we will be taking something valuable from them: part of their livelihood."

"How will we slip the women through this camp unseen?" I asked suddenly, realizing how little I'd actually considered the many fine details involved in our task.

"We will have to wait until the cover of night to sneak them onto the ship, and even then make a wide circuit around the camp," Marcus said. He sighed deeply, no trace of mirth left on his face. "Let's pray that we make it all the way back here."

We all retired to bed soon after, Zhara and I to her pavilion, and Danein and Marcus right outside to their small tent. Zhara attempted to convince me to sleep on the cot, but I was insistent that she have it, if only for the sake of appearances so as not to betray ourselves if anyone happened to look in on us. I made a small bed on the floor, which was not unlike many of the places I'd slept throughout my life. Zhara's breathing evened out quickly, and I could tell she had fallen asleep right away. From the men's tent outside came soft snoring sounds. I, however, didn't fall asleep as quickly or easily. My mind ran with too many thoughts, and my stomach jittered with nerves. As the evening wore on, the sounds from the workers' camp lessened more. Finally work stopped altogether for the night, but it was still some time before quiet settled over the place. It was only then, past the middle of the night, that the gentle sound of lapping waves from the sea reached my ears. When I listened closely, I could even hear the creaking of the captain's ship as it bobbed on the water. Only then did I finally fall asleep.

Morning came quickly enough. I was awakened by the bright light pouring in through the open canvas flaps of the tent windows. I sat up abruptly. Zhara's cot was empty, and her personal bag of belongings was gone. On the table stood a ceramic basin with a pitcher of water. I leaped up and made myself presentable as best as I could, then exited the tent. A bustle of activity and noise greeted me. Everyone was up and readying for our journey.

I recognized many of the shipmates moving back and forth, carrying barrels, boxes, and crates, and setting them on five large wagons that were lined up nearby. I glanced around for any sign of Danein, Marcus, or Zhara. Finally a hand came down gently on my shoulder.

"We're just about ready to go," Danein said.

"Why didn't you wake me?"

"I wanted to let you sleep. I'm surprised you slept as long as you did, through all this noise. Did you not sleep well?"

"No, I didn't. It took me a long while to fall asleep."

"Well, that explains your deep slumber well into the morning."

"I wish I could've helped with something," I said, looking around for any unfinished task. My eyes fell on Marcus helping Zhara up into the saddle of a horse. He waved us over when he saw us.

"It's time to go," Danein said, taking my hand and leading me to Liora, who stood next to Zhara's horse, all saddled and ready for me. "Allow me, dear lady-in-waiting."

I pursed my lips in a tight-lipped smile and allowed him to hand me up.

"I thought you would ride Liora," I told Zhara.

"Well, I tried, but she would not let me up. She's a strange, stubborn mare. Besides, I hoped to flatter the foreman by riding one of his horses." She smiled and patted the neck of her steed.

Marcus shared a few words of parting and instruction with Captain Lynch before our party set off. Marcus and Danein took the lead, guiding by foot two mules hitched to wagons. Zhara and I followed on our horses with three of Lynch's men behind us, also leading wagons. We followed the rough, rocky path southeastward, along the line of rising land to our left. It wasn't long before the cool sea breeze was far behind us and we were fully enveloped by the heat. I looked back and saw nothing but the rocky, sandy desert all around us.

The mountains loomed up as we approached them, and we soon made our way into their hold. We followed the path of a shallow valley that eventually turned into a deep canyon as steep, stark walls of sandstone and limestone rose up on either side. Once the sun began its descent in the west, our path was swathed in shadow, which cooled the air. A few tufts of dry grass, brittlebush, and sagebrush were tucked into corners and crags in the rocks. Every so often, a snake or scorpion would skitter across the path, upsetting the mules, and often in the distance there would come a faint howling. The sound made me shiver with trepidation.

"What is that?" I asked after I'd heard it the first time. "A coyote?"

Marcus and Danein had pulled back during the journey and were walking alongside our horses. Marcus listened intently when the next howl came. He frowned.

"No, it's a desert hound—something like a dog or wolf, but thin and hairless. We have them in our deserts in Coralind."

"Are they dangerous?" I asked as another howl drifted through the canyon on the wind.

"There should be no danger for us in the daylight since the hounds hunt at night."

"And what about when we make camp for the night?"

"We build a fire. That will keep the hounds away, though I'm not sure how they react to humans. Danein?"

Danein shook his head. "Nor I. The Outlands is the only desert in Zaphon, and very few people come out here. I've never encountered one of these creatures before."

"Well, I'm certain we pose more of a threat to the hounds than they do to us." Marcus smiled confidently. Upon seeing that I wasn't pacified, he added, "I wouldn't worry about it. We are armed, and we will have a watch throughout the night."

The howling eventually faded out of hearing altogether, yet I couldn't help but wonder what other unknown dangers of the desert might come upon us suddenly. How little we knew about the landscape we were currently traversing!

The canyon widened and leveled out again into a more open valley. A few desert trees grew along the base of the hills. We stopped to make camp when dusk settled in. Once our tents were set up and a fire built, we gathered around it eagerly. Though the day had been extremely warm, the air had grown very cool at the setting of the sun. From our stores and supplies, we were able to put together a modest meal. We all retired to bed soon after eating, except for two of the captain's men who were to take the first watch.

The noises of the desert seemed magnified at night in the stillness under that wide open sky. I lay awake, tense and alert, sensitive to every croaking insect or rush of wind through the valley. Every so often the men at watch, or Danein and Marcus in the nearby tent, would talk quietly to one another, and my heart would settle.

Just as I was finally dozing off, an abrupt sound of laughter followed by a shushing whisper jolted me awake. I turned onto my opposite side to find Zhara fully awake with a smile on her face.

"Danein and Marcus seem to be having quite the conversation," she said.

"What do you think they're talking about?"

"I can't make it out, but apparently, it must be something amusing."

I lifted myself onto an elbow. "I've noticed that you and Marcus have also been sharing a lot of conversation lately. What do you think of him?" I tried to appear disinterested as I asked, but I couldn't help turning up the corners of my mouth a little. Zhara didn't seem to notice or mind.

"I like him a lot. He has a good, noble heart. He seems to truly care about making a difference for the good of others, and he knows how to put others before himself. He weighs matters very thoughtfully and earnestly. Oh, he teases at times, but he knows how to gauge the situation and doesn't consider everything or everyone a joke for his own amusement." Zhara's eyes seemed to look through me as she spoke, and I had the impression that her mind was fully fixed on Marcus. "I do like that he can laugh, though, when the circumstances suit. He has such a lovely laugh—very resonant and manly."

"I think that is a very good picture of him," I agreed. "I'm pleased that you two are getting along."

"As am I." Her last words were spoken with the trace of a sigh, and it was unmistakable to me then that she had fallen in love with Marcus. I knew that sigh carried with it anxiety, so I was compelled to bring her any amount of peace or comfort I could.

"You don't have to fear," I told her suddenly, surprised at my own boldness, yet confident in my words.

Zhara seemed taken aback, and her eyes refocused in the dark on me. "Pardon?"

"Marcus is a transparent and honest man. He won't lead you to believe anything that's not true. He says and does what he means. He won't hurt you."

Silence followed, and I saw the gleam of a tear streak down Zhara's face. "Is it too much to hope that he may think of me in that way, Alonya?"

I reached out and touched her hand. "Not at all."

Just then, another burst of laughter issued forth from the men's tent, and Zhara and I caught it like a contagious disease. We began laughing as well, which silenced the men.

"What are you ladies discussing that's so amusing?" Danein called out.

I turned over on my belly and lifted myself onto my forearms. "Oh, we're merely laughing at you men," I called back. "You know, you really shouldn't talk so loudly. Others may eavesdrop without intending to. You ought to keep your secrets more secret."

Neither Marcus nor Danein responded, and that brought a fresh stream of laughter from Zhara and me.

"She's teasing!" Zhara finally admitted. "We didn't hear anything."

"Well, we have nothing to hide," Marcus replied. "If you must know, we were speaking of the events of the day and our plans for tomorrow. Naturally you two came up in conversation."

"Oh, *naturally*," I mocked.

I didn't worry about desert hounds any more that night.

The following day was much like the first. Against the protests of Danein, I walked most of the morning and afternoon alongside Liora to gain some exercise and give Liora a rest from carrying me. Danein stayed back with me. Zhara did likewise, but remained with Marcus at the head of our train. They conversed together easily, though their words were indistinct from our place behind them.

"The prince and princess have been getting along well, don't you think?" I asked Danein.

"Yes, I always thought they would. They do have a lot in common—similar passions, a like heart, same indomitable spirit."

"Yes, though I think her spirit is a little stronger to tame his." I giggled at that, my eyes falling on Zhara as she watched Marcus intently while he spoke, absorbing his every word, offering nods and smiles and laughter. My countenance grew staid. "I just hope Marcus is careful with her."

Danein seemed to weigh my words a moment before replying, as though deciding how much he ought to divulge. "He will be. You don't need to fear."

"That's what I told Zhara last night."

"Oh, so you ladies *were* speaking of us, then?"

"Well, *naturally* you came up in conversation."

Danein gave me a playful nudge, toppling me over into Liora. She snorted with irritation and moved over slightly.

"He does care for her, Alonya. You need not fear."

I nodded gratefully. "Thank you."

—∽∽—

We journeyed deeper into the mountains; our way included a vast deal of sloping paths as the landscape continued to rise higher. There was little vegetation to be found to offer a splash of color against that brown and gray palette. We were well into the heights at the close of the day. After we'd made camp, one of Lynch's men took Zhara's horse to ride onward and determine the distance remaining to the slaving camps. Upon his return, we learned that the camps were a mere two hours away. Wearied by two days in the sun and dust, we ate our meal quickly and retired to our tents. The howls of the desert hounds reappeared on the swell of the wind, but I was too fatigued to pay them any heed. I fell asleep instantly.

30

The Camps

The slave camps were nestled in a wide mountain alcove just along the base of a sheer rock wall that rose up to great heights and enclosed the slaving headquarters on three sides, towering over the inhabitants like a glaring, angry god. My jaw dropped as we entered through the high wrought-iron gates into the wide stone courtyard. The camps were much larger than I had imagined. Various people milled about in all directions, bent on any number of assorted tasks. Large wooden buildings and huts had been erected against the wall; there were also several large caverns dug into the mountain face itself. I wondered in awe at the series of tunnels and number of rooms those caverns must contain. How far back did they go, and to what other parts of the mountains?

Zhara atop her horse leaned in toward me as I rode beside her. "This is much more than I had anticipated, even with the descriptions from my spies."

"That's exactly what I was thinking," I said.

"It's much larger and more enclosed than I thought it would be. There seem to be no other outlets for exit except the gate through which we just entered, unless you want to attempt a climb."

I craned my neck back to catch a glimpse of the cliff towering above us. "I think climbing is out of the question."

Zhara lowered her voice as a man began to approach us in welcome. "We will have only one chance at this, Alonya. We must not fail."

The man was tall and skinny with a beak for a nose; he greeted us as we were being helped down from our horses. "Welcome, Your Highness. I am the headmaster here. We are honored you have chosen to grace us with your presence." He bowed low.

Zhara gave a little snort, barely acknowledging him with her eyes. "Let's make no pretense at polite conversation, sir. I have not come for you. I have come for these poor unfortunates that you have enslaved. If there is to be such an institution in Zaphon as this, I will do everything in my power to make certain that the people are treated humanely and given what they need."

The headmaster was caught off guard by the princess's brusque manner. He rose and cleared his throat. "My dear princess, I believe you are mistaken in believing these people slaves. What we do here is more akin to social reform. Those that Zaphon would cast out for being old or poor or disabled or unchosen, we take in. We give to them a home and good, honest work. We bring hope and purpose to these people. They are not slaves." He gave a pretentious laugh.

Zhara and I turned our eyes to scan the crowd. Some of the people had stopped to watch the exchange between their master and the royal visitor. Their eyes were blank and their smudged faces devoid of expression or emotion.

Zhara turned back to the tall man. "I see no hope before me. Please do not insult my intelligence, sir. I know just what's going on here, and it's *not* social reform."

The headmaster smirked and narrowed his eyes. "I understand your concern being that Your Highness is a sensitive, nurturing woman, and thus I will not take offense at what you have just said."

"Perhaps not, but I *will* take offense at you classifying my concern as mere womanly sensibilities. I assure you, there are many in Zaphon who know of this so-called secret slaving headquarters and would do something about it."

The headmaster nodded briefly as he scratched at the stubble on his face. He then broke out in a thin-lipped grin. "I seriously doubt that, Your Highness. I do seriously doubt that."

This disarmed and silenced Zhara. She set her gaze forward and motioned to me to come to her side.

"Alonya?"

I bowed as we had rehearsed. "Yes, Your Highness?"

"Tell this man what we require, please."

"Accommodations for the night, I presume," he said with a slight air of annoyance.

"Hardly," Zhara huffed. "I wouldn't spend a night here if my life depended on it." She turned a firm, steady gaze on the headmaster. "If we did, we might find ourselves unable to leave, taken against our will."

The man spat out a laugh. "Well, we do have unchosens here. You would certainly be a great prize to join our little enclave, Your Highness."

Out of the corner of my eye, I saw Marcus take a step forward, his face red with anger. Danein held him back. Nobody seemed to notice the action but me. Zhara kept her unflinching gaze on the headmaster, her head held aloft, maintaining stature and dignity. "I will be sure to let my father know that you think so."

The man's face blanched white, and he backed away slightly, lowering his gaze to the floor. Through grated teeth he said, "Forgive a poor fool like myself, Your Highness, for rash, foolish words. Please, what is it that you require while here?"

"I require proper respect due to the daughter of the king!"

The man nodded.

"My lady will give you further instructions while I take a tour of these grounds. Good day, sir." She signaled to Marcus, who was immediately at her side to chaperone her through the throngs of people in the courtyard. Danein crept close to me while I instructed the headmaster.

"These men will unload the provisions we have brought for the sla…uh…residents," I told him as firmly as I could manage. I heard a slight tremor in my voice and swallowed it, speaking with more authority next. "We desire to see each house and distribute the provisions ourselves. Some are material possessions—clothing, blankets, and such—and should *not* be taken away or denied the people once we have left. Most, however, is food, and some medical supplies. We have also brought a small offering of supplies for the workers here."

"You and your mistress are too generous, m'lady."

I let my gaze shift to where Zhara and Marcus were threading their way through the people. They were a dirty bunch, unlike the workers at the canal dig who had looked mostly muscular, strong, and well-fed. These people were thin and wore soiled, ragged clothing; their lank hair was oily and their skin smudged from a lack of washing. There were old, frail-looking women; bedraggled men with their bodies slumped from a life of difficulty and woe; people who limped or walked with crutches, some even missing limbs who crawled or dragged themselves along the ground; and children of various ages, subdued, walking shyly with heads down. Many had stopped to bow or kneel before the princess. She held their hands and touched their heads, speaking words of comfort to them.

My eyes searched frantically for Taralyn, for any sign of the other women from the Colony, but I saw none at all that indicated they were unchosen women. The youngest women there, besides children, looked middle-aged at the least.

Danein nudged me; I heard a throat being cleared and realized the headmaster was trying to speak to me. I turned to him and spoke before he could.

"I notice something very curious here, headmaster. Where are all the young women? You mentioned earlier that you kept unchosens—where are they?"

The man seemed to hesitate before speaking. He wrung his hands together. "Ah, yes, the women—we consider the unchosen women very precious. They are, after all, in a very precarious situation, what with their...*condition*...and thus we keep them separate from the rest of the inhabitants here. We wouldn't want the male residents taking advantage of them, if you understand my meaning."

"Oh, I understand you perfectly," I said, the blood rising to my face. "How very compassionate of you to think of the women's welfare in that way. The princess will be very pleased to learn that the women are in no way being taken advantage of."

The man attempted a smile, which looked more like a sneer. My heart hammered in my chest, and I felt near sick with disgust just standing in his presence. I waved him away, telling him we would call for him if he was required. Danein helped the captain's men unload some of the barrels and boxes from the wagons. Several people gathered around while we distributed water, dried beef, and fruit.

The afternoon sped by quickly as we made our rounds, walking the wide circumference of the mountain alcove, visiting each resident house—there were separate houses for the men, women, and children—the working houses, and the kitchens. Women and children were busy at all sorts of trades: cooking, laundering, spinning, weaving, sewing, candle making, and soap-making as well as bottling wine and mixing herbs and medicines. The men were working more labor-intensive trades. There were smiths forging swords, bowers making crossbows and arrows, carpenters building furniture, wheelwrights producing wheels, potters crafting ceramic jugs and pots, glassblowers fashioning windows, stone-cutters working the rock, and cobblers making shoes.

We walked amongst them. They were all hard at work, their heads bent low; they occasionally dared a sidelong glance at the princess and her small entourage. Danein, Marcus, and the captain's men walked behind us, distributing our provisions to those who were brave enough to leave their work and approach us. Few spoke, even when Zhara attempted to engage them in conversation. She asked questions about their work and their lives, but they didn't answer. They occasionally nodded or shook their heads, but we were unable to determine anything definitive about the nature of the camp from those vague answers.

As we left one of the working houses to return to the courtyard, Zhara motioned to the headmaster, who immediately approached us. "You—headmaster—for what reason are all these goods made? Where do they go?"

He bowed, his hands folded tightly together. "Some stay here with the residents, but most go back into Zaphon. Some we give away for charitable causes, and some we sell."

Zhara's brows rose at that news. "Some you sell? So you make a profit?"

"No, Your Highness, we do not profit. What little we make goes into buying and shipping more supplies to keep our good institution running."

"But surely you must profit something by having free labor available through all these people."

"If it were only so. However, as I described earlier, we are a charitable institution ourselves. The main reason we produce such goods is to give honest, valuable work to these unfortunates, as you labeled them earlier."

"I wonder, sir, why a charitable institution such as this would choose a location in the Outlands, so far removed from civilization. Surely shipping and transportation of all these goods is costly and inconvenient from this location."

"As I said, any profit we make goes to the shipping and transportation of these goods. We think only of our residents. As you well know, the people of Zaphon have very little sympathy with outcasts such as these. We chose the Outlands so that they need not be bothered by the cruelty of others who would ostracize them. Here they can live in peace and security amongst others like them."

Zhara's head gave a slow shake, and she frowned just before turning her back on the man. He flared his nostrils in irritation and walked away. I watched him stalk to the other end of the courtyard to a small group of men and begin speaking fervently to them. Some of their gazes fell across the wide open space to where Zhara and I were standing.

I leaned in to the princess as we moved to another area of the camps. "Zhara, perhaps we ought to retreat a little with the veiled accusations. I think the masters here are starting to become suspicious, which is not going to help us find the women."

Zhara stopped and closed her eyes, sighing heavily. "You're right, of course." She looked me square in the eyes. "Speaking of the women, where are all the unchosens?"

"The headmaster told me they're kept in a separate part of the camps for their protection."

"Hmph! I don't believe that one bit, just as I don't believe his speech about this being a charitable institution and producing goods at little to no profit. But you are right when you say we don't want to create suspicion. Come, let us continue looking."

The mountain alcove was truly akin to a small village. All evidence pointed to an institution of social sanctuary and reform, as the headmaster had told us. Yet as we continued our tour, there grew an unsettled, troubled feeling in my heart. The people were all so silent. Their bodies were frail and thin, bent with the weight of oppression and injustice. Nobody smiled. Somehow it seemed that everything we could see was a façade, that the truth was still lurking somewhere underneath it all.

We watched some of the larger, stronger men at work digging a new tunnel through a rock face, their arms and necks shiny with sweat. A few were bare-chested, but most wore tunics. A man paced behind them, calling out harsh orders.

Marcus came up beside Zhara. "Look at that man," he said, gesturing with a tilt of his chin. We all looked on as the foreman angrily scolded one of the workers, pulling at his tunic and then shoving him back to his place.

"What happened?" I asked.

"That man tried to remove his tunic, and the foreman got angry, yelled at him, and pulled it back down. It's a warm day today, and those men are engaging in hard labor. Why would the foreman forbid him from removing his tunic?"

"Perhaps he doesn't want the princess to be offended by a shirtless man," I offered, knowing it was a weak guess.

"Yes, but those men over there are shirtless. It doesn't make any sense."

"Unless he's hiding something that he doesn't want us to see," Danein said from behind me.

I shook my head. "On the outside, this place seems to be just what the headmaster described, but something doesn't add up."

"The man is lying," Zhara said. "We know from my sources that these people have been brought here and made to work against their will. I would stake my life they are producing these goods to sell to private buyers and clients. That way all the money goes to the masters here to line their pockets and enlarge this business. It's all for personal gain and profit. Why hire workers when you can just enslave the outcasts of society? They have no one and no law to protect them, to say otherwise."

"You are speaking my thoughts exactly," Marcus added quietly, with an affirming nod from Danein. "The man's story is just a front he hides behind for what's really going on here. And anybody who didn't know better would just take him at his word."

"These people have all been silenced," I said. "That's why they're so quiet and look so fearful."

"They've been threatened with punishment if they speak," added Zhara.

"And these men," Danein said, indicating the diggers, "their backs are most likely covered with whip marks and scars. The tunics are to hide any evidence of poor treatment."

"Well, let us gain some proof of that fact," Zhara suggested. "I will go share some words with the foreman to keep his attention averted while you men check the workers' backs."

Without waiting for affirmation, she immediately stepped forward and addressed the foreman, who moved aside to speak with her, his back to his workers. Danein and Marcus quickly ran toward the workers and lifted the backs of their tunics without their consent. Puzzled, the men stopped their work but didn't say anything or resist. Marcus and Danein returned just as Zhara, smiling and laughing, turned away from the foreman. She soon resumed her place beside us.

"Well?"

"It is as we guessed."

She nodded, her face grave. "I believe we've seen every inch of this place. Where do you suppose the unchosen women are?"

"What about those tunnels in the mountain?" Marcus said. "We've passed several. Some are dens that look like housing and storage, but perhaps some actually lead to another part of the mountain."

"I can think of no other explanation," Zhara said, shaking her head. She inhaled deeply, her brows furrowed in thought. "I must go speak with the headmaster and convince him to let me see the unchosen camp. Wait here." She left us to seek out the beak-nosed man. Marcus made to follow her, but Danein held him back.

"We can watch her from here. She'll be fine."

We watched Zhara as she crossed the courtyard and found the headmaster. She seemed to approach him timidly, but once she had his attention, she pasted a smile onto her face and spoke to him with expressive hands to accompany her words. They conversed for several minutes before Zhara nodded to him and turned, finding her way back to us. The smile on her face disappeared once her back was to the man.

"I told him that I was sorry for my behavior earlier today, for insinuating that the residents here were being kept as slaves, that I had been misinformed, and that I desired his pardon. After that he seemed to warm up to me quickly."

We glanced at one another, smiling.

"I thought you didn't want to lie," I reminded her.

"Well, it's not a complete lie," she explained with a small roll of her eyes. "I *am* sorry for my earlier behavior insofar as it might have created suspicion against us and made our errand more difficult. But what else can I say? May the High King forgive me. I'm not perfect."

"You did well," Danein said.

Zhara went on. "After a little persuasion, he agreed to let us see the unchosens. He's going to find a man to escort us there, but I believe it will be a quick visit, and we will have very little time."

I looked upward to where the sun was just lowering beneath the tops of the towering peaks. The day was quickly waning. "Can we go now, please, and find Taralyn?"

Within half an hour we were following our escort through one of the cold, drafty mountain tunnels. Zhara and I kept in front while Danein, Marcus, and the few captain's men trailed behind us, leading the mules and wagons on which were held the remaining crates and barrels. Most were empty.

There were several twists, inclines, and descents along that dark corridor, as well as a few side tunnels branching off into other parts of the mountain, but we stayed along the main way. We emerged into another open space in the mountain, smaller than the main camp behind us, but similar in appearance. There were housing structures and huts topped with twigs and thatch. Unlike the larger camp, however, this one was quiet, seemingly abandoned but for the smoke coming from the chimneys within the houses; no people milled about in the outer courtyard. A few stray women were seen crossing from one building to the next, carrying baskets. There was less sun filtering down into the enclosed space, and the air was duskier and cooler than it had been on the other side of the tunnel.

We looked to our guide for instruction, but the small round man said nothing. He merely nodded to prod us forward. I swallowed hard, my heart beating wildly for the possibility of seeing Taralyn again.

"Which are the women's houses?" Zhara asked. The man pointed to three of the larger structures on the opposite end to where we stood. We moved forward tentatively. Outside the structures were several armed men standing guard.

"How are we going to do this?" I asked with my voice lowered.

Zhara shook her head. "I am not sure. I fear that if we do manage to get some of the women, it won't be very many. It seems they keep a much closer watch on them than they do on the rest of their slaves."

The first house was built high against the rock face atop a stone plateau. Zhara and I ascended steps to reach the door and entered without knocking, followed by the men bringing in two large crates and two barrels. We found ourselves in a large open room with a loft just above. The furniture consisted of cots lined against the walls for sleeping, and a couple tables and chairs. Several women sat on these cots and in the chairs, and just as in the other houses, their faces were indifferent and unsmiling as we introduced ourselves. We ladled out water for those who would drink and handed out a few garments. As before, few women were willing to speak freely and openly with us. They seemed tense and frightened. It was difficult to make out their faces in the low candlelight, but I could see enough to discern that these women were better groomed and clothed than the people at the larger camp had been.

I scanned the faces for Taralyn or any other woman I might recognize. I knew none. We moved on quickly from there to the next house. Luckily, the guards kept outside and didn't go in with us. In the second house, we tried again to elicit a few words from some of the women.

"Why is it that you women are all kept inside the houses in the middle of the day? Surely there is no danger to you here in this abandoned place?"

They looked back and forth at one another but said nothing. Zhara asked again and stared hard at each woman individually, as though demanding an answer.

Finally, a woman sitting close spoke up. "We are having our rest period. We do work in the mornings and evenings, but we get a rest in the afternoon."

"Yes," piped up another, a little too eagerly. "We have much more freedom here. We have regular exercise and baths. We are well taken care of."

"And why should you women be treated with such favor and the other residents not?"

There was a long pause before a stifled sob came from the back of the house, followed by an abrupt shushing whisper.

Zhara moved quickly to the back of the room from where the sounds came. "What is it? What are you trying to hide? You must know we are here to help you."

"Don't say anything," a woman hissed.

"Who's speaking? I demand to know!"

Uncontrollable sobbing suddenly broke forth, presumably from the woman who was being shushed. She sat curled atop her cot in the back of the room, bathed in shadow. Zhara sat next to her and put her arms around the woman.

"It's all right, dear, let it out."

Some of the other women began grumbling and shaking their heads. "Now she'll get us into trouble," someone said above the discontented murmurings.

"Quiet, all of you!" Zhara scolded. "Let this woman alone. She only desires truth and freedom, something that's been denied her for too long, I imagine."

That seemed to get everybody's attention, and they finally stopped their restless shuffling. I moved slowly to the back of the room toward Zhara, making sure I glanced closely at each woman I passed. Still I saw none I recognized. When I reached Zhara, the sobbing woman had calmed down a bit and was just wiping the damp hair from her face. My eyes nearly bulged when I recognized the face.

31

Eloise

"Eloise!" I called out, running to her side. Through watery eyes, she looked at me with confusion and curiosity; her face brightened once she realized she knew me.

"Alonya—is it really you?" she asked, her voice heavy with emotion. I fell on the cot and embraced her.

"Look, look, Danein's here too!" I said, waving him over. He came quickly, and it only took Eloise a moment to recognize him before she stood and threw her arms around his neck. Zhara laughed, her eyes glistening with tears.

"Oh, I cannot believe this!" Eloise exclaimed, glancing back and forth between the two of us. "How did you…what happened… you were never caught, Alonya?"

"No. I wandered alone until Danein found me and rescued me."

Eloise gave Danein a look of awe. "You always were a great hero."

He blushed and lowered his head.

"What happened after you were caught?" I asked.

"We were taken here, and this is where I've been all along."

"What about the others? Are they here too?"

Eloise dropped back down to her cot, lowering her eyes to her lap. The entire room was silent with tension. "Some made it, but most either died along the journey, or died during their time here. There are very few of us left."

"They treat you poorly then," said Zhara, her face grave.

Eloise nodded, tears pooling once more. "We're not supposed to speak of it."

"You best hush now, Ellie!"

"We're all going to be whipped!"

"Silent!" Zhara called out. "Let her speak."

Eloise began shaking. Marcus brought over a thick woolen blanket from our supplies and handed it to me. I covered her shoulders with it. "Do not fear, Eloise. We're here to help. We're going to get you out of here. That's why we've come."

The frightened woman looked at me with large, surprised eyes, and I could see a glimmer of hope. It was only then I noticed how thin and gaunt she had become. Her skin was sallow and her cheekbones much more defined from loss of weight in her face. She had never been a large girl, but the healthy glow and plumpness was gone, as it was from most of these women.

Eloise seemed to gain courage from my words. "Yes, they treat us poorly. It is true we are given more freedom and exercise than the slaves on the other side of the camp, but that is because… because they want us to please the clients."

Zhara's jaw tightened and she put her head down. I inhaled deeply. Marcus and Danein looked on with grave faces while the captain's men remained near the door at the other end of the room.

"And Taralyn," I said, "is she also here?"

"She was, but she's not anymore."

My heart nearly stopped in my chest. "She's dead then?"

"No—she was sold three or four months ago. She's gone."

My shoulders slumped and I looked at Danein. He was as stricken as I was. Eloise went on to give a description of the man who had bought Taralyn. Many of the women inserted their own descriptions and information about where they thought he came from in Zaphon, but none knew for sure. His name, as known amongst the women, was Roark.

Zhara rose to her feet and looked around the room, addressing each woman. There were at least twenty present as there had been in the other house. "We have come to rescue you women, to bring out of slavery as many as will come."

There was a sudden spark of energy in the room as the women whispered and mumbled amongst themselves. Zhara silenced them before continuing.

"To be honest, we didn't anticipate there being so many of you. I'm afraid we don't have enough crates and barrels to smuggle you all out, but for those that cannot make it on this trip, we will return for you."

A woman with long, tar-black hair and matching eyes rose. Her features were harsh. "Boxes and barrels, you say? You came here to smuggle us out in boxes and barrels? What do you take us for?"

Zhara stood her ground. "I take you for unfortunate women who have been abandoned and cast out by society, only to be taken against your will and abused, your bodies and hearts plundered by evil, ruthless men who treat you like animals, empty of heart or soul." Zhara approached the woman slowly. "But I know better. We—my friends and I—we have come in the name of the High King, to tell you that you do have a heart and a soul, that it is valuable and of great worth. You no longer need to live as slaves. There is freedom for you, and we are offering it to you now."

From across the room came sounds of soft sobbing. I watched the woman Zhara had addressed. Her lips tightened and her eyes momentarily filled with tears, but she lifted her head stubbornly. "And what are we to do with this freedom once we've gained it? Go on the run again? Go into hiding? Scrape together a semblance of a living while we wait to be recaptured? There is no true life for an unchosen woman. We have become nothing to the world. Here, at least, we are something."

"What are you here?" I asked, moving forward to Zhara's side.

"We are…provided for. We have shelter here, and food, and we are given nicer clothes and greater freedom than the other slaves."

This speech elicited nods of assent from many of the women.

"Here we have a place to be, some sense of belonging. Out there we are nothing."

"That's not true!" I said. "You *will* have somewhere to go and some place to belong out there. You can find sanctuary with the High King. He will be your refuge, your place of shelter and safety!"

The black-haired woman snorted derisively. "You are speaking of fairy tales. If the High King truly did rule, what would he want with the likes of us?"

"He does rule! I was there. I am an unchosen like you, and the High King accepted me and took me in! He offers a new beginning, a new start! There is hope for women like us."

There was more murmuring. The bold woman shook her head and sat down. "It's too late. And too dangerous. I'm not going to risk my life trying to escape when there's no guarantee out there for us."

Murmurs of assent came from all around.

"And what about our babies?" spoke up another woman.

"What babies?" Zhara asked.

"Some of us have children. We can't leave our children."

"Children that were brought here with you?"

A very young woman—hardly more than a girl—spoke up timidly from the other side of the room. "No. Some of us have conceived and borne children here as a result of our…our trade," she admitted.

We all stood shocked and stunned at the news. When neither Zhara nor I spoke, the timid girl went on.

"They are kind enough here to let us bear the children and not take them out of us before they are born."

"And what happens to these children?" I asked through a lump in my throat.

"They are kept in another part of the camps, in a nursery, tended to by some of the older women, until they are old enough to work. If we behave and do our work well, they let us see our children. But sometimes, if our children grow to be beautiful or strong, they are sold."

I bit my lip, and I could see Zhara's face quickly drain of color. She sat on a nearby cot and closed her eyes tightly, her hand going to her head. Marcus was quickly at her side, but she motioned that she was well enough, and he backed away.

"How many of you women have children here?" she asked.

Several hesitant hands rose into the air.

"And how many are expecting?"

More hands went up. Only about three or four in the group hadn't raised their hands.

Zhara took another moment of silence then sighed deeply. "I understand your predicament, and would not compel any here to leave their children. For those who are interested in leaving with us today, we urge you to come. For all the rest—believe me when I say it will be my life's work and mission to see you and your children all freed. You will not be forgotten, and I will not give up until I have accomplished it."

The room was silent in thought and anticipation. We waited for any women to come forward. One of the captain's men who had stayed nearby the door during the entire exchange announced that it was late afternoon and we still had one more house to visit.

"Please, who will come with us?" Zhara implored.

I moved to Eloise and took her hand, squeezing it tightly. She nodded and stood up. "I'll come. And though Taralyn is not here, there are a few women from the Colony left here who live in the third house. I'm sure they'll come when they see that you're here for them."

Three more women from Eloise's house volunteered to leave with us. We quickly emptied the boxes and barrels and stowed the women inside as best we could, imploring them to remain quiet and still. The men carried them down the outside steps, setting them onto the wagons. We were watched gingerly by the house guards, but none spoke to us. We quickly visited the third house with a new set of crates and barrels. Danein and I were reunited with five more women from the Colony, but only three chose to come with us, making seven in all. We again emptied the crates and barrels and stowed the women inside, then carried them out to the wagons.

The clip-clopping of the mules' hooves on the stone masked any other noise, and we were able to cross the courtyard and enter the tunnel undetected. The women had told us that they were never made to account for their presence unless a client had come to call. Hopefully the seven we had taken would not be missed.

We moved quickly once we made it through the tunnel into the main courtyard near the gates. My heart was beating rapidly against my chest and I was near faint with anxiety. I saw freedom in those gates, and I longed to be through them. Just as we were mere feet away from our exit, the headmaster called us to stop and began approaching our train. When I saw the smile on his face, my pulse relaxed. I swallowed hard and smiled broadly, just as I saw Zhara was doing.

"Your Highness, will you not consider staying? The day is nearly over, and it is a long journey back to the coast."

"Thank you for your hospitality, sir, but I must decline the invitation. I have done what I came to do. I see that you are doing some good work here, and I am satisfied with my findings. Thank you again."

"Of course, Your Highness. Have a safe return journey, and we hope you will visit again soon." He bowed and turned abruptly, walking away with what I considered to be an air of relief.

Zhara's smile melted. "Hmph. No true gentleman would let the princess of Zaphon journey close to evening. You can see how eager he is to be rid of us. He fears we will discover his secret."

"Which we have," Marcus said. "Come, we must go."

We had only taken a few steps when I grabbed Danein's arm and stopped.

"What about Taralyn? We need to find out where she went."

"We have a name and a description from the girls," Danein assured me, but I was not pacified.

"But we have no idea where they went, where he lives. We have to try and get more information."

Zhara and Marcus had stopped and turned to me. I looked to each of them with entreaty. Finally Marcus stepped forward and said, "I'll go with you. We will speak with the headmaster and see if we cannot find out anything. Danein, you and the men take Zhara and follow the road back. We'll be along shortly."

"Be careful," Zhara said.

Danein squeezed my hand and they began moving again. Marcus and I waited until they were outside the gates and around the corner; we turned and sought out the headmaster. Several men were lighting torches and braziers throughout the courtyard, signaling evening's approach.

We found the headmaster in his private quarters—a large, luxurious room cut out of the rock face, like the antechamber of a great fortress. Vertical wooden beams reached high from the floor to reinforce the rock ceiling. Lavish rugs covered the cold stone floor, and thick brocade drapes hung from the ceiling to the floor in flowing folds, partitioning off the back portion of the room from the front. Several wall braziers with glowing red coals circled the perimeter of the room, providing light and warmth. The headmaster sat at a table, making notes on a piece of parchment paper. He stood to receive us.

"Hello again, and so soon. Has the princess changed her mind about sleeping accommodations?"

"No. I actually had a question of a personal nature that I wanted to put to you."

The man's brows rose. "Oh?" He stood and walked to the side of the table, leaning a hand atop it. "What can I help you with?"

"When we were visiting the unchosen camp, I heard of a woman with whom I used to be acquainted. It seems she is no longer here…that she, uh, was brought back into Zaphon. Her name is Taralyn, and I wondered if you might give me any information about her."

The man's face froze, expressionless. I feared I had said too much. I didn't want to get any of the women in trouble, nor give this man any reason to make a detailed inquiry into the unchosen camp, lest he discover the missing girls. He ran a finger along the edge of the table and slowly moved back to his chair, though he did not sit.

"Taralyn," he said, drawing the name out slowly. "We have so many women here, you must understand. Can you give me a description of her?"

I told him what I knew—how Taralyn had looked the last time I'd seen her, although I knew she might have changed significantly during her time at the camp. The headmaster pursed his lips as if in thought.

"Yes, this girl you describe is familiar to me. She was here. But I'm afraid I cannot tell you where she went."

"Do you not know?" Marcus cut in, stepping forward.

The headmaster seemed taken aback that Marcus had addressed him. He gave him an affronted look. "Of course I know, but I'm not at liberty to say."

"Why not?"

"For the protection of our women, as I mentioned before. It is confidential information."

I looked to Marcus, uncertain what to do next. A bulky man stepped out of the shadows behind the headmaster and approached him. Marcus pulled back next to my side while the two men spoke in hushed whispers, occasionally glancing in my direction. A shock of fear rippled through my body when I recognized the big man. I turned sideways and tapped Marcus's arm.

"Marcus, that man there. I think I know him."

"What do you mean?"

"He was one of the men that captured me when my sister-in-law gave me up in Fynn Harbor. He was wounded when Danein rescued me. I'm sure he must recognize me."

Marcus nodded in understanding. "I see. Don't worry, Alonya. I won't let anything happen to you."

The two men finished speaking, and the headmaster turned back to me, beaming as though quite pleased with himself.

"It seems my man here knows you," he said. I stiffened, and Marcus instinctively moved closer to me. My only comfort was in feeling his arm next to mine. The headmaster continued. "Apparently you know this Taralyn because you, too, were once an unchosen. Perhaps the true reason you came here was to find her and rescue her. Am I close?" He scrutinized me closely, and I did my best to remain calm under his unnerving stare.

"Why should I want to rescue someone from here," I said, "when this is a charitable institution and the residents are not slaves, as you have previously explained?"

"It seems to me, my dear lady, that you may know more than you should. You were bound for this place once, but you had a little help. I can see now from looking at you that it was a shame to have lost you. You would have been a nice addition to our little community here."

He walked toward me; Marcus stepped forward to keep him from getting too close.

"You know, the world out there is not safe for unchosen women."

"Only because of men like you. And I'm not unchosen!"

"Then where is your token of marriage to prove otherwise?"

I pulled out the chain from under the neckline of my dress to show the silver ring dangling from it. The man snorted.

"You don't wear it. That is a ring of promise, not of marriage. You don't yet belong to anybody."

"I belong to the princess's convoy, and you would do best to remember it!" I declared boldly, though my voice shook.

The man glared down his large nose at me. "Yes, well, consider that your salvation. If it wasn't for that, you, my dear girl, would belong to me."

"Watch how you speak to the princess's lady!" Marcus warned, stepping forward nose-to-nose with the man. He matched him in height but ousted him in build and strength. "Now, you have valuable information that we desire. You are right to say we came seeking out the woman Taralyn. You will tell us where she is and how we can find her. If you do not, there will be trouble." He swished aside his cloak and revealed the dagger hiding beneath it. The headmaster didn't blink.

"You dare to threaten me, you—a mere servant, who has no better purpose in life than to wipe the princess's boots! I too can use force against you." He gestured to his guard, who once again stepped forth from the back of the room, pulling a large sword from its sheath. I began backing away toward the door.

Marcus quickly grabbed the headmaster by the collar of his garment and pulled him close, jabbing the tip of the dagger to his neck, drawing out a pin prick of blood. The guard moved forward quickly.

"Stop!" Marcus bellowed. "Come any closer and your master will die!" The guard stopped in his tracks. Marcus held the dagger to the headmaster's throat and spoke right into his face. "Alonya, put your hand inside the pocket of my cloak and pull out what's in there, please."

I did as I was told. Inside was a large, ornate, golden signet ring.

"Show it to the man," Marcus commanded. I held the ring up. "What do you see there?" Marcus asked the headmaster.

The man gurgled out the words. "I see a signet ring."

"With what seal?"

"A royal seal."

"That's right. That's the royal seal of Coralind. You are mistaken to assume that I am a mere servant, or that my purpose in life, as you say, is to wipe the princess's boots. How dare *you* address *me* thus! The princess of Zaphon is not the only royal visitor you have had today."

The man's face reddened and Marcus released his hold, lowering the dagger. "Tell your guard to back down."

The headmaster swallowed hard then nodded to the guard, who quickly re-sheathed his sword and stepped back into the shadows.

"Now, I do not wish trouble or violence, but you will have it if you do not give us the information we seek. I do not like this operation of yours, whatever you may label it, and I assure you that although Zaphon may turn a blind eye to what's going on here, Coralind will not."

"Coralind has no authority in Zaphon! What is that to me?"

"Oh, believe me, sir, there *is* going to be a close alliance between the royal houses of Coralind and Zaphon very soon, and you do not want Coralind as an enemy."

I stared incredulously at Marcus, wondering to what alliance he was alluding. I kept silent, however. The headmaster wiped the perspiration from his forehead.

"Now, tell us where the woman Taralyn was taken. That's all we want to know, and then we'll be gone, and you can return to your lucrative business in peace."

"The man's name is Roark, and he lives in the southwest of Zaphon, somewhere near Vickston. That's all I can tell you. I don't know anymore. Our clients are very secretive."

"I can't imagine why," I stated sardonically. The man sneered at me as though I was a bad taste in his mouth. He waved a hand toward us.

"Now get out of here. I've suffered your presence all day long, you and your princess!"

Marcus pointed a finger at him. "If we learn that you have given us false information, believe me, I will be back with a retinue of soldiers!"

We left the room, flying across the courtyard and through the main gates as quickly as we could manage. We did not look back.

Pursued

As soon as we were half an hour outside of the slaving camps, we let the women out. They stepped into the open air slowly, tentatively, gazing at their surroundings with wonder and disbelief. Once they realized they were free from their walls, they began crying for joy. We shared a brief reunion and re-introduction. Four women from the Colony we knew, the other three we met again. Of them all, Eloise was the most energetic. She became their appointed leader, and when we set out again, she took the head, walking alongside Zhara and I, who had given up our horses for two of the women. The others sat on the wagons, their bodies swaying back and forth from the motion of the wheels over the rough terrain. They spoke timidly with the captain's men who took the rear guard.

Instead of making camp where we had the night before, we continued on to put as much distance between ourselves and the slaving camps as possible. We were fortunate to find ourselves underneath a clear sky lit by a glowing half moon, stars sprinkling the black above. The cold air blew lightly around us, going before us like a guide and following behind like a guard; we walked even more briskly to keep warm, especially when the howls of the desert hounds chased the wind to reach our ears.

After a time we abandoned the empty crates and barrels along the roadside to lighten our load and provide space on the wagons for the women to lie down. Eloise retired with them and they were soon asleep. I continued walking alongside Danein though my legs were weak and my body was heavy with fatigue. Zhara had regained her position on her horse, but her body slumped and her head drooped. After much supplication, Marcus finally convinced her to lie down on the wagons with the other women.

I lost track of time on that dark, quiet road. When we were several hours outside of the camps, we decided to stop for a quick rest. The men divided into two watches. One watch stayed awake while the rest of us slept fitfully for two hours. We then proceeded on for another long stretch before stopping again so that the second watch could stay on the alert while the first watch slept. We traveled throughout the night in that way. I had tried staying up on Danein's watch with him but found my body uncooperative. I awoke atop one of the rocking wagons next to Zhara, a splinter of sunlight dancing into my eyes. We had traveled all night and were out of the heights, back in the low, shallow valleys of the mountains.

After a few more hours of travel, we came upon a friendly sight: Captain Lynch and his party. He had set up a camp with extra men, horses, and provisions to meet us. A large fire blazed nearby with a smoking iron cauldron hanging over it. The aroma of boiling meat and vegetables issued forth from the pot. My stomach grumbled loudly. At first, the women shrank back in timidity from the sight of the large party of men, but after quick introductions, there was soon an air of joviality across the camp. I sat next to Danein quietly, eating my stew and watching the bright faces of the women. My heart inflated with emotion, and though I was happy for them, I also felt a sense of urgency within. It had been an entire night since the women had gone missing from the slaving camps. If they had been discovered at all, riders could be fast upon us.

Captain Lynch and his men took a watch while the remainder of us rested from our long night journey. I slept little, being agitated and restless to leave. We finally set out just before midday. According to our planning, we were right on schedule. We would arrive back at the coast that evening just after nightfall, and once the canal workers' camp was silent, we would sneak the women on board and take to sea.

Liora seemed just as restless as I was. She would let nobody ride her, not even me. I walked most of the day beside her, though occasionally she would shoot forward for a gallop or fall behind, often running out of sight for several minutes at a time. The others thought this strange behavior, but I assured them that Liora was a special horse; she would not run off indefinitely, and she would always find her way back. I didn't notice when a large span of time elapsed and she did not yet return.

As the day waned, we worked the horses and mules harder to make it to the coast on time. A gusty wind had come up as the sun descended, and suddenly there was a new sound with it—not that of the distant howl of desert hounds, but something more eerie, something that caused my heart to fall into my stomach—a deep, low grumbling, like a growl. The horses whinnied and kicked in fright; the mules stamped their hooves and shook their heads.

"Assume formation, men!" Captain Lynch yelled, his voice echoing in the hills. All the men began moving in concert, pulling the animals and the wagons around into a circle. They pushed us women into the center of the circle while they took defensive positions on the outer edge, swords and daggers unsheathed and held at the ready.

The women huddled in the center, crying out in fear and confusion.

"What's happening?" I called out.

"The slave traders have come to get us," one of the women cried.

"No, it's something else. Didn't you hear that noise?"

All grew quiet for a long, tense moment. Once more there came the unmistakable sound of scraping, then growling. We stared into the distance, anticipating something coming over the ridge at any moment. There seemed to be nothing at all at first, and then, whether because of truth or an illusion of the light, the very rocks—the ground itself—seemed to be moving, to be crawling slowly and steadily toward us. Upon closer inspection, I saw it was not the ground at all but creatures moving along the ground, creatures of dull brown and slate gray that resembled the very rocks of the hills. Their bodies were long and low to the ground, their backs scaly, their snouts long and rounded, and their teeth sharp.

"What are they?" screamed one of the women.

"Desert dragons!" roared Marcus. "Be on the alert!"

Three of the creatures approached us from the east. There was a repeated clicking sound from one, and then a blast of fire suddenly shot out of its mouth and nostrils. Two of the men dodged sideways out of the path of the fire.

"It can only shoot once every minute! Attack now!"

There was a roar and a scuffle as men charged the beast that had just shot fire. Another blast of fire erupted from one of the other dragons. There was a wild scurrying of men and beast, flesh and scale, as the battle waged. Two more of the creatures came over the ridge from the south side and closed in. I was speechless with shock and fear, though the women all around me screamed. I saw little; everything seemed to happen in a blur. I heard fragments of words and phrases.

"To the south!"

"Two more!"

"Wait until they fire!"

"You cannot pierce the armor!"

A man screamed in pain and fell to the ground, rolling back toward the inner circle where the women sat. His face and hands were blackened, his eyes closed. One of the creatures had gotten another man's foot in a firm grip between its teeth. The man yelled in pain and stabbed ceaselessly at the creature's face, to no avail. Zhara suddenly jumped from the ring of women. She took the fallen man's sword, dodged a breath of fire, and plunged the weapon into the eye of one of the creatures. Marcus leapt to her side and knocked her out of the way as another dragon came toward her with its mouth open and clicking. He shoved his sword into its jaws. It gagged and fell over, writhing in pain.

Three men were down, then four, but only one of the creatures had been dispatched. I was about to follow Zhara into the melee, though I didn't know how to fight, when a flash of white streaked over the eastern ridge right toward the fight. Liora rose up on her back hooves, flailing her front and bringing them down hard on the head of a dragon. It went down instantly. One of the women beside me suddenly gasped. I turned to her. Her mouth had dropped open and her eyes were wide with wonder, watching Liora. I noticed then that Liora had again assumed her unicorn shape. I smiled broadly and watched her with pride.

The men backed up to the inner circle as Liora took charge, stamping the creatures with her hooves and impaling them with her horn; it was the only thing that could pierce the armor of their scales. After she had killed two, the others slunk away quickly. She went after them, chasing them over the ridge and out of sight. An awed hush fell over everyone as we stared after her, waiting for her to reappear. She didn't.

We quickly gathered the wounded and loaded them onto the wagons. One man had been killed, and we buried him amongst tears in the failing light of the setting sun. We still had several miles to go and were behind schedule. We discussed our options—staying and resting for the remainder of the night and attempting escape the following day, or continuing on. If we continued on, we would still be able to make it to the coast before daybreak. After much debate we decided to continue on so as not to postpone our escape any longer.

We had only been back on the road for an hour when there came from behind us a new sound—not that of the desert dragons, but of hooves crashing against the rock. We had been pursued by the slave traders. We slowed and stopped, knowing it was futile to run ahead or hide. Danein, Marcus, Captain Lynch, and the men who had not been wounded by the desert dragons moved to the back of our train, hands on the hilts of their swords as riders descended upon us. The women huddled together on the wagons, clutching one another's hands, some closing their eyes as their lips moved in silent prayer and entreaty. Zhara and I stood in front of them as if to shield them with our bodies.

Seven men—one for each missing woman—flew down on horses, their swords unsheathed. They were led by the headmaster's guard—the man that had recognized me. His eyes were cold, his mouth curled into a grimace. He stopped suddenly as he saw the wall of men before him; with our wounded we still matched them in number of men. The guard held up a hand to signal his riders. They stopped as well.

"You have property that belongs to us, and we're here to get it back," he said. His eyes roved over the line of men, then behind them to the cowering women. His glance strayed to me and he sneered. "And this time, *you* won't get away from me so easily, girl. I'll be taking you as a consolation prize."

Danein whipped out his blade and stepped forward. "You will not be taking back any of these women, especially not *her*. She's my betrothed. You have no claim to her."

The man eyed Danein carefully before recognition dawned. "You—I know you. You shot me and stole my quarry from me."

"She's not game, and she's not yours."

Zhara stepped forward amongst the throng of men. "That woman is my lady-in-waiting. She belongs to the royal court, and you will not take her."

The guard leveled an icy, hateful stare on Zhara. "Princess, you are not exactly a favorite with the headmaster at this point. You deceived him, and he does not like to be made a fool of."

"*He* was deceived? And what about us? What about me? Was I not deceived in being told that your little slaving operation was a charitable institution for the outcasts of society? You do not care for those people. You abuse and exploit them."

The man rolled his eyes. "It's obvious, Princess, that you were not deceived in the least by anything that was told you. You knew exactly to where you were going, and you came here with a hidden agenda. Be assured you will no longer be making any 'diplomatic' visits here." He let those words linger in order for Zhara to better absorb them before going on. "And just because you can hide behind your father for protection doesn't mean that *she*"—he pointed at me—"or any of these other women can! You cannot threaten or scare me, so I suggest you kindly step out of the way before you get hurt!"

Zhara was about to protest when Marcus grabbed her arm and pushed her back behind the line of men. "You will be cut down before you touch any of these women!" he challenged.

"Very well!" He stretched his sword out behind him then brought it up and over his head, finally pointing it straight toward us. "Charge!"

Our men fanned out as the slavers came forward on their steeds, drawing their swords and swinging them down from side to side. Their blows were dodged, and several horses reared up, tossing their riders down. It was hand-to-hand combat, metal clashing and clanging, the harsh sounds echoing through the hills in the twilight of the evening. Two of the slavers were cut down. I watched terrified as both Marcus and Danein fought the large guard. He knocked aside their thrusts and dodged their blows as easily as a child playing at a game. One of our wounded men had managed to sit up on the wagon next to the women and string a bow; he let arrows fly one after another at the slavers. Many missed due to the poor light, but one of the slavers caught an arrow in his leg and fell to the ground. Two slavers managed to get through the line of fighting men and dodge the arrows to approach the women. We all jumped from the wagons and ran like streaking lightning in all directions.

The battle then turned and followed us for a while. Screaming, clashing, shuffling, and scraping came from all around. Zhara had fallen back to fight with the men but had been knocked to the ground, where she lay still. I ran toward her to help and found myself face-to-face with the big guard. My breath caught in my throat, and my eyes scanned frantically for Danein and Marcus as I backed away from the large man. He eyed me with a hungry wrath. Blood seeped through his fingers as he clutched a wounded arm. He took a step toward me. I turned and fled. I saw little but the ground before me. There were quick flashes of women running. One of our men lay motionless on the ground. Swords glinted in the last vestiges of twilight. And then I was shoved hard from behind and knocked down. I went sprawling onto my stomach, my hands scraping along the rocky ground to catch my fall. Before I could regain my bearings, I was suddenly yanked up from behind by the neck of my garment. A strong, muscular arm had pulled me in and was holding me closely, tightly, and the blade of a dagger was at my throat.

"Halt!" the guard screamed loudly just above my ear. All action stopped and all eyes turned toward us. The man had me pinned against his body, and he turned, dragging me with him, for all to see. "Halt, or I will hurt the girl!"

I felt the ring on the chain round my neck digging into my chest where the man's arm pushed against it. I closed my eyes; tears trickled down. Faces stared back at me: self-satisfied smirks and sneers from the slavers, large eyes full of worry and fear from the women. Marcus knelt on the ground next to Zhara, who was just sitting up, her hand on her head. More tears fell, blurring my vision. Bodies lay along the ground, some motionless, others undulating with pain. I could not see Danein anywhere.

The guard called his men—of the original seven, there were four remaining—to tie up the women. When our men made to prevent it, the guard held the dagger more tightly to my throat. I gasped, holding as still as possible. The women cried and protested, but hesitantly allowed themselves to be herded up. I noticed that three of them were missing, including Eloise.

"Where are the others?" the guard shouted.

"They got away, sir."

The guard cursed. "Well, we'll take what we've got, including *this* one."

He pulled me backward, my feet nearly dragging along the ground, and tossed me up quickly on his black horse, jumping up behind me. His men did the same with the other women. They turned and fled into the darkening evening.

"If anyone tries to follow, I will kill her!" The guard screamed before spurring his horse onward, following the others. I turned my gaze, still hoping to catch a glimpse of Danein, but saw only a blur of faces and desert and mountain. My tears blinded me.

We bounded ahead into the night, the cold air sharp on my face. The guard behind me sat close, one arm on the reins, the other clutched tightly around me as if he feared I might jump off the horse at any moment. He pulled me forcefully against himself. "You're not getting away this time, lovely," he whispered harshly into my ear. "I never cared for the other girls much, but I think I'll like you."

I closed my eyes, praying, comprehending very little except my fear, my confusion, and my grief.

There was a whoop of victory from up ahead. In the distance between us and the other riders, I could just make out the dark shapes of their horses and hear one of the men shout, "We're going to have fun tonight, boys!"

We rode on, though the others ahead of us rode harder and faster, and were soon nearly out of sight. There seemed to be no sound of pursuit from behind, so the guard slowed after about ten minutes. He put his face in my hair and pressed his body close to mine. I squirmed fiercely to get loose, but he held me tightly, laughing at my vain attempts to escape.

"You're a fiery one!"

I flailed and squirmed and kicked harder. The horse grew disturbed and reared up slightly. The guard loosened his hold on me in order to gain control of the reins. I swung my legs over to jump down but was caught once more, though in my new position the guard had a more difficult time keeping me stationary. The horse was stepping forward and backwards in agitation. I balled my hands into fists and punched out at my captor. He smacked me hard across the face, stunning me momentarily, then grabbed my wrists and held them tightly. They were like fragile twigs in his big burly hands, and I knew he could break them as easily as he could a branch.

"Woman, don't make me throw you down and teach you a lesson!"

All at once, from out of the shadows next to us, Liora charged forward, her head down and her sharp horn exposed. I had just an instant to recognize Danein astride her before she plunged her horn into the side of the guard's horse; all three of us went down. I hit the ground hard, rolling backward. Danein leapt from Liora's back and was quickly at my side. He helped me up just as the guard also regained his feet, his hand going to his sword hilt. Danein was unarmed. Just as the guard sprang at us, Liora stepped in front of him, blocking his path. He stopped as his eyes travelled across her brilliant white body up to her spiral, ivory horn. Even he was shocked into a mesmerized awe. Liora held his gaze, lowering her horn toward him. He dropped his sword and took two steps backward.

"Come on!" Danein said, pushing me toward Liora and helping me onto her back. He jumped up behind, and we turned and fled back to our party.

33

A Promise

Everybody cried with joy upon seeing us reappear so unexpectedly, believing we'd been lost for good. Another of our men had died and had already been buried; nobody else was seriously injured. We wasted no time in setting off for the coast once again, though it seemed unlikely the slavers would return, what with the head guard now horseless and his other riders well ahead of him. They might yet ride for several more miles before turning to notice their captain absent. By the time they returned, if they were to return, we would be far gone. Besides that, they had their captives to mind.

Danein held me close as we quickly trotted ahead, riding atop Liora. She made no fuss over carrying two of us. I leaned back into Danein, shedding silent tears for the women we'd lost and for how close I'd come to losing Danein again. In the comfort of the High King's palace and the security of Danein's love, I'd forgotten how real the danger was out in the world. As soon as Danein and I married, the danger would pass for me, but for many others like me, it was still very real and very present.

As the landscape flattened out and became less rocky, we were able to travel more quickly. Eloise had eluded capture along with two other of the women. They sat together with Zhara in one wagon, flanked on all sides by our men, some riding horses, others walking briskly alongside. Our three wounded men lay in another wagon; the third wagon, which had carried our provisions, we abandoned to speed our travel. I fancied the air smelled clearer and fresher as we drew closer to the coast. The sun had disappeared hours before, so we moved along in darkness, the points of light in the night sky our only guide as they'd been the night before. All was quiet from behind, yet still we marched on in haste.

Halfway through the night, there came from up ahead the unmistakable sound of waves on shore. We had arrived. Three men were appointed as sentinels; they crept forward to the outskirts of the laborers' camp. We could see their silhouettes against the dying embers of the campfires dotting the landscape. They returned within minutes, reporting that the camp was quiet; besides a few inebriated workers who were still awake, though disoriented, all had abandoned their activity in favor of their beds. We left the foreman's horses tied to a post outside the camp and took shifts stealing onto the ship in small groups of two and three. Our way was thankfully unhindered, and before the sun came up that morning, we had lifted anchor and were well along on our way, a strong wind from the east favoring us, causing us to glide along swiftly, smooth as ice.

Zhara immediately took to her bunk, still reeling slightly from her fall during the battle with the slavers. Marcus stayed by her side constantly, coming out only to visit the cook and bring Zhara meals. The captain's physician saw to her as well, but besides Marcus, Zhara saw nobody else for at least two days.

Eloise and the two other women spent their days on deck, growing more comfortable in their freedom, learning how to speak openly with the captain's men, occasionally laughing and jesting with them. In the evenings they would often play at cards or dice or other games with the men. Sometimes they would relieve the ship's cook by making the meals themselves or help out with the other chores. Before long, an air of gaiety dominated the atmosphere of the ship, much more lively than it had been on our journey to the Outlands. It was as if the freshness of the sea air washed away all the heavy burdens and cares those women had endured at the hands of their captors. The constant movement of the ship away from their old life and toward something new and promising restored in their hearts a sense of hope.

I told them all I could of the High King and his palace. Eloise and Anya, a woman only a few years my senior, always listened raptly, their eyes glistening with delight. They had plans upon reaching Fynn Harbor to travel to Haven Island in search of the High King. Coryn, a younger woman, would listen politely and ask a few questions before her gaze and attention drifted elsewhere. There was a young man among the ship's company that she constantly sought out. She would talk incessantly to him while watching him work. Anytime he was eating, resting, or engaging in recreation, she was sure to find her way to his side. He seemed to welcome her company and would allow her to join him, though for my part it was difficult to tell whether he truly felt any affection for her or merely tolerated her. Just the same, I wondered whether Coryn truly cared for him or was merely latching onto an opportunity to be loved and taken care of. I couldn't blame her. I myself understood the desperation that unchosen women could be driven to. It hadn't been long since I had been in that position. I just hoped one day she would discover sanctuary with the High King, as I had done.

Zhara was well enough to leave her room after three days of travel; she was accompanied by Marcus everywhere she went. They often took private strolls on deck or spent long hours sitting and conversing just out of reach of the ocean's spray. When Zhara wasn't with Marcus, she was with the women, joining them in their endeavors. Sometimes Eloise, Anya, and Coryn would find a cozy spot on deck, their shawls and blankets wrapped tightly around their shoulders against the sea chill, and sit at the princess's feet as she told them stories of her childhood and shared her experience of being an unchosen.

The days passed quickly in this way. The weather was fair, and we made swift headway back to Fynn Harbor without danger of pursuit.

I thought often of Taralyn. Vickston was due south several days' ride of Fynn Harbor. In my heart I planned on us leaving to fetch her as soon as we docked and were able to gather provisions for our travel. My eagerness and sense of urgency in seeing her again grew, ripening and widening inside of me until it filled me with restlessness and distraction. Danein did all he could to ease my mind, but I knew I would not be at peace until I could see my old friend again.

The evening before our arrival back in Fynn Harbor was merry with celebration. Down on the main deck, two shipmates were playing on a hornpipe and fiddle, stamping their feet to the tune, while a third shipmate sang a lively melody about sea adventurers. The women clapped their hands gaily, beginning to move to the music. Marcus took Zhara's hand and led her in a dance. Eloise, Anya, and Coryn found partners as well, and soon all were engaged in dancing—all except Danein, who was somewhere about the ship with the captain. I watched the dancers for a while before taking a short stroll up to the quarter deck. I stood at the railing and watched the water split out from underneath the ship in waves as we glided atop it. The music from down below mingled with the slap of water on wood, heavy in my ears at first, then distant like the mist of a dream. The face of the moon in the cloudless sky was reflected in the ocean, a spot of brilliance in the dark water.

I didn't immediately notice when Danein approached from behind and joined me quietly, leaning his arms on the railing and staring out into the night as I was. He sidled closer until his arm touched mine.

"Are you cold?" he asked.

"A little, but it's all right. I'll go below deck soon."

"We're almost home."

I smiled. Fynn Harbor was home. Danein was home.

"We can be married as soon as possible," Danein said. My heart leaped. "We can be married tomorrow, Alonya. What do you think about us getting married tomorrow?"

He put his arms around me and I settled into his embrace. "I would love to be married tomorrow," I said, "but Taralyn…"

"We will go for Taralyn as soon as we're married."

I shook my head, my heart battling between conviction and desire. "I cannot be settled until I know Taralyn is all right. I don't want to be married with that burden heavy in my heart and mind."

Danein sighed. "I understand." He turned back to the ocean trailing and spreading out behind us. "I have made you wait this long. I, too, can wait for a while longer."

"I'm sorry."

He smiled, though there was a trace of disappointment on his face. Disappointment and weariness.

"I wish this could all be over," he said, quite unexpectedly.

"What?"

"Though we've had a small victory, I know this is not the end of our mission. Until the laws in Zaphon change, there will always be work to do."

"And you'd rather be finished with it all?"

Danein sighed again. He took my hand and squeezed it, looking at me. "If life was simpler and easier, I would already be married to you. We would have a nice little cottage somewhere private in the woods, just outside of Fynn Harbor. We wouldn't have to travel. You wouldn't be on the run. I wouldn't have to peddle wares anymore." He stopped and smiled suddenly. "We'd already have one or two children."

Heat crept to my face and I lowered my head, but he took my face in his hands and turned my gaze back to him. His eyes were earnest, his mouth firm. "I mean it, Alonya. This is what I wish for most in the world. If there was nothing else in the world but you and me and our life together, I would be content."

I couldn't speak. He kissed me then, and it seemed forever that we were locked together. I let him hold me a long while before I spoke. "I used to wish that things were different, but I know that this is exactly what was meant to happen. And yes, unfortunately the problem with the unchosens will not be solved so easily. There will be work to do for a while yet, but while there is work to do, I am grateful to have you beside me along the journey. We will get to those dreams, Danein."

He held me close. "I know," he whispered. "I know."

We were interrupted by steps on the wooden planks behind us. Zhara and Marcus approached. I was surprised to see them hand in hand. It was obvious they had been close, especially during the journey back to Fynn Harbor, but they had never so openly displayed their affection before.

"There you two are!" Marcus exclaimed. He bounded up, pulling Zhara behind him. She laughed. "We have good news to share! We're going to be married!"

I tried to speak, but my words caught in my throat, and all I could manage was a squeak of excitement as I jumped forward to embrace Zhara. Danein clapped Marcus on the shoulder.

"I'm very happy for you two."

I finally found my voice. "I had hoped this would happen, but I didn't expect it to happen so suddenly!"

"We will marry as soon as I speak to Zhara's father, the king, and obtain his permission and blessing," Marcus explained.

"Wait!" My hands flew to my mouth, and I stared back and forth at the two of them.

"That's right! You can't marry without your father's consent, Zhara. Are you so confident that he'll give it?"

"I believe my father will not turn down an offer to make an alliance with Coralind through marriage. He spoke of the possibility often as I grew up, but since Coralind is such a distant country, it was never quite a practical or substantial possibility. Though he has been very selective and strict in allowing a husband for me, I believe he will yield in this matter."

Marcus jumped in. "There are a lot of political gains to be made through our marriage. Zaphon is little and obscure while Coralind is large and powerful, so connection with Coralind will give Zaphon a name and greatly enlarge its sphere of influence."

"It will also give my father a sense of renown, and he is too greedy to turn down such an opportunity."

"And once you are married, you will have rights to the throne, and opportunity to change policy?"

Marcus and Zhara exchanged glances. "I won't," she said, "but Marcus will. As my husband he will be named crown prince of Zaphon, so that in the event of my father's death he will take the throne and become king. And he will still have a voice in the court as a counselor. There is much we could do to help the outcasts of Zaphon in that position."

"I will pray that the High King grants your marriage," I said, again hugging Zhara.

"I have peace in my heart that he will," she said. "As strict as my father has been, and as much as he desires to clutch his power in his own fists, he knows he must allow me to marry sooner or later if there is to be an heir. My father has spoken of naming an heir, but I know he would rather have a blood heir." She gazed up at Marcus, her smile widening. "He will not turn down Marcus. Of course he won't allow the marriage for me—he'll do it for himself and for his own name because he won't be able to resist."

"Whatever happens, we have given our promise to each other," Marcus said. "Zhara is the woman I am meant to marry. Besides being in a position to help the outcasts of Zaphon, I love her. I, too, have a certainty and a peace in my heart that our marriage will come to pass."

"And how about you two?" Zhara asked, taking my hand in hers. "When will you be married?"

I sighed. "As soon as we can find Taralyn and bring her home."

"We will help you in that mission as well," Marcus said. "We began this together, and we will finish it together."

"I fear it'll never be finished, at least not soon enough," Danein said. "There will always be unchosens. We may save a few here or there, but there will always be slavers hunting them to take them back."

Marcus was not deterred. "And wherever the slavers are, we'll be right behind them. However long it takes, we will be there with you until the end. And that includes rescuing Taralyn."

The four of us stood together on that deck, once sundered as strangers but now united as family, having already lived lives full of fear and hope, failure and victory, joy and pain, yet just beginning life anew.

34

Rescued

In the valley between the forested foothills in the south of Zaphon was Vickston; even farther south, situated between a wild, hilly wood and flat, cultivated farmland was a large house. Unlike most of the rude one-story cottages and huts constructed from timber and thatch, this house had two stories. Its walls were composed of wattle and daub reinforced with a wooden frame. The house also boasted wooden shingles upon the roof, glass panes in the windows, and a stone chimney at one end. Marcus and Zhara, I knew, were not awed or intimidated by such a show of wealth; they were accustomed to even greater luxury. I pulled Liora's reins back and stopped abruptly to gaze at the house in the distance. Was this really the place Taralyn had been kept these last many months? It was clear that her master was a nobleman of sorts, or perhaps a rich merchant. I half wondered why the house wasn't made of brick or stone. Only the very wealthiest could afford such materials. Perhaps that was too affluent for his tastes.

A long, low field stretched down the hill from the house, and people busily went to and fro throughout it, bent over as they worked the land. As we spurred our horses onward toward the house, my eyes scanned the fields for any sign of Taralyn. I would rejoice if she had merely been bought as a field hand for the master's lands and nothing more. I prayed she would be there on that land or in that house somewhere, that all the long waiting and searching would not be in vain.

It had been an uneventful journey to Vickston. We four had embarked two days after arriving in Fynn Harbor. We went with little planning or preparation, taking our horses, bringing with us only a few belongings, and staying at inns along the way. Before acquiring lodgings upon arriving in Vickston, we inquired into the name of Roark. The first person we asked pointed to the road that led south out of town. Danein had suggested we wait until the following morning to make a visit since the day was waning, but I was insistent we go then. We stopped long enough to secure lodging and change out of our travel clothes before once more setting out. We followed the dirt road that led at a slight incline out of the village, up and up until arriving at the big house.

It wasn't until we had drawn closer that we saw several smaller buildings and huts sitting behind the house—the servants' and land workers' houses. I wondered whether Taralyn lived in one of those little huts or in the house proper. Several servants stopped and watched us as we approached. Marcus rode ahead a few strides and met a short, balding man coming out the front door. He wore simple clothes and thus could not be the master of the house.

Marcus sat very straight in the saddle, one hand wrapped around the reins and the other resting loosely on his sword hilt. "We desire to speak to the master of the house regarding one of his servants," he said.

The man's narrowed eyes roved up and down Marcus before turning toward the rest of us. "And who is it that inquires?"

"I am Prince Marcus Du'Karafin of Coralind. This is Princess Zhara of Zaphon, and these are our friends." The man seemed to start slightly at the sound of the names, and his eyes widened in surprise. Marcus continued. "We have traveled from Fynn Harbor in search of a woman we believe to be residing at this house."

The servant shuffled on his feet, looked behind him quickly, and opened his mouth as if to speak, then just as quickly closed it. He seemed to be having difficulty getting any words out. Finally he bumbled out, "I will fetch the master immediately. Please come in and rest from the road." He whistled to two nearby men who ran forward at the beckons. Zhara and I were helped down from our horses while Marcus and Danein jumped down from theirs. We were then led to a large furnished sitting room inside the house. We were given refreshment and left alone while the old servant went in search of the master.

Time went by in silence while we waited. None of us sat down, although there were cushioned chairs in the room. I strayed to the window and examined the glass panes with awe. I had never lived anywhere with glass panes and had rarely seen them. They were thick and sturdy. Through them I saw the old balding servant running across the yard, waving his arms to the men who were tending to our horses. I smiled, thinking of his flabbergasted reaction when he had learned only moments ago that he was in the presence of royalty.

"Did I look that foolish when I first discovered you were a prince?" I asked Marcus, turning away from the window and joining the others in the center of the room.

Marcus grinned. "Yes, you did."

"Do you ever grow irritated at such reactions?"

"No. I understand why they do it. To tell the truth, it quite fascinates me. I find great amusement in it."

Zhara nearly snorted. "I don't. I wish that people wouldn't make such a fuss about it—about me. Some people near faint with fear in my presence!" She shook her head then shared a smiling glance with Marcus. "You are better than I am, to try and understand it, to make light of it. I say I am like the people, yet I don't always understand them, and I can grow so impatient with them."

Marcus went to Zhara's side and took her hand tenderly. "Well, my dear, that is something we shall remedy together. But you must know you have infinitely more understanding and patience than you give yourself credit for."

A loud step was heard outside the room, and the door was suddenly flung open. A tall man in his early middle years stepped through the threshold. He bowed low when he saw us.

"Distinguished guests! I am honored to have the presence of Your Highnesses in my household this day."

I glanced over at Zhara. Her lips were tightened and her nostrils flared. She moved her gaze from the fawning man to me, and when she caught me staring at her, she nearly laughed.

The man rose and stepped closer to Marcus, who stood before all of us as the spokesman. Upon closer inspection, it was clear that the man could still be taken for young, and though he was not eye-catching, I would not have called him unhandsome. He was tall but broad-shouldered and thick. His clothes were neat and pressed, and his boots of good quality leather, polished to a sheen. I wondered absently if he always looked this spruce or if he had changed clothes quickly before meeting his royal guests. At his side hung a leather pouch; the jingle of coins within could be heard as he moved about—obviously a show of his wealth and power. He seemed to want to appear as favorably as possible.

"To what do I owe the pleasure of this visit? My man tells me it regards one of my servants." His face grew grave, though affectedly so. "I regret deeply if any of my servants have done wrong against Your Highnesses, and if that is the case, I can assure you the matter will be dealt with swiftly and assuredly."

"No, no, it is nothing like that."

The man heaved a sigh. "Well, I am relieved to hear it. I do hold my servants to the utmost standards of conduct. They represent me, after all, and I should be ashamed if any were to cast me in a wrongful light. But I have not properly introduced myself. My name is Larsen Roark." He gestured suddenly to the chairs behind us. "Please, sit, and we will discuss the business for which you came."

We all moved back quietly and found chairs, which we pulled together into a haphazard cluster before sitting down.

"I can call for a fire," the man offered.

Marcus held out his hand. "Thank you for the hospitality, sir, but that is not necessary. We don't plan on staying long. I'll get straight to the matter at hand. There is a woman by the name of Taralyn whom we have been led to believe resides in this house." Marcus stopped and paused. We all watched Roark's face, which hadn't reacted to Taralyn's name at all. He merely sat and listened as though awaiting more information. Marcus's brows rose in question.

"Yes?" the man finally spoke. "And this woman—Taralyn—is she in trouble with the law? Has she done anything to warrant arrest?"

"Well, no, she is actually a friend of ours," Marcus explained.

"She is a dear friend of mine," I jumped in, unable to remain silent. Somehow I felt this man must be stalling, playing games, and I wasn't going to play along. "We knew each other a while ago before she was kidnapped by slave traders and taken to a slaving camp for unchosens. I wish to find her and see her again."

Danein rose from his chair and stood behind mine, putting a hand gently on my shoulder. Heat burned my cheeks at my blunt outburst, but nobody chided me.

Still the man remained unmoved, unchanged but for his eyes, which narrowed in question as he looked me over very carefully. "If this woman was in a slaving camp, as you have said, why is it you believe her to be here?"

Zhara spoke before I could. "We visited said camp to find her, only to discover that she had been sold and taken to this area of the country."

"This area of the country? And why should that mean me? This is a large area, and I am only but a small part of it."

"We were given information that led to you," Zhara explained.

"Oh, I see," the man drew out slowly. He stood and walked to the window to gaze out of it. "I am a wealthy man with many acres of land, and I employ many servants, so it is only natural you would believe me to have acquired her, although if I was going to employ extra servants, I would not visit a slaving camp in order to hire them. I would hire locally."

Danein heaved an irritated sigh. "With all due respect, sir, she was not being sold as a household servant, and we do not believe she was bought as a household servant, if you get my meaning."

The man turned a calculated glare on Danein. "I do get your meaning, sir, and I do not appreciate the insinuation."

"So are you saying you do not have this woman?" Marcus asked suddenly.

Roark pursed his lips, put his hands behind his back, and sauntered slowly away from the window as if in thought. "I feel as though the answer to that question is irrelevant."

"What do you mean?"

"Well, would you believe me if I said no, she is not here?"

"Is that what you're saying?"

"Why shouldn't we believe you?" Zhara jumped in.

The man explained. "You seem to already believe she is here, so that it makes no difference what I say."

Marcus rose slowly from his chair with a sharp sigh. "Sir, we have made the purpose of our visit clear and desire a straight answer, yet it seems to me you drive around in circles."

A long pause hung in the air as the man considered his answer. He moved toward the door as if to dismiss us. "I am sorry you have wasted your time, Your Highnesses, but you have been given false information."

Marcus stepped forward, his jaw tight. "Again, sir, you evade the question and do not answer plainly."

Zhara followed Marcus. "We were not given false information. We were given your exact name and the location of your house. How could we come by that information hundreds of miles from here, in the Outlands?"

"I am well known in all parts of Zaphon. I am a businessman. I travel quite extensively."

"As extensively as the Outlands?" I asked. "If so, then you know what's there. Nothing but slaving encampments."

"What I mean is, I would not be surprised if my name and address get around to various parts of the country. I, on the other hand, do not. I don't wish to offend my royal guests, but it is nearing the evening meal, and I have much work to oversee. Now, if you will excuse me—"

"Sir, you are *not* excused," Zhara bellowed, moving forward.

The man stopped but did not look up at her, and though his face was stolid, I detected worry in his brows. A small bead of perspiration appeared along his hairline.

"I will have you know that by royal right I can search your house and the nearby premises without a warrant."

The man finally met Zhara's gaze, and there seemed to be a bit of a challenge in his eyes. "You are free to search my house and premises, Princess, but you won't find what you are looking for."

I jumped up from my chair. "Why not? What have you done with her?"

"I don't know what you're talking about," he said, again moving to leave.

Zhara stepped forward and grabbed his arm. "I will buy her from you," she said abruptly. "Whatever you paid for her, I will double it."

He glanced down his nose at Zhara, eyebrows rising. "I'm intrigued that this woman means so much to you. She is, after all, just an unchosen."

"You give yourself away, sir," Marcus said. "You couldn't know that unless she was here."

The man frowned. "I can guess by what you've told me—she was kidnapped and taken to a slaving camp in the Outlands. What else can she be?"

"You're not fooling anyone," Danein said. "We know she's here and that you have her. So what do you want? The princess has offered you double the price to buy Taralyn's freedom. Surely that's worth giving her up?"

The man looked furtively behind him then stepped fully back into the room and closed the door. He finally gave up the pretense. "Taralyn belongs to me. I visited her often in the Outlands, and I let no other man have her. I bought her to guarantee that she would belong to none other but me."

"She's not an animal," Zhara commented brusquely. "She belongs to no one and cannot be bought and sold and used like a common beast."

"So you say, Princess, and yet reality proves differently."

"If you loved her and wanted her so much," I said quietly from behind the others, still standing next to my chair, "why didn't you just marry her?"

The man let out a snort. "Who said anything about love? I'll put it another way for you to understand it, dear—I like what Taralyn does for me. She's too old to marry, anyway. Nobody marries an unchosen woman! Unchosen means unwanted goods, and like any good businessman or merchant knows, unwanted goods are usually sold cheap or given away in the end."

Tears stung my eyes. Knowing Taralyn was so close to me—that she was in this house—yet being unable to see her, was unbearable. My patience failed and anger boiled to the surface.

I rushed forward. "I want to see her!" I demanded, my voice rising to a scream. "I want to see Taralyn now!" Danein held me back.

The man laughed, ignored me, and turned back to Zhara. "Why should an unchosen woman be of such value to you? She's been cast out of society. She has no proper place, no purpose."

Though Zhara's face was red and her mouth tight, she kept herself composed. "You are wrong there. Not all people see as you do. There are other eyes besides the eyes of this world that see value in the unwanted and the unchosen, and a greater purpose than what we see around us each day. You should not deny this or mock it."

"That may be true, Princess, but it doesn't change anything. No matter what price you pay, I intend to keep Taralyn for myself. Whenever I'm through with her—if I tire of her—I will pass her on to you."

Danein stepped forward suddenly between Zhara and Marcus and threw a blow to the man's face. Roark reeled back against the wall, swearing oaths as he fell to the ground. Just then, the door to the sitting room flew open and the waifish figure of a woman ran inside, stopping suddenly at the sight of so many staring eyes. A servant ran in just behind and tried to grab her arm and pull her back, but she darted away quickly. When the servant saw his master on the floor nursing his jaw, his face blushed red.

"I'm sorry, sir, I tried to keep her upstairs as you instructed, but she fought me off. I've never seen her so lively. She was savage, she was. Quite took me by surprise." He produced an arm to show the scratches he had endured.

I looked again at the woman. She was in a plain woolen dress with a head scarf wrapped around her long dark hair. Anyone would have taken her for a usual servant, but when my eyes fell on her I saw immediately that it was Taralyn. My voice caught in my throat as I tried to say her name. She saw me at the same time and ran into my arms, sobbing heavily. I held her tightly, stroking her tangled hair as tears streamed down my face. Danein wrapped his arms around us both, and there we three stood together for several long moments.

"Oh, my dear friend," I whispered. "You are safe now."

She continued to cry, and I let her. "Just get it all out," I said. "Times have been dark and evil, but there will be stories and songs again, just like before. You had stories and songs for me in my time of trouble, and I will give them back to you, my friend. All will be well. You are safe."

Roark stood and dismissed his servant. I stole a glance at him to see his eyes storming with rage; yet he allowed Taralyn this reunion.

"Surely, sir," Zhara said, "you will find my offer fair and give up the woman to us."

He spit blood out of the corner of his mouth. "All right!" he shouted. "That's enough. You've seen her. You've had your time."

I let Taralyn go, but held her by the hand. Danein stood closely by us.

"Taralyn stays with me," Roark commanded. "Come on woman! Come here to me now!"

Taralyn's face was streaked with tears, but her eyes suddenly lit with a new fire. She wiped her face and stood her ground next to Danein and me. "I will not go to you, *sir*!" she spat out. "My friends have come for me and I will go with them."

"How dare you defy me! I bought you and you belong to me!" He stepped forward, but his way was blocked by Marcus, who lifted the hilt of his sword slightly. The blade scraped musically against the sheath and gleamed in the orange rays of the setting sun slanting in through the windows.

"You are not my master. I belong to no one but the High King!" Taralyn announced. I saw then that she was still there. Despite the sobbing and the tears and her wasted appearance, she was still the same Taralyn I had known before.

The man's face reddened, and he began to circle around the outside of our assembled group to reach Taralyn. We shifted as he did, and Danein and Marcus kept between him and Taralyn.

"Get out of my way! She belongs to me! I bought her! There is no law against that! You cannot take my rightful property from me!"

"There may be no law against it, but there's also no law for it!" Zhara said. "And there's no law against us taking her back!"

"You cannot threaten me. I don't care if you are of the royal houses! If you take what is mine, I will fight you for it. I will pursue you with an army, if need be!"

"That seems like an awful lot of trouble for a woman you referred to as 'unwanted goods,'" Danein pointed out.

Just then, the man's face softened, and he caught Taralyn's gaze, appealing to her with his eyes. "Please, Taralyn, stay with me. I know I can be a hard man, but have I not been fair to you? I give you everything you need. Warm clothes, good food, a bed—"

"Your bed! And I don't want it!"

"I know I have taken liberties with you, yet not treated you as a wife. If that's what you want, then I will give it to you. I will marry you, and your friends here may visit you as often as you'd like."

"I don't believe you," Taralyn said. "And besides, I would not have you. If ever I would have, that time has passed."

His face quivered again in anger. He grabbed a ceramic mug from a nearby table and threw it across the room. It crashed against the wall, splintering into shards that fell tinkling to the floor. Taralyn tensed and held my hand more tightly.

"What do you want from me, wench? You are nothing and yet I offer you the world!"

"You offer me scraps from your table! I am nothing but a dog to you, and so like an abused dog I will escape to seek kinder masters."

Danein ushered us to the door then. Zhara, Taralyn, and I moved in concert while Danein and Marcus held Roark at bay. The furious man went to a cabinet and pulled open a drawer. He withdrew a long, thin-bladed sword and held it out at Marcus.

"You do not want to fight me," Marcus warned. "You may be trained in fencing, but I assure you, no one is trained as well as a prince. I have held a sword since before I could speak in full sentences, and I have won many matches and competitions. I will not kill you, sir, but I will injure you severely."

"I can do just as much, Your Highness," the man threatened.

"You may at that, but if you do, the princess and I have the authority to put you behind bars for the rest of your life. It is a federal offense in every country of the Lands of the Seven Kingdoms to injure any of the royal house without due cause."

"I have due cause! You are stealing my property!"

"No, we are not!" Zhara spat out, throwing a purse full of coins onto the floor at the man's feet. "I have offered to pay you twice the price you paid for Taralyn, and there it is! Now we have bought her from you, and she no longer belongs to you! You would do well to leave the matter where it lies."

The man's arm drooped, and he let the tip of the sword clink to the ground. He eyed the purse, defeated, and we took that opportunity to steal away. Though we watched behind for any sign of pursuit from him or his servants, none came. Even so, we did not stay in the village of Vickston that night.

35

New Beginnings

From Vickston we all returned to the royal city with Zhara and Marcus; I was once again a guest at a palace. Taralyn remained with us only two short weeks before embarking on a journey out of Zaphon. She didn't know where she would go—to Kerith, she said, or beyond, perhaps toward Coralind. Though we entreated her to stay, and Zhara offered her a position at court, Taralyn declined. She felt a strong urge to go, saying she would be safer out of the country. I knew it was more than that, however. Taralyn had always wanted to help people—to use her gifts and skills and resources in helping people wherever she could find them. I knew she was ready to pick up that mission once more, to go where the needy were. Unfortunately, Zaphon was too dangerous for her to remain. I was angry at having to let her go so soon after finding her.

My throat was tight, and the tears behind my eyes burned as we all traveled to Fynn Harbor to see Taralyn safely off. I was barely able to look at her or speak for the sorrow in my heart. As grand and exciting as new beginnings are, they are always marked with some measure of loss and grief. Yet that is merely to create room for new gifts and blessings to enter in. In the end I said my good-bye to Taralyn, knowing she was making the right choice. After she'd gone, the rest of us spent some time with Janna before returning to the royal city.

Marcus, Danein, and I remained at the palace several weeks, during which time Marcus befriended Zhara's father, the king. Marcus and Zhara shared with him the plan for their marriage. The king was hard at first, employing Marcus on many tasks and small quests in order to prove himself as a man, a prince, and a future ruler of Zaphon. Those quests are meant for another story, for another time, but suffice it to say Marcus succeeded early on in winning the king's favor and approval. He and Zhara were married within half a year of our return. The wedding was large and festive, an occasion of which the entire city turned out for parades, games, and reveling. We had sent to Fynn Harbor for Janna and her son to join us, and she was agog with the wonder and excitement of it all. Marcus spoke to Havley as promised, and together they determined a plan for training Havley as the prince's ambassador between Zaphon and Coralind.

During those months at the palace, before the wedding, Danein continued to work. He went out almost every day in his cart, sometimes peddling, sometimes finding odd work in town. He also accompanied Marcus on several of his trips and errands for the king, and in that way, he became a kind of unofficial courtier of the prince. When they weren't away, Marcus and Danein often went into town together for work or play or some other purpose secretive in nature. Zhara and I would join them at times, but at other times the men wouldn't allow it, sometimes getting up and leaving early in the mornings before we had a chance to follow. When asked about their goings-on, they shrugged and exchanged furtive smiles with each other. Danein had said nothing to me since our return about our upcoming wedding. I hoped his and Marcus's secret had something to do with that, so I bit my tongue and kept quiet, just trusting that Danein would let me know when the time was right. I admit I grew uneasy. As though sensing my restlessness, Danein often reassured me of his love and his intention to marry me without me having to say anything. So I continued to wait. It was enough having a good friend in Zhara and being in similar circumstances—both of us having to wait on the men in our lives to be united with them. Despite the difficulty of that last long stretch, they were good months and good times.

For a few weeks, Liora had stayed with us in the stable on the palace grounds, and I had gone out on a few leisurely rides with her. Then one morning, I found her gone. I was taking a solitary stroll through the gardens, the morning air crisp and the ground flecked with dew, dampening the hem of my dress. My path eventually led me to the stables, and I entered to pay a visit to Liora. Her stall was empty. I looked for her and finally asked a stable hand if he'd seen her. Red-faced, he admitted that though she had been stabled the night before, she was gone early that morning when he arrived to work before dawn.

"I can't think what happened, miss," he said. "Guards walk these grounds at night, so she can't have been taken. If she had gotten loose, I can't see how she could have leapt the walls surrounding the palace. She could be wandering the grounds somewhere, miss, or perhaps she was taken out for a ride by someone else, though I can't think who would have authorized that, being that she's your horse."

I shook my head. "She wasn't mine."

The young man frowned. "Miss?"

I let out a prolonged sigh. "She was free—wild. She belonged to no one. She chose me for a short while, but it seems as though she's moved on."

Despite what the man had suggested, I knew Liora was gone. She hadn't been taken or gotten lost. She had moved on, had gone out of my life just as unexpectedly as she had entered it.

"Shall I try to find her for you, miss?" the stable hand asked, his face screwed into a mixture of worry and confusion. I smiled, though my heart broke inside me. The man seemed to relax at my softened features.

"No, thank you, sir. You may leave me."

He nodded and was gone.

Liora never returned, though I inadvertently waited for her, searched for her anytime we went out. I missed her as I would an old friend, but I comforted myself with the thought that perhaps one day I would see her again. She would find me like she had the first time, when I most needed her.

When Marcus and Zhara were finally married, the surprise came. That night, the festivities and revelries celebrating the royal wedding lasted late into the evening. Sometime well after dusk, after the number of guests had thinned out and the music quieted to a simple stringed melody, as I was sitting under a tent in the gardens, Danein, Marcus, and Zhara all accosted me at once.

"You two!" I reproached Zhara and Marcus. "I thought you would be leaving soon. You have a honeymoon trip to take!"

"We can't leave without seeing your wedding, of course!"

"What?" I had barely spoken the words when a blindfold was wrapped around my eyes from behind and Danein's strong hand took mine. He pulled me up from the bench.

"Come with me."

My whole body trembled with cold and excitement. A blanket was draped around my shoulders as I was whisked away over the cobblestone pavement and then lifted into a carriage—one of the royal carriages.

A whip snapped and the carriage began rattling down the driveway, out of the palace grounds. I tried to concentrate, to decipher the route we were traveling, but was unable due to nerves and excitement. Danein clasped my hand tightly, his warm arm firm against mine. Nobody said anything, and I could imagine my three comrades exchanging looks of silent amusement with one another.

We drove through the noisy city streets. Many people were still out celebrating, and they recognized the royal carriage as it passed. They cheered and laughed and sang. Soft strains from a flute and a harp floated on the air from somewhere in the distance. There was little traffic on those stone streets besides our carriage. All the sounds and the world they inhabited hushed and faded the farther and longer we drove.

"Zhara, when were you let in on this secret?" I asked, my nerves compelling me to speak, to fill the void caused by the silence.

"Shh, no talking."

I laughed then grew sober. The smile that had been stretched across my face slowly tired, and my tears soon wet the blindfold. I sniffed once, then twice.

"What is it, my love?" Danein asked, wrapping his arm around me. "Is this not what you want?"

The concern in his voice only brought more tears of gratitude. "No, it's not that. Yes, this is what I want, what I've been waiting for. I just…" But for the clacking of the horses' hooves and wheels against stone, it was quiet and still as though the whole world was holding its breath just for me.

"What are you trying to say, Alonya? Just say it."

"The waiting…all the waiting…I don't suppose I really believed that this would happen. I'm just so happy."

I burst into tears at the last word, and Danein cradled me close to him, pulling the soft fabric from my eyes. "I know, Alonya. I know. You don't have to wait anymore."

A hand from the seat across from me reached out and held my own. It was Zhara's.

Soon the stone-paved road smoothed out into a dirt track that led away from the royal city into what I conceived to be woodland. The city was surrounded with it. My heart continued to thump rapidly in my chest, and my mind burst with questions, yet I remained silent. Though the others didn't make me put the blindfold back on, they wouldn't allow me to look out the window, either. They had drawn the curtains over them. It was no matter—I had long ago lost my sense of direction.

Zhara yawned and dropped her head on Marcus's shoulder. He caught the yawn and settled down farther into the seat, closing his eyes. I wondered how late it was. Surely somewhere close to midnight. I glanced up at Danein next to me. He smiled and looked very awake.

Outside, the lantern affixed to the carriage creaked as it swung back and forth. Little of its light filtered in through the drawn curtains. It had grown much darker when we'd left the city. My eyes drooped and my head soon followed.

A sharp jerking motion awoke me. The carriage had come to a stop. I opened my heavy eyes as though walking through water, absently wondering how long I'd been asleep and curious as to the time.

"We're here," Danein said, sitting me upright.

I followed Marcus and Zhara out of the carriage into the cold, dark night. The chill air immediately washed away the remaining vestiges of sleepiness. We were on the edge of a wood in a small cove, and the sky was wide open where the land stretched out. The moon shone down on acres of grassy field, sheltered on all sides by low, soft hills. A light glowed in the distance. Without saying a word, Danein took my hand and began leading. Marcus and Zhara followed alongside.

"So is this part of your honeymoon?" I asked playfully to the newly married couple. Zhara shot me a sidelong glance and smirked.

"Alonya, don't worry about us. You, our friends, are more important than a honeymoon."

We crossed the field and came upon the light. Lanterns and torches came into view, illuminating the front side of a modest stone cottage. A vine-clad trellis stood nearby, the gateway into a small walled garden. I held my breath as we walked through it. More lanterns and torches threw soft light across the flowers, hedges, and trees that lined the garden. It was further adorned with painted wrought-iron benches, large decorative urns, and a few statues. A small pond with a fountain graced the center of the garden, and in front of the pond stood a robed man. We approached the man, and it was only then, in the dim light, that I saw he was a clergyman. He was there to marry us.

So we were married right there, in the garden, at the cottage, in the cove, on the edge of a wood, just outside the royal city. We were married with the prince and princess standing near as witnesses. I was half in a daze, and when the ceremony was completed, I expected that we would turn around, cross the cove once more, reenter the carriage, and drive back to the palace. Instead, we said good-bye to the clergyman just outside the front door of the cottage and dismissed him.

"Where is he going?" I asked as he walked away from the cottage. "Isn't this his house?"

The other three exchanged amused glances with one another before Zhara took both my hands in hers.

"Silly, this is your house. Yours and Danein's. This is the big secret the men were working on all those afternoons they left us. I only just discovered it a few days ago when I was let into the plot."

"Our house?"

Danein's smile seemed ready to dance off his face. "Yes. So now you understand why I made you wait just a little longer, and I hope you'll find it was all worth it."

Again, I could barely respond except with tears. As Danein held me, Zhara and Marcus quietly took their leave. When I again looked up, they were gone, and I was alone in the night with my new husband. Small blinking points of colored light danced in the field.

Two years later

The murmur of surprise from the ladies gradually swelled, alerting us to the arrival of the prince and princess. I turned from my seat on a log to see a crowd of women swarming at the Colony entrance. My eyes watched Danein cross the open space from the wood toward the rock wall where Zhara and Marcus had just emerged from a tunnel through the mountain. He parted the sea of women to welcome the two.

I dropped the linen I was folding into a nearby basket and grabbed up the baby boy sitting beside me on the ground. We stood and waited, watching Marcus and Zhara greet the unchosen women before making their way toward us.

"Alonya, look who's here!" Danein exclaimed as they approached.

My smile nearly danced off my face. "Welcome to the Colony," I said. "One of them anyway."

Zhara leaned in for a hug. "We're so glad we could finally make it!"

I used my free hand to embrace her. She kissed the eight-month-old sitting on my hip and ruffled his hair.

"Hi, Isak. You are growing so fast. Speaking of that"—she leaned back slightly and rubbed her protruding belly—"I can't imagine how this child can get any bigger, though I still have two months to go!"

I laughed and nodded. "I know. It's quite astonishing. Have you picked out names yet?"

"Goodness, no! There are so many we like. It's been difficult for us to come to an agreement, and then you have my father throwing in his opinions, as well."

"He wants us to name the baby after him," Marcus explained with a laugh.

"Well, only if it's a boy, of course," I said.

"Boy or girl!" Zhara exclaimed. "He doesn't care which. He just wants his name passed down."

"So how's the peddling business?" Marcus asked, clapping my husband on the back.

"It's great," Danein replied. "Two times a year we spend a few months making the rounds buying and selling, stopping off at the unchosen colonies along the way. The rest of the time we're at home restocking our wares. Of course peddling is much more enjoyable and meaningful now that I have a family to join me on the road."

"Have you been traveling with Isak?" Zhara asked.

I switched my baby from one hip to the other. "Oh yes. He does extremely well with all of it. He loves being on the move and looking at the scenery. And we find that he's actually good for business."

"People come near to admire our baby and end up buying some merchandise in the process," Danein explained, which elicited a laugh from the prince and princess. He then gestured us to a seat near the fire. "Come sit and we'll catch up."

A small cook fire was burning as two women oversaw the preparation of a midday meal. Various stumps and logs stood nearby in an open space underneath the cloudless blue sky, and we soon found seats. A light wind blowing through the forest carried with it the scent of wood smoke and pine. Zhara inhaled the aroma with a look of pure peace written on her face.

"This is delightful," she said. "I cannot believe it's taken us so long to come visit one of your unchosen colonies."

"Well, it's been a busy two years for you," I said. "You've made a couple trips to Coralind and back, and now you're expecting a child. There hasn't been a lot of time for social visits."

"Is this the colony where you stayed?" Marcus asked me.

I nodded and looked around as though reliving old memories. "Yes, I was here for almost a year. And in that time, I got to know Danein and fall in love with him." I glanced at my husband with a smile.

"This is where we fell in love with each other," he added.

"I'm so glad you've been able to reestablish it, along with the other colonies," Zhara said. "It's wonderful to witness the dreams and goals we spoke of so long ago actually coming to pass."

I nodded. "Some of them anyway." I sighed, thinking of the Outlands and all the outcasts still enslaved there. "We still haven't managed another visit to the slaving camps."

Danein took my hand. "We will, but it will take time, especially after being discovered the last time."

Marcus sat forward, resting his elbows on his knees. "I know we've been rather preoccupied with other concerns lately, but we *are* making headway in the council chamber with legislation concerning the camps. Because we've all been very active spreading the word about what happens there, greater awareness of the situation has arisen. More people are speaking up on behalf of the enslaved people, some even making royal petitions to the king himself. That has helped to put some extra pressure on the king and his advisors to do something about it."

When I wasn't pacified, Zhara jumped in. "Making people aware of this situation is the first step, and we've pretty well accomplished that, so you should be encouraged, Alonya."

"That's right," Danein added, squeezing my hand. "We need to focus on what we *have* achieved thus far, however small the feat may seem."

I sighed once again, nodding. "I know. But it's difficult to see the progress when we're constantly surrounded by unchosen women, for all of whom the injustice and danger is still very present. This is only one of seven colonies we help, and there are at least twenty women in each—not to mention all the unchosens still out there on their own, or the ones enslaved at the camps and elsewhere."

There was a brief pause before Zhara nodded. Her eyes glistened with tears. "The task before us seems insurmountable, I know. But even if nothing else changed, you are still doing an important work here. You have provided these women with a home, with family, with love and acceptance—the love and acceptance of the High King. He is working through you in this place to make his power known, and it will multiply and spread to other parts of Zaphon. Change for the better can happen, and it *will* happen, however slowly it seems to slink along."

Zhara smiled then, releasing an inner joy that reached out and gripped me with hope. That was the princess's way. And I thought in that moment that with such a princess to lead the cause, change was inevitable whether we saw it within our generation or not. We were laying a foundation in Zaphon that others would build upon. One day, when the High King returned to rule all the Lands of the Seven Kingdoms—as he certainly would—there would no longer be any who were unchosen or rejected or outcast or enslaved, for the High King would receive them all.

Isak squirmed on my lap, demanding to be let down. I set him on the ground next to my stump and handed him two large sticks to play with. He immediately began striking them together furiously, giggling at the clacking sound they made. Danein reached for an earthenware bowl nearby and set it down next to the baby along with a few large rocks. For a few minutes, we all watched Isak pick up the rocks one by one and drop them into the bowl before dumping them out again to start over.

I looked up from Isak's curly head to meet the shining eyes of my husband, who was watching me. His smile grew when our eyes locked. How could I ever doubt that change was possible with the love and power of the High King? My life had drastically changed in a way I never imagined it could. I was one unchosen who had been redeemed and given a new life of purpose. The women we had saved from the Outlands were a few more. These women we now tended to were still more.

Marcus and Zhara stayed with us for the midday meal and all through the afternoon. We gave them a tour of the Colony and visited with all of the women. As evening was approaching, everyone sat around the fire as Marcus and Zhara shared stories and songs. Though the women knew of our exploits in the

Outlands, they were eager to hear about it from the lips of the prince and princess. Overall, mine and Zhara's stories of being unchosens whose fortunes had turned really encouraged the women and gave them greater hope for their futures. Many spoke of leaving Zaphon like Eloise and Taralyn had done to make new lives for themselves in Kerith, Embury, or beyond. Indeed, we discussed a possible new scheme to help unchosen women leave the country safely with papers and resources to help them begin anew. Many other women, however, felt strongly that they were meant to stay in Zaphon to fight the injustice by working undercover as we were in helping others like them.

Whatever the women chose, I was happy to know that we were inspiring them to care about something bigger than themselves. We were helping them see the value in their lives and showing them that they each had a purpose despite what the laws of the kingdom told them. They were learning, like I had, that their worth was intrinsic, bestowed upon them by the High King himself.

When Marcus and Zhara left, it was time for us to go as well, and we set off with a promise to return to the women in a few months' time. The sky was darkening with the oncoming night, though it wasn't until we emerged from the forest that we were able to catch a glimpse of the star-filled sky. Danein and I, atop our peddler's wagon pulled by plain brown horses, rode alongside the royal couple's carriage until we came to the crossroads, where we parted ways. Once our current stint on the road was over, we were set to spend a short holiday at the palace in the royal city. I was looking forward to it.

There were so many things I was looking forward to. I was looking forward to spending a season back at home with my little family. I was looking forward to visiting the women again when once we set out on our next cross-country journey. I was looking forward to one day seeing Taralyn again, who had settled in Embury, and enjoying a nice long visit with her. I was looking forward to spending my days with Danein and growing our family. I was looking forward to witnessing the change in the unchosen laws in Zaphon, day by day, month by month, and year by year. I was looking forward to life.

My mind drifted as we turned toward the nearest village for an overnight stay at the inn. I thought of a conversation I had had with the High King. He had spoken of truly living, of going forth into the world and doing his work, of being a reflection of his glory. He said only then will we find the greatest reward.

I shuddered inwardly as I realized how close I'd come to missing out on what that meant. I had lost my way then, that day long ago in the Wild Lands when the enchanted toad offered me beauty. I hadn't known that all the toad's magic could have done for me was give me a shadow of what was real—a pale shade of a brighter color that already existed. I had only to open my blind eyes and see it. I had believed then that magic held the answer, that only magic could have helped me. I didn't see that there was a greater power that could do so much more, and did—the power of the one who sees the unseen and loves the unloved. There was magic in being held in Danein's arms, of burying my face in his shoulder and feeling his strong, warm arms tighten around me. That was magic without spell or enchantment, without condition or compromise.

But there was another besides Danein whose power to see and love was even stronger magic. The High King had shown me that I was a woman with a life of purpose, whose difficulties had been known and seen and taken into account, whose hard life had meant something and had been part of the course all along.

All the time I'd believed myself to be cursed, I'd actually been gifted. When I'd believed myself to be unchosen, I had really been chosen to help bring about the High King's purposes in Zaphon. I in turn had to choose it—to choose his way over my own. I could never have imagined, once upon a time, that my life could be so full.

I leaned my head on Danein's shoulder as he snapped the reins to urge the horses onward. Isak, cradled in my arms, nestled himself deeper into my embrace, having been lulled to sleep by the rocking and bumping of the wagon. The lullaby I softly hummed drifted behind us and seemed to echo off the faraway hills. Danein soon joined in, his sweet tenor mingling in harmony with the melody of my song. I smiled to myself.

This was the greatest reward ever, and I was filled to the brim indeed.

Journey to Coralind to see where it all started (and learn more about Prince Marcus's story) in *Once Upon a Wish*, also by Lisa Anne Nichols.

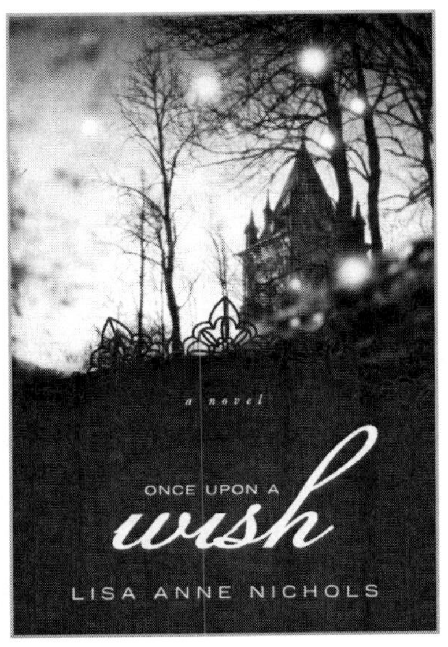